HOW THE LIGHT GETS IN

LOUISE PENNY

HOW THE LIGHT GETS IN

MINOTAUR BOOKS
NEW YORK

HOW THE LIGHT GETS IN. Copyright © 2013 by Three Pines Creations, Inc. All rights reserved. Printed in the United States of America. For information, address St. Martin's Press, 175 Fifth Avenue, New York, N.Y. 10010.

www.minotaurbooks.com

Excerpt from "Anthem" in *Stranger Music* by Leonard Cohen. Copyright © 1993 by Leonard Cohen. Reprinted by permission of McClelland & Stewart.

Excerpts from *Vapour Trails* by Marylyn Plessner (2000). Used by permission of Stephen Jarislowsky.

Library of Congress Cataloging-in-Publication Data

Penny, Louise.
   How the light gets in : Chief Inspector Gamache novel / Louise Penny.—First Minotaur Books edition.
      pages cm
   ISBN 978-0-312-65547-1 (hardcover)
   ISBN 978-1-4668-3470-5 (e-book)
   1. Gamache, Armand (Fictitious character)—Fiction.   2. Police—Québec (Province)—Fiction.   3. Missing persons—Fiction.   I. Title.
   PR9199.4.P464H69 2013
   813'.6—dc23

                                                                2013013622

Minotaur books may be purchased for educational, business, or promotional use. For information on bulk purchases, please contact Macmillan Corporate and Premium Sales Department at 1-800-221-7945, extension 5442, or write specialmarkets@macmillan.com.

First Edition: September 2013

10 9 8 7 6 5 4 3 2 1

ACKNOWLEDGMENTS

—

As with all my books, *How the Light Gets In* would not have been written without the help and support of Michael, my husband. No Michael, no books. It's simple and true, and I will be grateful to him through this life and into the next.

There are, in fact, many people who helped with this quite complex book. My friend Susan McKenzie and I spent two days at Hovey Manor, beside a lake in Québec, in a classic journalists' "story meeting" . . . hashing out ideas, thoughts, connections. Tossing out ideas, some crazy, some too sane and safe. Picking them up, examining each, taking out the best bits and building on them. When you find someone good at it, it's a magical process. But it demands being creative and constructive. Not finding flaws, but finding that hidden gem, recognizing a step to the better idea. It demands being an active and respectful listener. Susan is all those things. We're a great team and she helped make this book so much better.

I was also helped in many of the technical issues by Cassie Galante, Jeanne-Marie Hudson, Paul Hochman, and Denis Dufour. *Merci, mille fois.*

Lise Page, my assistant, is invaluable. She's an early reader, a constant cheerleader, a tireless workmate, a creative soul. I know my books and my career would not be where they are without Lise—and they sure wouldn't be as much fun!

My brother Doug is also an early reader, a gentle critic, and a wonderful support. You know, after a while in a career filled with blessings, it's difficult to keep calling up friends with more and more great news. I know without a doubt they're happy for me, but it can slip over into what might feel like (and might very well be) bragging. But still, when great things happen, I want to talk about them. Doug is the person I call. A man always happy for me (or kind enough not to tell me to be quiet and go away).

Linda Lyall designs and manages my website and newsletter and puts in long hours making sure the public face of the series does Gamache et al. justice. Thank you, Linda!

My agents, Teresa Chris and Patricia Moosbrugger, have shepherded the Gamache books over the sometimes rocky, and deeply unpredictable, terrain of today's publishing world. They've been sure and courageous and chosen their battles wisely . . . which allowed me to concentrate on my only real job. To write a book I'd be proud of.

I have no children. These Gamache books are not trivial to me. They're not a pastime, they're not cash cows. They are my dream come true. My legacy. My offspring. They are precious to me, and I put them into the hands of the great people at Minotaur Books and St. Martin's Press. Hope Dellon, my longtime editor and friend, who never fails to make the books far better. Andrew Martin, the publisher, who took a tiny book set in a little Québec village, and put it on the *New York Times* list. Sarah Melnyk, my publicist at Minotaur, who knows the books, knows me, and has been a ferocious and effective promoter of Chief Inspector Gamache.

Thank you!

And thank you to Jamie Broadhurst, Dan Wagstaff, and the people at Raincoast Books in Canada, who've put Gamache on bestseller lists in my own country. So exciting.

And thanks to David Shelley, the publisher of Little, Brown UK, for taking over the series. I know the books are in good hands with him.

Finally, I'd like to thank Leonard Cohen. The book is named after an excerpt from his poem/song—"Anthem."

> Ring the bells that still can ring,
> Forget your perfect offering,
> There's a crack in everything.
> That's how the light gets in.

I first used that stanza in my second book. When I contacted him to ask permission and find out what I'd have to pay for it, he got back through his agent to say he would give it to me for free.

Free.

I'd paid handsomely for other poetry excerpts, and rightly so. I'd expected to pay for this, especially given that at the time, six years ago, Mr. Cohen had just had most of his savings stolen by a trusted member of his team.

Instead of asking for thousands—he asked for nothing.

I cannot begin to imagine the light that floods into that man.

And now you're holding my imperfect offering. It was written with great love and gratitude and awareness of how very lucky I am.

HOW THE LIGHT GETS IN

ONE

———

Audrey Villeneuve knew what she imagined could not possibly be happening. She was a grown woman and could tell the difference between real and imagined. But each morning as she drove through the Ville-Marie Tunnel from her home in east-end Montréal to her office, she could see it. Hear it. Feel it happening.

The first sign would be a blast of red as drivers hit their brakes. The truck ahead would veer, skidding, slamming sideways. An unholy shriek would bounce off the hard walls and race toward her, all-consuming. Horns, alarms, brakes, people screaming.

And then Audrey would see huge blocks of concrete peeling from the ceiling, dragging with them a tangle of metal veins and sinews. The tunnel spilling its guts. That held the structure up. That held the city of Montréal up.

Until today.

And then, and then . . . the oval of daylight, the end of the tunnel, would close. Like an eye.

And then, darkness.

And the long, long wait. To be crushed.

Every morning and each evening, as Audrey Villeneuve drove through the engineering marvel that linked one end of the city with another, it collapsed.

"It'll be all right." She laughed to herself. At herself. "It'll be all right."

She cranked the music louder and sang loudly to herself.

But still her hands on the steering wheel tingled, then grew cold and numb, and her heart pounded. A wave of slush whacked her windshield. The wipers swept it away, leaving a half moon of streaky visibility.

Traffic slowed. Then stopped.

Audrey's eyes widened. This had never happened before. Moving through the tunnel was bad enough. Stopped in it was inconceivable. Her brain froze.

"It'll be all right." But she couldn't hear her voice, so thin was her breath and so great the howl in her head.

She locked the door with her elbow. Not to keep anyone out, but to keep herself in. A feeble attempt to stop herself from flinging open the door and running, running, screaming out of the tunnel. She gripped the wheel. Tight. Tight. Tighter.

Her eyes darted to the slush-spattered wall, the ceiling, the far wall.

The cracks.

Dear God, cracks.

And the half-hearted attempts to plaster over them.

Not to repair them, but hide them.

That doesn't mean the tunnel will collapse, she assured herself.

But the cracks widened and consumed her reason. All the monsters of her imagination became real and were squeezing out, reaching out, from between those faults.

She turned the music off so she could concentrate, hyper-vigilant. The car ahead inched forward. Then stopped.

"Go, go, go," she pleaded.

But Audrey Villeneuve was trapped and terrified. With nowhere to go. The tunnel was bad, but what waited for her in the gray December sunlight was worse.

For days, weeks, months—even years, if she was being honest—she'd known. Monsters existed. They lived in cracks in tunnels, and in dark alleys, and in neat row houses. They had names like Frankenstein and Dracula, and Martha and David and Pierre. And you almost always found them where you least expected.

She glanced into the rearview mirror and met two frightened brown eyes. But in the reflection she also saw her salvation. Her silver bullet. Her wooden stake.

It was a pretty party dress.

She'd spent hours sewing it. Time she could have, should have, spent wrapping Christmas gifts for her husband and daughters. Time she could have, should have, spent baking shortbread stars and angels and jolly snowmen, with candy buttons and gumdrop eyes.

Instead, each night when she got home Audrey Villeneuve went straight to the basement, to her sewing machine. Hunched over the emerald green fabric, she'd stitched into that party dress all her hopes.

She would put it on that night, walk into the Christmas party, scan the room and feel surprised eyes on her. In her clingy green dress, frumpy Audrey Villeneuve would be the center of attention. But it wasn't made to get everyone's attention. Just one man's. And when she had that, she could relax.

She'd hand over her burden, and get on with life. The faults would be repaired. The fissures closed. The monsters returned to where they belonged.

The exit to the Champlain Bridge was in sight. It wasn't what she normally took, but this was far from a normal day.

Audrey put on her signal and saw the man in the next car give her a sour look. Where did she think she was going? They were all trapped. But Audrey Villeneuve was more trapped. The man gave her the finger, but she took no offense. In Québec it was as casual as a friendly wave. If the Québécois ever designed a car, the hood ornament would be a middle finger. Normally she'd give him a "friendly wave" back, but she had other things on her mind.

She edged into the far right lane, toward the exit to the bridge. The wall of the tunnel was just feet away. She could have stuck her fist into one of the holes.

"It'll be all right."

Audrey Villeneuve knew it would be many things, but all right probably wasn't one of them.

TWO

~

"Get your own fucking duck," said Ruth, and held Rosa a little closer. A living eiderdown.

Constance Pineault smiled and stared ahead. Four days ago it would never have occurred to her to get a duck, but now she actually envied Ruth her Rosa. And not just for the warmth the duck provided on the bitter, biting December day.

Four days ago it would never have occurred to her to leave her comfortable chair by the bistro fireplace to sit on an icy bench beside a woman who was either drunk or demented. But here she was.

Four days ago Constance Pineault didn't know that warmth came in many forms. As did sanity. But now she knew.

"Deee-fenssssse," Ruth shouted at the young players on the frozen pond. "For God's sake, Aimée Patterson, Rosa could do better."

Aimée skated past and Constance heard her say something that might have been "duck." Or "puck." Or . . .

"They adore me," Ruth said to Constance. Or Rosa. Or the thin air.

"They're afraid of you," said Constance.

Ruth gave her a sharp assessing glance. "Are you still here? I thought you'd died."

Constance laughed, a puff of humor that floated over the village green and joined the wood smoke from the chimneys.

Four days ago she thought she'd had her last laugh. But ankle-deep in snow and freezing her bottom off beside Ruth, she'd discovered more. Hidden away. Here in Three Pines. Where laughter was kept.

The two women watched the activity on the village green in silence, except for the odd quack, which Constance hoped was the duck.

Though much the same age, the elderly women were opposites. Where

Constance was soft, Ruth was hard. Where her hair was silky and long, and done in a neat bun, Ruth's was coarse and chopped short. Where Constance was rounded, Ruth was sharp. All edges and edgy.

Rosa stirred and flapped her wings. Then she slid off Ruth's lap onto the snowy bench and waddled the few paces to Constance. Climbing onto Constance's lap, Rosa settled.

Ruth's eyes narrowed. But she didn't move.

It had snowed day and night since Constance had arrived in Three Pines. Having lived in Montréal all her adult life, she'd forgotten snow could be quite so beautiful. Snow, in her experience, was something that needed to be removed. It was a chore that fell from the sky.

But this was the snow of her childhood. Joyful, playful, bright and clean. The more the merrier. It was a toy.

It covered the fieldstone homes and clapboard homes and rose brick homes that ringed the village green. It covered the bistro and the bookstore, the boulangerie and the general store. It seemed to Constance that an alchemist was at work, and Three Pines was the result. Conjured from thin air and deposited in this valley. Or perhaps, like the snow, the tiny village had fallen from the sky, to provide a soft landing for those who'd also fallen.

When Constance had first arrived and parked outside Myrna's bookstore, she'd been worried when the flurries intensified into a blizzard.

"Should I move my car?" Constance had asked Myrna before they went up to bed. Myrna had stood at the window of her New and Used Bookstore and considered the question.

"I think it's fine where it is."

It's fine where it is.

And it was. Constance had had a restless night, listening for the sirens from the snow plows. For the warning to dig her car out and move it. The windows of her room had rattled as the wind whipped the snow against it. She could hear the blizzard howl through the trees and past the solid homes. Like something alive and on the hunt. Finally Constance drifted off to sleep, warm under the duvet. When she awoke, the storm had blown by. Constance went to the window, expecting to see her car buried, just a white mound under the foot of new snow. Instead, the road had been plowed and all the cars dug out.

It's fine where it is.

And so, finally, was she.

For four days and four nights snow had continued to fall, before Billy Williams returned with his plow. And until that happened, the village of Three Pines was snowed in, cut off. But it didn't matter, since everything they needed was right there.

Slowly, seventy-seven-year-old Constance Pineault realized she was fine, not because she had a bistro, but because she had Olivier and Gabri's bistro. There wasn't just a bookstore, there was Myrna's bookstore, Sarah's bakery, and Monsieur Béliveau's general store.

She'd arrived a self-sufficient city woman, and now she was covered in snow, sitting on a bench beside a crazy person, and she had a duck on her lap.

Who was nuts now?

But Constance Pineault knew, far from being crazy, she'd finally come to her senses.

"I came to ask if you'd like a drink," said Constance.

"For chrissake, old woman, why didn't you say that in the first place?" Ruth stood and brushed the flakes off her cloth coat.

Constance also rose and handed Rosa back to Ruth, saying, "Duck off."

Ruth snorted and accepted the duck, and the words.

Olivier and Gabri were walking over from the B and B, and met them on the road.

"It's a gay blizzard," said Ruth.

"I used to be as pure as the driven snow," Gabri confided in Constance. "Then I drifted."

Olivier and Constance laughed.

"Channeling Mae West?" said Ruth. "Won't Ethel Merman be jealous?"

"Plenty of room in there for everyone," said Olivier, eyeing his large partner.

Constance had had no dealings with homosexuals before this, at least not that she knew of. All she knew about them was that they were "they." Not "us." And "they" were unnatural. At her most charitable, she'd considered homosexuals defective. Diseased.

But mostly, if she thought of them at all, it was with disapproval. Even disgust.

Until four days ago. Until the snow began to fall, and the little village in the valley was cut off. Until she'd discovered that Olivier, the man she'd been cool to, had dug her car out. Unasked. Without comment.

Until she'd seen, from her bedroom window in Myrna's loft above the bookstore, Gabri trudging, head bent against the blowing snow, carrying coffee and warm croissants for villagers who couldn't make it to the bistro for breakfast.

As she watched, he delivered the food, then shoveled their porches and stairs and front walks.

And then left. And went to the next home.

Constance felt Olivier's strong hand on her arm, holding her secure. If a stranger came into the village at this moment, what would he think? That Gabri and Olivier were her sons?

She hoped so.

Constance stepped through the door and smelled the now familiar scent of the bistro. The dark wood beams and wide-plank pine floors were permeated with more than a century of maple-wood fires and strong coffee.

"Over here."

Constance followed the voice. The mullioned windows were letting in whatever daylight was available, but it was still dim. Her eyes went to the large stone hearths at either end of the bistro, lit with cheery fires and surrounded by comfortable sofas and armchairs. In the center of the room, between the fires and sitting areas, antique pine tables were set with silverware and mismatched bone china. A large, bushy Christmas tree stood in a corner, its red, blue, and green lights on, a haphazard array of baubles and beads and icicles hung from the branches.

A few patrons sat in armchairs nursing *cafés au lait* or hot chocolates, and read day-old newspapers in French and English.

The shout had come from the far end of the room, and while Constance couldn't yet clearly see the woman, she knew perfectly well who had spoken.

"I got you a tea." Myrna was standing, waiting for them by one of the fireplaces.

"You'd better be talking to her," said Ruth, taking the best seat by the fire and putting her feet on the hassock.

Constance hugged Myrna and felt the soft flesh under the thick sweater. Though Myrna was a large black woman at least twenty years her junior, she felt, and smelt, like Constance's mother. It had given Constance a turn at first, as though someone had shoved her slightly off balance. But then she'd come to look forward to these embraces.

Constance sipped her tea, watched the flames flicker, and half listened as Myrna and Ruth talked about the latest shipment of books, delayed by the snow.

She felt herself nodding off in the warmth.

Four days. And she had two gay sons, a large black mother, a demented poet for a friend and was considering getting a duck.

It was not what she'd expected from this visit.

She became pensive, mesmerized by the fire. She wasn't at all sure Myrna understood why she'd come. Why she'd contacted her after so many years. It was vital that Myrna understand, but now time was running out.

"Snow's letting up," said Clara Morrow. She ran her hands through her hair, trying to tame her hat head, but she only made it worse.

Constance roused and realized she'd missed Clara's arrival.

She'd met Clara her very first night in Three Pines. She and Myrna had been invited over for dinner, and while Constance yearned for a quiet dinner alone with Myrna, she didn't know how to politely decline. So they'd put on their coats and boots and trudged over.

It was supposed to be just the three of them, which was bad enough, but then Ruth Zardo and her duck had arrived and the evening went from bad to a fiasco. Rosa, the duck, had muttered what sounded like "Fuck, fuck, fuck" the whole night, while Ruth had spent the evening drinking, swearing, insulting and interrupting.

Constance had heard of her, of course. The Governor General's Award–winning poet was as close as Canada came to having a demented, embittered poet laureate.

Who hurt you once / so far beyond repair / that you would greet each overture / with curling lip?

It was, Constance realized as the evening ground on, a good question. One she was tempted to ask the crazy poet, but didn't for fear she'd be asked it in return.

Clara had made omelettes with melted goat cheese. A tossed salad and warm, fresh baguettes completed the meal. They'd eaten in the large kitchen, and when the meal was over and Myrna made coffee, and Ruth and Rosa retired to the living room, Clara had taken her into the studio. It was cramped, filled with brushes and palettes and canvasses. It smelled of oil and turpentine and ripe banana.

"Peter would've pestered me to clean this up," said Clara, looking at the mess.

Clara had talked about her separation from her husband over dinner. Constance had plastered a sympathetic look on her face and wondered if she could possibly crawl out the bathroom window. Surely dying in a snow bank couldn't be all that bad, could it?

And now here Clara was again talking about her husband. Her estranged husband. It was like parading around in her underwear. Revealing her intimates. It was unsightly and unseemly and unnecessary. And Constance just wanted to go home.

From the living room she heard, "Fuck, fuck, fuck." She didn't know, and no longer cared, whether it was the duck or the poet who was saying it.

Clara walked past an easel. The ghostly outline of what might become a man was just visible on the canvas. Without much enthusiasm, Constance followed Clara to the far end of her studio. Clara turned on a lamp and a small painting was illuminated.

At first it seemed uninteresting, certainly unremarkable.

"I'd like to paint you, if you don't mind," Clara had said, not looking at her guest.

Constance bristled. Had Clara recognized her? Did she know who Constance was?

"I don't think so," she'd replied, her voice firm.

"I understand," Clara had said. "Not sure I'd want to be painted either."

"Why not?"

"Too afraid of what someone might see."

Clara had smiled, then walked back to the door. Constance followed, after taking one last look at the tiny painting. It was of Ruth Zardo, who was now passed out and snoring on Clara's sofa. In this painting the old poet was clutching a blue shawl at her neck, her hands thin and claw-like. The veins and sinews of her neck showed through the skin, translucent, like onion paper.

Clara had captured Ruth's bitterness, her loneliness, her rage. Constance now found it almost impossible to look away from the portrait.

At the door to the studio she looked back. Her eyes weren't that sharp anymore, but they didn't have to be, to see what Clara had really captured. It was Ruth. But it was someone else too. An image Constance remembered from a childhood on her knees.

It was the mad old poet, but it was also the Virgin Mary. The mother of God. Forgotten, resentful. Left behind. Glaring at a world that no longer remembered what she'd given it.

Constance was relieved she'd refused Clara's request to paint her. If this was how she saw the mother of God, what would Clara see in her?

Later in the evening, Constance had drifted, apparently aimlessly, back to the studio door.

The single light still shone on the portrait, and even from the door Constance could see that her host hadn't simply painted mad Ruth. Nor had she simply painted forgotten and embittered Mary. The elderly woman was staring into the distance. Into a dark and lonely future. But. But. Just there. Just slightly out of reach. Just becoming visible. There was something else.

Clara had captured despair, but she'd also captured hope.

Constance had taken her coffee and rejoined Ruth and Rosa, Clara and Myrna. She'd listened to them then. And she'd begun, just begun, to understand what it might be like to be able to put more than a name to a face.

That had been four days ago.

And now she was packed and ready to leave. Just one last cup of tea in the bistro, and she'd be off.

"Don't go."

Myrna had spoken softly.

"I have to."

Constance broke eye contact with Myrna. It was altogether too intimate. Instead, she looked out the frosted windows, to the snow-covered village. It was dusk and Christmas lights were appearing on trees and homes.

"Can I come back? For Christmas?"

There was a long, long silence. And all Constance's fears returned, crawling out of that silence. She dropped her eyes to her hands, neatly folded in her lap.

She'd exposed herself. Been tricked into thinking she was safe, she was liked, she was welcome.

Then she felt a large hand on her hand and she looked up.

"I'd love that," Myrna said, and smiled. "We'll have such fun."

"Fun?" asked Gabri, plopping onto the sofa.

"Constance is coming back for Christmas."

"Wonderful. You can come to the carol service on Christmas Eve. We do all the favorites. 'Silent Night.' 'The First Noël'—"

"'The Twelve Gays of Christmas,'" said Clara.

"'It Came Upon a Midnight Queer,'" said Myrna.

"The classics," said Gabri. "Though this year we're practicing a new one."

"Not 'O Holy Night,' I hope," said Constance. "Not sure I'm ready for that one."

Gabri laughed. "No. 'The Huron Carol.' Do you know it?" He sang a few bars of the old Québécois carol.

"I love that one," she said. "But no one does it anymore."

Though it shouldn't have surprised her that in this little village she'd find something else that had been all but lost to the outside world.

Constance said her good-byes, and to calls of "*À bientôt!*," she and Myrna walked to her car.

Constance started it to warm up. It was getting too dark to play hockey and the kids were just leaving the rink, wobbling through the snow on their skates, using their hockey sticks for balance.

It was now or never, Constance knew.

"We used to do that," she said, and Myrna followed her gaze.

"Play hockey?"

Constance nodded. "We had our own team. Our father would coach us. Mama would cheer. It was Frère André's favorite sport."

She met Myrna's eyes. *There*, she thought. *Done*. The dirty secret was finally out in the open. When she returned, Myrna would have lots of questions. And finally, finally, Constance knew she would answer them.

Myrna watched her friend leave, and thought no more of that conversation.

THREE

"Think carefully," said Armand Gamache. His voice was almost neutral. Almost. But there was no mistaking the look in his deep brown eyes.

They were hard, and cold. And unyielding.

He stared at the agent over his half-moon reading glasses and waited.

The conference room grew quiet. The shuffling of papers, the slight and insolent whispering, died out. Even the amused glances stopped.

And all focused on Chief Inspector Gamache.

Beside him, Inspector Isabelle Lacoste shifted her glance from the Chief to the assembled agents and inspectors. It was the weekly briefing for the homicide department of the Sûreté du Québec. A gathering meant to exchange ideas and information on cases under investigation. Where once it had been collaborative, now it was an hour she'd come to dread.

And if she felt like that, how did the Chief Inspector feel?

It was hard to tell anymore, what the Chief really felt and thought.

Isabelle Lacoste knew him better than anyone else in the room. Had served with him longest, she realized with surprise. The rest of the old guard had been transferred out, either by request or on the orders of Chief Superintendent Francoeur.

And this rabble had been transferred in.

The most successful homicide department in the nation had been gutted, replaced with lazy, insolent, incompetent thugs. Or were they incompetent? Certainly as homicide investigators they were, but was that really their job?

Of course not. She, and she suspected Gamache, knew why these men and women were really there. And it wasn't to solve murders.

Despite this, Chief Inspector Gamache still managed to command them. To control them. Just barely. The balance was tipping, Lacoste could feel it.

Every day more new agents were brought in. She could see them exchanging knowing smiles.

Lacoste felt her bile rise.

The madness of crowds. Madness had invaded their department. And every day Chief Inspector Gamache reined it in and took control. But even that was slipping. How much longer could he hold out before losing his grip completely?

Inspector Lacoste had many fears, most to do with her young son and daughter. Of something happening to them. She knew those fears were for the most part irrational.

But the fear of what would happen if the Chief Inspector lost control was not irrational.

She caught the eye of one of the older agents as he slumped in his chair, his arms folded across his chest. Apparently bored. Inspector Lacoste gave him a censorious look. He lowered his eyes and turned red.

Ashamed of himself. As well he should be.

As she glared, he sat upright and uncrossed his arms.

She nodded. A victory, though small and doubtless temporary. But even those, these days, counted.

Inspector Lacoste turned back to Gamache. His large hands were folded neatly on the table. Resting on the weekly report. A pen, unused, lay beside it. His right hand trembled slightly, and she hoped no one else noticed.

He was clean-shaven and looked every inch what he was. A man on the far side of fifty. Not necessarily handsome, but distinguished. More like a professor than a cop. More like an explorer than a hunter. He smelled of sandalwood with a hint of rose and wore a jacket and tie in to work every day.

His dark hair was graying and groomed and curled a little at the temples and around his ears. His face was lined, from age and care and laughter. Though those lines weren't getting much of a workout lately. And there was, and always would be, that scar at his left temple. A reminder of events neither of them could ever forget.

His six-foot frame was large, substantial. Not exactly muscular, but neither was he fat. He was solid.

Solid, thought Lacoste. Like the mainland. Like a headland, facing a vast ocean. Was the now relentless buffeting beginning to wear deeper lines and crevices? Were cracks beginning to show?

At this moment Chief Inspector Gamache showed no sign of erosion. He stared at the offending agent, and even Lacoste couldn't help feeling just a little sympathy. This new agent had mistaken the mainland for a sandbar. And now, too late, realized what he'd come up against.

She could see the insolence turn to disquiet, then to alarm. He turned to his friends for support, but like a pack of hyenas, they backed off. Almost anxious to see him torn apart.

Until this moment, Lacoste hadn't realized how willing the pack was to turn on their own. Or, at least, to refuse to help.

She glanced at Gamache, at his steady eyes not leaving the squirming agent, and she knew that was what the Chief was doing. Testing them. Testing their loyalty. He'd cut one from the pack and waited to see if any would come to the rescue.

But they did not.

Isabelle Lacoste relaxed a little. Chief Inspector Gamache was still in control.

Gamache continued to stare at the agent. Now the others fidgeted. One even got up with a sullen "I've got work to do."

"Sit down," said the Chief, not looking at him. And he dropped like a rock.

Gamache waited. And waited.

"*Désolé, patron,*" said the agent at last. "I haven't interviewed that suspect yet."

The words slid down the table. A rotten admission. They'd all heard this agent lie about the interview, and now they waited to see what the Chief Inspector would do. How he'd maul this man.

"We'll talk about this after the meeting," said Gamache.

"Yessir."

The reaction around the table was immediate.

Sly smiles. After a display of strength on the Chief's part, they now sensed weakness. Had he ripped the agent to shreds they'd have respected him. Feared him. But now they only smelled blood.

And Isabelle Lacoste thought, God help me, even I wish the Chief had humiliated, disgraced this agent. Nailed him to the wall, as a warning to anyone else who'd cross Chief Inspector Gamache.

This far and no farther.

But Isabelle Lacoste had been in the Sûreté long enough to know how much easier it was to shoot than to talk. How much easier it was to shout than to be reasonable. How much easier it was to humiliate and demean and misuse authority than to be dignified and courteous, even to those who were themselves none of those things.

How much more courage it took to be kind than to be cruel.

But times had changed. The Sûreté had changed. It was now a culture that rewarded cruelty. That promoted it.

Chief Inspector Gamache knew that. And yet he'd just exposed his neck. Was it on purpose? Lacoste wondered. Or was he really so weakened?

She no longer knew.

What she did know was that over the past six months the Chief Inspector had watched his department being gutted, bastardized. His work dismantled. He'd watched those loyal to him leave. Or turn against him.

He'd put up a fight at first, but been pounded down. Time and again, she'd seen him return to his office after arguing with the Chief Superintendent. Gamache had come back defeated. And now, it seemed, he had little fight left in him.

"Next," said Gamache.

And so it went, for an hour. Each agent trying Gamache's patience. But the headland held. No sign of crumbling, no sign this had any effect at all on the Chief. Finally the meeting was over and Gamache rose. Inspector Lacoste rose too and there was a hesitation before first one then the rest of the agents got to their feet. At the door the Chief Inspector turned and looked at the agent who'd lied. Just a glance, but it was enough. The agent fell in behind Gamache and followed him to the Chief's office. Just as the door closed Inspector Lacoste caught a fleeting look on the Chief's face.

Of exhaustion.

Sit down." Gamache pointed to a chair, then he himself sat in the swivel chair behind his desk. The agent tried on some bravado, but that faded before the stern face.

When he spoke, the Chief's voice carried an effortless authority.

"Are you happy here?"

The question surprised the agent. "I suppose."

"You can do better than that. It's a simple question. Are you happy here?"

"I have no choice but to be here."

"You have a choice. You could quit. You're not indentured. And I suspect you're not the fool you pretend to be."

"I don't pretend to be a fool."

"No? Then what would you call failing to interview a key suspect in

16

a homicide investigation? What would you call lying about it to someone you must have known would see through that lie?"

But it was clear that the agent never thought he'd be caught. It had certainly never occurred to him that he'd find himself alone in the Chief's office, about to be chewed out.

But mostly, it never occurred to him that, instead of ripping into him, tearing him to shreds, Chief Inspector Gamache would simply stare at him, with thoughtful eyes.

"I would call it foolish," admitted the agent.

Gamache continued to watch him. "I don't care what you think of me. I don't care what you think of your assignment here. You're right, your being here wasn't your choice, or mine. You're not a trained homicide investigator. But you are an agent in the Sûreté du Québec, one of the great police forces in the world."

The agent smirked, then his expression shifted to mild surprise.

The Chief Inspector wasn't joking. He actually believed it. Believed the Sûreté du Québec was a great and effective police force. A breakwater between the citizens and those who would do them harm.

"You came from the Serious Crimes division, I believe."

The agent nodded.

"You must have seen some terrible things."

The agent sat very still.

"Difficult not to grow cynical," said the Chief quietly. "Here we deal with one thing. There's a great advantage in that. We become specialists. The disadvantage is what we deal with. Death. Every time the phone rings, it's about a loss of life. Sometimes accidental. Sometimes it's suicide. Sometimes it turns out to be natural. But most of the time it's very unnatural. Which is when we step in."

The agent looked deeply into those eyes and believed he saw, just for an instant, the terrible deaths that had piled up, day and night, for years. The young and the old. The children. The fathers and mothers and daughters and sons. Killed. Murdered. Lives taken. And the bodies laid at the feet of this man.

It seemed Death had joined their meeting, making the atmosphere stale and close.

"Do you know what I've learned, after three decades of death?" Gamache asked, leaning toward the agent and lowering his voice.

Despite himself, the agent leaned forward.

"I've learned how precious life is."

The agent looked at him, expecting more, and when no more came he slumped back in his chair.

"The work you do isn't trivial," said the Chief. "People are counting on you. I'm counting on you. Please take it seriously."

"Yessir."

Gamache rose and the agent got to his feet. The Chief walked him to the door and nodded as the man left.

Everyone in the homicide office had been watching, waiting for the explosion. Waiting for Chief Inspector Gamache to rip into the offending agent. Even Lacoste waited, and wanted it.

But nothing had happened.

The other agents exchanged glances, no longer bothering to hide their satisfaction. The legendary Chief Inspector Gamache was a straw man after all. Not quite on his knees, but close.

Gamache looked up from his reading when Lacoste knocked.

"May I come in, *patron*?" she asked.

"Of course." He got up and indicated the chair.

Lacoste closed the door, knowing some, if not all, of the agents in the large room would still be watching. But she didn't care. They could go to hell.

"They wanted to see you tear into him."

The Chief Inspector nodded. "I know." He looked at her closely. "And you, Isabelle?"

There was no use lying to the Chief. She sighed.

"Part of me wanted to see that too. But for different reasons."

"And what were your reasons?"

She jerked her head in the direction of the agents. "It would show them you can't be pushed around. Brutality is all they understand."

Gamache considered that for a moment, then nodded. "You're right, of course. And I have to admit, I was tempted." He smiled at her. It had taken him a while to get used to seeing Isabelle Lacoste sitting across from him, instead of Jean-Guy Beauvoir.

"I think that young man once believed in his job," said Gamache, looking through the internal window as the agent picked up his phone. "I think they all did. I honestly believe most agents join the Sûreté because they want to help."

"To serve and protect?" Lacoste asked, with a small smile.

"Service, Integrity, Justice," he quoted the Sûreté motto. "Old-fashioned, I know." He lifted his hands in surrender.

"So what changed?" asked Lacoste.

"Why do decent young men and women become bullies? Why do soldiers dream of being heroes but end up abusing prisoners and shooting civilians? Why do politicians become corrupt? Why do cops beat suspects senseless and break the laws they're meant to protect?"

The agent that Gamache had just been speaking with was talking on the phone. Despite the taunts of the other agents, he was doing what Gamache had asked of him.

"Because they can?" asked Lacoste.

"Because everyone else does," said Gamache, sitting forward. "Corruption and brutality are modeled and expected and rewarded. It becomes normal. And anyone who stands up to it, who tells them it's wrong, is beaten down. Or worse." Gamache shook his head. "No, I can't condemn those young agents for losing their way. It's a rare person who wouldn't."

The Chief looked at her and smiled.

"So you ask why I didn't rip him apart when I could have? That's why. And before you mistake it for heroics on my part, it wasn't. It was selfish. I needed to prove to myself that I hadn't yet fallen that far. I have to admit, it's tempting."

"To join Chief Superintendent Francoeur?" asked Lacoste, amazed at the admission.

"No, to create my own stinking mess in response."

He stared at her, seeming to weigh his words.

"I know what I'm doing, Isabelle," he said quietly. "Trust me."

"I shouldn't have doubted."

And Isabelle Lacoste saw how the rot started. How it happened, not overnight, but by degrees. A small doubt broke the skin. Then an infection set in. Questioning. Critical. Cynical. Distrustful.

Lacoste looked at the agent that Gamache had spoken to. He'd put down the phone and was making notes on his computer, trying to do his job. But his colleagues were taunting him, and as Inspector Lacoste watched, the agent stopped typing and turned to them. And smiled. One of them, again.

Inspector Lacoste returned her attention to Chief Inspector Gamache. Never, ever, would she have believed it possible for her to be disloyal to him. But if it could happen to those other agents, who'd been decent once, maybe it could happen to her. Maybe it already had. As more and more of Francoeur's agents were transferred in, as more and more of them challenged Gamache, believing him to be weak, maybe it was seeping into her too, by association.

Maybe she was beginning to doubt him.

Six months ago she'd never have questioned how the Chief disciplined a subordinate. But now she had. And part of her had wondered if what she'd seen, what they'd all seen, wasn't weakness after all.

"Whatever happens, Isabelle," said Gamache, "you must trust yourself. Do you understand?"

He was looking at her with great intensity, as though trying to place those words not simply in her head, but someplace deeper. Some secret, safe place.

She nodded.

He smiled, breaking the tension. "*Bon.* Is that what you came to say, or is there more?"

It took her a moment to remember and it was only in noticing the Post-it note in her hand that it came back to her.

"A call came in a few minutes ago. I didn't want to disturb you. I'm not sure if it's personal or professional."

He put on his glasses and read the note, then frowned.

"I'm not sure either." Gamache leaned back in his chair. His jacket opened and Lacoste noticed the Glock in the holster on his belt. She couldn't quite get used to seeing it there. The Chief loathed guns.

Matthew 10:36.

It was one of the first things she'd been taught when she'd joined the homicide division. She could still see Chief Inspector Gamache, sitting where he was now.

"Matthew 10:36," he'd said. "*And a man's foes shall be they of his own household.* Never forget that, Agent Lacoste."

She'd assumed he'd meant that in a murder investigation, the family was the place to start. But now she knew it meant much more than that. Chief Inspector Gamache wore a weapon. Inside Sûreté headquarters. Inside his own household.

Gamache picked the Post-it note off his desk. "Care for a drive? We can be there for lunch."

Lacoste was surprised but didn't need to be asked twice.

"Who'll be left in charge?" she asked, as she grabbed her coat.

"Who's in charge now?"

"You, of course, *patron.*"

"How nice of you to say that, but we both know it isn't true. I just hope we didn't leave any matches lying around."

As the door closed, Gamache heard the agent he'd spoken with say to the others, "It's about life . . ."

He was lampooning the Chief, in a high, childish voice. Making him sound idiotic.

The Chief walked down the long corridor to the elevator, and smiled.

In the elevator, they watched the numbers. 15, 14 . . .

The other person in the elevator got out, leaving them alone.

. . . 13, 12, 11 . . .

Lacoste was tempted to ask the one question that must never be overheard.

She looked at the Chief, watching the numbers. Relaxed. But she knew him enough to recognize the new lines, the deeper lines. The darker circles under his eyes.

Yes, she thought, let's get out of here. Cross the bridge, get off the island. As far from this damned place as we can.

8 . . . 7 . . . 6 . . .

"Sir?"

"*Oui?*"

He turned to her and she saw, again, the weariness that came in unguarded moments. And she hadn't the heart to ask what had happened to Jean-Guy Beauvoir. Gamache's second in command before her. Her own mentor. Gamache's protégé. And more than that.

For fifteen years Gamache and Beauvoir had been a formidable team. Twenty years younger than the Chief Inspector, Jean-Guy Beauvoir was being groomed to take over.

And then suddenly, coming back from a case at a remote abbey a few months earlier, Inspector Beauvoir had been transferred out, into Chief Superintendent Francoeur's own department.

It had been a mess.

Lacoste had tried to ask Beauvoir what'd happened, but the Inspector wanted nothing to do with anyone from homicide, and Chief Inspector Gamache had issued an order. No one in homicide was to have anything to do with Jean-Guy Beauvoir.

He was to be shunned. Disappeared. Made invisible.

Not only *persona non grata*, but *persona non exista*.

Isabelle Lacoste could hardly believe it. And the passage of time hadn't made it more believable.

3 . . . 2 . . .

That was what she wanted to ask.

Was it true?

She wondered if it was a ruse, a way to get Beauvoir into Francoeur's camp. To try to figure out what the Chief Superintendent was up to.

Surely Gamache and Beauvoir were still allies in this dangerous game.

But as the months passed, Beauvoir's behavior had grown more erratic and Gamache had grown more resolute. And the gulf between them had grown into an ocean. And now they appeared to inhabit two different worlds.

As she followed Gamache to his car, Lacoste realized she hadn't asked the question to spare his feelings, but her own. She didn't want the answer. She wanted to believe that Beauvoir remained loyal, and Gamache had a hope of stopping whatever plan Francoeur had in place.

"Would you like to drive?" Gamache asked, offering her the keys.

"With pleasure."

She drove through the Ville-Marie Tunnel, then up onto the Champlain Bridge. Gamache was silent, looking at the half-frozen St. Lawrence River far below. The traffic slowed almost to a stop once they approached the very top of the span. Lacoste, who was not at all afraid of heights, felt queasy. It was one thing to drive over the bridge, another thing to be stopped within feet of the low rail. And the long plunge.

She could see, far below, sheets of ice butting against each other in the cold current. Slush, like sludge, moved slowly under the bridge.

Beside her, Chief Inspector Gamache inhaled sharply, then exhaled and fidgeted. She remembered that he was afraid of heights. Lacoste noticed his hands were balled into fists, which he was tightening, then releasing. Tightening. Releasing.

"About Inspector Beauvoir," she heard herself say. It felt a bit like jumping from the bridge.

He looked as though she'd slapped him. Which was, she realized, her goal. To slap him. Break the squirreling in his head.

She couldn't, of course, physically hit Chief Inspector Gamache. But she could emotionally. And she had.

"Yes?" He looked at her but neither his voice nor his expression was encouraging.

"Can you tell me what happened?"

The car ahead moved a few feet, then put on its brakes. They were almost at the top of the span. The highest point.

"No."

He'd slapped her back. And she felt the sting.

They sat in uncomfortable silence for a minute or so. But Lacoste noticed the Chief was no longer flexing his fists. Now he just stared out the window. And she wondered if she might have hit him too hard.

Then his face changed and Lacoste realized he was no longer looking at the dark waters of the St. Lawrence, but to the side of the bridge. They'd crested and could now see what the delay was. Police cars and an ambulance were blocking the far right lane, just where the bridge connected with the south shore.

A covered body, strapped to a wire basket, was being hauled up the embankment. Lacoste crossed herself, through force of habit and not out of any faith that it would make a difference to the dead or the living.

Gamache did not cross himself. Instead he stared.

The death had occurred on the south shore of Montréal. It wasn't their territory, and not their body. The Sûreté du Québec was responsible for policing all of Québec, except those cities with their own forces. It still left them plenty of territory, and plenty of bodies. But not this one.

Besides, both Gamache and Lacoste knew that the poor soul was probably a suicide. Driven to despair as the Christmas holidays neared.

Gamache wondered, as they passed the body swaddled in blankets like a newborn, how bad life would have to be before the cold, gray waters seemed better.

And then they were past, and the traffic opened up, and soon they were speeding along the autoroute, away from the bridge. Away from the body. Away from Sûreté headquarters. Toward the village of Three Pines.

FOUR

⁓

The small bell above the door tinkled as Gamache entered the bookstore. He knocked his boots against the doorjamb, hoping to get some of the snow off.

It'd been snowing slightly in Montréal when they'd left, just flurries, but the snow had intensified as they'd climbed higher into the mountains south of the city. He heard a muffled thumping as Isabelle Lacoste knocked her boots and followed him inside.

Had the Chief Inspector been blindfolded he could have described the familiar shop. The walls were lined with bookcases filled with hardcovers and paperbacks. With fiction and biography, science and science fiction. Mysteries and religion. Poetry and cookbooks. It was a room filled with thoughts and feeling and creation and desires. New and used.

Threadbare Oriental rugs were scattered on the wood floor, giving it the feel of a well-used library in an old country home.

A cheerful wreath was tacked on the door into Myrna's New and Used Bookstore, and a Christmas tree stood in a corner. Gifts were piled underneath and there was the slight sweet scent of balsam.

A black cast-iron woodstove sat in the center of the room, with a kettle simmering on top of it and an armchair on either side.

It hadn't changed since the day Gamache had first entered Myrna's bookstore years before. Right down to the unfashionable floral slipcovers on the sofa and easy chairs in the bay window. Books were piled next to one of the sagging seats and back copies of *The New Yorker* and *National Geographic* were scattered on the coffee table.

It was, Gamache felt, how a sigh might look.

"*Bonjour?*" he called and waited. Nothing.

Stairs led from the back of the bookstore into Myrna's apartment above.

He was about to call up when Lacoste noticed a scribbled note by the cash register.

Back in ten minutes. Leave money if you buy anything. (Ruth, this means you.)

It wasn't signed. No need. But there was a time written at the top. 11:55.

Lacoste checked her watch while Gamache turned to the large clock behind the desk. Noon almost exactly.

They wandered for a few minutes, up and down the aisles. There were equal parts French and English books. Some new, but most used. Gamache became absorbed in the titles, finally selecting a frayed book on the history of cats. He took off his heavy coat and poured himself and Lacoste mugs of tea.

"Milk, sugar?" he asked.

"A bit of both, *s'il vous plaît*," came her reply from across the room.

He sat down by the woodstove and opened his book. Lacoste joined him in the other easy chair, sipping her tea.

"Thinking of getting one?"

"A cat?" He glanced at the cover of the book. "*Non.* Florence and Zora want a pet, especially after the last visit. They fell for Henri's charms and now want a German shepherd of their own."

"In Paris?" asked Lacoste, with some amusement.

"Yes. I don't think they quite realize they live in Paris," laughed Gamache, thinking of his young granddaughters. "Reine-Marie told me last night that Daniel and Roslyn are considering getting a cat."

"Madame Gamache is in Paris?"

"For Christmas. I'll be joining them next week."

"Bet you can hardly wait."

"*Oui,*" he said, and went back to his book. Hiding, she thought, the magnitude of his longing. And how much he was missing his wife.

The sound of a door opening brought Gamache out of the surprisingly riveting history of the tabby. He looked up to see Myrna coming through the door connecting her bookstore to the bistro.

She carried a bowl of soup and a sandwich, but stopped as soon as she saw them. Then her face broke into a smile as bright as her sweater.

"Armand, I didn't expect you to actually come down."

Gamache was on his feet, as was Lacoste. Myrna put the dishes on her desk and hugged them both.

"We're interrupting your lunch," he said apologetically.

"Oh, I only nipped out quickly to get it, in case you called back." Then

26

she stopped herself and her keen eyes searched his face. "Why're you here? Has something happened?"

It was a source of some sadness for Gamache that his presence was almost always greeted with anxiety.

"Not at all. You left a message and this is our answer."

Myrna laughed. "What service. Did you not think to phone?"

Gamache turned to Lacoste. "Phone. Why didn't we think of that?"

"I don't trust phones," said Lacoste. "They're the devil's work."

"Actually, I believe that's email," said Gamache, returning to Myrna. "You gave us an excuse to get out of the city for a few hours. And I'm always happy to come here."

"Where's Inspector Beauvoir?" Myrna asked, looking around. "Parking the car?"

"He's on another assignment," said the Chief.

"I see," said Myrna, and in the slight pause Armand Gamache wondered what she saw.

"We need to get you both some lunch," said Myrna. "Do you mind if we eat it here? More private."

A bistro menu was produced, and before long Gamache and Lacoste also had the *spécial du jour*, soup and a sandwich. Then all three sat in the light of the bay window, Gamache and Lacoste on the sofa and Myrna in the large easy chair, which retained her shape permanently and looked like an extension of the generous woman.

Gamache stirred the dollop of sour cream into his borscht, watching the deep red turn soft pink and the chunks of beets and cabbage and tender beef mix together.

"Your message was a little vague," he said, looking up at Myrna across from him.

Beside him, Isabelle Lacoste had decided to start with her grilled tomato, basil, and Brie sandwich.

"I take it that was intentional," said the Chief.

He'd known Myrna for a number of years now, since he'd first come to the tiny village of Three Pines on a murder investigation. She'd been a suspect then, now he considered her a friend.

Sometimes things changed for the better. But sometimes they didn't.

He placed the yellow slip of paper on the table beside the basket of baguette.

Sorry to bother you, but I need your help with something. Myrna Landers

Her phone number followed. Gamache had chosen to ignore the

number, partly as an excuse to get away from headquarters, but mostly because Myrna had never asked for help before. Whatever it was might not be serious, but it was important to her. And she was important to him.

He ate the borscht while she considered her words.

"This really is probably nothing," she started, then met his eyes and stopped. "I'm worried," Myrna admitted.

Gamache put down his spoon and focused completely on his friend.

Myrna looked out the window and he followed her gaze. There, between the mullions, he saw Three Pines. In every way. Three huge pines dominated the little village. For the first time he realized that they acted as a windbreak, taking the brunt of the billowing snow.

But still, a thick layer blanketed everything. Not the filthy snow of the city. Here it was almost pure white, broken only by footpaths and the trails of cross-country skis and snowshoes.

A few adults skated on the rink, pushing shovels ahead of them, clearing the ice while impatient children waited. No two homes around the village green were the same, and Gamache knew each and every one of them. Inside and out. From interrogations and from parties.

"I had a friend visit last week," Myrna explained. "She was supposed to come back yesterday and stay through Christmas. She called the night before to say she'd be here in time for lunch, but she never showed."

Myrna's voice was calm. Precise. A perfect witness, as Gamache had come to realize. Nothing superfluous. No interpretation. Just what had happened.

But her hand holding the spoon shook slightly, so that borscht splashed tiny red beads onto the wood table. And her eyes held a plea. Not for help. They were begging him for reassurance. To tell her she was overreacting, worrying for nothing.

"About twenty-four hours then," said Isabelle Lacoste. She'd put down her sandwich and was paying complete attention.

"That's not much, right?" said Myrna.

"With adults we don't generally start to worry for two days," said Gamache. "In fact, an official dossier isn't opened until someone's been missing for forty-eight hours." His tone held a "but," and Myrna waited. "But if someone I cared about had disappeared, I wouldn't wait forty-eight hours before going looking. You did the right thing."

"It might be nothing."

"Yes," said the Chief. And while he didn't say the words she longed to hear, his very presence was reassuring. "You called her, of course."

"I waited until about four yesterday afternoon, then called her home.

28

She doesn't have a cell phone. I just got the answering machine. I called"—Myrna paused—"a lot. Probably once an hour."

"Until?"

Myrna looked at the clock. "The last time was eleven thirty this morning."

"She lives alone?" Gamache asked. His voice had shifted, from serious conversation into inquiry. This was now work.

Myrna nodded.

"How old is she?"

"Seventy-seven."

There was a longer pause as the Chief Inspector and Lacoste took that in. The implication was obvious.

"I called the hospitals, both French and English, last night," said Myrna, rightly interpreting their train of thought. "And again this morning. Nothing."

"She was driving out here?" Gamache confirmed. "Not taking the bus, and not being driven by someone else?"

Myrna nodded. "She has her own car."

She was watching him closely now, trying to interpret the look in his deep brown eyes.

"She'd have been alone?"

She nodded again. "What're you thinking?"

But he didn't answer. Instead he reached in his breast pocket for a small notebook and pen. "What's the make and model of your friend's car?"

Lacoste also brought out a pad and pen.

"I don't know. It's a small car. Orangy color." Seeing that neither wrote that down, Myrna asked, "Does that help?"

"I don't suppose you know the license plate number?" asked Lacoste, without much hope. Still, it needed to be asked.

Myrna shook her head.

Lacoste brought out her cell phone.

"They don't work here, you know," said Myrna. "The mountains."

Lacoste did know that, but had forgotten that there remained pockets of Québec where phones were still attached to the walls. She got up.

"May I use your phone?"

"Of course." Myrna indicated the desk, and when Lacoste moved away, she looked at Gamache.

"Inspector Lacoste is calling our traffic patrol, to see if there were any accidents on the autoroute or the roads around here."

"But I called the hospitals."

When Gamache didn't respond Myrna understood. Not every accident victim needed a hospital. They both watched Lacoste, who was listening on the phone, but not taking notes.

Gamache wondered if Myrna knew that was a good sign.

"We need more information, of course," he said. "What's your friend's name?"

He picked up his pen and pulled his notebook closer. But when there was just silence he looked up.

Myrna was looking away from him, into the body of her bookstore. He wondered if she'd heard the question.

"Myrna?"

She returned her gaze to him, but her mouth remained shut. Tight.

"Her name?"

Myrna still hesitated and Gamache tilted his head slightly, surprised.

Isabelle Lacoste returned and, sitting down, she smiled at Myrna reassuringly. "No serious car accidents on the highway between here and Montréal yesterday."

Myrna was relieved, but it was short-lived. She returned her attention to Chief Inspector Gamache, and his unanswered question.

"You'll have to tell me," he said, watching her with increased curiosity.

"I know."

"I don't understand, Myrna," he said. "Why don't you want to tell me?"

"She might still turn up, and I don't want to cause her embarrassment."

Gamache, who knew Myrna well, knew she wasn't telling the truth. He stared at her for a moment, then decided to try another tack.

"Can you describe her for us?"

Myrna nodded. As she spoke Myrna saw Constance sitting exactly where Armand Gamache was now. Reading and occasionally lowering her book to gaze out the window. Talking to Myrna. Listening. Helping to make dinner upstairs, or sharing a Scotch with Ruth in front of the bistro fireplace.

She saw Constance getting into her car and waving. Then driving up the hill out of Three Pines.

And then she was gone.

Caucasian. Francophone. Approx. five foot four. Slightly overweight, white hair, blue eyes. 77 years of age.

That's what Lacoste had written. That's what Constance came down to.

"And her name?" Gamache asked. His voice, now, was firm. He held Myrna's eyes and she held his.

"Constance Pineault," she said at last.

"*Merci,*" said Gamache quietly.

"Is that her *nom de naissance*?" asked Lacoste.

When Myrna didn't answer Lacoste clarified, in case the French phrase had been lost on the Anglophone woman. "The name she was born with or her married name?"

But Gamache could tell that Myrna understood the question perfectly well. It was the answer that confused her.

He'd seen this woman afraid, filled with sorrow, joyful, annoyed. Perplexed.

But he'd never seen her confused. And it was clear by her reaction that it was a foreign state for her too.

"Neither," she finally said. "Oh, God, she'd kill me if I told anyone."

"We're not 'anyone,' " said Gamache. The words, while carrying a mild reproach, were said softly, with care.

"Maybe I should wait some more."

"Maybe," said Gamache.

He got up and fed two pieces of wood into the stove in the center of the room, then brought back a mug of tea for Myrna.

"*Merci,*" she said, and held it between her hands. Her lunch, partly eaten, would not now be finished.

"Inspector, would you mind trying the home number once more?"

"*Absolument.*" Lacoste got up and Myrna scribbled the number on a piece of paper.

They heard the beep, beep, beeps from across the room as she punched in the numbers. Gamache watched for a moment, then turned to Myrna, lowering his voice.

"Who is she if not Constance Pineault?"

Myrna held his eyes. But they both knew she'd tell him. That it was inevitable.

"Pineault's the name I know her by," she said quietly. "The name she uses. It was her mother's maiden name. Her real name, her *nom de naissance,* is Constance Ouellet."

Myrna watched him, expecting a reaction, but Armand Gamache couldn't oblige.

Across the room, Isabelle Lacoste was listening on the phone. Not talking. The phone rang and rang and rang, in an empty home.

The home of Constance Ouellet. Constance Ouellet.

Myrna was studying him closely.

He could have asked. Was tempted to ask. And he certainly would, if he had to. But Gamache wanted to get there on his own. He was curious to see if the missing woman lurked in his memory and, if she did, what his memory said about her.

The name did sound familiar. But it was vague, ill-defined. If Madame Ouellet lived in his memory, she was several mountain ranges away from today. He cast his mind back, moving rapidly over the terrain.

He bypassed his own personal life and concentrated on the collective memory of Québec. Constance Ouellet must be a public figure. Or had been. Someone either famous or notorious. A household name, once.

The more he looked, the more certain he became that she was in there, hiding in some recess of his mind. An elderly woman who didn't want to come out.

And now she was missing. Either by choice, or by someone else's design.

He brought his hand up to his face as he thought. As he got closer and closer.

Ouellet. Ouellet. Constance Ouellet.

Then he inhaled and his eyes narrowed. A faded black and white photo drifted into view. Not of a seventy-seven-year-old woman, but of a smiling, waving girl.

He'd found her.

"You know who I'm talking about," said Myrna, seeing the light in his eyes.

Gamache nodded.

But in his search he'd stumbled over some other memory, much more recent. And more worrisome. He got to his feet and walked over to the desk just as Lacoste hung up.

"Nothing, Chief," she said and he nodded, taking the receiver from her.

Myrna rose. "What is it?"

"Just a thought," he said, and dialed.

"Marc Brault." The voice was clipped, official.

"Marc, it's Armand Gamache."

"Armand." The voice became friendly. "How're you doing?"

"Fine, thank you. Listen, Marc, I'm sorry to bother you—"

"No bother at all. What can I help you with?"

"I'm in the Eastern Townships. As we crossed the Champlain Bridge this morning at about quarter to eleven"—Gamache turned his back on Myrna and lowered his voice—"we noticed your people bringing a body up from the south shore."

"And you want to know who it was?"

"I don't want to pry into your jurisdiction, but yes."

"Let me just look."

Gamache could hear the clicking of keys as the head of homicide for the Montréal police accessed his records.

"Right. Not much on her yet."

"A woman?"

"Yes. Been there for a couple days, apparently. Autopsy scheduled for this afternoon."

"Do you suspect murder?"

"Not likely. Her car was found up above. Looks like she tried to jump from the bridge into the water and missed. Hit the shore and rolled under the bridge. Some workers found her there this morning."

"Do you have a name?"

Gamache prepared himself. *Constance Ouellet.*

"Audrey Villeneuve."

"Pardon?" asked Gamache.

"Audrey Villeneuve, it says here. Late thirties. Husband reported her missing two days ago. Didn't show up for work. Hmmm . . ."

"What?" asked Gamache.

"It's interesting."

"What is?"

"She worked for the Ministry of Transport, in their roads division."

"Was she an inspector? Could she have fallen by accident?"

"Let me see . . ." There was a pause while Chief Inspector Brault read the file. "No. She was a senior clerk. Almost certainly suicide, but the autopsy will tell us more. Want me to send it to you, Armand?"

"No need, but thank you. *Joyeux Noël*, Marc."

Gamache hung up, then turned to face Myrna Landers.

"What is it?" she asked, and he could see her bracing for what he had to say.

"A body was brought up from the side of the Champlain Bridge this morning. I was afraid it might be your friend, but it wasn't."

Myrna closed her eyes. Then opened them again.

"So where is she?"

FIVE

—

Isabelle Lacoste and Chief Inspector Gamache sat in rush hour traffic, on the approach to the Champlain Bridge back into Montréal. It was barely four thirty, but the sun was down and it felt like midnight. The snow had stopped and Gamache looked past Isabelle Lacoste, out the window, and across the six lanes of traffic. To the spot where Audrey Villeneuve had chosen death over life.

By now her family had been told. Armand Gamache had done enough of that, and it never got easier. It was worse than looking into the faces of the dead. To look into the faces of those left behind, and to see that moment when their world changed forever.

It was a sort of murder he performed. The mother, the father, the wife or husband. They opened the door to his knock, believing the world a flawed but fundamentally decent place. Until he spoke. It was like throwing them off a cliff. Seeing them plummet. Then hitting. Dashed. The person they'd been, the life they'd known, gone forever.

And the look in their eyes, as though he'd done it.

Before they'd left, Myrna had given him Constance's home address.

"When she was here, how'd she seem?" Gamache had asked.

"As she always did. I hadn't seen her for a while, but she seemed her usual self."

"Not worried about anything?"

Myrna shook her head.

"Money? Health?"

Myrna shook her head again. "She was a very private person, as you might expect. She didn't tell me a lot about her life, but she seemed relaxed. Happy to be here and happy to be coming back for the holidays."

"You noticed nothing odd at all? Did she have an argument with anyone here? Hurt feelings?"

"You suspect Ruth?" asked Myrna, a shadow of a smile on her face.

"I always suspect Ruth."

"As a matter of fact, Constance and Ruth hit it off. They had a certain chemistry."

"Do you mean chemistry or medication?" asked Lacoste, and Myrna had smiled.

"Are they alike?" Gamache asked.

"Ruth and Constance? Completely different, but for some reason they seemed to like each other."

Gamache took that in, with some surprise. The old poet, as a matter of principle, disliked everyone. She'd have hated everyone if she could have worked up the energy hate required.

"Who hurt you once, / so far beyond repair / that you would greet each overture / with curling lip?" said Myrna.

"I'm sorry?" said Gamache, taken aback by the question.

Myrna smiled. "It's from one of Ruth's poems. Constance quoted it to me one night when she came back from visiting Ruth."

Gamache nodded and wondered if, when they eventually found her, Constance would have been hurt beyond repair.

Gamache crossed the bookstore to retrieve his coat. At the door he kissed Myrna on both cheeks.

She held him at arm's length, looking into his face. "And you? Are you all right?"

He considered the question, and all his possible responses, from flippant to dismissive, to the truth. It was, he knew, very little use lying to Myrna. But neither could he tell her the truth.

"I'm fine," he said, and saw her smile.

She watched them get into their car and drive up the hill out of Three Pines. Constance had taken that same route, and not returned. But Myrna knew Gamache would come back and bring with him the answer she had to hear.

The traffic started to creep forward, and before long the Sûreté officers were over the Champlain Bridge and driving through the city. Inspector Lacoste pulled up in front of a modest home in the Pointe-Saint-Charles *quartier* of Montréal.

Windows were lit in houses up and down the street. Christmas decorations were on, reflecting red and yellow and green in the fresh snow.

Except for here. This house was a hole in the cheerful neighborhood.

Chief Inspector Gamache checked the address he'd been given. Yes, this was where Constance Ouellet lived. He'd expected something different. Bigger.

He looked at the other homes. A snowman sat on a lawn across the street, his twig arms open in a hug. Gamache could see clearly through the front window. A woman was helping a child with homework. Next door, an elderly couple watched television while decorations on their mantelpiece blinked on and off.

Everywhere there was life. Except at the dark home of Constance Ouellet.

The clock on the dashboard said it was just after five.

They got out of the car. Inspector Lacoste grabbed a flashlight and swung a satchel over her shoulder. The Scene of Crime kit.

The path to Madame Ouellet's home had not been shoveled and there were no footprints in the snow. They mounted the steps and stood on the small concrete porch, their breaths puffing and disappearing into the night.

Gamache's cheeks burned in the slight breeze, and he could feel the cold sneak up his sleeves and past the scarf at his neck. The Chief ignored the chill and looked around. The snow on the windowsills was undisturbed. Inspector Lacoste rang the doorbell.

They waited.

A great deal of police work involved waiting. For suspects. For autopsies. For forensic results. Waiting for someone to answer a question. Or a doorbell.

It was, he knew, one of Isabelle Lacoste's great gifts, and one so easily overlooked. She was very, very patient.

Anyone could run around, not many could quietly wait. As they did now. But that didn't mean Chief Inspector Gamache and Inspector Lacoste did nothing. As they waited they took in their surroundings.

The little home was in good repair, the eaves troughs tacked in place, the windows and sills painted and without chips or cracks. It was neat and tidy. Christmas lights had been strung around the wrought-iron rail of the porch, but they remained off. A wreath was on the front door.

Lacoste turned to the Chief, who nodded. She opened the outer door and peered through the semi-circle of cut glass, into the vestibule.

Gamache had been inside many similar homes. They'd been built in the late forties and early fifties for returning veterans. Modest homes in

37

established neighborhoods. Many of the houses had since been torn down, or added to. But some, like this, remained intact. A small gem.

"Nothing, Chief."

"*Bon*," he said. Walking back down the stairs, he gestured to the right and watched Lacoste step into the deep snow. Gamache himself walked around the other side, noting that the snow there was also unmarred by footprints. He sank up to his shins. The snow tumbled down into his boots and he felt the chill as it turned to ice water and soaked his socks.

Like Lacoste, he looked into the windows, cupping his hands around his face. The kitchen was empty and clean. No unwashed dishes on the counter. He tried the windows. All locked. In the tiny backyard he met Lacoste coming around the other side. She shook her head, then stood on tiptoes and looked in a window. As he watched, she turned on her flashlight and shone it in.

Then she turned to him.

She'd found something.

Wordlessly, Lacoste handed the flashlight to Gamache. He shone it through the window and saw a bed. A closet. An open suitcase. And an elderly woman lying on the floor. Far beyond repair.

Armand Gamache and Isabelle Lacoste waited in the small front room of Constance Ouellet's home. Like the exterior, the interior was neat, though not antiseptic. There were books and magazines. A pair of old slippers sat by the sofa. This was no showroom reserved for special guests. Constance clearly used it. A television, the old box variety, was in a corner, and a sofa and two armchairs were turned to face it. Like everything else in the room, the chairs were well-made, once expensive but now worn. It was a comfortable, welcoming room. What his grandmother would have called a genteel room.

After they saw the body through the window, Gamache had called Marc Brault, then the two Sûreté officers had waited in their car for the Montréal force to arrive and take over. And when they did, the familiar routine started, only without the help of Chief Inspector Gamache and Inspector Lacoste. They were relegated to the front room, guests at the investigation. It felt odd, as though they were playing hookey. He and Lacoste filled the time by wandering around the modest room, noting the décor, the personal items. But touching nothing. Not even sitting.

Gamache noticed that three of the seats looked as though transparent people were still sitting in them. Like Myrna's armchair in the bookstore, they held the shape of the people who'd used them, every day, for years and years.

There was no Christmas tree. No decorations inside the home, but why would there be? thought Gamache. She was planning to go to Three Pines for the holidays.

Through the drawn curtains, Gamache saw a glow of headlights and heard a car stop, then a door slam and the measured crunch of boots on snow.

Marc Brault let himself into the home and found Gamache and Lacoste in the front room.

"I didn't expect to see you, Marc," said Gamache, shaking the hand of the head of the Montréal homicide squad.

"Well, I was about to head home, but since you called in the report I thought I should come along, in case someone needed to arrest you."

"How kind, *mon ami*," smiled Gamache.

Brault turned to Lacoste. "We're shorthanded. The holidays. Would you like to help my team?"

Lacoste knew when she was being politely dismissed. She left them and Brault turned his intelligent eyes on Gamache.

"Now, tell me about this body you found."

"Her name's Constance Ouellet," said Gamache.

"Is she the woman you were worried about this afternoon? The one you thought might be the suicide?"

"*Oui.* She was expected yesterday for lunch. My friend waited a day, hoping she'd show up, then she called me."

"Did you know the dead woman?"

It was an odd experience, Gamache realized, to be interrogated. For that's what this was. Gentle. Friendly. But an interrogation.

"Not personally, no."

Marc Brault opened his mouth to ask another question, then hesitated. He studied Gamache for a moment.

"Not personally, you say. But did you know her any other way? By repu-tation?"

Gamache could see Brault's sharp mind working, listening, analyzing.

"Yes. And so did you, I think." He waited a moment. "She's Constance Ouellet, Marc." He repeated the name. He'd tell Brault who she was, if necessary, but he wanted his colleague to come to it himself, if he could.

He saw his friend scan his memory, just as Gamache had done. And he saw Brault's eyes widen.

He'd found Constance Ouellet. Brault turned and stared out the door, then he left, walking rapidly down the hall. To the bedroom and the body.

Myrna hadn't heard anything from Gamache, but she didn't expect to so soon. No news was good news, she told herself. Over and over.

She called Clara and asked her around for a drink.

"There's something I need to tell you," said Myrna, once they had their glasses of Scotch and were sitting by Myrna's fireplace in her loft.

"What?" asked Clara, leaning toward her friend. She knew Constance was missing, and like Myrna, she was worried.

"It's about Constance."

"What?" She steeled herself for bad news.

"About who she really is."

"What?" asked Clara. Her panic evaporated, replaced by confusion.

"She went by the name of Constance Pineault, but that was her mother's maiden name. Her real name was Constance Ouellet."

"Who?"

"Constance Ouellet."

Myrna watched her friend. By now, after Gamache's reaction, she was used to that pause. Where people wondered two things. Who Constance Ouellet was, and why Myrna was making such a big deal about it.

Clara's brow furrowed and she sat back in her chair, crossing her legs. She sipped her Scotch and looked into the distance.

And then Clara gave a slight jerk as the truth hit her.

Marc Brault returned to the front room, walking slowly this time.

"I told the others," he said, his voice almost dream-like. "We searched her bedroom. You know, Armand, if you hadn't told us who she was we wouldn't have known. Not until we ran her through the system."

Brault looked around the small front room.

"There's nothing at all to suggest she was one of the Ouellets. Not here, not in the bedrooms. There might be papers or photographs some- where, but so far nothing."

The two men looked around the front room.

There were china figurines and books and CDs and crossword puzzles and worn boxes of jigsaw puzzles. Evidence of a personal life, but not of a past.

"Is she the last one?" Brault asked.

Gamache nodded. "I think so."

The coroner poked his head in and said they were about to leave with the body, and did the officers want one last look? Brault turned to Gamache, who nodded.

The two men followed the coroner down the narrow corridor, to a bedroom at the very back of the home. There, a Scene of Crime team from the Montréal homicide squad was collecting evidence. When Gamache arrived, they stopped and acknowledged him. Isabelle Lacoste, who'd simply been observing the operation, saw their eyes widen when they realized who he was.

Chief Inspector Gamache, of the Sûreté. The man most Québec cops dreamed of working with. With the exception of the very cops who were now assigned to the Chief's own homicide division. She stepped around the tape marking Madame Ouellet's body and joined the two men at the door. The little room was suddenly very crowded.

The bedroom, like the front room, had many personal touches, including her suitcase, open and packed, on the neatly made bed. But also like the front room, there wasn't a single photograph.

"May I?" Gamache asked the Scene of Crime investigator, who nodded. The Chief knelt beside Constance. She wore a dressing gown, buttoned up. He could see a flannel nightie underneath. She'd clearly been killed in the act of packing the night before leaving for Three Pines.

Chief Inspector Gamache held her cold hand and looked into her eyes. They were wide. Staring. Very blue. Very dead. Not surprised. Not pained. Not fearful.

Empty. As though her life had simply run out. Drained, like a battery. It would have been a peaceful scene, except for the blood under her head and the broken lamp, its base covered in blood, beside her body.

"Looks unpremeditated," said one of the investigators. "Whoever did this didn't bring a weapon. The lamp came from there." She pointed to the bedside table.

Gamache nodded. But that didn't make it unpremeditated. It only meant the killer knew where a weapon could be found.

He looked back down at the woman at his feet and wondered if her murderer had any idea who she was.

Are you sure?" Clara asked.

"Pretty sure," said Myrna, and tried not to smile.

41

"Why didn't you tell us?"

"Constance didn't want anyone to know. She's very private."

"I thought they were all dead," said Clara, her voice low.

"I hope not."

Frankly," Marc Brault admitted as they prepared to leave the Ouellet home, "this couldn't come at a worse time. Every Christmas husbands kill wives, employees kill employers. And some people kill themselves. Now this. Most of my squad is going on holiday."

Gamache nodded. "I'm off to Paris in a week. Reine-Marie's already there."

"I'm heading to our chalet in Sainte-Agathe on Friday." Brault gave his colleague an appraising look. They were out on the sidewalk now. Neighbors had begun to gather and stare. "I don't suppose . . ." Marc Brault rubbed his gloved hands together for warmth. "I know you have plenty of your own cases, Armand . . ."

Brault knew more than that. Not because Chief Inspector Gamache had told him, but because every senior cop in Québec, and probably Canada, knew. The homicide department of the Sûreté was being "restructured." Gamache, while publicly lauded, was being privately and professionally marginalized. It was humiliating, or would be except that Chief Inspector Gamache continued to behave as though he hadn't noticed.

"I'll be happy to take it over."

"*Merci*," said Brault, clearly relieved.

"*Bon*." The Chief Inspector signaled to Lacoste. It was time to leave. "If your team can complete the interviews and forensics, we'll take over in the morning."

They walked to the car. Some of the neighbors asked for information. Chief Inspector Brault was vague, but reassuring.

"We can't keep her death quiet, of course," he said to Gamache, his voice low. "But we won't announce her real name. We'll call her Constance Pineault, if the press asks." Brault looked at the worried faces of the neighbors. "I wonder if they knew who she was?"

"I doubt it," said Gamache. "She wouldn't have erased all evidence of who she was, including her name, just to tell her neighborhood."

"Maybe they guessed," said Brault. But, like Gamache, he thought not. Who would guess that their elderly neighbor was once one of the most famous people not just in Québec, or Canada, or even North America, but in the world?

Lacoste had started the car and put the heat on to defrost the windshield. The two men stood outside the vehicle. Instead of walking away, Marc Brault lingered.

"Just say it," said Gamache.

"Are you going to resign, Armand?"

"I've been on the case for two minutes and you're already asking for my resignation?" Gamache laughed.

Brault smiled and continued to watch his colleague. Gamache took a deep breath and adjusted his gloves.

"Would you?" he finally asked.

"At my age? I have my pension in place, and so do you. If my bosses wanted me out that badly, I'd be gone like a shot."

"If your bosses wanted you out that badly," said Gamache, "don't you think you'd wonder why?"

Behind Brault, Gamache could see the snowman across the street, its arms raised like the bones of an ill-formed creature. Beckoning.

"Take retirement, *mon ami*," said Brault. "Go to Paris, enjoy the holidays, then retire. But first, solve this case."

SIX

—

"Where to?" Isabelle Lacoste asked.

Gamache checked the dashboard clock. Almost seven.

"I need to get home for Henri, then back to headquarters for a few minutes."

He knew he could ask his daughter Annie to feed and walk Henri, but she had other things on her mind.

"And Madame Landers?" Lacoste asked, as she turned the car toward the Chief's home in Outremont.

Gamache had been wondering about that too.

"I'll head down later tonight, and tell her in person."

"I'll come with you," she said.

"*Merci*, Isabelle, but that isn't necessary. I might stay over at the B and B. Chief Inspector Brault said he'd send over what files he has. I'd like you to download them tomorrow morning. I'll find out what I can in Three Pines."

They didn't stay long at his home, only long enough for the Chief to pack an overnight bag for himself and Henri. Gamache beckoned the large German shepherd into the backseat of the car and Henri, his satellite ears forward, received this command with delight. He leapt in, then, fearing Gamache might change his mind, immediately curled into as tight a ball as he could manage.

You can't see me. Yoooou can't seeeee meeee.

But in his excitement, and having eaten too fast, Henri gave himself away in an all-too-familiar fashion.

In the front seat, both the Chief Inspector and Isabelle Lacoste cracked open their windows, preferring the bitter cold outside to what threatened to melt the upholstery inside.

"Does he do that often?" she gasped.

"It's a sign of affection, I'm told," said the Chief, not meeting her eyes. "A compliment." Gamache paused, turning his head to the window. "A great compliment."

Isabelle Lacoste smiled. She was used to similar "compliments" from her husband and now their young son. She wondered why the Y chromosome was so smelly.

At Sûreté headquarters, Gamache clipped Henri on the leather leash and the three of them entered the building.

"Hold it, please!" Lacoste called as a man got into the elevator at the far end of the corridor. She walked rapidly toward it, Gamache and Henri a pace behind, then she suddenly slowed. And stopped.

The man in the elevator hit a button. And hit it again. And again.

Lacoste stopped a foot from the elevator. Willing the doors to close so they could take the next one.

But Chief Inspector Gamache didn't hesitate. He and Henri walked past Lacoste and into the elevator, apparently oblivious to the man with his finger pressed hard against the close button. As the doors began to close Gamache put his arm out to stop them and looked at Lacoste.

"Coming?"

Lacoste stepped inside to join Armand Gamache and Henri. And Jean-Guy Beauvoir.

Gamache acknowledged his former second in command with a small nod.

Jean-Guy Beauvoir did not return the greeting, preferring to stare straight ahead. If Isabelle Lacoste didn't already believe in things like energy and vibes when she entered the elevator, she would have when she left. Inspector Beauvoir was throbbing, radiating strong emotion.

But what emotion? She stared at the numbers—2 . . . 3 . . . 4—and tried to analyze the waves pounding out of Jean-Guy Beauvoir.

Shame? Embarrassment? She knew she'd certainly be feeling both of those if she was him. But she wasn't. And she suspected what Beauvoir felt and radiated was baser. Coarser. Simpler.

What poured out of him was rage.

6 . . . 7 . . .

Lacoste glanced at Beauvoir's reflection in the pocked and dented door. She'd barely seen him since he'd transferred out of homicide and into Chief Superintendent Francoeur's department.

Isabelle Lacoste remembered her mentor as lithe, energetic, frenetic at times. Slender to Gamache's more robust frame. Rational to the Chief's intuitive. He was action to Gamache's contemplation.

Beauvoir liked lists. Gamache liked thoughts, ideas.

Beauvoir liked to question, Gamache liked to listen.

And yet there was a bond between the older man and the younger that seemed to reach through time. They held a natural, almost ancient, place in each other's lives. Made all the more profound when Jean-Guy Beauvoir fell in love with Annie, the Chief's daughter.

It had surprised Lacoste slightly that Beauvoir would fall for Annie. She wasn't anything like Beauvoir's ex-wife, or the parade of gorgeous Québécoise he'd dated. Annie Gamache chose comfort over fashion. She was neither pretty nor ugly. Not slender, but neither was she fat. Annie Gamache would never be the most attractive woman in the room. She never turned heads.

Until she laughed. And spoke.

To Lacoste's amazement, Jean-Guy Beauvoir had figured out something many men never got. How very beautiful, how very attractive, happiness was.

Annie Gamache was happy, and Beauvoir fell in love with her.

Isabelle Lacoste admired that in him. In fact, she admired many things about her mentor, but what she most admired were his passion for the job and his unquestioned loyalty to Chief Inspector Gamache.

Until a few months ago. Though, if she was being honest, fissures had begun to appear before that.

Now she shifted her glance to Gamache's reflection. He seemed relaxed, holding Henri's leash loosely in his hands. She noticed the scar at his graying temple.

Nothing had been the same since the day that had happened. It couldn't be. It shouldn't be. But it had taken Lacoste a while to realize just how much everything had changed.

She was standing in the ruins now, amid the rubble, and most of it had fallen from Beauvoir. His clean-shaven face was sallow, haggard. He looked much older than his thirty-eight years. Not simply tired, or even exhausted, but hollowed out. And into that hole he'd placed, for safekeeping, the last thing he possessed. His rage.

9 . . . 10 . . .

The faint hope she'd held, that the Chief and Inspector Beauvoir were just pretending to this rift, vanished. There was no harbor. No hope. No doubt.

Jean-Guy Beauvoir despised Armand Gamache.

This wasn't an act.

Isabelle Lacoste wondered what would have happened if she hadn't been in the elevator with them. Two armed men. And one with the advantage, if it could be called that, of near bottomless rage.

Here was a man with a gun and nothing more to lose.

If Jean-Guy Beauvoir loathed Gamache, Lacoste wondered how the Chief felt.

She studied him again in the scratched and dented elevator door. He seemed perfectly at ease.

Henri chose, if such a thing is a choice, to hand out another great compliment at that moment. Lacoste brought her hand to her face, in an involuntary survival instinct.

The dog, oblivious to the curdled air, looked around, his tags clinking cheerily together. His huge brown eyes glanced up at the man beside him. Not the one who held his leash. But the other man.

A familiar man.

14 . . . 15.

The elevator stopped and the door opened, bringing with it oxygen. Isabelle wondered if she'd have to burn her clothes.

Gamache held it open for Lacoste and she left as quickly as possible, desperate to get out of that stink, only part of which could be blamed on Henri. But before Gamache could step out, Henri turned to Beauvoir, and licked his hand.

Beauvoir pulled it back, as though scalded.

The German shepherd followed the Chief from the elevator. And the doors closed behind them. As the three walked toward the glass doors into the homicide division, Lacoste noticed that the hand that held the leash trembled.

It was slight, but it was there.

And Lacoste realized that Gamache had perfect control over Henri, if not Henri's bowels. He could have held the leash tight, preventing the German shepherd from getting anywhere close to Beauvoir.

But Gamache hadn't. He'd allowed the lick. Allowed the small kiss.

The elevator reached the top floor of Sûreté headquarters and the doors clunked open to reveal a couple of men standing in the corridor.

"Holy shit, Beauvoir, what a stink." One of them scowled.

"It wasn't me." Beauvoir could feel Henri's lick, moist and warm on his hand.

48

"Right," said the man, and caught the eye of the other agent.

"Fuck you," Beauvoir mumbled as he pushed between them and into the office.

Chief Inspector Gamache looked at his homicide department. Where busy agents would once have sat into the night, the desks were now empty.

He wished the tranquillity was because all the murders had been solved. Or, better yet, there were no more murders. No more pain so great it made a person take a life. Someone else's, or his own.

Like Constance Ouellet. Like the body below the bridge. Like he'd felt in the elevator just now.

But Armand Gamache was a realist, and knew the long list of homicides would only grow. What had diminished was his capacity to solve them.

Chief Superintendent Francoeur didn't get up. Didn't look up. He ignored Beauvoir and the others as they took seats in his large private office.

Beauvoir was used to that now. Chief Superintendent Francoeur was the most senior cop in Québec and he looked it. Distinguished, with gray hair and a confident bearing, he exuded authority. This was a man not to be trifled with. Chief Superintendent Francoeur associated with the Premier, had meals with the Public Security Minister. He was on a first-name basis with the Cardinal of Québec.

Unlike Gamache, Francoeur gave his agents freedom. He didn't worry about how they got results. *Just get it done*, was what he said.

The only real law was Chief Superintendent Francoeur. The only line not to be crossed was drawn around him. His power was absolute and un-questioned.

Working with Gamache was always so complicated. So many gray areas. Always debating what was right, as though that was a difficult question.

Working with Chief Superintendent Francoeur was easy.

Law-abiding citizens were safe, criminals weren't. Francoeur trusted his people to decide who was who, and to know what to do about it. And when a mistake was made? They looked out for each other. Defended each other. Protected each other.

Unlike Gamache.

Beauvoir rubbed his hand, trying to erase the lick, like a lash. He thought about the things he should have said, could have said, to his former Chief. But hadn't.

Just drop your things and head home," said Gamache at the door to his office.

"Are you sure you don't want me to drive down with you?" asked Lacoste.

"I'm sure. As I said, I'll probably stay over. Thank you, Isabelle."

As he looked at her now he saw, as he almost always did, a brief image. Of Lacoste bending over him. Calling to him. And he felt again her hands gripping either side of his head as he lay sprawled on the concrete floor.

There'd been a crushing weight on his chest and a rush in his head. And two words that needed to be said. Only two, as he stared at Lacoste, desperate for her to understand him.

Reine-Marie.

That was all there was left to say.

At first, when he'd recovered and remembered Isabelle's face so close to his, he'd been embarrassed by his vulnerability.

His job was to lead them, to protect them. And he'd failed. Instead, she'd saved him.

But now when he looked at her, and that brief image exploded between them, he realized they were fused together forever by that moment. And he felt only great affection for her. And gratitude. For staying with him and hearing those barely whispered words. She was the vessel into which he'd poured his last thoughts.

Reine-Marie.

Armand Gamache would always remember the enormous relief when he'd realized she'd understood. And he could go.

But, of course, he hadn't gone. In large part thanks to Isabelle Lacoste, he'd survived. But so many of his agents hadn't, that day.

Including Jean-Guy Beauvoir. The swaggering, annoying smartass had gone into that factory, and something else had come out.

"Go home, Isabelle," said Gamache.

The Superintendent continued to read the document in front of him, slowly turning a page.

Beauvoir recognized the report on the raid he'd been on a few days earlier.

"I see here," Francoeur said slowly in his deep, calm voice, "that not all the evidence made it to the locker."

He met Beauvoir's eyes, which widened.

"Some drugs seem to be missing."

Beauvoir's mind raced, while the Superintendent again lowered his eyes to the report.

"But I don't think that will affect the case," Francoeur said at last, turning to Martin Tessier. "Remove it from the report."

He tossed the paper across to his second in command.

"Yessir."

"I have a dinner in half an hour with the Cardinal. He's very worried about the biker gang violence. What can I tell him?"

"It's unfortunate that girl was killed," said Tessier.

Francoeur stared at Tessier. "I don't think I need to tell him that, do you?"

Beauvoir knew what they were talking about. Everyone in Québec did. A seven-year-old child had been blown up along with a few members of the Hell's Angels when a car bomb exploded. It was all over the news.

"Up until then, we'd been pretty successful at feeding rival gangs information," said Tessier, "and having them go at each other."

Beauvoir had come to appreciate the beauty of this strategy, though it had shocked him at first. Let the criminals kill each other. All the Sûreté had to do was guide them a little. Drop a bit of information here. A bit there. Then get out of the way. The rival gangs took care of the rest. It was easy and safe and, above all, effective. True, sometimes a civilian got in the way, but the Sûreté would plant suggestions in the media that the dead man or woman wasn't perhaps as innocent as their family claimed.

And it worked.

Until this child.

"What're you doing about it?" Francoeur asked.

"Well, we need to respond. Hit one of their bunkers. Since the Rock Machine planted the bomb that killed the kid, we should plan a raid against them."

Jean-Guy Beauvoir lowered his eyes, studying the carpet. Studying his hands.

Not me. Not me. Not again.

"I'm not interested in the details." Francoeur got up and they all rose. "Just get it done. The sooner the better."

"Yessir," said Tessier, and followed him out the door.

Beauvoir watched them go, then exhaled. Safe.

At the elevator the Chief Superintendent handed Tessier a small vial.

"I think our newest recruit is a little anxious, don't you?" Francoeur pressed the pill bottle into Tessier's hand. "Put Beauvoir on the raid."

He got in the elevator.

Beauvoir sat at his desk, staring blankly at the computer screen. Trying to get the meeting out of his mind. Not with Francoeur, but with Gamache. He'd structured his days, done everything he could, to avoid seeing the Chief. And for months it had worked, until tonight. His whole body felt bruised. Except for one small patch, on his hand. Which still felt moist and warm no matter how hard he rubbed it dry.

Beauvoir sensed a presence at his elbow and looked up.

"Good news," said Inspector Tessier. "You've impressed Francoeur. He wants you on the raid."

Beauvoir's stomach curdled. He'd already taken two OxyContin, but now the pain returned.

Leaning over the desk, Tessier placed a pill bottle by Beauvoir's hand.

"We all need a little help every now and then." Tessier tapped the top of the bottle, his voice light and low. "Take one. It's nothing. Just a little relaxant. We all take them. You'll feel better."

Beauvoir stared at the bottle. A small warning sounded, but it was too deep and too late.

SEVEN

—

Armand Gamache turned off the lights, then he and Henri walked down the corridor, but instead of pressing the down button, he pressed up. Not to the very top floor, but the one just below it. He looked at his watch. Eight thirty. Perfect.

A minute later he knocked on a door and went in without waiting for a response.

"*Bon*," said Superintendent Brunel. "You made it."

Thérèse Brunel, petite and soignée as always, rose and indicated a chair next to her husband, Jérôme, who was also on his feet. They shook hands and everyone sat.

Thérèse Brunel was beyond the Sûreté retirement age, but no one had the stomach, or other organs, to tell her. She'd come late to the force, been trained by Gamache, then rapidly lapped him, partly through her own hard work and ability, but partly, they all knew, because his career had hit a wall, constructed by Chief Superintendent Francoeur.

They'd been friends since the academy, when she was twice the age of any other recruit and he was her professor.

The roles, the offices, the ranks they now enjoyed should have been reversed. Thérèse Brunel knew that. Jérôme knew that. And Gamache knew that, though he alone didn't seem to care.

They sat on the formal sofa and chairs, and Henri stretched out between Gamache and Jérôme. The older man dropped an arm, absently stroking the shepherd.

Jérôme, hovering on the far side of seventy, was almost completely round, and had he been slightly smaller, Henri would have been tempted to chase him.

53

Despite the difference in their ranks, it was clear that Armand Gamache was in charge. This was his meeting, if not his office.

"What's your news?" he asked Thérèse.

"We're getting closer, I think, Armand, but there's a problem."

"I've hit a few walls," Jérôme explained. "Whoever's done this is clever. Just when I get up a head of steam, I find I'm actually in a *cul-de-sac*."

His voice was querulous, but his manner was jovial. Jérôme had rolled forward, his hands clasped together. His eyes were bright and he was fighting a smile.

He was enjoying himself.

Dr. Brunel was an investigator, but not with the Sûreté du Québec. Now retired, he'd been the head of emergency services for the Hôpital Notre-Dame in Montréal. His training was to quickly assess a medical emergency, triage, diagnose. Then treat.

Retired a few years now, he'd refocused his energy and skills toward solving puzzles, cyphers. Both his wife and Chief Inspector Gamache had consulted him on cases involving codes. But it was more than a retired doctor passing the time. Jérôme Brunel was a man born to solve puzzles. His mind saw and made connections that might take others hours or days, or never, to find.

But Dr. Brunel's game of choice, his drug of choice, was computers. He was a cyber junkie, and Gamache had brought him uncut heroin in the form of this gnarly puzzle.

"I've never seen so many layers of security," said Jérôme. "Someone's tried very hard to hide this thing."

"What thing, though?" Gamache asked.

"You asked us to find out who really leaked that video of the raid on the factory," Superintendent Brunel said. "The one you led, Armand."

He nodded. The video was taken from the tiny cameras each of the agents wore, attached to their headphones. They recorded everything.

"There was an investigation, of course," Superintendent Brunel continued. "The conclusion of the Cyber Crimes division was that a hacker had gotten lucky, found the files, edited them, and put them on the Internet."

"Bullshit," said Dr. Brunel. "A hacker could never have just stumbled on those files. They're too well guarded."

"So?" Gamache turned to Jérôme. "Who did?"

But they all knew who'd done it. If not a lucky hacker, it had to be someone inside the Sûreté, and high enough up to cover his trail. But Dr. Brunel had found that trail, and followed it.

They all knew it would lead to the office right above them. To the very highest level in the Sûreté.

But Gamache had long since begun to wonder if they were asking the right question. Not who, but why. He suspected they'd find that the video was simply the disgusting dropping of a much larger creature. They'd mistaken the *merde* for the actual menace.

Armand Gamache looked at the gathering. A senior Sûreté officer, past her retirement age. A rotund doctor. And himself. A middle-aged, marginalized officer.

Just the three of them. And the creature they sought seemed to grow each time they caught a glimpse of it.

Gamache knew, though, that what was a disadvantage was also an advantage. They were easily overlooked, dismissed, especially by people who believed themselves invisible and invincible.

"I think we're getting closer, Armand, but I keep hitting dead ends," said Jérôme. The doctor suddenly looked a little furtive.

"Go on," said Gamache.

"I'm not certain, but I think I detected a watcher."

Gamache said nothing. He knew what a watcher was, in physical as well as cyber terms. But he wanted Jérôme to be more precise.

"If I have, he's very cunning and very skilled. It's possible he's been watching me for a while."

Gamache rested his elbows on his knees, clasping his large hands in front of him. Like a battleship plowing toward its target.

"Is it Francoeur?" Gamache asked. No need to pretend otherwise.

"Not him personally," said Jérôme, "but I think whoever it is is within the Sûreté network. I've been doing this for a long time now, and I've never seen anything this sophisticated. Whenever I stop and look, he fades into the background."

"How do you even know he's there?" asked Gamache.

"I don't for sure, but it's a sense, a movement, a shift."

Brunel paused and for the first time Gamache saw in the cheerful doctor a hint of concern. A sense that as good as he was, Dr. Brunel might be up against someone better.

Gamache sat back in his chair as though something had walked by him, and pushed. *What have we uncovered?*

Not only were they hunting the creature, it seemed the creature might now be hunting them.

"Does this watcher know who you are?" he asked Jérôme.

"I don't think so."

"Think?" asked Gamache, his voice sharp, his eyes hard.

"No," Jérôme shook his head. "He doesn't know."

Yet. The word was unspoken, but implied. Yet.

"Be careful, Jérôme," said Gamache, as he rose and picked up Henri's leash. He said his good-byes, left them, and headed into the night.

The lights of the cities and towns and villages faded in his rearview mirror as they drove deeper into the forest. After a while the darkness was complete, except for the beams of his headlights on the snowy roads. Eventually he saw a soft glow ahead, and knew what it was. Gamache's car crested a hill, and there in the valley he saw three huge pines lit with green and red and yellow Christmas lights. Thousands of them, it seemed. And around the village cheery lights were hung along porches and picket fences and over the stone bridge.

As his car descended, the signal on his device disappeared. No phone reception, no emails. It was as though he and Henri, asleep on the backseat, had fallen off the face of the earth.

He parked in front of Myrna's New and Used Bookstore and noted the lights still on upstairs. So often he'd come here to find death. This time he'd brought it with him.

EIGHT

⌒

Clara Morrow was the first to notice the car arrive.

She and Myrna had had a simple dinner of reheated stew and a salad, then she'd gotten up to do the dishes, but Myrna soon joined her.

"I can do them," said Clara, squirting the dishwashing liquid into the hot water and watching it foam. It was always strangely satisfying. It made Clara feel like a magician, or a witch, or an alchemist. Not, perhaps, as valuable as turning lead into gold, but useful all the same.

Clara Morrow was not someone who liked housework. What she liked was magic. Water into foam. Dirty dishes into clean. A blank canvas into a work of art.

It wasn't change she liked so much as metamorphosis.

"You sit down," she said, but Myrna took the tea towel and reached for a warm, clean dish.

"It helps take my mind off things."

They both knew drying the dinner dishes was a fragile raft on a rough sea, but if it kept Myrna afloat for a while Clara was all for it.

They fell into a reassuring rhythm. She washed and Myrna dried.

When Clara was finished she drained the water, wiped the sink, and turned to face the room. It hadn't changed in the years since Myrna had given up her psychologist's practice in Montréal and packed her tiny car with all her worldly possessions. When she rolled into Three Pines she looked like someone who'd run away from the circus.

Out she climbed, an immense black woman, surely larger than the car itself. She'd gotten lost on the back roads, and when she found the unexpected village she'd stopped for a coffee, a pastry, a bathroom break. A pit stop on her way somewhere else. Somewhere more exciting, more promising. But Myrna Landers never left.

57

Over *café au lait* and patisserie in the bistro, she realized that she was fine where she was.

Myrna had unpacked, leased the empty shop next to Olivier's Bistro, and opened a new and used bookstore. She'd moved upstairs, into the loft space.

That's how Clara had first really gotten to know Myrna. She'd dropped by to check out how the new bookstore was going and heard sweeping and swearing from above. Climbing the stairs at the back of the shop, Clara had found Myrna.

Sweeping and swearing.

They'd been friends ever since.

She'd watched Myrna work her magic, turning an empty store into a bookshop. Turning an empty space into a meeting place. Turning a disused loft into a home. Turning an unhappy life into contentment.

Three Pines might be stable but it was never still.

When Clara surveyed the room, seeing the Christmas lights through the windows, she wasn't sure she'd seen that brief flash. Headlights.

But then she heard the car engine. She turned to Myrna, who'd also heard it.

They were both thinking the same thing.

Constance.

Clara tried to stomp down the relief, knowing it was premature, but found it bubbled up and around her caution.

There was the tinkle of the door downstairs. And steps. They could hear a person, one person, walking across the floor below them.

Myrna grabbed Clara's hand and called out, "Hello?"

There was a pause. And then a familiar voice.

"Myrna?"

Clara felt Myrna's hand grow cold. It wasn't Constance. It was the messenger. The telegraph man, pulled up on his bicycle.

It was the head of homicide for the Sûreté.

Myrna held the mug of tea, untouched, in both hands. The purpose was to warm, not to drink.

She stared into the window of the woodstove, at the flames and embers. They reflected off her face, giving it more animation than it actually held.

Clara was on the sofa and Armand sat in the armchair across from Myrna. He too held a cup of tea in his large hands. But he watched Myrna, not the fire.

Henri, after sniffing around the loft, had come to rest on the rug in front of the hearth.

"Do you think she suffered?" Myrna asked, her eyes not leaving the fire.

"I don't."

"And you don't know who did it?"

It. It. Myrna couldn't yet bring herself to say out loud what "it" was.

When a day had gone by and Constance hadn't shown up, hadn't even called, Myrna had prepared herself for the worst. That Constance had had a heart attack. A stroke. An accident.

It had never occurred to her that it could be even worse. That her friend hadn't lost her life, but that it had been taken from her.

"We don't know yet, but I'll find out." Gamache was sitting forward now.

"Can you?" asked Clara, speaking for the first time since he'd broken the news. "Didn't she live in Montréal? Isn't that out of your jurisdiction?"

"It is, but the head of homicide for Montréal's a friend. He handed the case over to me. Did you know Constance well?" he asked Myrna.

Myrna opened her mouth, then looked over at Clara.

"Oh," said Clara, with sudden understanding. "Would you like me to leave?"

Myrna hesitated then shook her head. "No, sorry. Force of habit, to not talk about a client."

"She was a client then," said Gamache. He didn't take out his notebook, preferring to listen intently. "Not just a friend."

"A client first, then a friend."

"How did you meet?"

"She came for counseling a number of years ago."

"How long ago?"

Myrna thought. "Twenty-three years." She seemed a little amazed by that. "I've known her for twenty-three years," Myrna marveled, then forced herself back to the reality. "After she stopped coming for therapy, we stayed in touch. We'd go for dinner, a play. Not often, but as two single women we found we had a lot in common. I liked her."

"Was that unusual," Gamache asked, "becoming personal friends with a client?"

"A former client, but yes, extremely. It's the only time it's happened with me. A therapist has to have clear boundaries, even with former clients. People already get into our heads—if they also get into our lives, there's a problem."

"But Constance did?"

Myrna nodded. "I think we were both a little lonely, and she seemed pretty sane."

"Pretty?" Gamache asked.

"Who among us is totally sane, Chief Inspector?"

They looked at Clara, whose hair was again standing on end, the terrible convergence of hat head, static electricity, and the habit of running her hands through it.

"What?" asked Clara.

Gamache turned back to Myrna. "Had you seen Constance since you moved to Three Pines?"

"A couple of times, when I went in to Montréal. Never out here. Mostly we kept in touch through cards and phone calls. The truth is, we'd drifted apart in recent years."

"So what brought her down for a visit now?" the Chief asked. "Did you invite her?"

Myrna thought about that, then shook her head. "No, I don't think so. I think it was her idea, though it's possible she hinted she'd like to come and I invited her."

"Did she have any particular reason for wanting to visit?"

Again, Myrna considered before answering. "Her sister died in October, as you probably heard—"

Gamache nodded. It had been in the news, as Constance's death would be. The murder of Constance Pineault was a statistic. The murder of Constance Ouellet was headline news.

"With her sisters gone there was no one else in her life," said Myrna. "Constance was very private. Nothing wrong with that, but it had become a sort of mania with her."

"Can you give me the names of some of her friends?"

Myrna shook her head.

"You don't know any?" he asked.

"She didn't have any."

"*Pardon?*"

"Constance had no friends," said Myrna.

Gamache stared at her. "None?"

"None."

"You were her friend," said Clara. "She was friends with everyone here. Even Ruth."

Though even as she said it, Clara realized her error. She'd mistaken being friendly for being friends.

Myrna was quiet for a moment before she spoke.

"Constance gave the impression of friendship and intimacy without actually feeling it."

"You mean that was all a lie?" asked Clara.

"Not totally. I don't want you to think she was a sociopath or anything. She liked people, but there was always a barrier."

"Even for you?" asked Gamache.

"Even for me. There were large parts of her life she kept well hidden."

Clara remembered their exchange in the studio, when Constance had refused to let Clara paint her portrait. She hadn't been rude, but she had been firm. It was certainly a shove back.

"What is it?" Gamache asked, seeing the look of concentration on Myrna's face.

"I was just thinking about what Clara said, and she's right. I think Constance was happy here, I think she genuinely felt comfortable with everyone, even Ruth."

"What does that tell you?" Gamache asked.

Myrna thought. "I wonder . . ."

She stared across the room, out the window, to the pines lit for Christmas. The bulbs bobbed in the night breeze.

"I wonder if she was finally opening up," said Myrna, bringing her gaze back to her guests. "I hadn't thought about it, but she seemed less guarded, more genuine, especially as the days went on."

"She wouldn't let me paint her portrait," said Clara.

Myrna smiled. "But that's understandable, don't you think? It was the very thing she and her sisters most feared. Being put on display."

"But I didn't know who she was then," said Clara.

"Wouldn't matter. She knew," said Myrna. "But I think by the time she left, she felt safe here, whether her secret was out or not."

"And was her secret out?" Gamache asked.

"I didn't tell," said Myrna.

Gamache looked at the magazine on the footstool. A very old copy of *Life*, and on the cover a famous photo.

"And yet you obviously knew who she was," he said to Clara.

"I told Clara this afternoon," Myrna explained. "When I began to accept that Constance would probably never show up."

"And no one else knew?" he repeated, picking up the magazine and staring at the picture. One he'd seen many times before. Five little girls, in muffs and pretty little winter coats. Identical coats. Identical girls.

61

"Not that I know of," said Myrna.

And once again, Gamache wondered if the man who'd killed Constance knew who she was, and realized he was killing the last of her kind. The last of the Ouellet quintuplets.

NINE

———

Armand stepped outside into the cold, crisp night. The snow had long since stopped and the sky had cleared. It was just past midnight, and as he stood there, taking deep breaths of the clean air, the lights on the trees went out.

The Chief Inspector and Henri were the lone creatures in a dark world. He looked up, and slowly the stars appeared. Orion's Belt. The Big Dipper. The North Star. And millions and millions of other lights. All very, very clear now, and only now. The light only visible in the dark.

Gamache found himself uncertain what to do and where to go. He could return to Montréal, though he was tired and would rather not, but he hadn't made any arrangements to stay at the B and B, preferring to go straight to Myrna. And now it was past midnight and all the lights were out at the B and B. He could only just make out the outline of the former coach inn against the forest beyond.

But as he watched, a light, softened by curtains, appeared at an upstairs window. And then, a few moments later, another downstairs. Then he saw a light through the window in the front door, just before it opened. A large man stood silhouetted on the threshold.

"Come here, boy, come here," the voice called, and Henri tugged at the leash.

Gamache dropped it and the shepherd took off along the path, up the stairs and into Gabri's arms.

When Gamache arrived, Gabri struggled to his feet.

"Good boy." He embraced the Chief Inspector. "Get inside. I'm freezing my ass off. Not that it couldn't use it."

"How'd you know we were here?"

"Myrna called. She thought you might need a room." He regarded his unexpected guest. "You do want to stay, don't you?"

"Very much," said the Chief, and had rarely meant anything more.

Gabri closed the door behind them.

Jean-Guy Beauvoir sat in his car and stared at the closed door. He was slumped down. Not so far as to disappear completely, but far enough to make it look like he was trying to be discreet. It was calculated and, somewhere below the haze, he knew it was also pathetic.

But he didn't care anymore. He just wanted Annie to look out her window. To recognize his car. To see him there. To open the door.

He wanted . . .

He wanted . . .

He wanted to feel her in his arms again. To smell her scent. He wanted her to whisper, "It'll be all right."

Most of all, he wanted to believe it.

Myrna told us that Constance was missing," said Gabri, reaching for a hanger for Gamache's coat. He took the parka from the Chief and paused. "Are you here about her?"

"I'm afraid so."

Gabri hesitated just an instant before asking, "She's dead?"

The Chief nodded.

Gabri hugged the parka and stared at Gamache. While he longed to ask more questions, he didn't. He could see the Chief's exhaustion. Instead he finished hanging up the coat and walked to the stairs.

Gamache followed the immense, swaying dressing gown up the stairs.

Gabri led them along the passage and stopped at a familiar door. He flicked a switch to reveal the room Gamache always stayed in. Unlike Gabri, this room, indeed the entire bed and breakfast, was a model of restraint. Oriental throw rugs were scattered on the wide-plank floor. The dark wood bed was large and inviting and made up with crisp white linens, a thick white duvet, and down pillows.

It was uncluttered and comforting. Simple and welcoming.

"Have you had dinner?"

"No, but I'll be fine until morning." The clock on the bedside table said 12:30.

Gabri crossed to the window, opened it a sliver to let the fresh, cold air in, and pulled the curtains closed.

"What time would you like to get up?"

"Six thirty too early?"

Gabri blanched. "Not at all. We're always up at that hour." At the door he paused. "You do mean six thirty P.M., right?"

Gamache placed his satchel on the floor by the bed.

"*Merci, patron,*" he said with a smile, holding Gabri's eyes for a moment.

Before changing, Gamache looked at Henri, who was standing by the door.

The Chief stood in the middle of the room, looking from the warm, soft bed to Henri and back again.

"Oh, Henri, you'd better want to do more than just play," he sighed, and fished in Henri's satchel for the tennis ball and a bag.

They went quietly down the stairs. Gamache put his parka, gloves, and hat back on, unlocked the door and the two headed into the night. He didn't put Henri on the leash. There was very little danger he'd run away, since Henri was among the least adventurous dogs Gamache knew.

The village was completely dark now, the homes just hinted at in front of the forest. They walked over to the village green. Gamache watched with satisfaction and a silent prayer of thanks as Henri did his business. The Chief picked it up with the bag, then turned to give Henri his treat.

But there was no dog. Every walk, over hundreds of walks, Henri had stood beside Gamache, looking up expectantly. One treat deserved another. A quid pro quo.

But now, inconceivably, Henri wasn't there. He'd disappeared.

Gamache cursed himself for a fool and looked at the empty leash in his hand. Had Henri gotten a whiff of deer or coyote, and taken off into the woods?

"Henri," the Chief called. "Come here, boy."

He whistled and then noticed the paw prints in the snow. They headed back across the road, but not toward the bed and breakfast.

Gamache bent over and followed them at a jog. Across the road, over a snow bank. Onto a front lawn. Down an unshoveled walkway. For the second time that day, the Chief felt snow tumble down his boots and melt into his socks. Another soaker. But he didn't care. All he wanted was to find Henri.

Gamache stopped. There was a dark figure, with immense ears, looking up expectantly at a door. His tail wagging. Waiting to be let in.

The Chief felt his heart simmer down and he took a deep, calming breath.

"Henri," he whispered vehemently. "*Viens ici.*"

The shepherd looked in his direction.

Gone to the wrong house, thought Gamache, not altogether surprised. While Henri had a huge heart, he had quite a modest brain. His head was taken up almost entirely by his ears. In fact, his head seemed simply a sort of mount for those ears. Fortunately Henri didn't really need his head. He kept all the important things in his heart. Except, perhaps, his current address.

"Come here," the Chief gestured, surprised that Henri, so well trained and normally so compliant, hadn't immediately responded. "You'll scare the people half to death."

But even as he spoke, the Chief realized that Henri hadn't made a mistake at all. He'd meant to come to this house. Henri knew the B and B, but he knew the house better.

Henri had grown up here. He'd been rescued and brought to this house as a puppy, to be raised by an elderly woman. Emilie Longpré had saved him, and named him, and loved him. And Henri had loved her.

This had been, and in some ways always would be, Henri's home.

Gamache had forgotten that Henri knew Three Pines better than he ever would. Every scent, every blade of grass, every tree, every one.

Gamache looked down at the paw and boot prints in the snow. The front walk hadn't been shoveled. The steps up to the verandah hadn't been cleaned. The home was dark. And empty.

No one lived there, he was sure, and probably hadn't in the years since Emilie Longpré had died. When Armand and Reine-Marie had decided to adopt the orphan puppy.

Henri hadn't forgotten. Or more likely, thought Gamache as he climbed the snowy steps to retrieve the dog, he knew this home by heart. And now the shepherd waited, his tail swishing back and forth, for a woman long dead to let him in and give him a cookie, and tell him he was a good boy.

"Good boy," whispered Gamache into the immense ears, as he bent down and clipped the leash on Henri. But before going back down the stairs, the Chief peered into a window.

He saw furniture covered in sheets. Ghost furniture.

Then he and Henri stepped off the porch. Under a canopy of stars he and Henri walked slowly around the village green.

One of them thinking, one of them remembering.

Thérèse Brunel got up on one elbow and looked over the lump in the bed that was Jérôme, to the clock on the bedside table.

It was past one in the morning. She lowered herself onto the mattress and watched her husband's easy breathing, and envied him his calm.

She wondered if it was because he really didn't grasp the seriousness of the situation, though he was a thoughtful man and should.

Or, perhaps most likely, Jérôme trusted his wife and Armand to know what to do.

For most of their married life, Thérèse had been comforted by the thought that as an emergency room physician Jérôme would always be able to help. If she or one of the children choked. Or hit their head. Or were in an accident. Or had a heart attack. He'd save them.

But now she realized the roles were reversed. He was counting on her. She hadn't the heart to tell him she had no idea what to do. She'd been trained to deal with clear targets, obvious goals. Solve the crime, arrest the criminal. But now everything seemed blurry. Ill-defined.

As Superintendent Brunel stared at the ceiling, listening to the heavy, rhythmic breathing of her husband, she realized it came down to two possibilities. That Jérôme had not been found in cyber space. Had not been followed. That it was a mirage.

Or that he had been found. And followed.

Which meant someone high up in the Sûreté had gone to a great deal of trouble to cover up what they were doing. More trouble than a viral video, no matter how vile, warranted.

Lying in bed, staring at the ceiling, she thought the unthinkable. What if the creature they hunted had been there for years, growing and scheming? Putting patient plans in place?

Is that what they'd stumbled upon? In following the hacked video, had Jérôme found something much larger, older, even more contemptible?

She looked at her husband and noticed that he was awake after all and also staring at the ceiling. She touched his arm and he rolled over, bringing his face very close to hers.

Taking both her hands in his, he whispered, "It'll be all right, *ma belle*."

She wished she could believe him.

On the far side of the village green, the Chief Inspector paused. Henri, on his leash, stood patiently in the cold as Gamache studied the dark and empty house where Henri had been raised. Where Henri had taken him that evening.

And a thought formed.

After a minute or so Gamache noticed that the shepherd was raising and lowering his front paws, trying to get them away from the snow and ice underfoot.

"Let's go, *mon vieux*," he said, and walked rapidly back to the B and B.

In the bedroom, the Chief found a plate of thick ham sandwiches, some cookies, and a hot chocolate. He could hardly wait to crawl into bed with his dinner.

But first he knelt down and held Henri's cold paws in his warm hands. One after the other. Then into those ears he whispered, "It'll be all right."

And Henri believed him.

TEN

⌐◦

A tap on the door awakened Gamache at six thirty the next morning.

"*Merci, patron,*" he called, then threw off the duvet and went gingerly across the cold room to shut the window.

After showering, he and Henri headed downstairs, following the scent of strong coffee and maple-smoked bacon. A fire popped and leapt in the grate.

"One egg or two, *patron*?" called Gabri.

Gamache looked into the kitchen. "Two eggs, please. Thank you for the sandwiches last night." He put the empty plates and mug in the sink. "They were delicious."

"Slept well?" Gabri asked, looking up from pushing the bacon around the skillet.

"Very."

And he had. It had been a deep and restful sleep, his first in a very long time.

"Breakfast will be ready in a few minutes," said Gabri.

"I'll be back by then."

At the front door he met Olivier and the two men embraced.

"I heard you were here," said Olivier, as they bent to put on their boots.

Straightening up, Olivier paused. "Gabri told me about Constance. What a terrible thing. Heart?"

When Gamache didn't respond, Olivier's eyes slowly widened, trying to take in the enormity of what he saw in the Chief's somber face.

"It's not possible," he whispered. "Someone killed her?"

"I'm afraid so."

"My God." Olivier shook his head. "Fucking city."

"Glass houses, monsieur?" asked Gamache.

Olivier pursed his lips and followed Gamache onto the front porch, where the Chief clipped Henri onto his leash. They were approaching the winter solstice, the shortest day of the year. The sun wasn't yet up, but villagers were beginning to stir. Even as the two men and the dog stood there, lights appeared at windows around the green and there was a faint scent of wood smoke in the air.

They walked together toward the bistro, where Olivier would prepare for the breakfast crowd.

"How?" Olivier asked.

"She was attacked in her home. Hit on the head."

Even in the dark, Gamache could see his companion grimace. "Why would anyone do that?"

And that, of course, was the question, thought Gamache.

Sometimes it was "how," almost always it was "who." But the question that haunted every investigation was "why."

Why had someone killed this seventy-seven-year-old woman? And had they killed Constance Pineault, or Constance Ouellet? Did the murderer know she was one of the celebrated Ouellet Quints? And not just a Quint, but the last one?

Why?

"I don't know," Gamache admitted.

"Is it your case?"

Gamache nodded, his head dipping in rhythm with his steps.

They came to rest in front of the bistro and Olivier was about to say good-bye when the Chief reached out and touched his arm. Olivier looked down at the gloved hand, then up into the intense brown eyes.

Olivier waited.

Gamache lowered his hand. He was far from certain that what he was about to do was wise. Olivier's handsome face was turning pink in the cold, and his breath was coming in long, easy puffs.

The Chief broke eye contact and concentrated on Henri, rolling in the snow, his feet thrashing in the air.

"Will you walk with me?"

Olivier was a little surprised, and more than a little guarded. It was rarely a good sign, in Olivier's experience, when the head of homicide asked to speak privately.

The hard-packed snow of the road squeaked as they walked with a measured pace around the village green. A tall, substantial man and a shorter, slighter, younger man. Heads bent together, sharing confidences. Not about the murder, but about something else entirely.

70

They stopped in front of Emilie Longpré's home. There was no smoke from the chimney. No light at the windows. But it was filled with memories of an elderly woman Gamache had greatly admired and Henri had loved. The two men looked at the house, and Gamache explained what he wanted.

"I understand, *patron*," said Olivier after listening to the Chief's request.

"Thank you. Can you keep this to yourself?"

"Of course."

They parted, Olivier to open his bistro, Gamache and Henri for breakfast at the B and B.

A large bowl of *café au lait* was waiting for the Chief on the worn pine table in front of the fireplace. After feeding Henri and giving him fresh water, Gamache settled at the table, sipping his café and making notes. Henri lay at his feet but looked up when Gabri arrived.

"*Voilà.*" The innkeeper put a plate with two eggs, bacon, toasted English muffins, and fresh fruit on the table, then he made himself a *café au lait* and joined the Chief.

"Olivier called a few moments ago from the bistro," said Gabri. "He told me that Constance had been killed. Is it true?"

Gamache nodded and took a sip of his own café. It was rich and strong. "Did he tell you anything else?" Gamache kept his voice light, but studied Gabri.

"He said she'd been at home."

Gamache waited, but it seemed Olivier had kept the rest of their conversation secret, as he'd promised.

"It's true," said Gamache.

"But why?" Gabri reached for one of the toasted English muffins.

There it was again, thought Gamache. Like his partner, Gabri hadn't asked who, but why.

Gamache, of course, could answer neither of those questions yet.

"What did you think of her?"

"She was only here a few days, you know," said Gabri. Then he considered the question. Gamache waited, curious to hear the answer.

"When she arrived she was friendly but reserved," said Gabri, finally. "She didn't like gays, that was obvious."

"And did you like her?"

"I did. Some people just haven't met many queers, that's their problem."

"And once she had met you and Olivier?"

"Well, she didn't exactly become a fag hag, but the next best thing."

"Which is?"

Instead of a clever quip, Gabri grew serious. "She became very motherly, to both of us. To all of us, I think. Except Ruth."

"And with Ruth, what was she like?"

"At first Ruth wouldn't have anything to do with her. Hated Constance on sight. As you know, it's a point of pride for Ruth, that she hates everyone. She and Rosa kept their distance and muttered obscenities from afar."

"Ruth's normal reaction, then," said Gamache.

"I'm glad Rosa's back," Gabri confided in a whisper, then looked around in exaggerated concern. "But does she look a little like a flying monkey to you?"

"I wonder if we can stick to the point, Dorothy," said Gamache.

"The funny thing is, after treating Constance like something Rosa pooped, Ruth suddenly warmed to her."

"Ruth?"

"I know. I'd never seen anything like it. They even had dinner together one night, at Ruth's home. Alone."

"Ruth?" Gamache repeated.

Gabri put marmalade on his muffin and nodded. Gamache studied him, but Gabri didn't seem to be hiding anything. And the Chief realized Gabri did not know who Constance was. If he did, he'd have said something by now.

"So as far as you can tell, nothing that happened here would explain her death?" asked Gamache.

"Nothing."

Gamache finished his breakfast, with Gabri's help, then he got up and called Henri.

"Should I keep your room for you?"

"Please."

"And one for Inspector Beauvoir, of course. He'll be joining you?"

"No, actually. He's on another assignment."

Gabri paused, then nodded. "Ahh."

Neither man really knew what the "ahh" was supposed to mean.

Gamache wondered how long it would be before people stopped looking at him and seeing Beauvoir standing beside him. And how long would it be before he himself stopped expecting to see Jean-Guy there? It wasn't the ache that was so difficult to bear, thought Gamache. It was the weight.

When the Chief Inspector and Henri arrived at the bistro, it was full with the breakfast rush, though "rush" might have been the wrong word. No one seemed in much of a hurry.

Many of the villagers were lingering over coffee, settling into seats by the fires with their morning papers, which came in a day late from Montréal. Some sat at the small round tables, eating French toast or crêpes or bacon and eggs.

The sun was just coming up on what would be a brilliant day.

As he walked through the door, all eyes turned to him. He was used to that. They would, of course, know about Constance. They knew she was missing, and now they'd know she was dead. Murdered.

The eyes that met his, as he scanned the open room, were curious, some pained, some searching, some simply inquisitive, as though he carried a sack of answers slung over his shoulder.

As he hung up his parka, Gamache noticed a few smiles. The villagers had recognized his companion, he of the ears. A returning son. And Henri recognized them, and greeted them with licks and wags and inappropriate sniffs as they walked through the bistro.

"Over here."

Gamache saw Clara standing by a group of armchairs and a sofa. He returned the wave and threaded his way between tables. Olivier joined him there, a tea towel slung over his shoulder and a damp cloth in his hand. He wiped the table as the Chief greeted Myrna, Clara, and Ruth.

"Do you mind if Henri stays, or would you rather I leave him in the B and B?" Gamache asked.

Olivier looked over at Rosa. The duck was sitting in an armchair by the fire, a copy of the Montréal *Gazette* beneath her and *La Presse* slung over the arm, waiting to be read.

"I think it'll be fine," said Olivier.

Ruth whacked the seat beside her on the sofa, in what could only be interpreted as an invitation. It was like receiving a personalized Molotov cocktail.

Gamache sat.

"So, where's Beauvoir?"

The Chief had forgotten that, against all odds and nature, Jean-Guy and Ruth had struck up a friendship. Or, at least, an understanding.

"He's on another assignment."

Ruth glared at the Chief and he held her eyes, calmly.

"Finally saw through you, did he?"

Gamache smiled. "Must have."

"And your daughter? Is he still in love with her, or did he make a balls-up of that too?"

Gamache continued to hold the cold, old eyes.

73

"I'm happy to see Rosa back," he said at last. "She looks well."

Ruth looked from Gamache to the duck, then back to the Chief. Then she did something he'd rarely seen before. She relented.

"Thank you," she said.

Armand took a deep breath. The bistro smelled of fresh pine and wood smoke and a hint of candy cane. A wreath hung over the mantel and a tree stood in the corner, decorated with mismatched Christmas ornaments and candies.

He turned to Myrna. "How're you this morning?"

"Pretty awful," she said with a small smile. And indeed, she looked as though she hadn't had much sleep.

Clara reached out and held her friend's hand.

"Inspector Lacoste will get all the hard evidence this morning from the Montréal police," he told them. "I'll drive into the city and we'll go over the interviews. One main question is whether the person who killed Constance knew who she really was."

"You mean, was it a stranger?" asked Olivier. "Or someone who targeted Constance on purpose?"

"That's always a question," admitted Gamache.

"Do you think they meant to kill her?" asked Clara. "Or was it a mistake? A robbery that got out of control?"

"Was there *mens rea*, a guilty mind, or was it an accident?" said Gamache. "Those are questions we'll be asking."

"Wait a minute," said Gabri, who'd joined them, but been uncharacteristically quiet. "What did you mean, 'who she really was'? Not 'who she was,' but 'who she really was.' What did you mean by that?"

Gabri looked from Gamache to Myrna, then back again.

"Who was she?"

The Chief Inspector sat forward, about to answer, then he looked over at Myrna, sitting quietly in her chair. He nodded. It was a secret Myrna had kept for decades. It was her secret to give up.

Myrna opened her mouth, but another voice, a querulous voice, spoke.

"She was Constance Ouellet, shithead."

ELEVEN

⁓

"Constance Ouellet-Shithead?" asked Gabri.

Ruth and Rosa glared at him.

"Fuck, fuck, fuck," muttered the duck.

"She's Constance Ouellet," Ruth clarified, her voice glacial. "You're the shithead."

"You knew?" Myrna asked the old poet.

Ruth picked up Rosa, placing the duck on her lap and stroking her like a cat. Rosa stretched her neck, straining her beak upward toward Ruth, and making a nest of the old body.

"Not at first. I thought she was just some boring old fart. Like you."

"Wait a minute," said Gabri, waving his large hand in front of him as though trying to clear away the confusion. "Constance Pineault was Constance Ouellet?"

He turned to Olivier.

"Did you know?" But it was clear his partner was equally amazed.

Gabri looked around the gathering and finally came to rest on Gamache.

"Are we talking about the same thing? The Ouellet Quints?"

"*C'est ça,*" said the Chief.

"The quintuplets?" Gabri insisted, still unable to fully grasp it.

"That's it," Gamache assured him. But it only seemed to increase Gabri's bafflement.

"I thought they were dead," he said.

"Why do people keep saying that?" Myrna asked.

"Well, it all seems so long ago. Once upon a time."

They sat in silence. Gabri had nailed it. Exactly what most of them had been thinking. Not so much amazement that one of the Ouellet Quints was dead, but that any were still alive. And that one had walked among them.

The Quints were legend in Québec. In Canada. Worldwide. They were a phenomenon. Freaks, almost. Five little girls, identical. Born in the depths of the Depression. Conceived without fertility drugs. In vivo, not in vitro. The only known natural quintuplets to survive. And they had survived, for seventy-seven years. Until yesterday.

"Constance was the only one left," said Myrna. "Her sister, Marguerite, died in October. A stroke."

"Did Constance marry?" asked Olivier. "Is that where Pineault came from?"

"No, none of the Quints married," said Myrna. "They went by their mother's maiden name, Pineault."

"Why?" asked Gabri.

"Why do you think, numb nuts?" asked Ruth. "Not everyone craves attention, you know."

"So how did you know who she was?" Gabri demanded.

That shut Ruth up, much to everyone's amazement. They'd expected a brusque retort, not silence.

"She told me," Ruth finally said. "We didn't talk about it, though."

"Oh, come on," said Myrna. "She told you she was a Ouellet Quint and you didn't ask a single question?"

"I don't care if you believe me," said Ruth. "It's the truth, alas."

"Truth? You wouldn't know the truth if it bit you on the alas," said Gabri.

Ruth ignored him and focused on Gamache, who'd been watching her closely.

"Was she killed because she was a Ouellet Quint?" Ruth asked him.

"What do you think?" he asked.

"I can't see why," Ruth admitted. "And yet . . ."

And yet, thought Gamache, as he rose. And yet. Why else would she be killed?

He looked at his watch. Almost nine. Time to get going. He excused himself to make a phone call from the bar, remembering in time that his cell phone didn't work in Three Pines, and neither did email. He almost expected to see messages fluttering back and forth in the sky above the village, unable to descend. Waiting for him to head up the hill out of Three Pines, and then dive-bombing him.

But as long as he was here, none could reach him. Armand Gamache suspected that partly explained his good night's sleep. And he suspected it also explained Constance Ouellet's growing ease in the village.

She was safe there. Nothing could reach her. It was only in leaving that she'd been killed.

Or . . .

As the phone rang his thoughts sped along.

Or . . .

She hadn't been killed when she left, he realized. Constance Ouellet had been murdered when she'd tried to return to Three Pines.

"*Bonjour, patron.*" Inspector Lacoste's bright voice came down the landline.

"How'd you know it was me?" he asked.

"The caller ID said 'Bistro.' It's our code word for you."

He paused for a moment, wondering if that was true, then she laughed.

"You're still in Three Pines?"

"Yes, just leaving. What do you have?"

"We got the autopsy and forensics from the Montréal police, and I'm reading through the statements from the neighbors. It's all been sent to you."

Among the messages hovering overhead, thought Gamache.

"Anything I should know?"

"Not so far. It seems the neighbors didn't know who she was."

"Do they now?"

"We haven't told them. Want to keep it quiet for as long as possible. There'll be a media storm when it comes out that the last Quint hasn't just died, but been murdered."

"I'd like to see the scene again. Can you meet me at the Ouellet home in an hour and a half?"

"*D'accord,*" said Lacoste.

Gamache looked up, into the mirror behind the bar. In it he saw himself reflected, and behind him the bistro, with its Christmas decorations, and the window into the snowy village. The sun was now up, cresting the tree line, and the sky was the palest of winter blues. Most of the patrons of the bistro had gone back to their conversations, excited now, animated by the news that they'd met, in person, a Ouellet Quint. Gamache could sense the ebb and flow of their emotions. Excitement at the discovery. Then remembering she was dead. Then back to the Quint phenomenon. Then the murder. It was like atoms racing between poles. Unable to rest in any one place.

Around the fireplace, the friends were commiserating with Myrna. And yet— He'd had the impression that as he'd looked into the reflection, there'd been a movement. Someone had been staring at him and had quickly dropped their eyes.

But one set of eyes remained on him. Staring, unyielding.

Henri.

The shepherd sat perfectly contained, oblivious to the hubbub around him. He stared at Gamache. Transfixed. Waiting. He would wait forever, secure in the absolute certainty that Gamache would not forget him.

Gamache held the shepherd's eyes and smiled into the mirror. Henri's tail twitched, but the rest of his body remained stone still.

"What now, *patron*?" asked Olivier, coming around the bar as Gamache replaced the phone.

"Now I head back to Montréal. Work to do, I'm afraid."

Olivier picked up the phone. "And I have work to do as well. Good luck, Chief Inspector."

"Good luck to you, *mon vieux*."

Chief Inspector Gamache met Isabelle Lacoste just outside Constance's home and they went in together.

"Where's Henri?" she asked, turning on the lights in the house. It was a sunny day, but the home felt dull, as though the color was draining from it.

"I left him in Three Pines with Clara. They both seemed pretty happy about that."

He'd assured Henri he'd be back, and the shepherd had believed him.

Gamache and Lacoste sat at the kitchen table and went over the interviews and forensics. The Montréal police had been thorough, taking statements and samples and fingerprints.

"Only her prints, I see," said Gamache, not looking up as he read the report. "No sign of forced entry and the door was unlocked when we arrived."

"That might not mean anything," said Lacoste. "When you get to the statements by the neighbors, you'll see that most don't lock their doors during the day, when they're at home. It's an old, established neighborhood. No crime. Families have lived here for years. Generations in some cases."

Gamache nodded but suspected Constance Ouellet had probably locked her doors. Her most valued possession seemed to be privacy, and she wouldn't have wanted any well-meaning neighbor stealing it.

"Coroner confirms she was killed before midnight," he read. "She'd been dead a day and a half by the time we found her."

"That also explains why no one saw anything," said Lacoste. "It was dark and cold and everyone was inside asleep or watching television or wrapping gifts. And then it snowed all day and covered any tracks there might've been."

"How did he get in?" Gamache asked, looking up and meeting Lacoste's eyes. Around them the dated kitchen seemed to be waiting for one of them to make a pot of tea, or eat the biscuits in the tin. It was a hospitable kitchen.

"Well, the door was unlocked when we arrived, so either she left it unlocked and he let himself in, or she had it locked, he rang, and she let him in."

"Then he killed her and left," said Gamache, "leaving the door unlocked behind him."

Lacoste nodded and watched as Gamache sat back and shook his head.

"Constance Ouellet wouldn't have let him in. Myrna said she was almost pathologically private, and this confirms it." He tapped the forensics report. "When was the last time you saw a house with only one set of prints? No one came into this home. At least, no one was invited in."

"Then the door must've been unlocked and he let himself in."

"But an unlocked door was also against her nature," said the Chief. "And let's say she'd gotten into the habit of keeping her door unlocked, like the rest of the neighborhood. It was late at night and she was getting ready for bed. She'd have locked the door by then, *non*?"

Lacoste nodded. Constance either let her killer in, or he let himself in.

Neither possibility seemed likely, but one of them was the truth.

Gamache read the rest of the reports while Inspector Lacoste did her own detailed search of the house, starting in the basement. He could hear her down there, moving things about. Beyond that, though, there was just the clunk, clunk as the clock above the sink noted the passing moments.

Finally he lowered the reports and took off his glasses.

The neighbors had seen nothing. The oldest of them, who'd lived on the street all her life, remembered when the three sisters moved into the home, thirty-five years ago.

Constance, Marguerite, and Josephine.

As far as she knew, Marguerite was the oldest, though Josephine was the first to die, five years ago. Cancer.

The sisters had been friendly, but private. Never having anyone in, but always buying boxes of oranges and grapefruit and Christmas chocolate from the children when they'd canvassed to raise money, and stopping to chat on warm summer days as they gardened.

They were cordial without being intrusive. And without allowing intrusion.

The perfect neighbors, the woman had said.

She lived next door and had once had a lemonade with Marguerite. They'd sat together on the porch and watched as Constance washed the car. They'd called encouragement and jokingly pointed out areas she'd missed.

Gamache could see them. Could taste the tart lemonade and smell the cold water from the hose as it hit the hot pavement. He wondered how this elderly neighbor could not have known she was sitting with one of the Ouellet Quints.

But he knew the answer to that.

The Quints only existed in sepia photographs and newsreels. They lived in perfect little castles and wore impossibly frilly dresses. And came in a cluster of five.

Not three. Not one.

Five girls, forever children.

The Ouellet Quints weren't real. They didn't age, they didn't die. And they sure didn't sip lemonade in Pointe-Saint-Charles.

That's why no one recognized them.

It helped, too, that they didn't want to be recognized. As Ruth said, not everyone seeks attention.

"It's the truth, alas," Ruth had said.

Alas, thought Chief Inspector Gamache. He left the kitchen and began his own search.

Clara Morrow placed a bowl of fresh water on the floor but Henri was too excited to notice. He ran around the home, sniffing. Clara watched, her heart both swelling and breaking. It hadn't been all that long ago that she'd had to put her golden retriever, Lucy, down. Myrna and Gabri had gone with them, and yet Clara felt she'd been alone. Peter wasn't there.

She'd debated calling to tell him about Lucy, but Clara knew that was just an excuse to make contact.

The deal was, they'd wait a year, and it hadn't been six months since he'd left.

Clara followed Henri into her studio, where he found an old banana peel. Taking it from him, she paused in front of her latest work, barely an outline so far.

This ghost on the canvas was her husband.

Some mornings, some evenings, she came in here and talked to him. Told him about her day. She even, sometimes, fixed dinner and brought a candle in and ate by candlelight, in front of this suggestion of Peter. She ate, and chatted with him, told him the events of her day. The little events only a good friend would care about. And the huge events. Like the murder of Constance Ouellet.

Clara painted and talked to the portrait. Adding a stroke here, a dab there. A husband of her own creation. Who listened. Who cared.

Henri was still sniffing and snorting around the studio. Having found one banana peel, there was reason to hope there'd be more. Pausing in her painting for a moment, Clara realized he wasn't looking for a banana peel. Henri was looking for Armand.

Clara reached into her pocket for one of the treats Armand had left, then she bent down and called the dog over. Henri stopped his scurrying and looked at her, his satellite ears turning toward her voice, having picked up his favorite channel. The treat channel.

He approached, sat, and gently took the bone-shaped cookie.

"It's okay," she assured him, resting her forehead against his. "He'll be back."

Then Clara returned to the portrait.

"I asked Constance to sit for me," she said to the wet paint. "But she refused. I'm not really sure why I asked. You're right, I am the best artist in Canada, perhaps the world, so she should've been pleased."

Might as well exaggerate—this Peter couldn't roll his eyes.

Clara leaned away from the canvas and put the brush in her mouth, smearing raw umber paint on her cheek.

"I stayed over at Myrna's last night." She described for Peter how she'd pulled the warm duvet around her, rested the old *Life* magazine on her knees, and studied the cover. As she'd looked at it, the image of the girls moved from endearing, to uncanny, to vaguely unsettling.

"They were all the same, Peter. In expression, in mood. Not just similar, but exactly the same."

Clara Morrow, the artist, the portraitist, had searched the faces for any hint of individuality. And found none. Then she'd sat back in bed and remembered the elderly woman she'd met. Clara didn't ask many people to sit for a portrait. It demanded too much of her to be done on a whim. But, apparently on a whim, she'd popped the question to Constance. And been firmly rebuffed.

She hadn't really exaggerated to Peter. Clara Morrow had become surprisingly famous for her portraits. At least, it surprised her. And it had sure surprised her artist husband.

She remembered what John Singer Sargent had said.

Every time I paint a portrait I lose a friend.

Clara had lost her husband. Not because she'd painted him, but because she'd outpainted him. Sometimes, on dark winter nights, she wished she'd stuck to gigantic feet and warrior uteruses.

"But my paintings didn't send you from our home, did they?" she asked the canvas. "It was your own demons. They finally caught up with you."

She considered him closely.

"How much that must have hurt," she said quietly. "Where are you now, Peter? Have you stopped running? Have you faced whatever ate your happiness, your creativity, your good sense? Your love?"

It had eaten his love, but not Clara's.

Henri settled on the worn piece of carpet at Clara's feet. She picked up her brush and approached the canvas.

"He'll be back," she whispered, perhaps to Henri.

Chief Inspector Gamache opened drawers and closets and cupboards, examining the contents of Constance Ouellet's home. In the front hall closet he found a coat, a small collection of hats, and a pair of gloves.

No hoarding here.

He looked at the bookshelves and mantelpiece. He got on his hands and knees and looked under furniture. From what the Montréal police could tell, Constance hadn't been robbed. Her purse was still there, money and all. Her car sat on the road. There were no blank spots on the walls where a painting might have once hung, or gaps in the curio cabinet where a surprisingly valuable knickknack might have sat.

Nothing was taken.

But still he looked.

He knew he was going over territory the Montréal police had already covered, but he was looking for something different. Their initial search was for clues to the killer. A bloody glove, an extra key, a threatening note. A fingerprint, a footprint. Signs of theft.

He was looking for clues to her life.

"Nothing, Chief," said Lacoste, wiping her hands of the dust from the basement. "They didn't seem a sentimental lot. No baby clothes, no old toys, no sleds or snowshoes."

"Snowshoes?" asked Gamache, amused.

"My parents' basement is full of that sort of stuff," Lacoste admitted. "And when they die, mine will be."

"You won't get rid of it?"

"Couldn't. You?"

"Madame Gamache and I kept a few things from our parents. As you know, she has three hundred siblings so there was no question of it all coming to us."

Isabelle Lacoste laughed. Every time the Chief described Madame Gamache's family, the number of siblings grew. She supposed for an only child like the Chief, it must have been overwhelming to suddenly find himself in a large family.

"What was downstairs?" he asked.

"A cedar chest with summer clothing, the outdoor furniture brought in for the winter. Mostly that cheap plastic stuff. Garden hoses and tools. Nothing personal."

"Nothing from their childhood?"

"Nothing at all."

They both knew that, even for people who were rigorously unsentimental, that was unusual. But for the Quints? Whole industries had been built around them. Souvenirs, books, dolls, puzzles. He was fairly sure if he looked hard enough in his own home he'd find something from the Quints. A spoon his mother collected. A postcard from Reine-Marie's family with the girls' smiling faces.

At a time when the Québécois were just beginning to turn from the Church, the Quints had become the new religion. A fantastic blend of miracle and entertainment. Unlike the censorious Catholic Church, the Quints were fun. Unlike the Church, whose most powerful symbol was of sacrifice and death, the lingering image of the Ouellet Quints was of happiness. Five smiling little girls, vibrant and alive. The world fell to its knees before them. It seemed the only ones not enamored of the Quints were the Quints themselves.

Gamache and Lacoste walked down the hall, each one taking a bedroom. They met up a few minutes later and compared notes.

"Nothing," said Lacoste. "Clean. Tidy. No clothing and no personal effects."

"And no photographs."

She shook her head.

Gamache exhaled deeply. Had their lives really been so antiseptic? And yet, the home didn't feel cold. It felt like a warm and inviting place. There were personal possessions, but no private ones.

They walked into Constance's bedroom. The bloodstained carpet was still there. The suitcase sat on the bed. The murder weapon had been taken away, but there was police tape indicating where it had been dropped.

Gamache walked over to the small suitcase and lifted items out, putting them neatly on the bed. Sweaters, underwear, thick stockings, a skirt and comfortable slacks. Long underwear and flannel nightgown. All the things you'd pack for Christmas in a cold country.

Packed between warm shirts he found three gifts, covered in candy cane wrapping paper. He squeezed and the paper crinkled. Whatever was inside was soft.

Clothing, he knew, having received his share of socks and ties and scarves from his children. He looked at the tags.

One for Clara, one for Olivier, and one for Gabri.

He handed them to Lacoste. "Can you unwrap these, please?"

While she did he felt around the suitcase. One of the sweaters didn't give as much as it should. Gamache picked it up and unrolled the wool.

"A scarf for Clara," said Lacoste, "and mittens for Olivier and Gabri."

She wrapped them up again.

"Look at this," said Gamache. He held up what he'd found in the center of the sweater. It was a photograph.

"That wasn't listed in the search by the Montréal cops," said Lacoste.

"Easy to miss," said Gamache. And he could imagine their thinking. It was late, it was cold, they were hungry, and this would soon not even be their case.

They hadn't been so much incompetent as less than thorough. And the small black and white photo was almost hidden in the thick wool sweater.

He took it over to the window, and he and Lacoste examined it.

Four women, in their thirties Gamache guessed, smiled at them. Their arms were around each other's waists, and they looked directly at the camera. Gamache found himself smiling back, and noticed Lacoste was as well. The girls' smiles weren't big, but they were genuine and infectious.

Here were four happy people.

But while their expressions were identical, everything else about them was different. Their clothes, their hair, their shoes, their style. Even their bodies were different. Two were plump, one skinny, one average.

"What do you think?" he asked Lacoste.

"It's obviously four of the sisters, but it looks like they've done all they can to make sure they're not alike."

Gamache nodded. That was his impression as well.

He looked at the back of the picture. There was nothing there.

"Why only four?" Lacoste asked. "What happened to the other one?"

"I think one died quite young," he said.

"Shouldn't be hard to find out," said Lacoste.

"Right. Sounds like a job for me, then," said Gamache. "You can look after the hard stuff."

Gamache put the photograph in his pocket and they spent the next few minutes searching Constance's room.

A few books were stacked on the bedside table. He went back to the suitcase and found the book she was reading. It was *Ru* by Kim Thúy.

He opened it to the bookmark and deliberately turned the page. He read the first sentence. Words Constance Ouellet would never get to.

As a man who loved books, a bookmark placed by the recently dead always left him sad. He had two books like that in his possession. They were in the bookcase in his study. They'd been found by his grandmother, on the bedside table of his parents' room, after they'd been killed in a car accident when Armand was a child.

Every now and then he pulled the books out and touched the bookmarks, but hadn't yet found the strength to pick up where they left off. To read the rest of the story.

Now he lowered Constance's book and looked out the window into the small backyard. He suspected that, beneath the snow, there was a small vegetable garden. And in the summer the three sisters would sit on the cheap plastic chairs in the shade of the large maple and sip iced tea. And read. Or talk. Or just be quiet.

He wondered if they ever talked about their days as the Ouellet Quints. Did they reminisce? He doubted it.

The home felt like a sanctuary, and that was what they were hiding from.

Then he turned back to look at the stain on the carpet, and the police tape. And the book in his hand.

Soon he'd know the full story.

"So, I can understand why the Ouellet sisters might not want everyone to know they were the Quints," said Lacoste, when they were ready to leave. "But why not have personal photographs and cards and letters in the privacy of their own home? Does that strike you as strange?"

Gamache stepped off the porch. "I think we'll find that very little about their life could be considered normal."

They walked slowly down the snow-packed path, squinting against the brilliant sun bouncing off the snow.

"Something else was missing," the Chief said. "Did you notice?"

Lacoste thought about that. She knew this wasn't a test. The Chief Inspector was beyond that, and so was she. But her mind was drawing a blank.

She shook her head.

"No parents," he said.

Damn, thought Lacoste. No parents. She'd missed that. In the crowd of Quints, or missing Quints, she'd missed something else.

Monsieur et Madame Ouellet. It was one thing to blank out a part of your own past, but why also erase your parents?

"What do you think it means?" she asked.

"Perhaps nothing."

"Do you think that's what the killer took?"

Gamache thought about that. "Photographs of the parents?"

"Family photographs. Of the parents and the sisters."

"I suppose it's possible," he said.

"I'm just wondering . . ." she said when they reached her car.

"Go on."

"No, it's really too stupid."

He raised his brows, but said nothing. Just stared at her.

"What do we really know about the Ouellet Quints?" she asked. "They deliberately dropped from view, became the Pineault sisters. They were private in the extreme . . ."

"Just say it, Inspector," said Gamache.

"Maybe Constance wasn't the last."

"*Pardon?*"

"How do we know the others are dead? Maybe one isn't. Who else could get into the house? Who else even knew where they lived? Who else might take family photographs?"

"We don't know if the killer even realized she was a Quint," the Chief

Inspector pointed out. "And we don't know that family photos were stolen."

But as he drove away, Lacoste's statement grew in his mind.

Maybe Constance wasn't the last.

TWELVE

———

Pay attention, Jean-Guy Beauvoir begged himself. *For chrissake, hold it together.*

His knee jittered up and down and he placed his hand on it. Pressing down.

At the front of the room, Martin Tessier was instructing the Sûreté agents who'd soon be raiding the biker gang stronghold.

"These aren't tattooed thugs," said Francoeur's second in command, turning away from the graphics on his tablet to face them. "Too many dead cops and mob bosses have underestimated the bikers. These're soldiers. They might look like yahoos, but make no mistake, they're disciplined and committed and highly motivated to protect their territory."

Tessier went on, flashing images, schematics, plans.

But all Beauvoir heard was his own voice, pleading.

Dear God, don't let me die.

Chief Inspector Gamache knocked on the door, then stepped into Thérèse Brunel's office. She looked up from her desk as he entered.

"Close the door, please," she said, removing her glasses. Her voice and manner were uncharacteristically brusque.

"I got your message but was out of town." He glanced at the clock on her desk. Just past noon.

She indicated a seat. He hesitated a moment, then sat. She took the chair beside him. She looked tired, but was still perfectly turned out, and perfectly in command of herself and him.

"We've come to the end, Armand. I'm sorry."

"What do you mean?"

"You know what I mean. I've been thinking about it, and speaking with Jérôme, and we think there's nothing there. We've been chasing our own tails."

"But—"

"Don't interrupt me, Chief Inspector. This whole video thing has gotten out of control and out of proportion. It's done. The video's out there, nothing we can do will get it back. You need to let it go."

"I don't understand . . ." He searched her face.

"It's quite simple. You were hurt and angry and wanted revenge. Perfectly natural. And then you became convinced there was more there than just the video. You got yourself rattled and managed to rattle everyone around you. Including me. That's my fault, not yours. I allowed myself to believe you."

"What's happened, Thérèse?"

"Superintendent," she said.

"*Désolé*. Superintendent." He lowered his voice. "Has something happened?"

"It certainly has. I've come to my senses and I advise you to do the same. I hardly slept last night, then I finally got up and made notes. Would you like to see them?"

Gamache nodded, watching her closely. She handed him a handwritten note. He put his reading glasses on and studied it. Then he carefully folded it in half.

"As you see, I listed all the evidence in favor of your contention that Chief Superintendent Francoeur leaked the video of the raid and has a larger, more malevolent purpose—"

"Thérèse!" Gamache exclaimed, leaning forward suddenly as though to physically stop her from saying more.

"Oh, for God's sake, Chief Inspector, give it up. The office isn't bugged. No one's listening to us. No one cares. It's all in your head. Look at my notes. There's no evidence. The weight of our friendship and my respect for you clouded my judgment. You've connected dots that you yourself created." She leaned toward him in a manner almost threatening. "Driven almost certainly by your own personal loathing for Francoeur. If you keep this up, Armand, I'll go to him myself with evidence of your actions."

"You wouldn't," said Gamache, barely finding his voice.

"I'm tired, Armand," she said, getting up and taking her seat behind her desk. "Jérôme is exhausted. You've dragged us both into this fantasy of yours. Give it up. Better still, retire. Go to Paris for Christmas, think about it, and when you come back . . ."

She let the sentence hang in the air between them.

He stood up. "You're making a mistake, Superintendent."

"If I am, I'll be making it in Vancouver with our daughter. And while there, Jérôme and I will also discuss my future. It's time to step aside, Armand. The Sûreté isn't falling apart, you are. We're dinosaurs and the meteor has struck."

Ready?" Tessier clapped Beauvoir on the back.

No.

"Ready," said Beauvoir.

"Good. I want you to lead the team into the second level of the bunker."

Tessier was smiling as though he'd just given the Inspector a ticket to the Bahamas.

"Yessir."

He just managed to get to a bathroom. Locking the stall door, he retched, and retched. Until only fetid air burped up, from deep down inside him.

Call for you, Chief."

"Is it important?"

His secretary looked through the open door into his office. In all the years she'd worked for Chief Inspector Gamache, he'd never asked that question. He'd trusted that if she put a call through, it was, in her judgment, worth taking.

But he'd seemed distracted since he'd returned from his meeting with Superintendent Brunel and had spent the past twenty minutes staring out the window.

"Would you like me to take a message?" she asked.

"No, no." He reached for the phone. "I'll take it."

"*Salut, patron,*" came Olivier's cheerful voice. "Hope I'm not disturbing you." He went on without waiting for an answer. "Gabri asked me to call to make sure you still want your room for tonight."

"I thought I'd already spoken with him about that." The Chief heard the slight annoyance in his voice, but did nothing to change his tone.

"Look, I'm just passing along the message."

"Has he double-booked or something?"

"No, it's still available, but he wants to know how many you'll be."

"What do you mean?"

"Well, will Inspector Beauvoir be coming down?"

Gamache exhaled sharply into the receiver.

"*Voyons*, Olivier," he began, then reined himself in. "Listen, Olivier, I've been through this as well. Inspector Beauvoir's on another assignment. Inspector Lacoste will be staying in Montréal to continue the investigation from here, and I'll be coming down to Three Pines, to look into that end of the case. I've left Henri with Madame Morrow so I have to come down anyway."

"No need to get all upset, Chief," snapped Olivier. "I was just asking."

"I'm not upset"—though it was clear he was—"I'm just busy and have no time for this. If the B and B is available, fine. If not, I'll collect Henri and come back to Montréal."

"*Non, non.* It's available. And stay as long as you want. Gabri isn't taking any bookings leading up to Christmas. Too involved with the concert."

Gamache wasn't going to be dragged into that conversation. He thanked Olivier, hung up, and looked at the small clock on his desk. Almost one thirty.

The Chief Inspector leaned back in his chair, then he swung it around so that his back was to the office and he faced the large window that looked out onto snowy Montréal.

One thirty.

It was one thirty.

Beauvoir took another deep breath and leaned back against the rumbling van. He tried closing his eyes, but that made the nausea worse. He turned his face so that the cold metal was against his hot cheek.

An hour and a half and the raid would begin. He wished the van had windows, so he could see the city. The familiar buildings. Solid, predictable. Jean-Guy was always more comfortable with the man-made than the natural. He tried to imagine where they were. Were they over the bridge yet? Were there buildings outside, or forests?

Where was he?

Gamache knew where Beauvoir was. He was on a raid scheduled to begin at three.

Another raid. An unnecessary raid, ordered by Francoeur.

The Chief closed his eyes. *Deep breath in. Deep breath out.*

Then he put on his coat. At the door to his office he watched Inspector Lacoste give orders to a group of agents. Or try to.

They were among the new agents, transferred in when Gamache's own people had been transferred out and spread around the other divisions of the Sûreté. To everyone's surprise, the Chief Inspector hadn't protested. Hadn't fought it. Had barely seemed to care or notice as his division was gutted.

It went beyond unflappable. Some had begun to wonder, quietly at first and then more boldly, whether Armand Gamache even cared anymore. But still, as he approached the group, they grew quiet and watchful.

"A word, Inspector," he said, and smiled at the agents.

Isabelle Lacoste followed Gamache back to his office, where he closed the door.

"For chrissake, sir, why do we have to put up with that?" She jerked her head toward the outer office.

"We just have to make the best of it."

"How? By giving up?"

"No one's giving up," he said, his voice reassuring. "You need to trust me. You're a great investigator. Tenacious, intuitive. Smart. And you have limitless patience. You need to use that now."

"It's not limitless, *patron.*"

He nodded. "I understand." Then, hands gripping the edges of his desk, he leaned toward her. "Don't be bullied off course. Don't be pushed from your center. And always, always trust your instinct, Isabelle. What does it tell you now?"

"That we're screwed."

He leaned back and laughed. "Then trust mine. All is not as I'd have wished, that much is certain. But it isn't over. This isn't inaction, this is simply a deep breath."

She glanced out at the agents lounging at their desks, ignoring her orders.

"And while we're catching our breath they're taking over. Destroying the division."

"Yes," he said.

She waited for the "but," but none came.

"Maybe I should threaten them," she suggested. "The only thing a lion respects is a bigger lion."

"Those aren't lions, Isabelle. They're irritating, but tiny. Ants, or toads. You step over them, or around them. But there's no need to step on them. You don't make war on toads."

Toads, or turds. The droppings of some larger beast, thought Lacoste as she left. But Chief Inspector Gamache was right. These new agents weren't worth her effort. She'd step around them. For now.

Gamache pulled his car into the reserved parking spot. He knew the employee who normally parked there wouldn't need it. She was in Paris.

It was two o'clock. He paused, closing his eyes. Then he opened them, and with resolve he walked along the icy path to the rear entrance of the Bibliothèque nationale. At the door, he punched Reine-Marie's code into the keypad and heard the clunk as the door unbolted.

"Monsieur Gamache." Lili Dufour looked up from her desk, understandably perplexed. "I thought you were in Paris with Reine-Marie."

"No, she went ahead."

"What can I do for you?" She stood up and walked around to greet him. She was slender, self-contained. Pleasant but cool, bordering on officious.

"I have some research to do and I thought you might be able to help."

"On what?"

"The Ouellet Quints."

He saw her brows rise.

"Really. Why?"

"You don't expect me to tell you that, do you?" asked Gamache, with a smile.

"Then you don't expect me to help you, do you?"

His smile faded. Reine-Marie had told him about Madame Dufour, who guarded the documents in the National Library and Archives as though they were her own private collection.

"Police business," he said.

"Library business, Chief Inspector," she said, nodding toward the large, closed doors.

He followed her gaze. They were in the back offices, where the head librarians worked. Through those doors was the public area.

Most of the time, when he'd visited his wife, he'd contented himself with waiting in the huge new public library, where row after row of desks and reading lamps held students and professors, researchers and those simply

94

curious. The desks had plugs for laptops, and wireless Internet gave access to the files.

But not all the files. The Bibliothèque et Archives nationales du Québec contained tens of thousands of documents. Not just books, but maps, diaries, letters, deeds. Many of them hundreds of years old. And most of them not in the computer system yet.

Scores of technicians were working long hours to scan everything in, but it would take years, decades.

He loved walking the aisles, imagining all the history contained there. Maps drawn by Cartier. Diaries written by Marguerite d'Youville. The bloodstained plans for the Battle of the Plains of Abraham.

And maybe, maybe, the story of the Ouellet Quints. Not the one for public consumption, but their private lives. Their real lives, when the cameras turned off.

If it was anywhere, it was here.

And he needed it.

He turned back to Madame Dufour. "I'm researching the Ouellet Quints for a case, and I need your help."

"I guessed that much."

"I need to look at what you have in the private archives."

"Those are sealed."

"Why?"

"I don't know, I haven't read them. They're sealed."

Gamache felt a stroke of annoyance until he noticed a slight look of amusement on her face.

"Would you like to read them?" he asked.

Now she hesitated, caught between the correct response and the truthful one.

"Are you trying to bribe me?" she asked.

Now it was his turn to be amused. He knew her currency. It was the same as his. Information, knowledge. Finding things out that no one else knew.

"Even if I let you, you couldn't use what you found in court," she said. "It would be illegally obtained. The principals are still alive."

By that she meant the Quints themselves, he knew.

When he said nothing she grew quiet, her intelligent eyes assessing him, and the silence.

"Come with me."

She turned away from the large doors that led to the glass and metal public library, and took him in the opposite direction. Along a corridor. Down some stairs. And finally, she tapped a code into a keypad and a large metal door clicked open with a slight whoosh.

Incandescent lights went on automatically when the door opened. It was cool inside the windowless room.

"Sorry for the lighting," she said, locking the door behind them and moving farther into the room. "We try to keep it to a minimum."

As his eyes adjusted he realized he was in a large room, but only one of many. He looked right. Then left. Then ahead of him. Room after room, all connected, had been constructed under the bibliothèque.

"Coming?" she said, and walked away. Gamache realized if he lost her, he'd be lost. So he made sure not to lose her.

"The rooms are set out according to quarter centuries," she said as she walked quickly from one to another.

Gamache tried to read the labels on the drawers as they walked by, but the dull lighting made it difficult. He thought he saw *Champlain* on one, and he wondered if Champlain himself was actually filed there. And later, in another room, *War of 1812*.

After a while he kept his eyes ahead of him, concentrating on Madame Dufour's thin back. It was best not to know the treasures he was walking by.

Finally she stopped and he almost bumped into her.

"There." She nodded to a drawer.

The label read *Ouellet Quintuplets*.

"Has anyone else seen the documents?" he asked.

"Not that I know of. Not since they were collected and sealed."

"And when was that?"

Madame Dufour went to the drawer and looked closely at the label.

"July 27, 1958."

"Why then?" he wondered.

"Why now, Chief Inspector?" she asked, and he realized that she was standing between him and what he needed to know.

"It's a secret," he said, his voice light, but his eyes not leaving hers.

"I'm good at keeping secrets," she said, glancing down the long line of files.

He considered her for a moment. "Constance Ouellet died two days ago."

Madame Dufour took in that information, her face troubled. "I'm sorry to hear that. She was the last of them, I believe."

Gamache nodded, and now she studied him more closely.

"She didn't just die, did she?"

"No."

Lili Dufour took a long breath, and sighed. "My mother went to see them, you know, at that home that was built for them here in Montréal. She lined up for hours. They were just children at the time. She talked about it until the day she died."

Gamache nodded. There'd been something magical about the Quints, and their extreme privacy later in life only added to the mystique.

Madame Dufour stepped aside, and Gamache reached for the drawer where their private life lived.

Beauvoir looked at his watch. Ten minutes to three. He was plastered against a brick wall. Three Sûreté officers were behind him.

"Stay here," he whispered, and stepped around the corner. He had a brief glimpse at the surprise in their faces. Surprise and concern. Not about the biker gang they were about to raid, but the officer who was supposed to lead them.

Beauvoir knew they had reason to be afraid.

He leaned his head again the brick, hitting it lightly. Then he crouched down so that his knees were against his chest, and he began rocking himself. As he rocked he heard the rhythmic squeaking of his heavy boots on the snow. Like a rocking horse in need of oiling. In need of something.

Eight minutes to three.

Beauvoir reached into the pocket of his Kevlar vest. The one that held bandages and tape to staunch wounds. He pulled out two pill bottles and, twisting the top off one, he quickly swallowed two OxyContin. He'd thrown up the earlier ones and now he could barely think for the pain.

And the other. The other. He stared at the pill bottle, and felt like a man halfway across a bridge.

Afraid to take the pill and afraid not to. Afraid of going into the bunker, afraid of running away. He was afraid of dying and he was afraid of living.

Mostly, he was afraid that everyone would find out just how frightened he really was.

Beauvoir twisted off the cap and shook the bottle. Pills cascaded out, bouncing off his trembling hand, and were lost in the snow. But one was saved. It sat in the center of his palm. His need was so great, and it was so tiny. He couldn't get it into his mouth fast enough.

Five minutes to three.

Gamache sat at a desk in the archive room, reading and making notes. Captivated by what he'd found so far. Diaries, personal letters, photographs. But now he took off his glasses, rubbed his eyes, and looked at the books and documents still to be read. There was no way he'd get through them that afternoon.

Madame Dufour had shown him the buzzer, and now he pressed it. Three minutes later he heard footsteps on the sealed concrete floor.

"I'd like to take it with me." He nodded to the stacks on the desk.

She opened her mouth to say something, but closed it again. And considered.

"Constance Ouellet really was murdered?" she asked.

"She was."

"And you think something in there"—she looked at the documents on the desk—"might help you?"

"I think it might."

"I retire next August, you know. Mandatory retirement."

"I'm sorry," he said as she looked around her.

"Shelved," she said with a smile. "I suspect neither I, nor that file, will be missed. Feel free to take it, monsieur. But please bring it back. Quite a steep fine, you know, if you lose it, or your dog eats it."

"*Merci*," he said, and wondered if Madame Dufour had met Henri. "There's something else I need from you."

"A kidney?"

"A code."

A few minutes later they stood by the rear door. Gamache had his coat on, and held the heavy box in both hands.

"I hope you find what you're looking for, Chief Inspector. Give my best to Reine-Marie when you see her. *Joyeux Noël.*"

But before the door closed and locked, she called him back.

"Be careful," she said. "Light and moisture can do permanent damage." She regarded him for a moment. "And I think, monsieur, you know something about permanent damage."

"*Oui*," he said. "*Joyeux Noël.*"

It was dark by the time Armand Gamache reached Three Pines. He parked not far from the B and B and barely had time to open the door before

Olivier and Gabri appeared from the bistro. It seemed to Gamache that they must have been watching for his arrival.

"How was the drive?" Gabri asked.

"Not bad," said Gamache, picking up his satchel and the heavy cardboard box. "Except for the Champlain Bridge, of course."

"Always hellish," agreed Olivier.

"Everything's ready for you," said Gabri, leading the way up the steps and along the verandah to the front door. He opened it, and Chief Inspector Gamache, instead of stepping inside, stepped aside to let his two companions in first.

"Welcome," said Olivier.

Thérèse and Jérôme Brunel walked into Emilie Longpré's home. The home Henri had found for them.

THIRTEEN

Olivier and Gabri brought the luggage in and took it to the bedrooms, then left.

"*Merci, patron*." Gamache stepped onto the cold verandah with them.

"You're welcome," said Olivier. "You played your role well on the phone. I almost believed you were annoyed."

"And you were very convincing," said Gamache. "Worthy of the Olivier award."

"Well, as luck would have it," said Gabri, "I planned to reward him to-night."

Gamache watched them cross to the bistro, then he closed the door and faced the room. And smiled.

He could finally relax.

Thérèse and Jérôme were safe.

And Jean-Guy was safe. He'd monitored the Sûreté frequency the entire drive down and heard no calls for ambulances. Indeed, what chatter he picked up led him to believe the bunker had been abandoned. The Rock Machine was no longer there.

The informant had lied. Or, more likely, there was no informant.

Gamache was both relieved and grim as he absorbed that news.

Jean-Guy was safe. For now.

Gamache looked at Emilie Longpré's home.

Two sofas faced each other on either side of the stone fireplace. They were slip-covered in faded floral fabric. A pine blanket box sat in the space between them. On it was a game of cribbage and some playing cards.

A couple of armchairs were tucked in a corner, a table between them and a hassock in front, to be shared by weary feet. A standing lamp with tasseled shade was on and held the chairs in soft light.

The walls were painted a soothing light blue, and one had floor-to-ceiling bookcases.

It felt quiet and calm.

Olivier had spent the morning finding out who now owned Emilie's home, and whether he could rent it. Seemed a distant niece in Regina owned the home and hadn't yet figured out what to do with it. She readily agreed to rent it over Christmas.

Olivier then called Gamache and gave him the agreed-upon phrase— *Gabri asked me to call to make sure you still want your room for tonight*—that would tell Gamache he could have Emilie's home.

Then Olivier had rounded up others in the village to help. The result was this.

Sheets had been pulled off the furniture, beds were made and clean towels put out, the home was vacuumed and dusted and polished. A fire was laid in the grate, and judging by the aroma, dinner was warming in the oven.

It was as though he and the Brunels had just stepped out for a few hours and were returning home.

Two of Sarah's fresh-baked baguettes sat in a basket on the marble kitchen counter, and Monsieur Béliveau had stocked the pantry and fridge with milk and cheese and butter. With homemade jams. Fruit sat in a wooden bowl on the harvest table

There was even a Christmas tree, decorated and lit.

Gamache loosened his tie, knelt down and struck a match to the wood and paper in the hearth, watching mesmerized as it caught and flared.

He exhaled. It felt as though a cloak, like the ghostly sheets over the furniture, had been lifted from him.

"Thérèse," he called. "Jérôme."

"*Oui?*" came the distant response.

"I'm going out."

He put on his boots and coat and walked quickly through the crisp evening, toward the little cottage with the open gate and winding path.

Armand," said Clara, opening the door to his knock. Henri was so excited he didn't know whether to jump up or curl into a ball at Gamache's feet. Instead, the shepherd threaded his way in and out and around Gamache's legs, crying with excitement.

"I beat him, of course," said Clara, looking with mock disgust at Henri.

Gamache knelt down and played with Henri for a moment.

"You look like you could use a Scotch," said Clara.

"Don't tell me I look like Ruth," said Gamache, and Clara laughed.

"Just around the edges."

"Actually, I don't need anything, *merci*." He took off his coat and boots and followed her into the living room, where a fire was lit.

"Thank you for looking after Henri. And thank you for helping to get Emilie's home ready for us."

There was no way to explain how that home looked to weary travelers who'd come to the end of the road.

He wondered, in a moment that startled him, whether that's what this little village was. The end of the road? And, like most ends, not an end at all.

"A pleasure," said Clara. "Gabri combined it with a rehearsal for the Christmas concert and had us sing 'The Huron Carol' over and over. I suspect if you hit one of the pillows that song will come out."

Gamache smiled. The idea of a home infused with music appealed to him.

"It's nice to see lights in Emilie's home again," said Clara.

Henri crawled onto the sofa. Slowly. Slowly. As though, if he crept up and averted his eyes, no one would see. He laid out his full length, taking up two thirds of the sofa, and slowly put his head in Gamache's lap. Gamache looked at Clara apologetically.

"It's OK. Peter was never a fan of the dogs getting up on the furniture, but I like it."

This provided Gamache the opening he was hoping for.

"How are you doing without Peter?"

"It's the strangest feeling," she said, after a moment's reflection. "It's like our relationship isn't dead, but neither is it alive."

"The undead," said Gamache.

"The vampire of marriages," laughed Clara. "Without all the fun blood-sucking part."

"Do you miss him?"

"The day he left, I watched him drive out of Three Pines and then I came back here and leaned against the door. I realized I was actually pushing against it, in case he returned and wanted back in. The problem is, I love him. I just wish I knew if the marriage was over and I needed to get on with my life," said Clara, "or if we can repair it."

Gamache looked at her for a long moment. Saw her graying hair, her comfortable and eclectic clothes. Her confusion.

"May I make a small suggestion?" he asked quietly.

She nodded.

"I think you might try leading your life as though it's just you. If he comes back and you know your life will be better with him, then great. But you'll also know you're enough on your own."

Clara smiled. "That's what Myrna said too. You're very alike, you know."

"I'm often mistaken for a large black woman," Gamache agreed. "I'm told it's my best feature."

"I never am. It's my one great failing," said Clara.

Then she noticed his thoughtful brown eyes. His stillness. And the hand that trembled, just a little. But enough.

"Are you all right?" she asked.

He smiled, nodded, and rose. "I'm fine."

He clipped Henri onto his leash and slung Henri's bag over his shoulder.

They walked back across the village, man and dog, in the red and green and golden light of the three huge Christmas pines, making prints in the stained-glass snow. Gamache realized he'd just said to Clara the exact words he'd said to Annie.

When everything had failed—the counseling, the intervention, the pleas to return to treatment—Annie had asked Jean-Guy to leave their home.

Armand had sat in the car that damp autumn evening, across the street from their apartment. Wet leaves were falling from the trees, caught in gusts of wind. They scudded across the windshield and the road. He'd waited. Watched. There in case his daughter needed him.

Jean-Guy had left without needing to be forced, but as he left he'd seen Gamache, who wasn't trying to hide. Beauvoir had stopped, in the middle of the glistening street, dead leaves swirling around him, and had poured all his venom into a look so vile it had shocked even the Chief Inspector of homicide. But it had also comforted him. Gamache knew in that moment that if Jean-Guy was going to hurt any Gamache, it would not be Annie.

It was with relief that he'd driven home that night.

That was several months ago and as far as he knew Annie had had no further contact with Jean-Guy. But that didn't mean she didn't miss him. The man Beauvoir once was, and might be again. Given a chance.

As Gamache entered Emilie's home, Thérèse struggled out of her seat by the fire.

"Someone knows you well," she said, handing a cut glass to Armand. "They left a fine bottle of Scotch on the sideboard and a couple of bottles of wine and beer in the fridge."

"And coq au vin in the oven," said Jérôme, coming in from the kitchen carrying a glass of red wine. "It's just warming up."

He raised his glass. "*À votre santé.*"

"To your good health," Gamache echoed, raising his own glass to the Brunels.

Then, after Thérèse and Jérôme had resumed their seats, Gamache sat down with a grunt, trying not to spill his Scotch in the descent. A soft pillow sat on the sofa beside him and, on a whim, he fluffed it.

No sound came out, but he softly hummed the first few notes of "The Huron Carol."

"Armand," said Thérèse. "How did you find this place?"

"Henri found it," said Gamache.

"The dog?" Jérôme asked.

Henri raised his head upon hearing his name, then lowered it again.

The Brunels exchanged glances. Henri, while a handsome dog, would never get into Harvard.

"It was his home, you see," said Gamache. "He'd been adopted from a shelter by Madame Longpré, when he was a puppy. So he knew the house. Madame Longpré died shortly after I met her. That's how Reine-Marie and I came to have Henri."

"Who owns the house now?" asked Thérèse.

Gamache explained about Olivier and the sequence of events that morning.

"You're a sneak, Armand." She leaned back in her seat.

"No more sneaky than that little charade in your office."

"*Oui,*" she admitted. "Sorry about that."

"What did you do?" Jérôme asked his wife.

"She called me into her office and gave me a dressing-down," said Gamache. "Told me I was delusional and she wasn't going to be sucked in anymore. She even threatened to go to Francoeur and tell him everything."

"Thérèse," said Jérôme, impressed. "You tormented and tricked this poor feeble man?"

"Had to, in case anyone was listening."

"Well, you had me convinced," said Gamache.

"Did I really?" She seemed pleased. "Good."

"He is easily fooled, I hear," said Jérôme. "Famous for his credulity."

"Most homicide detectives are," agreed Gamache.

"How'd you finally catch on?" Jérôme asked.

105

"Years of training. A keen knowledge of human nature," said Gamache. "And she gave me this."

From his pocket he took a piece of paper, neatly folded, and handed it over.

If Jérôme really has found something, I have to presume our home and my office are bugged. Have told Jérôme to pack for Vancouver, but don't want to involve our daughter. Suggestions?

"After Olivier called and said we could use this home, I wrote a note on the one Thérèse gave me," said Gamache, "and asked Inspector Lacoste to show it to her."

Jérôme turned the note on its side. Scribbled there, in Gamache's hand, was *Go to the airport for your flight, but don't board. Take a taxi to the Dix-Trente mall in Brossard. I'll meet you there. I know a safe place.*

Dr. Brunel handed the note back to Gamache. He'd noticed the first line of his wife's message. *If Jérôme really has found something . . .*

As the other two talked, he sipped his wine and looked into the fireplace. It was no longer a matter of *if*.

He hadn't told Thérèse, but after she'd finally fallen back to sleep, he'd done something foolish. He'd gone to his computer and tried again. He'd dug deeper and deeper into the system. Partly to see what he could find, but also to see if he could attract the watcher. If there was one. He wanted to tempt him out into the open.

And he had. The watcher appeared, but not where Jérôme Brunel expected. Not behind him, following, but in front of him. Luring Jérôme on, and in.

Trapping him.

Jérôme Brunel had fled, erasing, erasing, erasing his electronic footprints. But still the watcher followed. With sure, swift, relentless steps. He'd followed Jérôme Brunel right to their home.

There was no *if* about it. He'd found something. And he'd been found.

"A safe place," said Thérèse. "I didn't think one existed."

"And now?" Armand asked.

She looked around and smiled.

Jérôme Brunel, though, did not smile.

The debriefing was over and the Sûreté teams were heading home.

Beauvoir sat at his desk, his head lolling. His mouth open, each shallow breath unnaturally loud. His eyes were partly open and he felt himself sliding forward.

The raid was over. There were no bikers. He'd almost wept with relief, and would have, right there in that shithole of a bunker, had no one been watching.

It was over. And now he was back, safe in his office.

Tessier walked by, then backed up and looked in.

"I was hoping to catch you, Beauvoir. The informant fucked up, but what can we do? The boss feels badly about that, so he's put you on the next raid."

Beauvoir stared at him, barely focusing. "What?"

"A drug shipment heading for the border. We could let Canada Customs or the RCMP intercept it, but Francoeur wants to make up for today. Rest up. It looks big."

Beauvoir waited until he no longer heard footsteps down the corridor. And when there was only silence he put his head in his hands.

And cried.

FOURTEEN

⁓

After a dinner of coq au vin, green salad, and fruit and meringue, the three of them washed up. Chief Inspector Gamache was up to his elbows in suds in the deep enamel sink, while the Brunels dried.

It was an old kitchen. No dishwasher, no special mixer taps. No upper cabinets. Just dark wood shelves for plates, over the marble counters. And dark wood cabinets underneath.

A harvest table, where they'd eaten, doubled as the kitchen island. The windows looked out onto the back garden, but it was dark outside, so all they could see were their own reflections.

The place felt like what it was. An old kitchen, in an old home, in a very old village. It smelled of bacon and baking. It smelled of rosemary and thyme and mandarin oranges. And coq au vin.

When the dishes were done Gamache looked at the Bakelite clock above the sink. Almost nine o'clock.

Thérèse had returned to the living room with Jérôme. He stoked the embers of the fire while she found the record player and turned it on. A familiar violin concerto started playing softly in the background.

Gamache put his coat on and whistled for Henri.

"Evening stroll?" asked Jérôme, who stood by the bookcase, browsing.

"Want to come?" Gamache clipped Henri onto the leash.

"Not me, *merci*," said Thérèse. She sat by the fire and looked relaxed, but tired. "I'm going to have a bath and head for bed in a few minutes."

"I'll come with you, Armand," said Jérôme, and laughed at the look of surprise on the Chief's face.

"Don't let him stand still for too long," Thérèse called after them. "He looks like the bottom half of a snowman. Kids are constantly trying to put big snowballs on top of him."

"That's not true," said Jérôme, as he got into his coat. "Once it happened." He closed the door behind them. "Let's go. I'm curious to see this little village you like so much."

"It won't take long."

The cold hit them immediately, but instead of being shocking or uncomfortable, it felt refreshing. Bracing. They were well insulated against it. A tall man and a small, round man. They looked like a broken exclamation mark.

Once down the wide verandah steps, they turned left and strolled along the plowed road. The Chief unclipped Henri, tossed a tennis ball, and watched as the shepherd leapt into the snow bank, furiously digging to retrieve the precious ball.

Gamache was curious to see his companion's reaction to the village. Jérôme Brunel, as Gamache had grown to appreciate, was not easily read. He was a city man, born and bred. Had studied medicine at the Université de Montréal, and before that he'd spent time at the Sorbonne in Paris, where he'd met Thérèse. She'd been deep into an advanced degree in art history.

Village life and Jérôme Brunel did not, Gamache suspected, naturally mix.

After one quiet circuit, Jérôme stopped and stared at the three huge pine trees, lit up and pointing into the sky. Then, while Gamache threw the ball to Henri, Jérôme looked around at the homes surrounding the village green. Some were redbrick, some were clapboard, some were made of fieldstone, as though expelled from the earth they sat on. A natural phenomenon. But instead of commenting on the village, Jérôme's glance returned to the three huge pines. He tilted his head back, and followed them. Up, up. Into the stars.

"Do you know, Armand," he said, his face still turned to the sky, "some of those aren't stars at all. They're communication satellites."

His head, and gaze, dropped to earth. He met Gamache's eyes. Between them there was a haze of warm breath in the freezing air.

"*Oui*," said Armand. Henri sat at his feet staring at the tennis ball, encrusted with frozen drool, in Gamache's gloved hand.

"They orbit," Jérôme continued. "Receiving signals and sending them. The whole earth is covered."

"Almost the whole earth," said Gamache.

In the light from the trees the Chief saw a smile on Jérôme's moon face.

"Almost," Jérôme nodded. "That's why you brought us here, isn't it? Not just because it's the last place anyone would think to look for us, but because this village is invisible. They can't see us, can they?" He waved to the night sky.

"Did you notice," Gamache asked, "as soon as we drove down that hill, our cell phones went dead."

"I did notice. And it's not just cells?"

"It's everything. Laptops, smart phones. Tablets. Nothing works here. There's phone service and electricity," said Gamache. "But it's all land-lines."

"No Internet?"

"Dial-up. Not even cable. Not worth it for the companies to try to get through that."

Gamache pointed and Jérôme looked beyond the small circle of light that was Three Pines. Into the darkness.

The mountains. The forest. The impenetrable woods.

That was the glory of this place, Jérôme realized. From a telecommunications point of view, from a satellite's point of view, this would be complete darkness.

"A dead zone," said Jérôme, returning his eyes to Gamache.

The Chief tossed the ball again, and again Henri bounded into the snow bank, only his furiously wagging tail visible.

"*Extraordinaire*," said Jérôme. He'd started walking again, but now he looked down, concentrating on his feet. Walking and thinking.

Finally he stopped.

"They can't trace us. They can't find us. They can't see us and they can't hear us."

There was no need for Jérôme to explain who "they" were.

Gamache nodded toward the bistro. "Would you like a nightcap?"

"Are you kidding, I'd like the entire outfit." Jérôme rolled quickly toward the bistro, as though Three Pines had suddenly tilted. Gamache was delayed by a minute or two when he noticed that Henri was still bottom up in the snow drift.

"Honestly," said Armand when Henri popped his head out, covered in snow. But without the ball. Gamache dug down with his hands and finally found it. Then he made a snowball and tossed it into the air, watching as Henri jumped, grabbed it, bit down and was, yet again, surprised when it disappeared in his mouth.

No learning curve at all, marveled Gamache. But he realized Henri already knew all he'd ever need. He knew he was loved. And he knew how to love.

"Come along," he said, handing the tennis ball to Henri and clipping him back on his leash.

Jérôme had secured seats in the far corner, away from the other patrons. Gamache greeted and thanked a few of the villagers, whom he knew had helped get Emilie's home ready for them, then he took the armchair beside Jérôme.

Olivier showed up almost immediately to wipe the table and take their order.

"Everything okay?" he asked.

"It's perfect, thank you."

"My wife and I are deeply grateful to you, monsieur," said Jérôme, solemnly. "I understand you were the one who arranged for us to stay here."

"We all helped," said Olivier. But he looked pleased.

"I was hoping to see Myrna." Gamache looked around.

"You just missed her. She had dinner with Dominique but left a few minutes ago. Want me to call her?"

"*Non, merci,*" said the Chief. "*Ce n'est pas nécessaire.*"

Gamache and Jérôme ordered, then the Chief excused himself and returned a few minutes later to find cognacs on their table.

Jérôme looked content, but thoughtful.

"Something troubling you?" asked the Chief, as he warmed his glass between his hands.

The older man took a deep breath and closed his eyes. "Do you know, Armand, I can't remember the last time I felt safe."

"I know what you mean," said Gamache. "It feels as though this has been going on forever."

"No, I don't mean just this mess. I mean all my life." Jérôme opened his eyes, but didn't look at his companion. Instead he looked at the beamed ceiling with its simple Christmas pine boughs. He took a deep, deep, profound breath, held it for a moment, then exhaled. "I think I've been afraid most of my life. Schoolyards, exams, dating. Medical school. Every time an ambulance rolled into my ER I was afraid I'd screw up and someone would die. I was afraid for my children, afraid for my wife. Afraid something would happen to them."

Now he dropped his gaze to Gamache.

"Yes," said the Chief. "I know."

"Do you?"

The two men held each other's gaze, and Jérôme realized that the Chief knew something about fear. Not terror. Not panic. But he knew what it was to be afraid.

"And now, Jérôme? Are you feeling safe?"

Jérôme closed his eyes and leaned back in his armchair. He was quiet so long, Gamache thought maybe he'd nodded off.

The Chief sipped his cognac, leaned back in his own chair, and let his mind wander.

"We have a problem, Armand," said Jérôme after a few minutes, his eyes still closed.

"And what's that?"

"If they can't get in, we can't get out."

Jérôme opened his eyes and leaned forward.

"It's a beautiful village, but it's a little like a foxhole at Vimy, isn't it? We might be safe, but we're stuck. And we can't stay here forever."

Gamache nodded. He'd bought them time, but not eternity.

"I don't want to spoil the moment, Armand, but Francoeur and whoever's behind him will find us eventually. Then what?"

Then what? It was a good question, Gamache knew. And he didn't like the answer. He knew, as a man used to fear, the great danger of letting it take control. It distorted reality. Consumed reality. Fear created its own reality.

He leaned forward in his seat, toward Jérôme, and lowered his voice.

"Then we'll just have to find them first."

Jérôme held his eyes, not wavering. "And how do you propose to do that? Telepathy? We're fine here, for now. For tomorrow even. Maybe for weeks. But as soon as we arrived a clock started ticking. And no one, not you, not me, not Thérèse, not even Francoeur, knows how long we have before they find us."

Dr. Brunel looked around the bistro, at the villagers lingering over their drinks. Some chatting. Some playing chess or checkers. Some just sitting, quietly.

"And now we've dragged them into this," he said softly. "When Francoeur finds us, that'll be it for our peace and quiet. And theirs."

Gamache knew Jérôme wasn't being melodramatic. Francoeur had proven he was willing to do anything to achieve his goal. What preoccupied the Chief, what gnawed at him, was that he hadn't yet figured out what that goal was.

He needed to keep his fear at bay. A little was good. Kept him sharp. But fear, unchecked, became terror and terror grew into panic and panic created chaos. And then all hell broke loose.

What he needed, what they all needed, and what they could only find here in Three Pines, was peace and peace of mind and the clarity that came with it.

Three Pines had given them time. A day. Two. A week. Jérôme was right, it wouldn't last forever. But please, Lord, prayed Gamache, let it be enough.

"The problem, Armand," Jérôme continued, "is that the very thing that keeps us safe is what will eventually be our undoing. No telecommunications. Without that, I can't make any progress. I was getting close, that much is certain."

He lowered his eyes and swirled his cognac in the bulbous glass. Now was the time to tell Armand what he'd done. What he'd found. Who he'd found.

He looked up into Gamache's thoughtful eyes. Beyond his companion, Dr. Brunel saw the cheerful fire, the frosted mullioned windows, the Christmas tree with the presents underneath.

Dr. Brunel realized he had no desire to stick his head out of this pleasant foxhole. Just for this one night, he wanted peace. Even if it was pretend peace. An illusion. He didn't care. He wanted just this one quiet night, without fear. Tomorrow he'd face the truth and tell them what he'd found.

"What do you need to continue the search?" Gamache asked.

"You know what I need. A high-speed satellite link."

"And if I could get you one?"

Dr. Brunel studied his companion. Gamache was looking relaxed. Henri lay at his feet beside the chair and Armand's hand was stroking the dog.

"What're you thinking?" asked Jérôme.

"I have a plan," said Gamache.

Dr. Brunel nodded thoughtfully. "Does it involve spaceships?"

"I have another plan," said Gamache, and Jérôme laughed.

"You said we can't stay and we can't leave," said the Chief, and Jérôme nodded. "But there's another option."

"And what's that?"

"Create our own tower."

"Are you mad?" Jérôme glanced furtively around and dropped his voice. "Those towers go up hundreds of feet. They're engineering marvels. We can hardly ask the schoolchildren of Three Pines to make one out of Popsicle sticks and pipe cleaners."

"Not Popsicle sticks perhaps," said Gamache with a smile. "But you're close."

Jérôme downed the last of his cognac, then examined Gamache. "What're you thinking?"

"Can we talk about it tomorrow? I'd like to run it by Thérèse at the same time. Besides, it's getting late and I still need to speak with Myrna Landers."

"Who?"

"She owns the bookstore." Gamache nodded toward the internal door connecting the bistro with the bookstore. "I popped by while Olivier was getting our drinks. She's expecting me."

"Is she going to give you a book on building your tower?" Jérôme asked as he put on his parka.

"She was friends with a woman who was killed yesterday."

"Oh, *oui*, I'd forgotten you're actually here on business. I'm sorry."

"Not at all. The sad fact is, it's a perfect cover. If anyone asks, it explains why I'm in Three Pines."

They said their good nights, and while Jérôme walked back to Emilie Longpré's and a warm bed next to Thérèse, Armand and Henri entered the bookstore.

"Myrna?" he called, and realized he'd done exactly the same thing, at almost exactly the same time, the night before. But this time he wasn't bringing news of Constance Ouellet's murder—this time he came bearing questions, and lots of them.

FIFTEEN

—

Myrna greeted him at the top of the stairs.

"Welcome back," she said.

She wore an enormous flannel nightie covered in scenes of skiers and snowshoers, frolicking all over Mont Myrna. The nightie went down to her shins, and thick knitted slippers met it there. A Hudson's Bay blanket was spread across her shoulders.

"Coffee? Brownie?"

"*Non, merci*," he said, and took the comfortable chair she pointed to beside the fire, while she poured herself a mug and brought over a plate of fudge brownies, in case he changed his mind.

Her home smelled of chocolate and coffee, and something else musky and rich and familiar.

"You made the coq au vin?" he asked. He'd presumed it was Olivier or Gabri.

She nodded. "Ruth helped. Rosa, however, was no help at all. It was very nearly canard au vin."

Gamache laughed. "It was delicious."

"I thought you could use something comforting," she said, watching her guest.

He held her eyes. Waiting for the inevitable questions. Why was he here? Why did he bring the elderly couple? Why were they hiding, and who from?

Three Pines had taken them in. Three Pines could, reasonably, expect answers to those questions. But Myrna simply took a brownie and bit into it. And he knew then he really was safe, from prying eyes and prying questions.

Three Pines, he knew, was not immune to dreadful loss. To sorrow and pain. What Three Pines had wasn't immunity but a rare ability to heal. And that's what they offered him, and the Brunels. Space and time to heal.

And comfort.

But, like peace, comfort didn't come from hiding away or running away. Comfort first demanded courage. He picked up one of the brownies and took a bite, then he reached into his pocket for his notebook.

"I thought you'd like to hear what we've found so far about Constance."

"I take it that doesn't include whoever killed her," said Myrna.

"Unfortunately not," he said as he put on his reading glasses and glanced at his notebook. "I spent much of the day researching the Quints—"

"Then you think that had something to do with her death? The fact she was a Ouellet Quintuplet?"

"I don't really know, but it's extraordinary, and when someone is murdered we look for the extraordinary, though, to be honest, we often find the killer hiding in the banal."

Myrna laughed. "Sounds like being a therapist. People normally came into my office because something happened. Someone had died, or betrayed them. Their love wasn't reciprocated. They'd lost a job. Gotten divorced. Something big. But the truth was, while that might've been the catalyst, the problem was almost always tiny and old and hidden."

Gamache raised his brows in surprise. It did sound exactly like his job. The killing was the catalyst, but it almost always started as something small, invisible to the naked eye. It was often years, decades, old. A slight that rankled and grew and infected the host. Until what had been human became a walking resentment. Covered in skin. Passing as human. Passing as happy.

Until something happened.

Something had happened in Constance's life, or the life of her killer, that provoked the murder. It might have been big, clearly visible. But more likely it was tiny. Easily dismissed.

Which was why Gamache knew he had to look closely, carefully. Where other investigators bounded ahead, dramatically covering ground, Armand Gamache took his time. Indeed, he knew that to some it might even appear as inactivity. Walking slowly, his hands behind his back. Sitting on a park bench, staring into space. Sipping coffee in the bistro or brasserie, listening.

Thinking.

And while others, in glorious commotion, raced right by the killer, Chief Inspector Gamache slowly walked up to him. Found him hiding, in plain sight. Disguised as everyone else.

"Shall I tell you what I know?" he asked.

Myrna leaned back in her large armchair, pulled the Hudson's Bay blanket around her, and nodded.

"This is culled from all sorts of sources, some of them public, but most came from private notes and diaries."

"Go on," said Myrna.

"Her parents were Isidore Ouellet and Marie-Harriette Pineault. They were married in the parish church of Saint-Antoine-sur-Richelieu in 1928. He was a farmer. Twenty when they married, and Marie-Harriette was seventeen years old."

He looked up at Myrna. Whether this was news to her or not, he couldn't tell. It was, he had to admit, not exactly headline grabbing. That came later.

"The girls were born in 1937." He took off his glasses and leaned back in his chair, as though done. But they both knew he, and the story, were far from finished. "Now, why that gap? Almost ten years between the marriage and the first child. Children. It's inconceivable, so to speak, that they weren't trying to have children. This was a time when the Church and the parish priest were the greatest influences in people's lives. It was considered the duty of any couple to conceive. In fact, the only reason to get married and have sex was to procreate. So why didn't Isidore and his young wife?"

Myrna held her coffee mug and listened. She knew he wasn't asking her anything. Not yet.

"Families at that time routinely had ten, twelve, even twenty children. My own wife comes from a family of twelve children, and that was a generation on. In a small village, in the country, in the 1920s? It would have been their sacred duty to have children. And any couple that failed to conceive would be shunned. Considered unblessed. Even, perhaps, evil."

Myrna nodded. This attitude no longer existed in Québec, but it had until fairly recently. Well within living memory. Until the Quiet Revolution gave women back their bodies and Quebeckers back their lives. It invited the Church to leave the womb and restrict itself to the altar. It almost worked.

But in a farming community, in the twenties and thirties? Gamache was right. Every year that passed without children, the Ouellets would be more and more ostracized. Viewed with either pity or suspicion. Shunned, as though their childless state was communicable and would curse them all. People, animals, land. All would become infertile, barren. Because of one young couple.

"They'd have been desperate," said Gamache. "Marie-Harriette describes spending most of her days in the village church, praying. Going to confession. Doing penance. And then, finally, eight years on, she made the long journey to Montréal. It would have been a horrendous trip for a woman alone, from the Montérégie area all the way into Montréal. And then this farmer's wife, who'd never been outside her village, walked from the train station all the way to Saint Joseph's Oratory. That alone would've taken her most of a day."

As he spoke, he watched Myrna. She'd stopped sipping her coffee. Her brownie sat on her plate, half eaten. She listened, wholly and completely. Even Henri, at Gamache's feet, seemed to listen, his satellite ears turned to his master's voice.

"It was May of 1936," he said. "Do you know why she went to the Oratoire Saint-Joseph?"

"Brother André?" Myrna asked. "Was he still alive?"

"Barely. He was ninety years old and very ill. But he continued to see people. They came from all over the world by then," said Gamache. "Have you been to the Oratory?"

"Yes," said Myrna.

It was an extraordinary sight, the great dome, illuminated at night, visible from much of Montréal. The designers had created a long, wide pedestrian boulevard that ran from the street straight to the front door. Except that the church had been built on the side of the mountain. And the only way in was up. Up, up the many stone stairs. Ninety-nine of them.

And once inside? The walls were lined, floor to ceiling, with crutches and canes. Left because they were no longer needed.

Thousands of weak and crippled pilgrims had dragged themselves up those stone steps into the presence of the tiny old man. And Brother André had healed them.

He was ninety years old when Marie-Harriette Ouellet made her pilgrimage, and walking off the end of his life. It would be understandable if he conserved what strength he had left. But the wizened little man in the simple black robes continued to heal others while growing weaker himself.

Marie-Harriette Ouellet had traveled alone from her small farm to beg the saint for a miracle.

Gamache spoke without need of his notes. What happened next was not easily forgotten.

"Saint Joseph's Oratory wasn't what it is today. There was a church there, and a long promenade and stairs, but the dome wasn't completed. Now it's overrun with tourists, but back then almost everyone who visited was a pilgrim. The sick, the dying, the crippled, desperate for help. Marie-Harriette joined them."

He paused and took a deep breath. Myrna, who'd been looking into the dying fire, met his eyes. She knew what almost certainly came next.

"At the gate, the foot of the long pedestrian boulevard, she dropped to her knees and said the first of the Hail Marys," said Gamache.

His voice was deep and warm, but neutral. There was no need to infuse his words with his own feelings.

The images came alive as he spoke. Both he and Myrna could see the young woman. Young by their standards, elderly by the judgment of her time.

Twenty-six-year-old Marie-Harriette, dropped to her knees.

Hail Mary, full of grace, the Lord is with thee, she prayed. *Blessed art thou amongst women and blessed is the fruit of thy womb.*

Into the quiet loft, Armand Gamache spoke the familiar prayer.

"All night she crawled on her knees along the promenade, stopping to say the Hail Mary at every step," said Gamache. "At the bottom of the stairs Marie-Harriette didn't hesitate. She headed up them, her bloody knees staining her best dress."

It must have looked, thought Myrna, like menstruation. Blood staining a woman's dress. As she prayed for children.

Blessed is the fruit of thy womb.

She imagined the young woman, exhausted, in pain, desperate, crawling up the stone stairs on her knees. Praying.

"Finally, at dawn, Marie-Harriette reached the top," said Gamache. "She looked up, and standing at the door of the church was Brother André, apparently waiting for her. He helped her up and they went in together and prayed. He listened to her pleas, and he blessed her. Then she left."

The room fell silent and Myrna took a deep breath. Relieved the long climb was over. She could feel the sting in her knees. Could feel the ache in her own womb. And she could feel Marie-Harriette's belief, that with the help of a chaste priest and a long-dead virgin, she might finally have a child.

"It worked," said Gamache. "Eight months later, in January 1937, the day after Brother André died, Marie-Harriette Ouellet gave birth to five healthy daughters."

Even though she knew how the story ended, Myrna was still amazed.

She could see how this would be considered a miracle. Proof that God existed and was kind. And generous. Almost, thought Myrna, to a fault.

SIXTEEN

———

"It was, of course," said Gamache, voicing Myrna's thoughts, "considered a miracle. The first quintuplets to have ever survived childbirth. They became sensations."

The Chief leaned forward and placed a photograph on the coffee table.

It showed Isidore Ouellet, their father, standing behind the babies. He was unshaven, his farmer's face weather-beaten, his dark hair unkempt. It looked like he'd spent the night running his immense hands through it. Even in the grainy picture, they could see the dark circles under his eyes. He wore a light shirt with a collar, and a frayed suit jacket, as though he'd thrown on his Sunday best at the last minute.

His daughters lay on the rough kitchen table in front of him. They were tiny, newborn, wrapped in hastily brought sheets and dish towels and rags. He was looking at his children in amazement, his eyes wide.

It would be comical if there wasn't so much horror in that beaten face. Isidore Ouellet looked as though God had come for dinner and burned down the house.

Myrna picked up the picture and took a close look. She'd never seen it before.

"You found this in her home, I imagine," she said, still distracted by the look in Isidore's eyes.

Gamache put another photograph on the table.

She picked it up. It was slightly out of focus, but the father had disappeared and now standing behind the babies was an older woman.

"Midwife?" asked Myrna, and Gamache nodded.

She was stout, no-nonsense, her hands on her hips and a stained pinafore covering her large bosom. She was smiling. Weary and happy. And, like Isidore, amazed, but without his horror. Her responsibility, after all, was over.

Then Gamache put down a third black and white picture. The older woman had disappeared. The rags and wooden table had disappeared, and now each newborn was neatly wrapped in her own warm, clean flannel blanket and laid on a sterile table. A middle-aged man, dressed head to toe in white, stood proudly behind them. This was the famous photo. The world's introduction to the Ouellet Quintuplets.

"The doctor," said Myrna. "What was his name? Bernard. That's it. Dr. Bernard."

It was a testament to the Quints' fame that almost eight decades on, Myrna would know the name of the doctor who'd delivered them. Or not.

"You mean," she said, going back to the original pictures, "Dr. Bernard didn't deliver the Quints after all?"

"He wasn't even there," said Gamache. "And when you think about it, why would he be? In 1937 most farmers' wives had midwives at their deliveries, not doctors. And while they might have suspected Marie-Harriette was carrying more than one child, no one could have guessed there were five of them. It was the Depression, the Ouellets were dirt-poor, they could never have afforded a doctor even if they knew they needed one."

They both looked down at the iconic picture. The smiling Dr. Bernard. Confident, assured, paternal. Perfectly cast for a role he'd play for the rest of his life.

The great man who'd delivered a miracle. Who, because of his skill, had done what no other doctor had managed. He'd brought five babies into the world, alive. And kept them alive. He'd even saved their mother.

Dr. Bernard became the doctor every woman wanted. The poster boy for competence. A point of pride for Québec, that they had trained and produced a physician of such skill and compassion.

A shame, thought Gamache as he put on his glasses and studied the photo, that it was a lie.

He put it aside and went back to the original photograph, of the Quints and their horrified father. It was the first of what would prove to be thousands of pictures of the girls taken during their lifetimes. The babies were imperfectly wrapped in sheets soiled with their mother's blood and feces and mucus and membranes. It was a miracle, but it was also a mess.

It was the first picture, but it was also the last time the real girls were photographed. Within hours of the Quints being born, they were manufactured. The lies, the role-playing, the deceit, had begun.

He turned the original photo over. There, scrawled in neat, rounded schoolchild letters, were the children's names.

Marie-Virginie, Marie-Hélène, Marie-Josephine, Marie-Marguerite, Marie-Constance.

They must have been quickly wrapped in whatever the midwife and Monsieur Ouellet could find, and laid on the kitchen table in the order in which they were born.

Then he picked up the picture with Dr. Bernard, taken just hours later. On the back someone had written *M-M, M-J, M-V, M-C, M-H.*

No longer their full names, now they were just initials. Today it would have been bar codes, thought the Chief. He could guess whose handwriting he was seeing, and again he looked at the kindly country doctor whose life had also changed that night. A whole new Dr. Bernard had been born.

Gamache pulled one more photo from his breast pocket and placed it on the coffee table. Myrna picked it up. She saw four young women, probably in their early thirties, arms around each other and smiling for the camera.

She turned the photograph over, but nothing was written on the back.

"The girls?" she asked, and Gamache nodded.

"They all look so different," she marveled. "Hairstyles, taste in clothing, even their bodies." She looked over the picture, to Gamache, who was watching her. "It's impossible to tell they're even sisters. Do you think that was on purpose?"

"What do you think?" he said.

Myrna went back to the photo, but she knew the answer. She nodded.

"That's what I think too," said the Chief, taking off his glasses and leaning back in his armchair. "They were obviously very close. They didn't do it to distance themselves from each other, but from the public."

"They're in disguise," she said, lowering the picture. "They made their bodies a costume, so no one would know who they were. More like armor really, than a costume." She tapped the photo. "There're four of them. Where's the other one?"

"Dead."

Myrna tilted her head at the Chief. *"Pardon?"*

"Virginie," said Gamache. "She died in her early twenties."

"Of course. I forgot." She scoured her memory. "It was an accident, wasn't it? Car? Drowning? I can't quite remember. Something tragic."

"She fell down the stairs at the home they shared."

Myrna was quiet for a moment before she spoke. "I don't suppose it was more than that? I mean, twenty-year-olds don't normally just fall down stairs."

"What a suspicious mind you have, Madame Landers," said Gamache.

"Constance and Hélène saw it happen. They said she lost her footing. There was no autopsy. No obituary notice in the paper. Virginie Ouellet was quietly buried in the family plot in Saint-Antoine-sur-Richelieu. Someone at the mortuary leaked the news a few weeks later. There was quite a public outpouring of grief."

"Why hush up her death?" asked Myrna.

"From what I gather, the surviving sisters wanted to grieve in private."

"Yes, that would fit," said Myrna. "You said, 'They said she lost her footing.' There seems a bit of a qualifier there. They said it, but is it true?"

Gamache smiled slightly.

"You're a good listener." He leaned forward so that they looked at each other across the coffee table, their faces half in the firelight, half in darkness. "If you know how to read police reports and death certificates, there's a lot in what isn't said."

"Did they think she might've been pushed?"

"No. But there was a suggestion that while her death was an accident, it wasn't altogether a surprise."

"What do you mean?" asked Myrna.

"Did Constance tell you anything about her sisters?"

"Only in general terms. I wanted to hear about Constance's life, not her sisters'."

"It must have been a relief for her," said Gamache.

"I think it was. A relief and a surprise," said Myrna. "Most people were only interested in the Quints as a unit, not as individuals. Though, to be honest, I didn't realize she was a Quint until about a year into therapy."

Gamache stared at her and tried to contain his amusement.

"It isn't funny," said Myrna, but she too smiled.

"No," agreed the Chief, wiping the smile from his face. "Not at all. Did you really not know she was one of the most famous people in the country?"

"OK, so here's the thing," said Myrna. "She introduced herself as Constance Pineault and mentioned her family, but only in response to my questions. It didn't occur to me to ask if she was a quintuplet. I almost never asked that of my clients. But you didn't answer my question. What did you mean when you said the youngest Quint's death was an accident but not a surprise?"

"The youngest?" asked Gamache.

"Well, yes . . ." Myrna stopped herself and shook her head. "Funny that. I think of the one who died first—"

"Virginie."

"—as the youngest, and Constance as the oldest."

"I suppose it's natural. I think I do too."

"So, Chief, why wasn't Virginie's death such a surprise?"

"She wasn't diagnosed or treated, but it seems Virginie almost certainly suffered from clinical depression."

Myrna inhaled slowly, deeply, then exhaled slowly, deeply. "They thought she killed herself?"

"It was never said, not so clearly, but the impression I got was that they suspected it."

"Poor one," said Myrna.

Poor one, thought Gamache, and was reminded of the police cars on the Champlain Bridge and the woman who'd jumped to her death the morning before. Aiming for the slushy waters of the St. Lawrence. How horrible must the problem be when throwing yourself into a freezing river, or down a flight of stairs, was the solution?

Who hurt you once, he thought, looking at the photo of the newborn Virginie on the harvest table, crying next to her sisters, *so far beyond repair?*

"Did Constance tell you anything about her upbringing?"

"Almost nothing. She'd taken a big step in admitting who she was, but she wasn't ready to talk about the details."

"How did you even find out she was one of the Ouellet Quints?" asked Gamache.

"Wish I could say it was my remarkable insight, but I think that ship has sailed."

"And sunk, I'm afraid," said Gamache.

Myrna laughed. "Too true. Looking back, I realize she was a great one for hints. She dropped them all over the place, for a year. She said she had four sisters. But I never thought she meant all the same age. She said her parents were obsessed with Brother André, but that she and her sisters were told not to talk about him. That it would get them into trouble. She said people were always trying to find out about their lives. But I thought she just had snoopy neighbors, or was paranoid. Never occurred to me she meant all of North America, including newsreels, and that it was the truth. She must have been pretty exasperated with me. I'm embarrassed to admit I might never have twigged if she hadn't finally just told me."

"I'd like to have been there for that conversation."

"I'll never forget it, that's for sure. I thought we were going to talk about intimacy issues again. I sat there with my notebook on my knee, pen in hand"—Myrna aped it for him now—"and then she said, 'My mother's name was Pineault. My father's name was Ouellet. Isidore Ouellet.' She was looking at me as though this was supposed to mean something. And the funny thing was, it did. There was a sort of vague stirring. Then when I didn't respond she said, 'I go by the name Constance Pineault. I actually think of myself as that now, but most people know me as Constance Ouellet. My four sisters and I share a birthday.' I'm ashamed to say even then it took me a moment or two to understand."

"I'm not sure I'd have believed it either," said Gamache.

She shook her head, still in some disbelief. "The Ouellet Quintuplets were almost fictional. Certainly mythical. It was as though the woman I knew as Constance Pineault announced she was a Greek goddess, Hera come to life. Or a unicorn."

"It seemed unlikely?"

"It seemed impossible, delusional even. But she was so composed, so relaxed. Almost relieved. A more sane person would be hard to find. I think she could see I was struggling to believe her, and I think she found it amusing."

"Was she also suffering from depression? Is that why she came to you?"

Myrna shook her head. "No. She had moments of depression, but everyone does."

"Then why did she come to you?"

"It took us a long time to figure that out," admitted Myrna.

"You make it sound as though Constance herself didn't know."

"She didn't. She was there because she was unhappy. She wanted me to help her figure out what was wrong. She said she felt like someone who suddenly realizes they're color-blind, and everyone else lives in a more vibrant world."

"Color-blindness can't be cured," said Gamache. "Could Constance?"

"Well, first we had to get at the problem. Not the brass band banging away on the surface, but the barb beneath."

"And did you get at the barb?"

"I think so. I think it was simple. Most problems are. Constance was lonely."

Chief Inspector Gamache thought about that. A woman never alone. Sharing a womb, sharing a home. Sharing parents, sharing a table, sharing clothing, sharing everything. Living in a constant crowd. People around all the time, inside the house, and outside. Gawking.

"I'd have thought what she'd crave was privacy," he said.

"Oh, yes, they all craved that. Oddly enough, I think that's what made

Constance so lonely. As soon as they could, the girls retreated from the attention, but they retreated too far. Became too private. Too isolated. What started as a survival mechanism turned against them. They were safe in their little home, in their private world, but they were alone. They were lonely children who grew into lonely adults. But they knew no other life."

"Color-blind," said Gamache.

"But Constance could see there was something else out there. She was safe, but she wasn't happy. And she wanted to be." Myrna shook her head. "I wouldn't wish celebrity on my worst enemy. And parents who do it to their children should be tied up by their nuts."

"You think the Quints' parents were to blame?"

Myrna considered that. "I think Constance thought so."

Gamache nodded to the pictures on the coffee table between them. "You asked if I found those in Constance's home. I didn't. There were no personal photos there at all. None in frames, none in albums. I found those in the national archives. Except"—he picked up the one of the four young women—"this one. Constance had packed it, to bring down."

Myrna stared at the small picture in his hand. "I wonder why."

Jérôme Brunel closed his book.

The curtains were drawn and the eiderdown comforter lay on top of them in the large bed. Thérèse had fallen asleep reading. He watched her for a few moments, breathing deeply, evenly. Her chin on her chest, her active mind at rest. At peace. At last.

He put his book on the nightstand and, reaching over, took off her glasses and lifted the book from her hand. Then he kissed her forehead and smelled her night cream. Soft and subtle. When she went away on business trips he would spread some on his hands and go to sleep with them to his face.

"Jérôme?" Thérèse roused. "Is everything all right?"

"Perfect," he whispered. "I was just going to turn off the lights."

"Is Armand back?"

"Not yet, but I left the porch lights on and some lamps in the living room."

She kissed him and rolled over.

Jérôme turned off the bedside lamp, and pulled the duvet up around them. The window was open, letting in cold, fresh air, and making the warm bed all the more welcome.

"Don't worry," he whispered into his wife's ear. "Armand has a plan."

129

"I hope it doesn't involve spaceships or time travel," she mumbled, half asleep again.

"He has another plan," said Jérôme, and heard her chuckle before the room fell back into silence, except for the little cracks and groans as the home settled around them.

Armand Gamache stood at the window of Myrna's bookstore and saw the light go out in the upstairs bedroom at Emilie's home.

He'd followed Myrna downstairs into her shop, and now she was standing, baffled, in the middle of an aisle of her bookstore.

"I'm sure it was here."

"What was?" He turned around, but Myrna had disappeared into the rows of bookshelves.

"The book Dr. Bernard wrote, about the Quints. I had it here, but I can't find it."

"I didn't know he'd written a book," said Gamache, walking down another aisle, scanning the shelves. "Is it any good?"

"I haven't read it," she mumbled, distracted by looking at the spines. "But I can't believe it was, given what we now know."

"Well, we know he didn't deliver them," said Gamache, "but he still devoted most of his life to them. Probably knew them better than anyone."

"I doubt it."

"Why do you say that?"

"I think they barely knew themselves. At best the book might give you an insight into the routine of their days, but not into the girls themselves."

"Then why're you looking for it?"

"I thought even that might help."

"It might," he agreed. "Why didn't you read it?"

"Dr. Bernard took what should've been private and made it public. He betrayed them at every turn, as did their parents. I wanted no part of that."

She rested her large hand on a shelf, perplexed.

"Could someone have taken it out?" Gamache suggested, from the next aisle over.

"This isn't a lending library. They'd have had to buy it from me." There was silence before Myrna spoke again. "Fucking Ruth."

It struck Gamache that maybe that was Ruth's real name. It was certainly her given name. He considered the christening.

"What do you name this child?" the minister asked.

"Fucking Ruth," her godparents replied. It would have been a prescient choice.

Myrna interrupted his reverie. "She's the only one who seems to think this's a library. She takes out books, then returns them and takes out others."

"At least she returns them," said Gamache, and got a rude look from Myrna. "You think Ruth took Bernard's book on the Quints?"

"Who else would have?"

It was a good question.

"I'll ask her about it tomorrow," he said, putting on his coat. "You know that poem of Ruth's you quoted?"

"*Who hurt you once?* That one?" asked Myrna.

"Do you have it?"

Myrna found the slim volume and Gamache paid for it.

"Why did Constance stop coming to you as a client?" he asked.

"We hit an impasse."

"How so?"

"It became clear that if Constance really wanted to have close friends, she'd have to drop her guard, and let someone in. Our lives are like a house. Some people are allowed on the lawn, some onto the porch, some get into the vestibule or kitchen. The better friends are invited deeper into our home, into our living room."

"And some are let into the bedroom," said Gamache.

"The really intimate relationships, yes," said Myrna.

"And Constance?"

"Her home was beautiful to look at. Lovely, perfect. But locked. No one got inside," said Myrna.

He listened but didn't tell Myrna that the home analogy was perfect. Constance had barricaded herself in emotionally, but no one got past the threshold of her bricks and mortar home either.

"Did you tell her this?" he asked, and Myrna nodded.

"She understood and she tried, she really struggled with it, but the walls were just too high and thick. So the therapy had to end. There was nothing more I could do for her. But we stayed in touch. Acquaintances." Myrna smiled. "Even this visit, I thought maybe she'd finally open up. I'd hoped now that her last sister was dead she wouldn't feel she was betraying family secrets."

"But she didn't say anything?"

"No."

"Do you want to know what I think?" he asked.

131

Myrna nodded.

"I think when she first came down it was for a pleasant visit. When she decided to return it was for another reason altogether."

Myrna held his eyes. "What reason?"

He brought the pictures out of his pocket and selected the one of the four women.

"I think she was bringing this to you. Her most prized, most personal possession. I think she wanted to open the doors, the windows of her home, and let you in."

Myrna let out a long breath, then took the photograph from him.

"Thank you for that," she said quietly, and looked at the picture. "Virginie, Hélène, Josephine, Marguerite, and now Constance. All gone. Passed into legend. What is it?"

Gamache had picked up the very first picture ever taken of the Ouellet Quintuplets, when they were newborns, lined up like loaves of bread on the hacked harvest table. Their stunned father standing behind them.

Gamache turned the photograph over and looked at the words almost certainly written by their mother or father. Neatly, carefully. In a hand not used to making note of anything. In a life not very noteworthy, this was worth the effort. They'd written the names of their girls in the order in which they'd been placed on the table.

Marie-Virginie.

Marie-Hélène.

Marie-Josephine.

Marie-Marguerite.

Marie-Constance.

Almost certainly the order in which they were born, but also, he realized, the order in which they died.

SEVENTEEN

—

Armand Gamache woke to screams and shouts and a short, sharp explosion of sound.

Sitting bolt upright in bed, he went from deep sleep to complete awareness in a split second. His hand shot out and hovered over the nightstand where his gun sat in the drawer.

His eyes were sharp, his focus complete. He was motionless, his body tense.

He could see daylight through the curtains. Then he heard it again. An urgent shout. A cry for help. A command given. Another bang.

There was no mistaking that sound.

He put on his dressing gown and slippers, pulled back the curtain, and saw a pickup hockey game on the frozen pond, in the middle of the village green.

Henri was beside him, alert as well, nudging his nose out the window. Sniffing.

"This place's going to kill me," said the Chief Inspector to Henri. But he smiled as he watched the kids, skating furiously after the puck. Shouting instructions to each other. Howling in triumph, and screaming with pain, when a slap shot went in the net.

He stood, mesmerized for a moment, looking out the frosted pane of glass.

It was a brilliant day. A Saturday, he realized. The sun was just up, but the kids looked like they'd been at it for hours and could go on all day, with only short breaks for hot chocolate.

He lowered the window and opened the curtains all the way, then turned around. The house was quiet. It had taken him a moment to remember he wasn't in Gabri's bed and breakfast, but in Emilie Longpré's home.

This room was larger than the one he had at the B and B. There was a fireplace on one wall, the floors were wide-plank pine, and the walls were covered in floral paper that was anything but fashionable. There were windows on two sides, making it bright and cheerful.

He looked at the bedside clock and was shocked to see it was almost eight. He'd overslept. Hadn't bothered to set the alarm, sure he'd wake up on his own at six in the morning, as he normally did. Or that Henri would nudge him awake.

But both had fallen into a deep sleep and would still be in bed if it weren't for a sudden breakaway goal in the game below.

After a quick shower, Gamache took Henri downstairs, fed him, put the coffee on to perk, then clipped the leash on Henri for a walk around the village green. As they strolled they watched the hockey game, Henri straining, anxious to join the other kids.

"I'm glad you keep the dumb beast on a leash. He's a menace."

Gamache turned to see Ruth and Rosa closing in on them over the frozen road. Rosa wore little knitted boots and seemed to walk with a slight limp, like Ruth. And Ruth appeared to have developed a waddle, like Rosa.

If people really did morph into their pets, thought Gamache, any moment now he'd sprout huge ears and a playful, slightly vacant, expression.

But Rosa was more than a pet to Ruth, and Ruth was more than just another person to the duck.

"Henri is not a dumb beast, madame," said Gamache.

"I know that," snapped the poet. "I was talking to Henri."

The shepherd and the duck eyed each other. Gamache, as a precaution, tightened his grip on the leash, but he needn't have worried. Rosa thrust out her beak and Henri leapt back and cowered behind Gamache's legs, looking up at him.

Gamache and Henri raised their brows at each other.

"Pass," Ruth screamed at the hockey players. "Don't hog the puck."

Anyone listening would have heard the implied "dumbass" tacked to the end of that sentence.

A boy passed the puck, but too late. It disappeared into a snow bank. He looked over at Ruth and shrugged.

"That's OK, Etienne," said Ruth. "Next time keep your head up."

"*Oui*, coach."

"Fucking kids never listen," said Ruth, and turned her back on them, but not before a few had seen her and Rosa and stopped play to wave.

"Coach?" asked Gamache, walking beside her.

"It's French for asshole. *Coach.*"

Gamache laughed, a puff of humor. "Something else you taught them, then."

Small puffs came from Ruth's mouth and he presumed it was a chuckle. Or sulphur.

"Thank you for the coq au vin last night," said the Chief. "It was delicious."

"It was for you? Christ, I thought that librarian woman said it was for the people in Emilie's home."

"That's me and my friends, as you very well know."

Ruth picked up Rosa and walked in silence for a few paces.

"Are you any closer to finding out who killed Constance?" she asked.

"A little."

Beside them the hockey game continued, with boys and girls chasing the puck, some skating forward, some wiggling backward. As though life depended on what happened to that piece of frozen rubber.

It might appear trivial, but Gamache knew that this was where so much was learned. Trust and teamwork. When to pass, when to advance and when to retreat. And to never lose sight of the goal, no matter the chaos and distractions around you.

"Why did you take that book by Dr. Bernard?" he asked.

"What book?"

"How many books by a Dr. Bernard do you have?" he asked. "The one on the Ouellet Quints. You took it from Myrna's bookstore."

"It's a bookstore?" Ruth asked, looking over at the shop. "But it says 'library.'"

"It says *librairie*," said the Chief. "French for 'you're lying.'"

Ruth snorted with laughter.

"You know perfectly well *librairie* in French means bookstore," he said.

"Fucking confusing language. Why not just be clear?"

Gamache looked at her with amazement. "A very good question, madame."

He spoke without exasperation. He owed Ruth a great deal, not the least of which was patience.

"Yes, I took the book. As I said earlier, Constance told me who she was, so I wanted to read up on her. Morbid curiosity."

Gamache knew that Ruth Zardo might be morbid but she wasn't curious. That would demand an interest in others.

"And you figured you'd learn something from Dr. Bernard's account?"

135

"Well, I wasn't going to learn it from her, was I? It was the best I could do. Boring book. Talked mostly about himself. I hate self-centered people."

He let that one pass.

"Had some rude things to say about the parents, though," she continued. "All couched in polite terms, of course, in case they ever read it, which I suspect they did. Or had it read to them."

"Why do you say that?" asked Gamache.

"According to Bernard, they were poor and ignorant and dumb as a puck. And greedy."

"How so?"

"They basically sold their kids to the government, then got huffy when the money ran out. Figured they were owed more."

Chief Inspector Gamache had himself found the details of the accounting. It showed a large payment, or certainly large for the time, to Isidore Ouellet, disguised as an expropriation of his farm for a hundred times what it was really worth.

The dirt-poor farmer had won the lottery, in the form of five fantastical daughters. And all he'd had to do was sell them to the state.

Gamache had also come across letters. Lots of them. Written over a period of years in laborious longhand, demanding their daughters back, saying they were tricked. Threatening to go public. The Ouellets would tell everyone how the government had stolen their children. Isidore even invoked Frère André, who was dead by then, but an increasingly potent symbol in Québec.

In reading the letters it struck Gamache that what Isidore Ouellet really wanted was not the girls, but more money.

Then there were the letters in response from a newly formed branch of the government called Service de protection de l'enfance. They were addressed to the Ouellets, and while the language was extremely civil, Gamache could see the counter-threat.

If the Ouellets opened their mouths, so would the government.

And they had a great deal to say. They too invoked Brother André. It seemed the saint played for both teams. Or so they hoped.

Eventually the letters from the Ouellets petered out, but not before the tone became more pathetic, more demeaning. Begging. Explaining they had rights and needs.

And then the letters stopped.

"Did Constance tell you about her parents?" Gamache asked. It was their second time around the village green. He looked down at Henri, who was staying close to Gamache's legs, eyes fixed on Rosa. A spectacularly stupid expression on his face.

Could it be? Gamache wondered. *No. Surely not.*

He stole another look at Henri, who was all but slobbering as he watched Rosa. It was difficult to tell, but the shepherd either wanted to eat the duck, or had fallen in love with her.

Gamache decided not to explore either thought further. It was far too star-crossed.

"Honestly, you can't be that stupid," said Ruth. "I told you yesterday that I knew who Constance was but we didn't talk about it. You really aren't listening, are you?"

"To your sparkling conversation? Who wouldn't? No, I was paying attention, I just wondered if Constance had said something to you, but, alas, she didn't."

Ruth shot him a look, her blue eyes bleary but sharp. Like a knife in a cold, shallow stream.

They stopped in front of Emilie Longpré's home.

"I remember visiting Madame Longpré here," said Gamache. "She was a remarkable woman."

"Yes," said Ruth, and he waited for some snide qualifier, but none came.

"It's nice to see lights on, and smoke coming from the chimney again," she said. "It's been empty far too long. This home was meant for people." She turned to him. "It wants company. Even company as banal as yours."

"*Merci*," said the Chief, with a small bow. "Might I come over later and pick up the book?"

"What book?"

It was all Gamache could do to not roll his eyes. "The book by Dr. Bernard on the Ouellet Quintuplets."

"You still want that? You'd better pay that librarian woman for it then, now that she's changed her place from a library to a bookstore. Is that legal?"

"*À bientôt*, coach," said Gamache, and watched Ruth and Rosa limp and waddle next door.

Henri embarrassed himself by crying a little.

Gamache tugged on the leash and the shepherd reluctantly followed.

"And I thought you were in love with the arm of our sofa," said the Chief, as they entered the warm house. "Fickle brute."

Thérèse was in the living room in front of the fireplace, reading an old paper.

"From five years ago," she said, putting it down beside her. "But if I hadn't looked at the date I'd swear it was today's."

"*Plus ça change . . .*" said Gamache, joining her.

"The more it changes, the more it stays the same," Thérèse finished the quote, then thought about it. "Do you believe it?"

"No," he said.

"You're an optimist, monsieur." She leaned toward him and lowered her voice. "Neither do I."

"Café?" he asked, and went to the kitchen to pour them both a coffee. Thérèse followed him and leaned against the marble counter.

"I feel out of sorts without my phone and emails and laptop," she admitted, her arms around her body, like an addict in withdrawal.

"Me too," he said, passing her a mug of coffee.

"When you've come here for murder investigations, how did you connect?"

"Not much we could do except tap into the telephone lines and boost them."

"But that's still dial-up," said Thérèse. "Better than nothing, though. I know you also use hubs and mobile satellite dishes when you're in remote areas. Do they work here?"

He shook his head. "Not very reliable. The valley's too deep."

"Or the mountains too high," said Thérèse with a smile. "Perspective."

Gamache opened the fridge and found bacon and eggs. Thérèse brought a loaf out of the bread box and began slicing it while the Chief put bacon into a cast-iron skillet.

It sizzled and popped, while Gamache poked it and moved the slices around.

"Morning." Jérôme entered the kitchen. "I smelled bacon."

"Almost ready," said Gamache from the stove. He cracked the eggs into the frying pan while Jérôme put preserves on the table.

A few minutes later they all sat in front of plates of bacon, eggs over easy and toast.

Through the back window, over the sink, Gamache could see Emilie's garden and the forest beyond covered in snow so bright it looked more blue and pink than white. A more perfect place to hide would be impossible to find. A safer safe house did not exist.

They were safe, the Chief knew, but they were also stuck.

Like the Quints, he thought, as he took a sip of rich, hot coffee. While the rest of the world had been in the depths of the Depression, they'd been scooped up, taken away, and made safe. They were given everything they wanted. Except their freedom.

Gamache looked at his companions, eating bacon and eggs, and spreading homemade jam on homemade bread.

They too had everything they could want. Except their freedom.

"Jérôme?" he began, his voice uncertain.

"*Oui, mon ami.*"

"I have a medical question for you." The thought of the Quints reminded him of his conversation the night before with Myrna.

Jérôme lowered his fork and gave Gamache his full attention.

"Go on."

"Twins," said Gamache. "Do they generally share the same amniotic sac?"

"In the womb? Identical twins do. Fraternal twins don't. They have their own egg and their own sac."

He was clearly curious, but didn't ask why.

"Why?" But Thérèse did. "A happy announcement for you and Reine-Marie?"

Gamache laughed. "As wonderful as having twins at this stage in life would be, no. I'm actually interested in multiple births."

"How many?" asked Jérôme.

"Five."

"Five? Must've been IVF," he said. "Fertility drugs. Multiple eggs so almost certainly not identical."

"No, no, these are identical. Or were. And there was no IVF at the time."

Thérèse stared at him. "Are you talking about the Ouellet Quintuplets?"

Gamache nodded. "There were five of them, of course. From a single egg. They split off into twos in the womb and shared amniotic sacs. Except one."

"What a thorough investigator you are, Armand," said Jérôme. "You go all the way back to the womb."

"Well, no one suspects a fetus," said Gamache. "That's their great advantage."

"Though there are a few disadvantages." Jérôme paused to gather his thoughts. "The Ouellet Quints. We studied them in medical school. It was a phenomenon. Not simply a multiple birth, and identical at that, but the fact all five survived. Remarkable man, Dr. Bernard. I heard him lecture once, when he was a very old man. Still sharp, and still very proud of those girls."

Gamache wondered if he should say something, but decided against it. There was no need to throw dirt on that idol. Yet.

139

"What was your question, Armand?"

"The one Quint who was alone in the womb. Would that have made any difference once they were born?"

"What sort of difference?"

Gamache thought about that. What did he mean?

"Well, she would have looked like her sisters, but would she have been different in other ways?"

"It's not my specialty," Jérôme qualified, then answered anyway. "But I think it couldn't help but affect her. Not necessarily in a bad way. It could make her more resilient and self-reliant. The others would have a natural affinity for the girl they shared the sac with. Being that close physically, physiologically for eight months, they couldn't help but bond in ways that go beyond personality. But the girl who developed on her own? She might have been less dependent on the others. More independent."

He went back to spreading jam on his toast.

"Or not," said Gamache, and wondered what life would have been like for a perpetual outsider in a closed community. Would she have yearned for that bond? Seen their closeness, and felt left out?

Myrna had described Constance as lonely. Is this why? Had she been alone and lonely all her life, from before her first breath even?

Sold by her parents, excluded by her sisters. What would that do to a person? Could it twist her into something grotesque? Pleasant, smiling, the same as all the others on the outside, but hollow on the inside?

Gamache had to remind himself that Constance was the victim, not a suspect. But he also remembered the police report on the first sister's death. Virginie had fallen down the stairs. Or maybe, he thought, been pushed.

The sisters had entered into a conspiracy of silence. Myrna assumed it was in reaction to the extreme glare of publicity they'd suffered as children, but now Chief Inspector Gamache wondered if there was another reason for their silence. Something from within their own household, not from outside.

And yet, he had the impression that seventy-seven-year-old Constance was returning to Three Pines, to Myrna, and bringing with her not simply the only photo that existed of the grown-up girls, but also the story of what really happened in that home.

But Constance was killed before she could say anything.

"She'd have brought it on herself, of course," said Jérôme.

"What do you mean?"

"Well, she killed her sister."

Gamache gawked. How could Jérôme possibly know that, or know Gamache's suspicions?

"The reason she was alone in the sac. There were almost certainly six of them, two to a sac, but the singleton would have killed and absorbed her twin," Jérôme explained. "Happens all the time."

"Why do you want to know all this, Armand?" Thérèse asked.

"There's been no public announcement, but the last Quint, Constance Ouellet, was murdered two days ago. She was preparing to come down here, to Three Pines."

"Here?" asked Jérôme. "Why?"

Gamache told them. He could tell, as he spoke, that this was more than another death to them, even more than another murder. There was an added weight to this tragedy, as though Thérèse and Jérôme had lost someone they knew and cared about.

"Hard to believe they're all gone," said Thérèse, then she thought about it. "But they never seemed completely real. They were like statues. Looked human but weren't."

"Myrna Landers said it was like finding out her friend was a unicorn, or a Greek goddess. Hera, come to earth."

"An interesting thing to say," said Thérèse. "But how did this get to be your case, Armand? Constance Ouellet was found in Montréal. It would be the jurisdiction of the Montréal police."

"True, but Marc Brault handed it to me when he realized there was a connection."

"Lucky you," said Jérôme.

"Lucky all of us," said Gamache. "If not for that, we wouldn't be in this home."

"Which brings us to another issue," said Jérôme. "Now that we're here, how are we going to get out?"

"The plan?" asked Gamache.

They nodded.

The Chief paused to gather his thoughts.

Jérôme knew now would be the time to tell them what he'd found. The name. He'd only just glimpsed it in the moment before he realized he'd been caught. In the moment before he'd run. Run away. Back down the virtual corridor. Slamming doors, erasing his trail. Running, running.

He'd only just glimpsed it. And, thought Jérôme, maybe he got it wrong. In his panic, he must have gotten it wrong.

"Our only hope is to find out what Francoeur's doing and stop it. And to do that we have to get you reconnected to the Internet," Gamache said. "And not dial-up. It needs to be high-speed."

"Yes," said Thérèse, exasperated. "We know that. But how? There is no high-speed here."

"We create our own transmission tower."

Thérèse Brunel sat back and stared. "Have you hit your head, Armand? We can't do that."

"Why not?" he asked.

"Well, beside the fact it would take months and require all sorts of expertise, don't you think someone would notice we were building a tower?"

"Ahh, they'd notice that, but I didn't say 'build,' I said 'create.'" Gamache got up and walked to the kitchen window. He pointed, past the village green, past the three huge pine trees, past the homes covered in snow. And up the hill.

"What're we looking at?" Jérôme asked. "The hill over the village? We could put a tower on it, but again, that would take expertise."

"And time," said Thérèse.

"But the tower's already there," said Gamache, and they looked again. Finally Thérèse turned to him, astonished.

"You mean the trees," she said.

"*C'est ça*," said Gamache. "They make a natural tower. Jérôme?"

Gamache turned to the rotund man, wedged between the armchair and the window. His back to them. Staring up and out of the village.

"It might work," he said, uncertainly. "But we'd need someone to put a satellite dish on a tree."

They walked back to the breakfast table.

"There must be people who work with trees around here—what're they called?" Thérèse's city mind stumbled over itself. "Lumberjacks or something? We could get one of them to climb up with a dish. And from that height I bet we could find a transmission tower using line-of-sight. And from there we connect with a satellite."

"But where do we find a satellite dish?" Jérôme asked. "It can't be a regular one. It needs to be some satellite dish that can't be traced."

"Let's say we do get online," said Thérèse, her mind racing ahead, "we'd have another problem. We can't use the Sûreté log-ins to get into the system, Francoeur would be looking for those. So how do we get back in?"

Gamache placed a piece of notepaper on the wooden table.

"What is it?" Thérèse asked.

But Jérôme knew. "It's an access code. But using what network?"

Gamache turned the paper over.

"La Bibliothèque nationale," said Thérèse, recognizing the logo. "The national archives of Québec. Reine-Marie works there, doesn't she?"

"*Oui.* I did my research on the Ouellet Quints yesterday at the Bibliothèque nationale and I remembered Reine-Marie saying that the archive network goes all over the province, into the smallest library and into the massive archives at the universities. It's connected to every publicly funded library."

"It also goes into the Sûreté archives," said Thérèse. "The files of all the old cases."

"It's our way in," said Jérôme, his eyes glued to the bit of paper and the logo. "Is it Reine-Marie's? A code belonging to Reine-Marie Gamache would trip an alarm."

He knew he was looking for reasons this wouldn't work, because he knew what was waiting on the other side of that electronic door. Prowling. Pacing. Looking for him. Waiting for him to do something stupid. Like go back in.

"I thought of that," said Gamache, his voice reassuring. "It belongs to someone else. She's one of the supervisors, so no one will question if that code is logged on."

"I think it might work." Thérèse's voice was low, afraid to tempt the Fates.

Gamache pushed himself out of the chair. "I'm off to see Ruth Zardo, then I need to head in to Montréal. Can you speak with Clara Morrow and see if she knows anyone who puts up satellite dishes?"

"Armand," said Thérèse at the door, as he collected his car keys and put on his coat and gloves. "You must know that you might've solved two ends of the problem. The satellite connection and the access codes, but how do we get from one to the other? The whole middle part is missing. We'll need cables and computers and someone to connect it all."

"Yes, that's a problem. I might have an idea about that though."

Superintendent Brunel thought Gamache looked even unhappier about the solution than the problem.

After the Chief Inspector left, Thérèse Brunel walked back into the kitchen and found her husband sitting at the table, staring at his now cold breakfast.

"The worm has turned," she announced, joining him at the table.

"Yes," said Jérôme, and thought that was a perfect description of them.

EIGHTEEN

⌒

"You lied to me."

"You sound like a schoolgirl," said Ruth Zardo. "Are your feelings all hurt? I know what'll help. Scotch?"

"It's ten in the morning."

"I was asking, not offering. Did you bring Scotch?"

"Of course I didn't."

"Well then, why're you here?"

Armand Gamache was trying to remember that himself. Ruth Zardo had the strange ability to muddle even the clearest goal.

They sat in her kitchen, on white plastic preform chairs, at a white plastic table, all salvaged from a Dumpster. He'd been there before, including at the oddest dinner party he'd ever attended, where he'd been far from certain they'd all survive.

But this morning, while maddening, was at least predictable.

Anyone who placed himself within Ruth's orbit, and certainly within her walls, and wasn't prepared for dementia had only himself to blame. What often came as a surprise to people was that the dementia would be theirs, not Ruth's. She remained sharp, if not clear.

Rosa slept in her nest made from an old blanket, on the floor between Ruth and the warm oven. Her beak was tucked into her wing.

"I came for the Bernard book, on the Quints," he said. "And for the truth about Constance Ouellet."

Ruth's thin lips pursed, as though stuck between a kiss and a curse.

"Long dead and buried in another town," Gamache quoted, conversationally, *"my mother hasn't finished with me yet."*

The lips unpursed. Flatlined. Her entire face went limp, and for a moment Gamache was afraid she was having a stroke. But the eyes remained sharp.

"Why did you say that?" she asked.

"Why did you write that?" He brought a slim volume out of his satchel and placed it on the plastic table. Her eyes rested on it.

The cover was faded and torn. It was blue. Just blue, no design or pattern. And on it was written *Anthology of New Canadian Poetry*.

"I picked this up from Myrna's store last night."

Ruth lifted her eyes from the book to the man. "Tell me what you know."

He opened the book and found what he was looking for. "*Who hurt you once, / so far beyond repair / that you would greet each overture / with curling lip?* You wrote those words."

"Yes, so? I've written a lot of words."

"This was the first poem of yours to be published, and it remains one of your most famous."

"I've written better."

"Perhaps, but few more heartfelt. Yesterday, when we were talking about Constance's visit, you said she told you who she was. You also said you didn't ask her any more questions. Alas."

She met his eyes, then her face cracked into a weary smile. "I thought maybe you'd picked up on that."

"This poem is called 'Alas.'" He closed the book and quoted by heart, "*Then shall forgiven and forgiving meet again / or will it be, as always was, / too late?*"

Ruth held her head erect as though facing an attack. "You know it?"

"I do. And I think Constance knew it too. I know the poem because I love it. She knew it because she loved the person who'd inspired it."

He opened the book again and read the dedication, "*For V.*"

He carefully placed it on the table between them.

"You wrote 'Alas' for Virginie Ouellet. The poem was published in 1959, the year after her death. Why did you write it?"

Ruth was quiet. She bent her head and looked at Rosa, then she dropped her thin, blue-veined hand and stroked Rosa's back.

"They were my age, you know. Almost exactly. Like them, I grew up in the Depression and then the war. We were poor, my parents struggled. They had other things on their mind than an awkward, unhappy daughter. So I turned inward. Developed a rich imaginary life. In it, I was a Quint. The sixth quint," she smiled at him, and her cheeks reddened a bit. "I know. Six quints. Didn't make sense."

146

Gamache chose not to point out that that wasn't the only leap of logic.

"They always seemed so happy, so carefree," Ruth went on.

Her voice became distant and her face took on an expression Gamache had never seen before. Dreamy.

Thérèse Brunel followed Clara from the bright kitchen into her studio.

They passed a ghostly portrait on an easel. A work-in-progress. Thérèse thought it might be a man's face, but she wasn't sure.

Clara stopped in front of another canvas.

"I've just started this one," she said.

Thérèse was eager to see it. She was a fan of Clara's work.

The two women stood side-by-side. One disheveled, in flannel and a sweatshirt, the other beautifully turned out in slacks, a silk blouse, a Chanel sweater and thin leather belt. They both held steaming mugs of tisane and stared at the canvas.

"What is it?" Thérèse finally asked, after tilting her head this way and that.

Clara snorted. "Who is it, you mean? It's the first time I've done a portrait from memory."

Thérèse wondered how good Clara's memory could be.

"It's Constance Ouellet," Clara said.

"Ah, *oui*?" Again Thérèse tilted her head, but no amount of twisting could make this look like one of the famous Quints. Or any other human. "She never finished sitting for you."

"Or started. Constance refused," said Clara.

"Really? Why?"

"She didn't say, but I think she didn't want me to see too much, or reveal too much."

"Why did you want to paint her? Because she was a Quint?"

"No, I didn't know it then. I just thought she had an interesting face."

"What interested you? What did you see there?"

"Nothing."

Now the Superintendent turned from her study of the canvas to study her companion.

"*Pardon?*"

"Oh, Constance was wonderful. Fun and warm and kind. A great dinner guest. She came here a couple of times."

"But?" Thérèse prompted.

"But I never felt I got to know her better. There was a veneer over her, a sort of lacquer. It was as though she was already a portrait. Something created, but not real."

They stared at the blotch of paint on the canvas for a while.

"I wonder if you could suggest someone to put up a satellite dish," Thérèse asked, remembering her mission.

"I can, but it won't help."

"What do you mean?"

"Satellite dishes don't work here. You can try rabbit ears, but the TV signal's still pretty blurry. Most of us get our news from radio. If there's a big event we go up to the inn and spa and watch their TV. I can lend you a good book though."

"*Merci*," said Thérèse with a smile, "but if you could find the satellite person anyway that would be great."

"I'll make some calls." Clara left Thérèse alone in the studio contemplating the canvas, and the woman who'd been not quite real and now was dead.

Ruth held the volume of poetry in her thin hands, pressing it closed.

"Constance came to me the first afternoon she was here. She said she liked my poetry."

Gamache grimaced. There were two things you never, ever, said to Ruth Zardo. *We're out of alcohol*, and *I like your poetry*.

"And what did you say to her?" he was almost afraid to ask.

"What do you think I said?"

"I'm sure you were gracious and invited her in."

"Well, I invited her to do something."

"And did she?"

"No." Ruth sounded surprised still. "She stood at my front door and just said, 'Thank you.'"

"What did you do?"

"Well, what could I do after that? I slammed the door in her face. Can't say she didn't ask for it."

"You were provoked beyond reason," he said, and she gave him a keen, assessing look. "Did you know who she was?"

"Do you think she said, 'Hi, I'm a Quint. Can I come in?' Of course I didn't know who she was. I just thought she was some old fart who wanted something from me. So I got rid of her."

"And what did she do?"

"She came back. Brought a bottle of Glenlivet. Apparently she'd had a word with Gabri over at Chez Gay. He told her the only way into my home was through a bottle of Scotch."

"A gap in your security system," said Gamache.

"She sat there." Ruth pointed to his plastic chair. "And I sat here. And we drank."

"At what stage did she tell you who she was?"

"She didn't really. She told me I had the poem right. I asked her which poem and she quoted it to me. Like you did. Then she said that Virginie had felt exactly like that. I asked what Virginie she had in mind, and she said her sister. Virginie Ouellet."

"And that's when you knew?" Gamache asked.

"God, man, the fucking duck knew then."

Ruth got up and returned with the Bernard book on the Quints. She threw it on the table and sat back down.

"Vile book," she said.

Gamache looked at the cover. A photograph, in black and white, of Dr. Bernard sitting in a chair, surrounded by the Ouellet Quints, about eight years of age, looking at him adoringly.

Ruth was also looking at the cover. At the five little girls.

"I used to pretend I was adopted out and one day they'd come and find me."

"And one day," Gamache said quietly, "Constance did."

Constance Ouellet, at the end of her life, at the end of the road, had come to this falling-down old home, to this falling-down old poet. And here, finally, she'd found her companion.

And Ruth had found her sister. At last.

Ruth met his eyes, and smiled. *"Or will it be, as always was / too late?"*

Alas.

NINETEEN

⁓

Chief Inspector Gamache drove in to Montréal, and now sat at his computer reading the weekly roundup from Inspector Lacoste, from his homicide agents, from detachments around the province.

It was Saturday morning and he was alone in the office. He responded to emails, wrote notes, and sent off thoughts and suggestions on murder investigations under way. He called a couple of inspectors in remote areas with active cases, to talk about progress.

When all that was done, he looked at the last daily report. It was an executive summary of activities and cases from Chief Superintendent Francoeur's office. Gamache knew he didn't have to read it, knew if he opened it he was doing exactly as Sylvain Francoeur wanted. It was sent to Gamache not as information, and certainly not as a courtesy, but as an assault.

Gamache's finger rested on the open message command.

If he pressed down it would be flagged as opened, by him. At his desk, on his terminal. Using his security codes.

Francoeur would know he'd bested Gamache, again.

Gamache pressed anyway, and the words sprang up on the page.

He read what Francoeur wanted him to see. And he felt exactly what Francoeur wanted him to feel.

Impotent. Angry.

Francoeur had assigned Jean-Guy Beauvoir to another operation, this time a drug raid that could easily have been left to the RCMP and border guards. Gamache stared at the words and took a long, slow, deep breath in. Held it for a moment. Then he released it. Slowly. He forced himself to reread the report. To take it in, fully.

Then he closed the message and filed it.

He sat at his chair and looked through the glass between his office and the open room beyond. The empty room beyond. With its bedraggled strings of Christmas lights. The half-hearted tree, without gifts. Not even fake ones.

He wanted to swing his chair around, to turn his back on all that and stare at the city he loved. But instead he contemplated what he saw, and what he'd read. And what he felt. Then he made a call, got up, and left.

He probably should have driven, but the Chief wanted fresh air. The streets of Montréal were slushy underfoot and bustling with holiday shoppers, bumping each other and wishing each other anything but peace and good-will.

The Salvation Army was performing carols on one of the corners. As he walked, a boy soprano sang, "Once in Royal David's City."

But Chief Inspector Gamache heard none of it.

He wove his way between the shoppers, not meeting anyone's eyes. Deep in thought. Finally the Chief arrived at an office building, pressed a button and was buzzed in. An elevator took him to the top floor. He walked down the deserted corridor and opened a door into a familiar waiting room.

The sight of it, the scent of it, turned his stomach, and he was slightly surprised by the force of the memories that hit him, and the wave of nausea.

"Chief Inspector."

"Dr. Fleury."

The two men shook hands.

"I'm glad you could see me," said Gamache. "Especially on a Saturday. *Merci*."

"I'm not normally in on a weekend. I was just clearing my desk before heading off for holiday."

"I'm sorry," said the Chief. "I'm disturbing you."

Dr. Fleury regarded the man in front of him, and smiled. "I said I'd see you, Armand. You're not disturbing me at all."

He ushered the Chief into his office, a comfortable, bright space with large windows, a desk and two chairs facing each other. Fleury indicated one, but he needn't have. Armand Gamache knew it well. Had spent hours there.

Dr. Fleury was his therapist. Indeed, he was the main therapist for the Sûreté du Québec. His offices, though, weren't in headquarters. It was de-cided a neutral place would be better.

Besides, if Dr. Fleury's practice depended upon Sûreté agents coming for therapy, he'd starve. Sûreté agents were not known for admitting they needed help. And certainly not renowned for asking for it.

But after the raid on the factory, Chief Inspector Gamache had made it a condition of returning to work that all the agents involved, wounded physically or otherwise, needed to get therapy.

Including himself.

"I thought you didn't trust me," said Dr. Fleury.

The Chief smiled. "I trust you. It's others I'm not so sure about. There've been leaks about me, my personal life and relationships, but mostly leaks from sessions you had with my team. Information has been used against them, deeply personal information they only admitted to you."

Gamache's eyes remained on Dr. Fleury. His voice was matter-of-fact, but his gaze was hard.

"Your office was the only place it could've come from," he continued. "But I never accused you, personally. I hope you know that."

"I do. But you believed my files had been hacked."

Gamache nodded.

"Do you still?"

The Chief held the therapist's eyes. They were almost the same age, with Fleury perhaps a year or two younger. Experienced men. One who'd seen too much, and one who'd heard too much.

"I know you investigated thoroughly," said the Chief. "And there was no evidence of tampering with your patient files."

"But do you believe it?"

Gamache smiled. "Or am I paranoid?"

"I hope so," said Fleury, crossing his legs and placing his open notebook on his knee. "I'm eyeing a cottage in the Laurentians."

Gamache laughed, but the nausea had settled into his stomach, a sour, stagnant pool. He hesitated.

"Are you still not sure, Armand?"

Gamache could see the concern, almost certainly genuine, in Fleury's face, and could hear it in his voice.

"Someone else called me paranoid recently," admitted the Chief.

"Who was that?"

"Thérèse Brunel. Superintendent Brunel."

"A superior officer?" asked Fleury.

Gamache nodded. "But also a friend, and confidante. She thought I'd gone off the deep end. Seeing conspiracies all over the place. She, ah . . ." He looked briefly at his hands in his lap, then back up to Dr. Fleury's face.

Gamache smiled a little bashfully. "She refused to help me investigate and took off on holiday to Vancouver."

"You think her holiday plans had something to do with you?"

"Now you think I'm a narcissist?"

"I can see a new outboard motor in my future," admitted Fleury. "Continue, Chief Inspector."

But this time Gamache didn't smile. Instead he leaned forward.

"There's something going on. I know it, I just can't prove it. Yet. There's corruption inside the Sûreté, but it's more than that. I think a senior officer is behind it."

Dr. Fleury was unmoved. Unfazed.

"You keep saying, 'I think,'" said the therapist. "But are your fears really rational?"

"They're not fears," said Gamache.

"But they're not facts."

Gamache was silent, clearly trying to choose words that would convince this man.

"Is this about the leaked video again? You know there was an official investigation," said Dr. Fleury. "You need to accept their findings and let it go."

"Move on?" Gamache heard the tinge of bitterness, a slight whine, in his voice.

"Things you can't control, Armand," the therapist reminded him, patiently.

"It's not about control, it's about responsibility. Taking a stand."

"The white knight? The key is to know if you're tilting at a legitimate target or a windmill."

Chief Inspector Gamache glared at Fleury, his eyes hard, then he inhaled sharply as though from a sudden pain. He dropped his head into his hands and covered his face. Massaging his forehead. Feeling the rough scar.

Eventually Gamache raised his head and met patient and kind eyes.

My God, thought Gamache. *He feels sorry for me.*

"I'm not making this up," he insisted. "Something's going on."

"What?"

"I don't know," the Chief admitted, and realized how lame that sounded. "But it goes high up. To the top."

"Are these the same people who were supposed to have hacked into my files and stolen the notes on your therapy?"

Gamache could hear the slightly patronizing tone.

"Not just mine," said Gamache. "They stole the files of everyone who was involved in that raid. Who came to you for help. Who told you everything. All their fears, their vulnerabilities. What they want from life. What matters to them. A road map into their heads."

His voice was getting louder, more intense. His right hand started to tremble and he took hold of it with his left. Gripping it.

"Jean-Guy Beauvoir came to you. He sat right here, and opened up to you. He didn't want to, but I ordered him to. I forced him to. And now they know everything about him. Know how to get inside his head and under his skin. They turned him against me."

Gamache's tone slid from sulky to pleading. Begging this therapist to believe him. Begging just one person to believe him.

"So you still think my records have been hacked?" Fleury's normally steady voice was incredulous. "If you really believe that, why're you here now, Armand?"

That stopped the Chief. They held each other's eyes.

"Because there's no one else to talk to," Gamache finally said, his voice almost a whisper. "I can't talk to my wife, my colleagues. I can't tell my friends. I don't want to involve them. I could tell Lacoste. I've been tempted. But she has a young family . . ."

His voice trailed off.

"In the past, when things got bad, who did you speak to?"

"Jean-Guy." The words were almost inaudible.

"Now you're alone."

Gamache nodded. "I don't mind that. I prefer it." He was resigned now.

"Armand, you need to believe me when I say that my files haven't been stolen. They're secure. No one but me knows what we've talked about. You're safe here. What you're telling me now will go no further. I promise."

Fleury continued to regard the man in front of him. Sunken, sad. Trembling. This was what was beneath the façade.

"You need help, Armand."

"I do need help, but not the sort you think," said Gamache, rallying.

"There's no threat," said Fleury, his voice convincing. "You've created it in your mind, to explain things you don't want to see or admit."

"My department's been gutted," said Gamache, anger once again flaring. "I suppose that's my imagination. I spent years building it up, taking discarded agents and turning them into the best homicide investigators in the country. And now they've left. I suppose I'm imagining that."

"Maybe you're the reason they left," Fleury suggested quietly.

Gamache gaped at him. "That's what he wants everyone to believe."

"Who?"

"Syl—" but Gamache stopped himself and stared out the window. Trying to rein himself in.

"Why're you here, Armand? What do you want?"

"I didn't come for me."

Dr. Fleury nodded. "That's obvious."

"I need to know if Jean-Guy Beauvoir is still seeing you."

"I can't tell you that."

"This isn't a polite request."

"That day in the factory—" began Dr. Fleury before Gamache cut him off.

"This has nothing to do with that."

"Of course it does," said Dr. Fleury, impatience finally getting the better of him. "You felt you'd lost control, and your agents were killed."

"I know what happened, I don't need reminding."

"What you need to be reminded of," snapped Fleury, "is that it wasn't your fault. But you refuse to see that. It's willful and arrogant and you need to accept what happened. Inspector Beauvoir has his own life."

"He's being manipulated," said Gamache.

"By the same senior officer?"

"Don't patronize me. I'm also a senior officer, with decades of investigative experience. I'm not some delusional nutcase. I need to know if Jean-Guy Beauvoir is still seeing you, and I need to see his files. I need to see what he's told you."

"Listen." Dr. Fleury's voice was straining, trying to get back to calm, to be reasonable. But he was finding it difficult. "You have to let Jean-Guy live his own life. You can't protect him. He has his own road and you have yours."

Gamache shook his head and looked at his hands in his lap. One still, the other still trembling. He raised his eyes to meet Fleury's.

"That would make sense in normal circumstances, but Jean-Guy isn't himself. He's being influenced and manipulated. And he's addicted again."

"To his painkillers?"

Gamache nodded. "Superintendent—"

He stopped himself. Across from him Dr. Fleury was leaning forward slightly. This was the closest Gamache had come to naming his so-called adversary.

"The senior officer," said Gamache. "He's pushed OxyContin on him. I

156

know it. And Beauvoir's working with him now. I think he's trying to shove Jean-Guy over the edge."

"Why?"

"To get at me."

Dr. Fleury let the words sit there. To speak for themselves. About this man's paranoia and arrogance. His delusions.

"I'm worried about you, Armand. You say Inspector Beauvoir is being pushed over the edge, but so are you. And you're doing it to yourself. If you're not careful, I'll have to recommend you go on leave."

He looked at the gun attached to Gamache's belt.

"When did you start carrying that?"

"It's regulation issue."

"That wasn't my question. When you first came to me you made it clear how you felt about firearms. You said you never wore one unless you felt you might use it. So why are you wearing it now?"

Gamache's eyes narrowed and he got up.

"I can see it was a mistake coming here. I wanted to know about Inspector Beauvoir."

Gamache walked to the door.

"Worry about yourself," Dr. Fleury called after him. "Not Beauvoir."

Armand Gamache left the office, strode back down the corridor, and punched the down button. When the elevator arrived he got in. Breathing deeply, he leaned against the back wall and closed his eyes.

Once outside, he felt the bracing air against his cheeks and narrowed his eyes against the bright sunshine.

"Noel, noel," the small chorus on the corner sang. "Noooo-e-el, nooo-eee-elll."

The Chief walked back to headquarters, taking his time. His gloved hands held each other behind his back. The sound of Christmas carols in his ears.

And as he walked, he hummed. He'd done what he went there to do.

At Sûreté headquarters Chief Inspector Gamache pressed the up button, but when the elevator came he didn't get into it. By the time the elevator door closed, Gamache was in the stairwell. Walking down.

He could have taken the elevator, but he couldn't risk being seen descending so low.

Beyond the basement, beyond the sub-basement, below the parking garage, into an area of flickering fluorescent lights. Of cinder-block walls and metal doors. And a constant throb from the lights, and the boilers, heaters, air conditioners. The whir of hydraulics.

This was the physical plant. A place of machines and maintenance crews. And one agent.

All the way in to Montréal, Gamache had thought about his next move. He'd weighed the consequences of visiting Dr. Fleury, and visiting this agent. He'd considered what would happen if he did. What would happen if he didn't.

What was the best he could expect?

What was the worst?

And, finally, what was the alternative? What choice did he have?

And when he'd answered those questions, and made up his mind, Chief Inspector Gamache didn't hesitate. At the door, he gave a sharp rap, then opened it.

The young agent, her pale face a soft green from the bank of monitors around her, turned. He could see she was surprised.

No one came here to see her. Which was why Armand Gamache was there.

"I need your help," he said.

TWENTY

⌐

A note on the kitchen table greeted Gamache when he arrived back at Emilie's home.

Drinks at the bistro. Join us.

Even Henri was gone. Saturday night. Date night.

Gamache showered, changed into corduroys and a turtleneck, then walked over to join them. Thérèse stood as he entered and waved him over.

She was sitting with Jérôme, Myrna, Clara, and Gabri. Henri had been dozing by the fire, but sat up, tail wagging. Olivier brought over a licorice pipe.

"If any man looked like he could use a good pipe," said Olivier.

"Merci, patron." Gamache dropped onto the sofa with a groan and raised the candy to his companions. *"À votre santé."*

"You look like you had a long day," said Clara.

"A good day, I think," said the Chief. Then he turned to Jérôme. "You too?"

Dr. Brunel nodded. "It's restful here."

But he didn't look very rested.

"Scotch?" Olivier offered, but Gamache shook his head, not really sure what he felt like. Then he noticed a boy and girl with bowls of hot chocolate.

"I'd love one of those, *patron*," said the Chief, and Olivier smiled and left.

"What news from the city?" Myrna asked. "Any progress on Constance's murder?"

"Some," said Gamache. "I have to say that in most investigations progress isn't exactly linear."

"True," said Superintendent Brunel. And she told some humorous stories about art thefts and forgeries and confused identities, while Gamache sat back, half listening. Grateful that the Superintendent had leapt in, deflecting the conversation. So he needn't admit that he'd spent most of the day on something else.

His hot chocolate arrived and he raised it to his lips, and noticed that Myrna was watching him. Not examining, but simply looking at him, with interest.

She took a handful of mixed nuts.

"Ah, here's Gilles," said Clara, getting up and waving a large, red-bearded man over. He was in his late forties and dressed casually. "I've invited him and Odile for dinner," she said to the Chief Inspector. "You're coming too."

"*Merci*," he said, shoving himself off the sofa to greet the newcomer.

"Been a while," said Gilles, shaking Gamache's hand, then taking a seat. "I was sorry to hear about the Quint."

Gamache noticed that it wasn't even necessary to say Ouellet Quints. The five girls had lost their privacy, their parents, and their names. They were just the Quints.

"We're trying to keep that quiet for now," said the Chief.

"Well, Odile's writing a poem about them," Gilles confided. "She's hoping to get it into the *Hog Breeder's Gazette*."

"I think that'll be all right," said Gamache, and wondered if that was further up the food chain from her previous publishers. Her anthology, he knew, had been published, almost without edits, by the Root Vegetable Board of Québec.

"She's calling it 'Five Peas in a Gilded Pod,'" said Gilles.

Gamache was grateful Ruth wasn't there. "She knows her market. Where is Odile, by the way?"

"At the shop. She'll try to make it later."

Gilles made exquisite furniture from fallen trees and Odile sold it from the front of their shop. And wrote poetry that, Gamache had to admit, was barely fit for human consumption, despite the opinion of the Root Vegetable Board.

"Now"—Gilles whacked a huge hand onto Gamache's knee—"I hear you want me to install a satellite dish? You know they don't work here, right?"

The Chief stared at him, then over at the Brunels, who were also slightly perplexed.

"You asked me to get in touch with the guy who puts up satellite dishes in the area," said Clara. "That's Gilles."

"Since when?" asked Gamache.

"Since the recession," said the large, burly man. "The market for hand-made furniture tanked, but the market for five hundred television channels has skyrocketed. So I make extra bucks putting up the dishes. It helps that I have a head for heights."

"To put it mildly," said Gamache. He turned to Thérèse and Jérôme. "He used to be a lumberjack."

"Long time ago," said Gilles, looking into his drink.

"I have to put the casserole in the oven." Clara rose to her feet.

Gamache got up and they all followed.

"Maybe we can continue this discussion over at Clara's," said the Chief, and Gilles rocked himself out of the sofa. "Where it's a little more private."

"So," said Gilles as they walked the short distance to Clara's home, their feet crunching on the snow. "Where's your little buddy?"

A few kids were skating on the frozen pond. Gabri scooped up some snow, made it into a ball and tossed it for Henri, who sailed over the snow bank after it.

"Gilligan?" asked Gamache, keeping his voice light. In the darkness he heard Gilles guffaw.

"That's right, Skipper," said Gilles.

"He's on another assignment."

"So he finally made it off the island," said Gilles, and Gamache could hear the smile in his deep voice. But the words came as a bit of a shock.

Had he inadvertently made the famed homicide department of the Sûreté an island? Far from saving the careers of promising agents, had he in fact imprisoned them, kept them from the mainland of their peers?

The kids on the pond saw Gabri's snowball and stopped to make some of their own, throwing them at Gabri, who ducked but too late. Snowballs rained down on all of them and Henri was almost hysterical with excitement.

"You gol'darned kids," said Gabri. "Dagnabbit." He shook his fist at them in such a parody of anger that the kids almost peed themselves with laughter.

Jean-Guy Beauvoir couldn't be bothered to shower. He wanted one, but it was just too much effort. As was laundry. He knew he reeked, but he didn't care.

He'd come in to the office but had done no work. He only wanted to get away from his dreary little apartment. From the piles of dirty clothing, from the rotting food in the fridge, from the unmade bed and food-encrusted dishes.

And from the memory of the home he'd had. And lost.

No, not lost. It had been taken from him. Stolen from him. By Gamache. The one man he'd trusted had taken everything from him. Everyone from him.

Beauvoir got to his feet and walked stiffly to the elevator, then to his car.

His body ached and he was alternately famished and nauseous. But he couldn't be bothered to pick up anything from the cafeteria or any of the fast food joints he passed on his way.

He pulled into a parking spot, turned the car off, and stared.

Now he was hungry. Starving. And he stank. The whole car reeked. He could feel his clammy undershirt sticking to him. Molding itself there, like a second skin.

He sat in the cold, dark car and stared at the one lit window. Hoping for a glimpse of Annie. Even just a shadow.

Was a time he could conjure up her scent. A lemon grove on a warm summer day. Fresh and citrony. But now all he smelt was his own fear.

Annie Gamache sat in the dark, staring out the window. She knew this was unhealthy. It wasn't something she'd ever admit to her friends. They'd be appalled and look at her as though she was pathetic. And she probably was.

She'd kicked Jean-Guy out of their home when he refused to go back to rehab. They'd fought and fought, until there was nothing left to say. And then they fought some more. Jean-Guy insisted there was nothing wrong. That her father had made up the whole drug thing, as payback for him joining Superintendent Francoeur.

Finally, he'd left. But he hadn't actually gone. He was still inside her, and she couldn't get him out. And so she sat in her car and stared at the dark window of his tiny apartment. Hoping to see a light.

If she closed her eyes she could feel his arms around her, smell his scent. When she'd kicked him out she'd bought a bottle of his cologne and put a dab on the pillow next to hers.

She closed her eyes and felt him inside her skin. Where he was vibrant and smart and irreverent and loving. She saw his smile, heard his laugh. Felt his hands. Felt his body.

Now he was gone. But he hadn't left. And she sometimes wondered if that was him, beating on her heart. And she wondered what would happen if he stopped.

Every night she came here. Parked. And stared at the window. Hoping to see some sign of life.

It's hardly the first time you've had a ball in the face," said Ruth to Gabri. "Stop complaining."

Ruth was in Clara's living room when they arrived. Not really waiting for them. In fact, she'd looked pissed off when everyone came in.

"I was hoping for a quiet night," she muttered, swirling the ice cubes around in her glass so forcefully they created a Scotch vortex. Gamache wondered if one day the old poet would be sucked right into it. Then he realized she already had.

Henri ran to Rosa, who was seated on the footstool beside Ruth. Gamache grabbed his collar as he took off, but needn't have worried. Rosa hissed at the shepherd then turned away. If she could have raised one of her feathers to him, she would have.

"I didn't think ducks hissed," said Myrna.

"Are we sure it's a duck?" Gabri whispered.

Thérèse and Jérôme wandered over, fascinated.

"Is that Ruth Zardo?" Jérôme asked.

"What's left of her," said Gabri. "She lost her mind years ago, and never did have a heart. Her bile ducts are keeping her alive. That," said Gabri, pointing, "is Rosa."

"I can see why Henri's lost his heart," said Thérèse, looking at the smitten shepherd. "Who doesn't like a good duck?"

Silence met that remark by the elegant older woman. She smiled and raised her brow just a little, and Clara started to laugh.

The casserole was in the oven and they could smell the rosemary chicken. People poured their own drinks and broke into groups.

Thérèse, Jérôme and Gamache took Gilles aside.

"Did I understand correctly? You used to be a lumberjack?" Thérèse asked.

Gilles became guarded. "Not anymore."

"Why not?"

"Doesn't matter," said the burly man. "Personal reasons."

Thérèse continued to stare at him, with a look that had dragged uncomfortable truths from hardened Sûreté officers. But Gilles held firm.

She turned to Gamache, who remained mute. While he knew those reasons, he wouldn't break Gilles's confidence. The two large men held eyes for a moment and Gilles nodded a slight thanks.

"Let me ask you this, then," said Superintendent Brunel, taking another tack. "What's the tallest tree up there?"

"Up where?"

"On the ridge above the village," said Jérôme.

Gilles considered the question. "Probably a white pine. They can get to ninety feet or more. About eight stories high."

"Can they be climbed?" Thérèse asked.

Gilles stared at her as though she'd suggested something disgusting. "Why these questions?"

"Just curious."

"Don't treat me like a fool, madame. You're more than just curious." He looked from the Brunels to Gamache.

"We'd never ask you to cut down a tree, or even hurt one," said the Chief. "We just want to know if the tallest trees up there can be climbed."

"Not by me they can't," Gilles snapped.

Thérèse and Jérôme turned away from the former forester and looked at Gamache, perplexed by Gilles's reaction. The Chief Inspector touched Gilles's arm and drew him aside.

"I'm sorry, I should have spoken with you privately about this. We need to bring a satellite signal down into Three Pines—"

He held up his hand to ward off Gilles's protests, yet again, that it couldn't be done.

"—and we wondered if a dish could be attached to one of the tall trees, and a cable strung down to the village."

Gilles opened his mouth to protest again, but closed it. His expression went from aggressive to thoughtful.

"You're thinking someone could climb ninety feet up a pine tree, a frozen pine tree, hauling a satellite dish with him, then not only attach it up there, but adjust it to find a signal? You must love television, monsieur."

Gamache laughed. "It's not for television." He lowered his voice. "It's for the Internet. We need to get online, and we need to do it as . . . umm . . . quietly as possible."

"Steal a signal?" asked Gilles. "Frankly, you'd be far from the first to try it."

"Then it's possible?"

Gilles sighed and gnawed on his knuckles, deep in thought. "You're talk-

164

ing about turning a ninety-foot tree into a transmission tower, finding a signal, then laying cable back down."

"You make it sound difficult," said the Chief, with a smile.

But Gilles wasn't smiling. "I'm sorry, *patron*. I'd do anything to help you, but what you're describing I don't think can be done. Let's just say I could climb to the top of the tree with the dish and attach it—there's too much wind. The dish would blow around up there."

He looked at Gamache and saw the fact sink in. And it was a fact. There was no way around it.

"The signal would never hold," Gilles said. "That's why transmission towers are made of steel, and are stable. That's absolutely key. It's a good idea, in theory, but it just won't work."

Chief Inspector Gamache broke eye contact and looked at the floor for a moment, absorbing the blow. This wasn't just a plan, it was the plan. There was no Plan B.

"Can you think of another way to connect to high-speed Internet?" he asked, and Gilles shook his head.

"Why don't you just go into Cowansville or Saint-Rémi? They have high-speed."

"We need to stay here," said Gamache. "Where we can't be traced."

Gilles nodded, thinking. Gamache watched him, willing an answer to appear. Finally Gilles shook his head. "People have been trying to get it for years. Legal or bootleg. It just can't be done. *Désolé*."

And that's how Gamache felt, as he thanked Gilles and walked away. Desolated.

"Well?" asked Thérèse.

"He says it can't be done."

"He just doesn't want to do it," said Superintendent Brunel. "We can find someone else."

Gamache explained about the wind, and saw her slowly accept the truth. Gilles wasn't being willful, he was being realistic. But Gamache saw something else. While Thérèse Brunel looked disappointed, her husband did not.

Gamache wandered into the kitchen where Clara and Gabri were preparing dinner.

"Smells good," he said.

"Hungry?" Gabri asked, handing him a platter with pâté de campagne and crackers.

"I am, as a matter of fact," said the Chief, as he spread a cracker. He could smell the yeasty scent of baking bread. It mingled with the rosemary chicken and he realized he hadn't eaten since breakfast. "I have a favor to ask. I've transferred some old film onto a disk and I'd like to watch it, but Emilie's home doesn't have a DVD player."

"You want to use mine?"

When he nodded she waved a piece of cutlery like a wand in the direction of the living room. "It's in the room off the living room."

"Do you mind?"

"Not at all," she said. "I'll set you up. Dinner won't be for at least half an hour."

Gamache followed her through to a small room with a sofa and arm-chair. An old box television sat on a table, with a DVD player beside it. He watched while Clara pressed some buttons.

"What's on the DVD?" asked Gabri. He stood at the door holding the platter of crackers and pâté. "Let me guess. Your audition for *Canada's Got Talent*?"

"It would be very short if it was," said Gamache.

"What's going on?" Ruth demanded, pushing through, holding Rosa in one arm and a vase of Scotch in the other.

"The Chief Inspector's auditioning for *Canadian Idol*," Gabri explained. "This's his audition tape."

"Well, not—" Gamache began, then gave up. Why bother?

"Did someone say you're auditioning for *So You Think You Can Dance*?" asked Myrna, squeezing onto the small sofa between the Chief and Ruth.

Gamache looked plaintively over at Clara. Olivier had arrived and was standing next to his partner. The Chief sighed and pressed the play button.

A familiar black and white graphic swirled toward them on the small screen, accompanied by music and an authoritative voice.

"In a small Canadian hamlet a tiny miracle has occurred," said the grim newsreel announcer. The first grainy images appeared, and everyone in Clara's small television room leaned forward.

TWENTY-ONE

—

"Five miracles," the melodramatic narration continued, as though announcing Armageddon. "Delivered one bitter winter night by this man, Dr. Joseph Bernard."

There on the screen stood Dr. Bernard, in full surgical smock, a mask over his nose and mouth. He waved a little maniacally, but Gamache knew that was the effect of the old black and white newsreels, where people lurched and movements were either too static or too manic.

In front of the doctor lay the five babies, wrapped up tight.

"Five little girls, born to Isidore and Marie-Harriette Ouellet."

The sonorous voice struggled with the Québécois names. The first time they'd been pronounced on the newsreels, but would soon be on everyone's lips. This was the world's introduction to—

"Five little princesses. The world's first surviving quintuplets. Virginie, Hélène, Josephine, Marguerite, and Constance."

And Constance, noted Gamache with interest. She would go through life hanging off the end of that sentence. *And Constance.* An outlier.

The voice became suddenly excitable. "Here's their father."

The scene switched to Dr. Bernard standing in a modest farmhouse living room, in front of a woodstove. He was handing a large man one of his own daughters. Like a special favor. Not a gift, though. A loan.

Isidore, cleaned up for the camera and giving a gap-toothed smile, held his child awkwardly in his arms. Unused to infants but, Gamache could see, he was a natural.

Thérèse felt a familiar hand on her elbow, and was drawn, reluctantly, away from the television.

Jérôme led her to a corner of Clara's living room, as far from the gathering as possible, though they could still hear the Voice of Doom in the background. Now the Voice was talking about rustics, and seemed to imply the girls had been born in a barn.

Thérèse looked at her husband inquiringly.

Jérôme positioned himself so that he could see the guests standing around the doorway, focused on the television. He switched his gaze to his wife.

"Tell me about Arnot."

"Arnot?"

"Pierre Arnot. You knew him." His voice was low. Urgent. His eyes flickered between the other guests and his wife.

Thérèse could not have been more surprised had her husband suddenly stripped. She stared at him, barely comprehending.

"Do you mean the Arnot case? But that was years ago."

"Not just the case. I want to hear about Arnot himself. Everything you can tell me."

Thérèse stared, dumbfounded. "But that's absurd. Why in the world would you suddenly want to know about him?"

Jérôme's eyes shot to the other guests, their backs safely turned, before returning to his wife. He lowered his voice still further.

"Can't you guess?"

She felt her heart drop. *Arnot. Surely not.*

In the background the bleak voice implied that the hand of God had assisted in the delivery. But the hand of God felt very far from this little room, with the cheery fire and aroma of fresh baking. And the rancid name hanging foul in the air.

Goddamned Pierre Arnot.

Dr. Bernard is typically humble about his accomplishment," said the newsreel announcer.

On the screen now, Dr. Bernard was out of his hospital whites and in a suit and narrow black tie. His gray hair was groomed, he was clean-shaven and wore glasses with heavy black frames.

He was standing in the Ouellet living room, alone, holding a cigarette.

"Of course, the mother did most of the work." He spoke English with a soft Québécois accent and his voice was surprisingly high, especially compared to the cavern voice of the narrator. He looked at the camera and smiled at his little joke. The viewers were meant to believe only one thing. That Dr. Bernard was the hero of the moment. A man whose immense skill was only matched by his humility. And, thought Gamache with some admiration, he was perfectly cast for the role. Charming, whimsical even. Fatherly and confident.

"I was called out in the middle of a storm. Babies seem to prefer arriving in storms." He smiled for the camera, inviting the viewers into his confidence. "This was a big one. A five-baby blizzard."

Gamache glanced around and saw Gilles and Gabri and even Myrna smiling back. It was involuntary, almost impossible not to like this man.

But Ruth, at the far end of the sofa, was not smiling. Still, that was hardly telling.

"It must have been almost midnight," Dr. Bernard continued. "I'd never met the family but it was an emergency, so I took my medical bag and got here as fast as I could."

It was left vague as to how this man, who'd never been to the Ouellet farm, might have found it in the middle of the night, in the middle of a snowstorm, in the middle of nowhere. But perhaps that was part of the miracle.

"No one told me there were five babies." He corrected himself, and his tense. "There would be five babies. But I set the father to boiling water and sterilizing equipment and finding clean linen. Fortunately Monsieur Ouellet is used to helping his farm animals calve and drop foals. He was remarkably helpful."

The great man sharing credit, albeit by implying Madame Ouellet was no better than one of their sows. Gamache felt his admiration, if not his respect, grow. Whoever was behind this was brilliant. But, of course, Dr. Bernard was as much a pawn as the babies and the earnest, stunned Isidore Ouellet.

Dr. Bernard looked directly at the newsreel camera, and smiled.

The Arnot case was in all the papers," said Thérèse, lowering her own voice. "It was a sensation. You know it already. Everyone knows it."

It was true. Pierre Arnot was as infamous as the Ouellet Quints were famous. He was their antithesis. Where the five girls brought delight, Pierre Arnot brought shame.

If they were an act of God, Pierre Arnot was the son of the morning. The fallen angel.

And still, he haunted them. And now he was back. And Thérèse Brunel would give almost anything not to resurrect that name, that case, that time.

"*Oui, oui*," said Jérôme. He rarely showed his impatience, and almost never with his wife. But he did now. "It all happened a decade or so ago. I want to hear it again, and this time what didn't make the papers. What you kept from the public."

"I didn't keep anything from the public, Jérôme." Now she was herself impatient. Her voice was clipped and cold. "I was an entry-level agent at the time. Wouldn't it be better to ask Armand? He knew the man well."

They both, instinctively, turned to the group gathered around the door to the television.

"Do you really think that would be wise?" asked Jérôme.

Thérèse turned back to her husband. "Perhaps not." She stared at him for a moment, searching his eyes. "You need to tell me, Jérôme. Why are you interested in Pierre Arnot?"

Jérôme's breathing was labored, as though he'd been carrying something too heavy over too great a distance. Finally he spoke.

"His name came up in my search."

Thérèse Brunel felt herself suddenly light-headed. Goddamned Pierre Arnot.

"Are you kidding?" But she could see he was not. "Was that the name that tripped the alarms? If it was, you need to tell us."

"What I need, Thérèse, is to hear more about Arnot. His background. Please. You might have been entry-level then, but you're a superintendent now. I know you know."

She gave him a hard, assessing stare.

"Pierre Arnot was the Chief Superintendent of the Sûreté," she began, giving in, as she knew she would. "The top position, the job Sylvain Francoeur now holds. I'd just joined the Sûreté when it all came to light. I only met him once."

Jérôme Brunel remembered all too well the day his wife, the head curator at the Musée des beaux-arts in Montréal, came home announcing she wanted to join the provincial police. She was in her mid-fifties and might as well have said she'd signed up for Cirque du Soleil. But he could tell she wasn't joking, and to be fair, it hadn't come completely out of the blue. Thérèse had been a consultant for the police on a number of art thefts and had discovered an aptitude for solving crimes.

"As you said, this all happened more than ten years ago," said Thérèse. "Arnot had held the top post for many years by then. He was well liked. Respected. Trusted."

"You say you met him once," said Jérôme. "When was that?"

Her husband's eyes were sharp. Analytical. She knew this was exactly as he must have been in the hospital, when a particularly urgent case had been wheeled in.

Gathering information, absorbing, analyzing. Breaking it down rapidly so he'd know how to deal with the emergency. Here in Clara's living room, with the scent of fresh baking and rosemary chicken in the air, some sudden emergency had arisen. And brought with it the mud-covered, blood-covered name of Pierre Arnot.

"It was at a lecture at the academy," she recalled. "In the class Chief Inspector Gamache taught."

"Arnot was his guest?" asked Jérôme, surprised.

Thérèse nodded. By then both men were already famous. Arnot for being the respected head of a respected force, and Gamache for building and commanding the most successful homicide department in the nation.

She was in the packed auditorium, just one of hundreds of students, nothing, yet, to distinguish her from the rest, except her gray hair.

As Thérèse thought about it, the living room dissolved and became the amphitheater. She could see the two men below clearly. Arnot standing at the lectern. Older, confident, distinguished. Short and slender. Compact. With groomed gray hair and glasses. He looked anything but powerful. And yet, in that very humility there was force implied. So great was his power he needn't flaunt it.

And standing off to the side, watching, was Chief Inspector Armand Gamache.

Tall, substantial. Quiet and contained. As a professor he seemed endlessly patient with stupid questions and testosterone. Leading by example, not force. Here, Agent Brunel knew, was a born leader. Someone you'd choose to follow.

Had Arnot been alone at the front of the class, she would have been deeply impressed. But as his lecture went on, her eyes were drawn more and more to the quiet man off to the side. So intently listening. So at ease.

And slowly it dawned on Agent Brunel where the real authority lay.

Chief Superintendent Arnot might hold power, but Armand Gamache was the more powerful man.

She told Jérôme this. He thought for a moment before speaking.

"Did Arnot try to kill Armand?" he asked. "Or was it the other way around?"

The Movietone newsreel ended with the benign Dr. Bernard holding up one of the newborn Quints and flapping her arm at the camera.

"Bye-bye," said the announcer, as though announcing the Great Depression. "I know we'll be seeing a lot more of you and your sisters."

Out of the corner of his eye, Gamache noticed Ruth raise one veined hand.

Bye-bye.

The screen went blank, but only for a moment before another image, familiar to Canadians, came on. The black and white stylized eye and then the stenciled words, with no attempt at creativity or beauty.

Just facts.

National Film Board of Canada. The NFB.

There was no grim voice-over. No cheerful music. It was just raw footage taken by an NFB cameraman.

They saw the exterior of a charming cottage in summer. A fairy-tale cottage, with fish-scale shingles and gingerbread woodwork. Flower boxes were planted at each window and cheery sunflowers and hollyhocks leaned against the sunny home.

The little garden was ringed by a white picket fence.

It was like a doll's house.

The camera zoomed in on the closed front door, focused, then the door opened slightly and a woman's head poked out, stared at the camera, mouthed something that looked like *"Maintenant?"* Now?

She backed up and the door closed. A moment later it opened again and a little girl appeared in a short, frilly dress with a bow in her dark hair. She wore ankle socks and loafers. She was five or six years of age now, Gamache guessed. He did a quick calculation. It would be the early forties. The war years.

A hand appeared and pushed her further out into the sunshine. Not a shove, exactly, but a push strong enough that she stumbled a little.

Then an identical girl was expelled from the home.

Then another.

And another.

And another.

172

The girls stood together, clasping each other as though they'd been born conjoined. And their expressions were identical too.

Terror. Confusion. Almost exactly the same expression their father had had when he'd first gazed down at them.

They turned to the door, then returned to the door, flocking around it. Trying to get back in. But it wouldn't open for them.

The first little girl looked at the camera. Pleading. Crying.

The image flickered and went out. Then the pretty cottage reappeared. The girls were gone and the door was closed.

Again it opened and this time the little girl walked out on her own. Then her sister appeared, gripping her hand. And so on. Until the last one was out, and the door closed behind them.

As one, they stared back at it. A hand snaked through a crack in the door and waved them away, before disappearing.

The girls were rooted in place. Paralyzed.

The camera shook slightly and as one the girls turned to look into the lens. The cameraman, Gamache thought, must have called to them. Was perhaps holding up a teddy bear or candy. Something to draw their attention.

One of them began to cry, then the others disintegrated and the picture flickered and went to black.

Over and over, in Clara's back room, they watched, the pâté and drinks forgotten.

Over and over the girls came out of the pretty little house, and were hauled back in, to try it again. Until finally the first one appeared, a big smile on her face, followed by her sister, happily holding her hand.

Then the next and the next.

And the next.

They left the cottage and walked around the garden, along the border of white picket fence, smiling and waving.

Five happy little girls.

Gamache looked at Myrna, Olivier, Clara, Gilles, Gabri. He looked at Ruth, her tears following the crevices in her face, grand canyons of grief.

On the television, the Ouellet Quints smiled identical smiles, and waved identical waves into the camera, before the screen went dead. It was, Gamache knew, the scene that had come to define the Quints as perfect little girls, leading fairy-tale lives. Plucked from poverty, far from any conflict. This bit of footage had been sold to agencies around the world and was still used today in retrospectives of their lives.

As proof of how lucky the Ouellet Quints were.

Gamache and the others knew what they'd just witnessed. The birth of a myth. And they'd seen something broken. Shattered. Hurt beyond repair.

How'd you know about that?" Thérèse asked. "It never came out in the trial."

"I found references to something happening between the two men. Something near lethal."

"You really want to know?" she asked, examining him.

"I need to know," he said.

"This goes no further." She received a look caught between amusement and annoyance.

"I promise not to put it into my blog."

Thérèse didn't laugh. Didn't even smile. And Jérôme Brunel, not for the first time, wondered if he really wanted to hear this.

"Sit," she said, and he followed her to the comfortable sofa. They faced the door, watching the backs of the other guests.

"Pierre Arnot made his mark in the Sûreté detachment in the north of Québec," she confided. "On a Cree reserve on James Bay. Lots of alcohol. Sniff. The government-issue homes were a disgrace. The sewage and water systems overflowed into each other. There was terrible disease and violence. A cesspool."

"In the middle of paradise," said Jérôme.

Thérèse nodded. That, of course, heightened the tragedy.

The James Bay area was spectacularly beautiful and unspoiled. At the time. Ten thousand square miles of wildlife, of clear, fresh lakes, of fish and game and old-growth forests. This was where the Cree lived. This was where their gods lived.

But a hundred years ago they'd met the devil and made a deal.

In exchange for everything they could ever need—food, medical care, housing, education, the marvels of modern life—all they had to do was sign over the rights to their ancestral land.

But not all of it. They'd be given a nice plot on which to hunt and fish.

And if they didn't sign?

The government would take the land anyway.

A hundred years before Agent Pierre Arnot stepped off the floatplane onto the reserve, the Grand Chief and the head of Indian Affairs for Canada met.

The deed was signed.

The deed was done.

The Cree had everything they could want. Except their freedom.

They did not thrive.

"By the time Arnot arrived the reserve was a ghetto of open sewers and disease, addiction and despair," said Thérèse. "And lives so empty they raped and beat each other for distraction. Still, the Cree had held on to their dignity longer than anyone could have expected. It had taken several generations until finally there was no dignity, no self-respect, no hope left. The Cree thought their life couldn't get worse. But it was about to."

"What happened?" asked Jérôme.

"Pierre Arnot arrived."

Here the girls are asking their father for his blessing," the Movietone newsreel narrator said, as though announcing the bombing of London. "Like obedient children. It's a ritual still practiced in the hinterlands of Quebec."

He pronounced it Kwee-bek, and his voice was hushed, documenting a rare species caught in its natural habitat.

Gamache sat forward. The girls were now eight or nine years of age. They weren't in their fairy-tale cottage. This was back at the family farm-house. Through the windows he could see it was winter.

Their coats and hats and skates were neatly hung on pegs by the door. Hockey sticks formed a teepee in the corner. He recognized the wood-stove and braided rag rug and furnishings from the very first film, when the girls had been born. Almost nothing had changed. Like a museum.

The girls were kneeling, hands clasped in front of them, heads bowed, wearing identical dresses, identical shoes, identical bows. He wondered how anyone could tell them apart, and he wondered if they even bothered. As long as there were five of them, the details didn't seem to matter.

Marie-Harriette knelt behind her daughters.

It was the first time the newsreels had captured the Quints' mother. Gamache put his elbows on his knees and leaned further forward, trying to get a good look at this epic mother.

With surprise, Gamache realized this wasn't, in fact, the first time he'd seen her. It had been Marie-Harriette who'd pushed her daughters out that door. Then closed it on them.

Over and over. Until they got it right.

He'd presumed it was some NFB producer, or even a nurse or teacher. But it was their own mother.

Isidore Ouellet stood at the front of the room facing his family, his arms straight out in front of him. His eyes were closed. His face was in repose, like a zombie seeking enlightenment.

Gamache recognized the ritual. It was the New Year's Day blessing of the children by their father. It was a solemn and meaningful prayer, though one rarely practiced in Québec anymore. He'd never considered doing it and Reine-Marie, Annie and Daniel would have howled with laughter had he tried. He had a brief thought that the holidays were approaching and the whole family would be together in Paris. Perhaps on New Year's Day, with his children and grandchildren, he could suggest it. Just to see the looks on their faces. It would almost be worth it. Though Reine-Marie's mother had remembered, as a child, kneeling with her siblings for the blessing.

And here it was, being played out for the insatiable newsreel audience, sitting in dark theaters around the world in the mid-forties, the Quints' lives a prelude to the latest Clark Gable or Katharine Hepburn film.

There was a definite odor of the gaslights about what they were seeing on this grainy black and white film. A staged event, played for effect. Like the native drumming and dances performed for paying tourists.

Genuine, absolutely. But here more mercantile than spiritual.

The girls were supposedly praying for the paternal blessing. Gamache wondered what their father was praying for.

"The charming little ceremony over, the girls prepare to go outside to play," said the voice-over, as though announcing the tragic raid on Dieppe.

What followed were scenes of the Quints putting on their snowsuits, good-naturedly teasing each other, looking into the camera and laughing. Their father helped lace up their skates and handed them hockey sticks.

Marie-Harriette appeared, putting knitted tuques on their heads. Each hat, Gamache noticed, had a different pattern. Snowflakes, trees. She had one too many and threw the extra off camera. Not a casual toss. She whipped it, as though it had bitten her.

The gesture was revealing. It showed a woman at the end of her tether, where something as trivial as too many hats could spark anger. She was exasperated, exhausted. Worn down.

She turned to the camera and, in a look that chilled the Chief Inspector, she smiled.

It was one of those moments a homicide investigator looked for. The tiny conflict. Between what was said and what was done. Between the tone and the words.

Between Marie-Harriette's expression and her actions. The smile, and the thrown hat.

Here was a woman divided, perhaps even falling apart. It was through such a crack an investigator crawled to get to the heart of the matter.

Gamache watched the screen and wondered how the woman who'd struggled up the steps of Saint Joseph's Oratory on her knees, praying for children, came to this.

The Chief suspected her annoyance had been directed at the ubiquitous Dr. Bernard, trying to keep him out of the frame. To, just once, leave them alone with their children.

It had worked. Whoever she'd gestured to had backed off.

But Gamache could tell it was a rearguard action. No one that tired would prevail for long.

Long dead and buried in another town, Gamache remembered Ruth's seminal poem, *my mother hasn't finished with me yet.*

In just over five years, Marie-Harriette would be dead. And in just over fifteen years Virginie would possibly take her own life. And what had Myrna said? They would no longer be Quints. They would be a quartet, then triplets, twins. Then just one. An only child.

And Constance would become simply Constance. And now she was gone too.

He looked at the girls, laughing together in their snowsuits, and tried to pick out the little girl who now lay in the Montréal morgue. But he could not.

They all looked alike.

"Yes, these rugged Canadians pass the long winter months ice fishing, skiing and playing hockey," said the morose narrator. "Even the girls."

The Quints waved at the camera and wobbled on their skates out the door.

The film ended with Isidore waving merrily to them, then turning back into the cabin. He closed the door and looked into the camera, but Gamache realized his eyes were in fact slightly off. Catching not the lens, but the eye of someone just out of sight.

Was he looking at his wife? At Dr. Bernard? Or at someone else entirely?

It was a look of supplication, for approval. And once again Gamache wondered what Isidore Ouellet had prayed for, and whether his prayers had ever been answered.

But something was off. Something about this film didn't fit with what the Chief Inspector had learned.

He covered his mouth with his hand and stared at the black screen.

Let me ask you this," said Thérèse Brunel. "What's the surest way to destroy someone?"

Jérôme shook his head.

"First you win their trust," she said, holding his stare. "Then you betray it."

"The Cree trusted Pierre Arnot?" asked Jérôme.

"He helped restore order. He treated them with respect."

"And then?"

"And then, when plans for the new hydroelectric dam were unveiled, and it became clear it would destroy what was left of the Cree territory, he convinced them to accept it."

"How'd he do that?" asked Jérôme. As a Québécois, he'd always seen the great dams as a point of pride. Yes, he was aware of the damage up north, but it seemed a small price. A price he himself didn't actually have to pay.

"They trusted him. He'd spent years convincing them he was their friend and ally. Later, those who doubted him, questioned his motives, disappeared."

Jérôme's stomach churned. "He did that?"

Thérèse nodded. "I don't know if he started out so corrupt, or if he was corrupted, but that's what he did."

Jérôme lowered his eyes and thought about the name he'd found. The one buried below Arnot. If Arnot had fallen, this other man had fallen further. Only to be dug up, years later, by Jérôme Brunel.

"When did Armand get involved?" asked Jérôme.

"A Cree elder, a woman, was selected to travel to Quebec City, to ask for help. She wanted to tell someone in authority that young men and women were disappearing. Dying. They were found hanged and shot and drowned. The Sûreté detachment had dismissed the deaths as accidents or suicides. Some young Cree had disappeared completely. The Sûreté concluded they'd run away. Probably down south. They'd be found in some crack house or drunk tank in Trois-Rivières or Montréal."

"She came to Quebec City to ask for help in finding them?" asked Jérôme.

"No, she wanted to tell someone in authority that it was lies. Her own son was among the missing. She knew they hadn't run away, and the deaths weren't accidents or suicides."

Jérôme could see how dredging up these memories was affecting Thérèse. As a senior Sûreté officer. As a woman. As a mother. And it sickened him too, but they'd gone too far. They couldn't stop in the middle of this quagmire. They had to keep going.

"No one believed her," said Thérèse. "She was dismissed as demented. Another drunk native. It didn't help that she didn't know where to find the National Assembly, so she stopped people going into and out of the Château Frontenac."

"The hotel?" asked Jérôme.

Thérèse nodded. "It's such an imposing building, she thought it was where the leaders must be."

"But how did Armand get involved?"

"He was in Quebec City for a conference at the Château and saw her sitting on a bench, distraught. He asked her what was wrong."

"She told him?" asked Jérôme.

"Everything. Armand asked why she hadn't gone to the Sûreté with that information." Thérèse lowered her eyes to her manicured hands.

Out of the corner of his eye Jérôme could see the gathering in the TV room breaking up, but he didn't hurry his wife. They'd come to the bottom of the swamp at last, to the final words that needed to be dredged up. She was clearly struggling to speak the unspeakable.

"The Cree elder said she hadn't reported it to the Sûreté because the Sûreté were doing it. They were killing the young Cree. Including, probably, her own son."

Jérôme stared at his wife. Holding on to those familiar eyes. Not wanting to let go and slide into a world where such a thing was possible. He could tell that Thérèse was almost relieved. Believing she was near the end now. That the worst was over.

But Jérôme knew they were very far from the worst. And nowhere near the end.

"What did Armand do?"

He could see Clara heading to the kitchen and Olivier was making his way toward them. But still he held his wife's eyes.

She leaned toward him and whispered, just before Olivier arrived.

"He believed her."

TWENTY-TWO

~

"Dinner!" Clara called.

They'd watched to the end of the DVD. After the NFB footage and the newsreels, there were more clips of the Quints. At First Communion, meeting the young Queen, curtsying to the Prime Minister.

In unison, of course. And the great man laughing, delighted.

It was odd, thought Clara, as she took the casserole from the oven, to see someone she only knew as an elderly woman as an infant. It was odder still to see her grow up. To see so much of her, and so many of her.

Seeing those films one after the other went from charming, to disconcerting, to devastating. It was made even odder by not being able to tell which one was Constance. They were all her. And none were.

The films ended suddenly when the girls reached their late teens.

"Can I help?" asked Myrna, prying the warm bread from Clara's hand.

"What did you think of the film?" Clara asked, putting the baguette Myrna sliced into a basket. Olivier was placing plates on the long pine table while Gabri tossed the salad.

Ruth was either trying to light the candles or set the house on fire. Armand was nowhere to be seen, and neither were Thérèse or her husband Jérôme.

"I keep seeing that first sister, Virginie, I think, looking at the camera." Myrna paused in her slicing and stared ahead.

"You mean when their mother wouldn't let them back into the house?" Clara asked.

Myrna nodded and thought how strange it was that, when talking with Gamache, she'd used the house analogy, saying that Constance was locked and barricaded inside her emotional home.

What was worse, Myrna wondered. To be locked in, or locked out?

"They were so young," Clara said, as she took the knife from Myrna's suspended hand. "Maybe Constance didn't remember."

"Oh, she'd have remembered," said Myrna. "They all would. If not the specific event, they'd remember how it felt."

"And they couldn't tell anyone," said Clara. "Not even their parents. Especially not their parents. I wonder what that does to a person."

"I know what it does."

They turned to Ruth, who'd struck another match. She stared, cross-eyed, as it burned down. Just before it singed her yellowed nails she blew it out.

"What does it do?" Clara asked. The room was quiet, all eyes on the old poet.

"It turns a little girl into an ancient mariner."

There was a collective sigh. They'd actually thought maybe Ruth had the answer. They should have known better than to look for wisdom in a drunken old pyro.

"The albatross?" asked Gamache.

He was standing just inside the doorway between the living room and the kitchen. Myrna wondered how long he'd been listening.

Ruth struck another match and Gamache held her blazing eyes, looking beyond the flame to the charred core.

"What's that supposed to mean?" Gilles broke the silence. "An old sailor and a tuna?"

"That's albacore," said Olivier.

"Oh, for chrissake," snapped Ruth, and flicked her hand so that the flame went out. "One day I'll be dead and then what'll you do for cultured conversation, you stupid shits?"

"*Touché*," said Myrna.

Ruth gave Gamache one final, stern look, then turned to the rest of the room.

"*The Rime of the Ancient Mariner*?" When that was met with blank stares she went on. "Epic poem. Coleridge?"

Gilles leaned toward Olivier and whispered, "She's not going to recite it, is she? I get enough poetry at home."

"Right," said Ruth. "People are always confusing Odile's work with Coleridge."

"At least they both rhyme," said Gabri.

"Not always," Gilles confided. "In her latest, Odile has 'turnip' rhyming with 'cowshed.'"

Ruth sighed so violently her latest match blew out.

"OK, I'll bite," said Olivier. "Why does any of this remind you of *The Rime of the Ancient Mariner*?"

Ruth looked around. "Don't tell me Clouseau and I are the only ones with classical educations?"

"Wait a minute," said Gabri. "I remember now. Didn't the ancient mariner and Ellen DeGeneres save Nemo from a fish tank in Australia?"

"I think that was the Little Mermaid," said Clara.

"Really?" Gabri turned to her. "Because I seem to remember—"

"Stop it." Ruth waved them to be quiet. "The Ancient Mariner carried his secret, like a dead albatross, around his neck. He knew the only way to get rid of it was to tell others. To unburden himself. So he stopped a stranger, a wedding guest, and told him everything."

"And what was his secret?" asked Gilles.

"The mariner had killed an albatross at sea," said Gamache, stepping into the kitchen and taking the breadbasket to the table. "As a consequence of this cruel act, God took the lives of the entire crew."

"Jeez," said Gilles. "I'm no fan of hunting, but a bit of an overreaction, wouldn't you say?"

"Only the mariner was spared," said Gamache. "To stew. When he was finally rescued he realized that he could only be free if he talked about what had happened."

"That a bird died?" asked Gilles, still trying to wrap his mind around it.

"That an innocent creature was killed," said Gamache. "That he'd killed it."

"You'd think God should also have to answer for slaughtering the entire crew," Gilles suggested.

"Oh, shut up," snapped Ruth. "The Ancient Mariner brought the curse on himself and them. It was his fault, and he had to admit it, or carry it the rest of his life. Got it?"

"Still doesn't make sense to me," mumbled Gilles.

"If you think this is difficult, try reading *The Faerie Queene*," said Myrna.

"Fairy Queen?" asked Gabri, hopefully. "Sounds like bedtime reading to me."

They sat down for dinner, the guests jockeying not to sit next to Ruth, or the duck.

Gamache lost.

Or perhaps he wasn't playing.

Or perhaps he won.

"You think Constance had an albatross around her neck?" he asked Ruth as he spooned chicken and dumplings onto her plate.

"Ironic, don't you think?" Ruth asked, without thanking him. "Talking about the killing of an innocent bird while eating chicken?"

Gabri and Clara put down their forks. The rest pretended they hadn't heard. It was, after all, very tasty.

"So what was Constance's albatross?" asked Olivier.

"Why ask me, numb nuts? How would I know?"

"But you think she had a secret?" Myrna persevered. "Something she felt guilty about?"

"Look." Ruth laid down her cutlery and stared across at Myrna. "If I was a fortune-teller, what would I say to people? I'd look them in the eye and say . . ." She turned to Gamache and moved her spiny hands back and forth in front of his amused face. She took on a vague eastern European accent and lowered her voice. "You carry a heavy burden. A secret. Something you've told no living soul. Your heart is breaking, but you must let it go."

Ruth dropped her hands but continued to stare at Gamache. He gave nothing away, but became very still.

"Who doesn't have a secret?" Ruth asked quietly, speaking directly to the Chief.

"You're right, of course," said Gamache, taking a forkful of the delicious casserole. "We all carry secrets. Most to the grave."

"But some secrets are heavier than others," said the old poet. "Some stagger us, slow us. And instead of taking them to the grave, the grave comes to us."

"You think that's what happened with Constance?" asked Myrna.

Ruth held Gamache's thoughtful brown eyes for a moment longer, then broke off to stare across the table.

"Don't you, Myrna?"

More frightening than the thought was Ruth's use of Myrna's actual name. So serious was the suddenly and suspiciously sober poet that she'd forgotten to forget Myrna's name.

"What do you think her secret was?" asked Olivier.

"I think it was that she was a transvestite," said Ruth so seriously that Olivier's brows rose, then quickly descended and he glowered. Beside him, Gabri laughed.

"The Fairy Queen after all," he said.

"How the hell should I know her secret?" demanded Ruth.

Gamache looked across the table. Myrna was the wedding guest, he suspected. The person Constance Ouellet had chosen to unburden herself to. But she never got that chance.

And, more and more, Gamache suspected it wasn't a coincidence that Constance Ouellet, the last Quint, was murdered as she prepared to return to Three Pines.

Someone wanted to prevent her from getting here.

Someone wanted to prevent her from unburdening herself.

But then another thought struck Gamache. Maybe Myrna wasn't the only wedding guest. Maybe Constance had confided in someone else.

The rest of the meal was spent talking about Christmas plans, menus, the upcoming concert.

Everyone, except Ruth, cleared the table while Gabri took Olivier's trifle out of the fridge, with its layers of ladyfingers, custard, fresh whipped cream and brandy-infused jam.

"The love that dares not speak its name," Gabri whispered as he cradled it in his arms.

"How many calories, do you think?" asked Clara.

"Don't ask," said Olivier.

"Don't tell," said Myrna.

After dinner, when the table was cleared and the dishes done, the guests took their leave, getting on their heavy coats and sorting through the jumble of boots by the mudroom door.

Gamache felt a hand on his elbow and was drawn by Gilles into a far corner of the kitchen.

"I think I know how to connect you to the Internet." The woodsman's eyes were bright.

"Really?" asked Gamache, barely daring to believe it. "How?"

"There's a tower up there already. One you know about."

Gamache looked at his companion, perplexed. "I don't think so. We'd be able to see it, *non*?"

"No. That's the beauty of it," said Gilles, excited now. "It's practically invisible. In fact, you can barely tell it's there even from right under it."

Gamache was unconvinced. He knew those woods, not, perhaps, as intimately as Gilles, but well enough. And nothing came to mind.

"Just tell me," said the Chief. "What're you talking about?"

"When Ruth was talking about killing that bird, it made me think of hunting. And that reminded me of the blind."

The Chief's face went slack from surprise. *Merde*, he thought. The hunting blind. That wooden structure high up in a tree in the forest. It was a platform with wooden railings, built by hunters to sit comfortably and wait for a deer to walk past. Then they'd kill it. The modern equivalent of the Ancient Mariner in his crow's nest.

It was, for a man who'd seen far too many deaths, shameful.

But it might, this day, redeem itself.

"The blind," whispered Gamache. He'd actually been on it, when he'd first come to Three Pines to investigate the murder of Miss Jane Neal, but he hadn't thought of it in years. "It'll work?"

"I think so. It's not as high as a transmission tower, but it's on the top of the hill and it's stable. We can attach a satellite dish up there for sure."

Gamache waved Thérèse and Jérôme over.

"Gilles's figured out how to get a satellite dish up above."

"How?" the Brunels asked together and the Chief told them.

"That'll work?" asked Jérôme.

"We won't know until we try, of course," said Gilles, but he was smiling and clearly hopeful, if not completely confident. "When do you need it up by?"

"The dish and other equipment are arriving sometime tonight," said Gamache, and both Thérèse and Jérôme looked at him, surprised.

Gilles walked with them to the door. The others were just leaving, and the four of them put on their parkas and boots, hats and mitts. They thanked Clara, then left.

Gilles stopped at his car. "I'll be by tomorrow morning then," he said. "À demain."

They shook hands, and after he'd driven away Gamache turned to the Brunels.

"Do you mind walking Henri? I'd like a word with Ruth."

Thérèse took the leash. "I won't ask which word."

Good."

Sylvain Francoeur glanced from the document his second in command had downloaded, then went back to the computer. They were in the Chief Superintendent's study at home.

As his boss read the report, Tessier tried to read his boss. But in all the years he'd worked for the Chief Superintendent, he'd never been able to do that.

Classically handsome, in his early sixties, the Chief Superintendent could smile and bite your head off. He could quote Chaucer and Tintin, in either educated French or broad joual. He'd order poutine for lunch and foie gras for dinner. He was all things. To all people. He was everything and he was nothing.

But Francoeur also had a boss. Someone he answered to. Tessier had seen the Chief Superintendent with him just once. The man hadn't been introduced as Francoeur's boss, of course, but Tessier could tell by the way Francoeur behaved. "Grovel" would be too strong a word, but there'd been anxiety there. Francoeur had been as anxious to please that man as Tessier was to please Francoeur.

At first it had amused Tessier, but then the smile had burned away when he realized there was someone who scared the most frightening man he knew.

Francoeur finally sat back, rocking a little in the chair.

"I need to get back to my guests. I see it went well."

"Perfectly." Tessier kept his face placid, his voice neutral. He'd learned to mirror his boss. "We got completely kitted out, drove there in the assault van. By the time we got there Beauvoir could barely stand. I made sure some of the evidence ended up in a baggie in his pocket, with my compliments."

"I don't need to know the details," said Francoeur.

"Sorry, sir."

It wasn't, Tessier knew, because Francoeur was squeamish. It was that he just didn't care. All he cared about was that it was done. The details he left up to his subordinates.

"I want him sent on another raid."

"Another?"

"Do you have a problem with that, Inspector?"

"It's a waste of time, in my opinion, sir. Beauvoir's had it. He's past the edge now, hanging in midair. He just hasn't fallen. But he will. There's no way back for him and nothing to go back to. He's lost everything, and he knows it. Another raid is unnecessary."

"Is that so? You think this is about Beauvoir?"

The calm should have warned him. The slight smile certainly should have. But Inspector Tessier had taken his eyes off Francoeur's face.

"I realize this is about Chief Inspector Gamache."

"Do you?"

"But did you see here—" Tessier leaned forward and pointed to the computer screen. He didn't see that the Chief Superintendent's eyes never left him. Never wavered. Barely blinked.

"The psychologist's report, Dr. Fleury. Gamache was so upset he went to see him today. A Saturday."

Too late, he looked up into those glacier eyes. "We picked this off Dr. Fleury's computer late this afternoon."

He hoped for some sign of approval. A slight thaw. A sign of life. But all he met was the dead stare.

"He says Gamache is spinning out of control. Delusional even. Don't you see?" And even as he said that he could have shot himself. And might have. Francoeur saw everything, ten steps ahead of everyone else. Which was why they were on the verge of success.

There'd been a few unexpected setbacks. The raid on the factory was one. The dam plot discovered. Gamache again.

But that's what made this report all the sweeter. The Chief Superintendent should be pleased. Then why was he looking like that? Tessier felt his blood cool and grow thick and his heart labor.

"If Gamache ever tries to go public, his own therapist's report can be leaked. His credibility will be gone. No one will believe a man who . . ." Tessier looked over at the report, desperate to find that perfect sentence. He found it and read, ". . . *is suffering from persecution mania. Seeing conspiracies and plots.*"

Tessier scrolled down, reading fast. Trying to create a wall of reassuring words between himself and Francoeur.

"*Chief Inspector Gamache is not simply a broken man,*" he read, "*but shattered. When I return from Christmas vacation I will recommend he be relieved of duty.*"

Tessier looked up and met, again, those arctic eyes. Nothing had changed. Those words, if they penetrated, had only found more ice. Colder. Older. Endless.

"He's isolated," said Tessier. "Inspector Lacoste is the only one left of his original investigators. The rest have either transferred out on their own or been moved by you. His last senior ally, Superintendent Brunel, has even abandoned him. She also thinks he's delusional. We have the recordings from her office. And Gamache refers to it here."

Once again Tessier rifled through the therapist's report. "See? He admits they've left for Vancouver."

"They may have gone, but they got too close." Francoeur spoke at last. "Thérèse Brunel's husband turned out to be more than a weekend hacker. He almost figured it out."

The voice was conversational, at odds with the glacial look.

"But he didn't," said Tessier, eager to reassure his boss. "And it scared him shitless. Brunel shut down his computer. Hasn't turned it on since."

"He saw too much."

"He has no idea what he saw, sir. He won't be able to put it together."

"But Gamache will."

It was Tessier's turn to smile. "But Dr. Brunel didn't tell him. And now he and the Superintendent are in Vancouver, as far from Gamache as they could get. They've abandoned him. He's on his own. He admitted as much to his therapist."

"Where is he?"

"Investigating the murder of the Quint. He's spending most of his time in some small village in the Townships, and when he's not there he's distracted by Beauvoir. It's too late. He can't stop it now. Besides, he doesn't even know what's happening."

Chief Superintendent Francoeur got up. Slowly. Deliberately. And walked around his desk. Tessier twisted out of his chair and stood, then stepped back, back, until he felt his body against the bookcase.

Francoeur stopped within inches of his second in command, his eyes never leaving Tessier.

"You know what's at stake?"

The younger man nodded.

"You know what happens if we succeed?"

Again Tessier nodded.

"And you know what happens if we don't?"

It had never occurred to Tessier that they could possibly fail, but now he thought about it, and understood what that would mean.

"Do you want me to take care of Gamache, sir?"

"Not yet. It would raise too many questions. You need to make sure Dr. Brunel and Gamache don't come within a thousand kilometers of each other. Understood?"

"Yessir."

"If it looks like Gamache is coming close, you need to distract him. That shouldn't be difficult."

As Tessier walked to his car he knew Francoeur was right. It wouldn't be difficult. Just a tiny little shove and Jean-Guy Beauvoir would fall. And land on Chief Inspector Gamache.

TWENTY-THREE

Jérôme and Thérèse walked Henri around the village green. Their second circuit. Deep in conversation. It was biting cold, but they needed the fresh air.

"So Armand investigated what the Cree elder told him," said Jérôme. "And he found she was telling the truth. What did he do?"

"He made absolutely certain his case was seamless, then he took the proof to the council."

This was the council of superintendents, Jérôme knew. The leadership of the Sûreté. Thérèse sat on it now, but at the time she was a lowly agent, a new recruit. Oblivious to the earthquake that was about to shake everything the Sûreté felt was stable.

Service, Integrity, Justice. The Sûreté motto.

"He knew it would be almost impossible to convince the superintendents, and even if convinced, they'd want to protect Arnot and the reputation of the force. Armand approached a couple of members of the council he thought would be sympathetic. One was, one wasn't. And his hand was forced. He asked for a meeting with the council. By now Arnot and a few others suspected what it was about. They refused, at first."

"What changed their minds?" asked Jérôme.

"Armand threatened to go public."

"You're kidding."

But even as he said that, Jérôme knew it made sense. Of course Gamache would. He'd discovered something so horrific, so damning, he felt he no longer owed loyalty to the Sûreté leadership. His loyalty was to Québec, not a bunch of old men around a polished table looking at their own reflections as they made decisions.

"What happened at the meeting?" Jérôme asked.

"Arnot and his immediate deputies, the ones Armand had the most proof against, agreed to resign. They'd retire, the Sûreté would leave the Cree territory, and everyone would get on with their lives."

"Armand won," said Jérôme.

"No. He demanded more."

Their feet crunched over the snow as they made their slow circuit in the light of the three great trees.

"More?"

"He said it wasn't enough. Not even close. Armand demanded that Arnot and the others be arrested and charged with murder. He argued that the young Cree who died deserved that. That their parents and loved ones and their community deserved answers and an apology. And a pledge that it would never happen again. The council reluctantly agreed after a bitter debate. They had no choice. Armand had all the proof. They knew it would ruin the Sûreté when it all became public, when the very head of the force was tried for murder."

That was the Arnot case.

Jérôme, like the rest of Québec, had followed it. It was, in many ways, his introduction to Gamache. Seeing him on the news walk into court, alone, each day. Swarmed by the media. Answering impolite questions politely.

Testifying against his own brothers-in-arms. Clearly. Thoroughly. Hammering home, in his reasonable, thoughtful voice, the facts.

"But there's more," said Thérèse quietly. "What didn't make the papers."

"More?"

May I make you a tea, madame?" Gamache asked Ruth.

Once more they were in her small kitchen. Ruth had put Rosa to bed and taken off her cloth coat, but didn't offer to take Gamache's parka.

He'd found a bag of loose Lapsang souchong and held it up. Ruth squinted at it.

"That's tea? That would explain a few things . . ."

Gamache put the kettle on. "Do you have a pot?"

"Well, I thought . . ." Ruth jerked her head toward the baggie.

Gamache stared at her for a moment before decoding that.

"A pot," he said. "Not 'pot.'"

"Oh, in that case, yes. Over there."

Gamache poured hot water into the teapot and swirled it around before pouring it out. Ruth sprawled in a chair and regarded him as he spooned loose black tea into the chipped and stained pot.

"So, time to drop your albatross," said Ruth.

"Is that a euphemism?" Gamache asked, and heard Ruth snort.

He poured the just boiling water onto the tea and put the cover on. Then he joined her at the table.

"Where's Beauvoir?" Ruth asked. "And don't give me any of that crap about being on another assignment. What happened?"

"I can't tell you the specifics," said Gamache. "It's not my story to tell."

"Then why did you come here tonight?"

"Because I knew you were worried. And you love him too."

"Is he all right?"

Gamache shook his head.

"Shall I be mother?" asked Ruth, and Gamache smiled as she poured.

They sat and sipped in silence. Then he told her what he could, about Jean-Guy. And he felt his load was lightened.

The Brunels walked in silence except for the rhythmic sound of their boots crunching on the snow. What had once seemed annoying, a noise that broke the quietude, now seemed reassuring, comforting even. A human presence in this tale of inhumanity.

"The Sûreté council voted not to arrest Pierre Arnot and the others immediately," said Thérèse, "but to give them a few days to put their affairs in order."

Jérôme thought about that for a moment. The use of those particular words.

"Do you mean . . . ?"

Thérèse said nothing, forcing him to say it.

". . . kill themselves?"

"Armand was vehemently against it, but the council voted, and even Arnot could see it was the only way out. A quick bullet to the brain. The men would go to a remote hunting camp. Their bodies, and confessions, would be found later."

"But . . ." Again Jérôme was at a loss for words, trying to corral his racing thoughts. "But there was a trial. I saw it. That was Arnot, wasn't it?"

"It was."

"So what happened?"

"Armand disobeyed orders. He went to the hunting camp and arrested them. Brought them back to Montréal in handcuffs and filed the papers himself. Multiple charges of first-degree murder."

Thérèse stopped. Jérôme stopped. The comforting munching of the snow stopped.

"My God," Jérôme whispered. "No wonder the leadership hate him."

"But the rank and file adore him," said Thérèse. "Instead of bringing shame on the service, the trial proved that while corruption exists, so does justice. The corruption within the Sûreté shocked the public. At least, the degree of it did. But what also surprised them was the degree of decency. While the leadership privately rallied around Arnot, the body of the Sûreté sided with the Chief Inspector. And the public certainly did."

"Service, Integrity, Justice," Jérôme quoted the motto Thérèse had above her desk at home. She too believed in it.

"*Oui.* They suddenly became more than words for the rank and file. The only question left unanswered was why Chief Superintendent Arnot did it," said Thérèse.

"Arnot said nothing?" asked Jérôme, looking down at his feet. Not daring to look at his wife.

"He refused to testify. Proclaimed his innocence throughout the trial. Said it was a putsch, a lynching by a power-hungry and corrupt Chief Inspector."

"He never explained himself?"

"Said there was nothing to explain."

"Where is he now?"

"In the shoe."

"*Pardon?*"

"The shoe. It's where the worst offenders are kept," said Thérèse.

"You keep them in a shoe? Is that really wise?"

Thérèse stared at her husband, then for the first time since this conversation started, she laughed.

"I mean the Special Handling Unit at the maximum security penitentiary. The SHU."

"That would make more sense," agreed Jérôme. "And Francoeur?"

"He—"

Thérèse Brunel began to answer but stopped. There was another sound. Coming toward them, out of the darkness.

Crunch. Crunch. Crunch.

Neither fast, nor slow. Not hurried, but neither was it leisurely.

They stopped, two elderly people frozen in place. Jérôme drew himself up to his full height. He stared into the night and tried not to think that the very mention of the name had conjured the man.

And still the steps approached. Measured. Assured.

"That was where I made my mistake."

The voice came out of the darkness.

"Armand," said Thérèse with a nervous laugh.

"Christ," said Jérôme. "We almost needed the pooper-scooper."

"Sorry," said the Chief.

"How did it go with Madame Zardo?" asked Jérôme.

"We talked a bit."

"About what?" Thérèse asked. "The Ouellet case?"

"No." The three of them, and Henri, walked back toward Emilie Long-pré's home. "About Jean-Guy. She wanted to know what happened."

Thérèse was silent. It was the first time Armand had mentioned the young man's name, though she suspected he thought about him almost constantly.

"I couldn't tell her much, but I felt I owed her something."

"Why?"

"Well, she and Jean-Guy had developed a particular loathing for each other."

Thérèse smiled. "I can see that happening."

Gamache stopped and looked at the Brunels. "You were discussing the Arnot case. Why was that?"

Thérèse and Jérôme exchanged looks. Finally Jérôme answered.

"I'm sorry, I should have told you right away, but I was too . . ."

Afraid, admit it. Afraid.

". . . afraid," he said. "In my last search, I came across his name. It was in a file deeply buried."

"About the murders in the Cree territory?" asked Gamache.

"No. A more recent file."

"And you said nothing?" Armand's voice was clear and calm and dark like the night.

"I found his name just before we came here. I thought it was over. That we'd stay here for a while, lie low so Francoeur and the others would know we weren't a threat."

"And then what?" asked Gamache. He wasn't angry. Just curious. Sympathetic even. How often had he wished for the same thing? To offer his resignation and walk away. He and Reine-Marie would find a small place in Saint-Paul de Vence, in France. Far away from Québec. From Francoeur.

195

Surely he'd done enough. Surely Reine-Marie had done enough.

Surely it was someone else's turn.

But it wasn't. It was still his turn.

And he'd involved the Brunels. And neither they, nor he, could put down this burden just yet.

"It was a fool's dream," admitted Jérôme wearily. "Wishful thinking."

"What did the files say about Pierre Arnot?" Gamache asked.

"I didn't have a chance to read them."

Even in the dark, Jérôme could feel Gamache scrutinizing him.

"And Francoeur?" asked the Chief. "Was he mentioned?"

"Just suggestions," said Jérôme. "If I can get back online I can look deeper."

Gamache nodded toward the road. A vehicle drove slowly around the green, then came to a stop directly in front of them. It was a beat-up old Chevy truck, with cheap winter tires and rust. The door shrieked as it opened and the driver stepped out. Male or female, it was impossible to say.

Henri, who barely ever made a sound, emitted a low growl.

"Hope this is worth it," said the voice. Female. Petulant. Young.

Thérèse Brunel turned to Gamache.

"You didn't," she whispered.

"I had to, Thérèse."

"You could've just stuck a gun in our mouths," she said. "Would have been less painful."

She grabbed the Chief's arm, yanked him a few paces away from the truck, and whispered urgently into his face. "You do know she's one of the people we suspect of working with Francoeur, of leaking the video of the raid? She was in the perfect position to do that. She had the access, the ability and the personality to do it." Thérèse shot a look at the figure creating a dark hole against the cheerful Christmas lights. "She's almost certainly working with Francoeur. What've you done, Armand?"

"It was a risk I had to take," he insisted. "If she's working with Francoeur we're sunk, but we would've been anyway. She might be one of the few who could leak the video, but she's also one of the few who can get us back online."

The two senior Sûreté officers glared at each other.

"You know that, Thérèse," said Gamache urgently. "I had no choice."

"You had a choice, Armand," Thérèse hissed. "For one thing, you could have consulted me. Us."

"You haven't worked with her, I have," said Gamache.

"And you have such insight into people? Is that it, Armand? Is that why

196

Jean-Guy's where he is? Is that why your department deserted you? Is that why we're hiding here and our only hope is one of your own former agents, and you don't even know if she's loyal or not?"

Silence met those words. Silence and a long, long exhale of what looked like steam.

"Excuse me," he said at last, and walked past Thérèse Brunel to the road.

"Can I help?" Jérôme asked a little awkwardly. He'd heard what Thérèse had said. He suspected this young woman had too.

"Go inside, Jérôme," said Gamache. "I'll look after this."

"She didn't mean it, you know."

"She meant it," said Gamache. "And she was right."

When the Brunels had gone inside, he turned to the newcomer.

"You heard that?"

"I did. Fucking paranoid."

"Do not use that language with me, Agent Nichol. You'll be respectful of me, and the Brunels."

"So that's who that is," she said, peering into the night. "Superintendent Brunel. I couldn't tell. Heady company. She doesn't like me."

"She doesn't trust you."

"And you, sir?"

"I asked you down here, didn't I?"

"Yes, but you had no choice."

It was too dark to see her face, but Gamache was sure there was a sneer there. And he wondered just how big a mistake he might have made.

TWENTY-FOUR

The next morning all four of them worked to install the equipment Agent Yvette Nichol had brought with her from Montréal. They carried it up the hill, from Emilie's home to the old schoolhouse.

Olivier had given Gamache the key, but had asked no questions. And Gamache had offered no explanations. When he'd unlocked the door a puff of stale air met him, as though the one-room schoolhouse had been holding its breath for years. It was dusty and still smelled of chalk and textbooks. It was bitterly cold inside. A black potbellied woodstove sat in the middle of the floor, and the walls were lined with maps and charts. Math, science, spelling. A large blackboard above the teacher's desk dominated the front of the room.

Most of the students' desks had gone, but a couple of tables sat against the wall.

Gamache surveyed it and nodded. It would do.

Gilles showed up and helped them carry the cables and terminals and monitors and keyboards.

"Pretty old stuff," he commented. "Are you sure it still works?"

"It works," snapped Nichol, and studied the grizzled man. "I know you. We met when I was here last time. You talk to trees."

"He talks to trees?" Thérèse muttered to Gamache as she passed, carrying a box of supplies. "Two for two, Chief Inspector. Who's next? Hannibal Lecter?"

Within the hour all the equipment had been moved from Emilie's home to the old schoolhouse. Agent Nichol had proved more helpful than anyone, especially Gamache, could have hoped. Which only increased his discomfort. She only questioned his orders once.

"Really?" She'd turned to him when the Chief Inspector had told her what they needed to do. "That's your plan?"

199

"Do you have a better one, Agent Nichol?"

"Set it up in Emilie Longpré's living room. That way it's convenient."

"For you, yes," explained Gamache. "But the less distance the cables have to run, the better. You know that."

She reluctantly admitted he had a point.

He hadn't told her the other reason. If they were found out, if their signal was traced, if Francoeur and Tessier and others appeared on the brow of the hill, he wanted the target to be the abandoned schoolhouse. Not a home in the middle of Three Pines. The schoolhouse wasn't far removed, but perhaps enough.

If they were successful, it would be decided, he suspected, by moments and millimeters.

"You do know this probably won't work," said Nichol, as she crawled under the old teacher's desk.

The school had been decommissioned years earlier. No longer could the children of Three Pines walk to school and go home for lunch. Now they were bused to Saint-Rémi every day. Such was progress.

Once the equipment was in place, Gilles left them. Through the dirty schoolhouse window Gamache watched the red-bearded woodsman carry his snowshoes up the hill out of the village, in search of the hunting blind. It had been a long time since Gilles, or Gamache, had seen it, and Gamache hoped and prayed it was still there.

A clanking of metal on metal caught his attention and he turned to face the room. Superintendent Brunel was feeding old newspapers and kindling into the woodstove, trying to get it going. Right now the schoolhouse felt like a freezer.

While Agent Nichol and Jérôme Brunel worked to connect the equipment, Chief Inspector Gamache walked over to one of the maps of Québec tacked to a wall. He smiled. Someone had placed a tiny dot south of Montréal. Just north of Vermont. Beside the winding Rivière Bella Bella. Written there, in a small perfect hand, was one word. *Home.*

It was the only map in existence that showed the village of Three Pines.

Superintendent Brunel was now feeding quartered logs into the woodstove. Gamache could hear the crackle and pop of the long-dry wood and he could smell the slight sweet scent of the smoke. Soon, if Thérèse Brunel tended it, the stove would be radiating heat and they could remove their coats and hats and mitts. But not just yet. The winter had taken hold of the old building and wouldn't be easily evicted.

Gamache walked over to Thérèse.

"Can I help?"

She shoved another log in and poked it as embers flew up.

"You all right?" he asked.

She took her eyes off the stove and glared across the room. Jérôme was sitting at the desk, organizing a bank of monitors and keyboards and slim metal boxes. Agent Nichol's bottom could be seen under the desk, as she made connections.

Her eyes flashed back to Gamache.

"No, I'm not all right. This is crazy, Armand," Thérèse said under her breath. "Even if she doesn't work for Francoeur, she's unstable. You know that. She lies, she manipulates. She used to work for you and you fired her."

"I transferred her, to that basement."

"You should have fired her."

"For what? Being arrogant and rude? There'd barely be any Sûreté agents left if that was a dismissible offense. Yes, she's a piece of work, but look at her."

They both looked over. All they could see was her bottom, in the air, like a terrier burying a bone.

"Well, maybe not the best moment to make a judgment," said Gamache with a smile, but Thérèse saw nothing amusing. "I put her in the basement, monitoring communications, because I wanted her to learn how to listen."

"And did it work?"

"Not perfectly," he admitted. "But something else happened." He looked over at Agent Nichol again. Now she was seated, cross-legged, under the desk, carefully dissecting a mass of cables. Disheveled, unkempt, in clothes that didn't quite fit. The sweater was pilled and too tight, the jeans a bad cut for her body, her hair had a slightly greasy look. But her focus was intense.

"In the hours and hours of sitting there listening, Agent Nichol discovered a knack for communication," Gamache continued. "Not verbal, but electronic. She spent hours and hours refining techniques for gathering information."

"Spying." Thérèse refined what he meant. "Hacking. You do know you're making an argument for her collaborating with Francoeur."

"Oui," he said. "We'll see. The Cyber Crimes division suspected her, you know."

"What happened?"

"They rejected her for being unstable. I don't believe Francoeur would work with someone he couldn't control."

"And so you brought her here?"

"Not as a witty companion, but because of that."

He tipped a piece of wood in Nichol's direction and Superintendent Brunel followed it. And saw, again, the awkward young agent sitting under the desk. Quietly, intently, turning the chaos of wires and cables and boxes into orderly connections.

Thérèse turned back to Gamache, her eyes unyielding. "Agent Yvette Nichol may be good at her job, but the question I have, and the one you seem to have failed to ask, is what is her job? Her real job?"

Chief Inspector Gamache had no answer for that.

"We both know she's probably working for Francoeur. He gave the order and she did it. Found the video, edited it, and released it. To spite you. You're not universally loved, you know."

Gamache nodded. "I'm getting that impression."

Again, Thérèse failed to smile. "The very qualities you see in her, Francoeur also sees. With one exception." Superintendent Brunel leaned closer to the Chief Inspector and lowered her voice. He could smell her sophisticated eau de toilette, and the slight scent of mint on her breath. "He knows she's a sociopath. Without conscience. She'll do anything, if it amuses her. Or hurts someone else. Especially you. Sylvain Francoeur sees that. Cultivates that. Uses that. And what do you see?"

They both looked over at the pale young woman holding a cable up, with much the same expression as Ruth had when she held the flame the night before.

"You see another lost soul to be saved. You made your decision, you brought her here, without consulting us. Unilaterally. Your hubris has very likely cost us . . ."

Thérèse Brunel didn't finish that sentence. She didn't have to. They both knew what the price might be.

She slammed down the wrought-iron cover of the woodstove with such force the clank made Yvette Nichol jump and hit her head on the underside of the desk.

A series of filth exploded from under the teacher's desk, such as the little schoolhouse had probably never heard before.

But Thérèse didn't hear it. Neither did Gamache. The Superintendent had left the little building, slamming the door in Gamache's face as he followed her.

"Thérèse," he called, and caught up halfway down the shoveled path. "Wait."

She stopped, but her back was to him. Not able to face him.

"So help me, Armand, if I could fire you I would." She turned then and her face was angrier than he'd ever seen. "You're arrogant, egotistical. You think you have special insight into the human condition, but you're as flawed as the rest of us. And now look what you've done."

"I'm sorry, Thérèse, I should have consulted you and Jérôme."

"And why didn't you?"

He thought about that for a moment. "Because I was afraid you'd over-rule me."

She stared at him, still angry, but caught off guard by his candor.

"I know Agent Nichol's unstable," he continued. "I know she might be working with Francoeur and that she might have leaked the video."

"Christ, Armand, do you ever listen to yourself?" she demanded. "I know, I know, I know."

"What I'm trying to say is that there was no choice. She might be working for him, but if she isn't, she's our only hope. No one will miss her. No one ever goes into that basement. Yes, she's emotionally stunted, she's rude and insubordinate, but she's also exceptional at what she does. Finding information. She and Jérôme will make a formidable team."

"If she doesn't kill us."

"*Oui.*"

"And you thought, if you explained it, Jérôme and I would be too stupid to come to the same conclusion?"

He stared at her. "I'm sorry. I should have told you."

His sharp eyes looked around him, then up the road out of the village. Thérèse followed his gaze.

"If she's working with Francoeur," she said, "he's on his way. She'll have told him we're together, and she'll have told him what we're doing. And she'll have told him where to find us. If she hasn't yet, she soon will."

Gamache nodded, and continued to stare at the top of the hill, half expecting a bank of black vehicles to roll to a stop up there, like dung on the white snow.

But nothing happened. Not yet anyway.

"We have to assume the worst. That he now knows that Jérôme and I are not in Vancouver," said Thérèse. "That we didn't turn our backs on you." She looked like she now wished she had. "That we're all here in Three Pines, and still trying to gather information on him."

She turned back to Gamache and considered him.

"How can we trust you, Armand? How do we know you won't do something else without consulting us?"

203

"And I'm the only one holding back information?" he demanded, more angrily than even he expected. "Pierre Arnot."

He spat the name at her.

"Which is the more damning? The more dangerous?" he asked. "An agent who may or may not be working with Francoeur, or a mass murderer? A psychopathic killer who knows the workings of the Sûreté better than anyone else? Is Arnot involved in all of this somehow?"

He glared at her and her cheeks colored. She gave one curt nod.

"Jérôme thinks so. He doesn't know how yet, but if they can get that thing to work, he'll find out."

"And how long has he kept that name from you? From me? Do you not think it would have been helpful to know?"

His voice was rising, and he struggled to lower it, to bring himself under control.

"*Oui*," said Thérèse. "It would have been helpful."

Gamache gave a curt nod. "It's done now. His mistake doesn't excuse my own. I was wrong. I promise to consult you and Jérôme in the future." He held out a gloved hand to her. "We can't turn on each other."

She stared at it. Then took it. But she didn't return his thin smile.

"Why didn't you arrest Francoeur at the same time as Arnot and the others?" she asked, dropping his hand.

"I hadn't enough proof. I tried, but it was all insinuation. He was Arnot's second in command. It was inconceivable that Francoeur wouldn't have been involved in the Cree killings, or at the very least known about them. But I couldn't find a direct link."

"But you found a link to Chief Superintendent Arnot?" asked Thérèse.

She'd touched on something that had long troubled the Chief Inspector. How he could have found damning and direct evidence against the Chief Superintendent but not against his second in command.

It had worried him then. It worried him now. Even more.

It suggested that he'd not only missed all the rot, but he'd missed the source of it.

It suggested someone had protected Sylvain Francoeur. Covered for him. And hadn't covered for Arnot. Someone had thrown Arnot to the wolves.

Was that possible?

"*Oui*," he said. "It was hard to find, but evidence linking Arnot with the killings was there."

"He always maintained his innocence, Armand. You don't think . . ."

"That he really was innocent?" asked Gamache, shaking his head. "No. Not a chance."

But, he thought to himself, perhaps Pierre Arnot was not quite as guilty as he'd thought. Or, perhaps, there was someone who carried even more guilt. Someone still free.

"Why did Chief Superintendent Arnot do it?" asked Thérèse. "That never came out in court, or in any of the confidential documents. He seemed to respect, even admire the Cree at the beginning of his career. Then thirty years later he's involved in killing them. For no reason, apparently."

"Well, he didn't do the actual killing, as you know," said Gamache. "He created a climate where the use of lethal force was encouraged. Rewarded even."

"He did more than that, as your own investigation proved," said Thérèse. "There were documents showing he encouraged the killings, even ordered some. That was irrefutable. What was never clear was why a senior and apparently excellent officer would do such a thing."

"You're right," agreed Gamache. "From the evidence, the young men who were killed weren't even criminals. Just the opposite. Most had no record at all."

In a place with so much crime, why kill the ones who'd done nothing wrong?

"I need to visit Arnot," he said.

"In the SHU? You can't do that. They'll know we've found his name in our searches." She examined him closely. "That's an order, Chief Inspector. You're not to go. Understand?"

"I do. And I won't."

Still, she tried to read his familiar face. The worn and torn face. Behind his eyes she could sense activity. Just as her husband and that alarming young agent were busy trying to make connections, she could see Armand doing the same thing. In his mind. Sifting through old files, names, events. Trying to find some connection he'd missed.

A man appeared at the brow of the hill and waved.

It was Gilles and he looked pleased.

Here she is."

Gilles laid a hand on the rough bark of the tree. They were in the forest above the village. He'd brought snowshoes for all of them, and now Thérèse,

205

Jérôme, Nichol, and Gamache stood beside him, only sinking a few inches into the deep snow.

"Isn't she magnificent?"

They tilted their heads back, and Jérôme's tuque fell off as he looked up.

"She?" asked Nichol.

Gilles chose to ignore the sarcasm in her voice. "She," he confirmed.

"Hate to think how he came to that conclusion," said Nichol, not quite under her breath. Gamache gave her a stern look.

"She's at least a hundred feet tall. White pine. Old growth," Gilles continued. "Hundreds of years old. There's one in New York State that they figure is almost five hundred years old. The three white pines down in the village may have seen the first loyalists come across during the American Revolution. And this one"—he turned to it, his nose touching the mottled bark, his words soft and warm against the tree—"might have been a seedling when the first Europeans arrived."

The woodsman looked at them, a bit of bark on the tip of his nose and in his beard. "Do you know what the aboriginals called the white pine?"

"Ethel?" asked Nichol.

"The tree of peace."

"So what're we doing here?" asked Nichol.

Gilles pointed and they looked up again. This time Gamache's hat fell off as he tilted his head. He picked it up and struck it against his leg to knock the soft snow off.

There, nailed twenty feet up in the tree of peace, was the hunting blind. Made for violence. It was rickety and rotten, as though the tree was punishing it.

But it was there.

"What can we do to help?" asked Gamache.

"You can help me haul the satellite dish up there," said Gilles.

Gamache blanched.

"I think we have the answer to that request," said Jérôme. "And you're not going to be doing any of the wiring."

Gamache shook his head.

"Then I suggest you and Thérèse get out of the way," said Jérôme.

"Banished to the bistro," said Gamache, and now Thérèse Brunel did smile.

TWENTY-FIVE

—

Mugs of steaming apple cider were placed in front of Thérèse Brunel and the Chief Inspector.

Clara and a friend were sitting by the fireplace and motioned them over, but after thanking Clara for dinner the night before, the Sûreté officers moved off to the relative privacy of the easy chairs in front of the bay window.

The mullions were frosted slightly but the village was still easily seen, and the two stared out in slightly awkward silence for a minute or two. Thérèse stirred her cider with the cinnamon stick, then took a sip.

It tasted of Christmas, and skating, and long winter afternoons in the country. She and Jérôme never had cider in Montréal, and she wondered why not.

"Will it be all right, Armand?" she finally asked. There was no neediness, no fear in her voice. It was strong and clear. And curious.

He also stirred his cider. Looking up, he held her eyes and once again she marveled at the quality of calm in them. And something else. Something she'd first noticed in that packed amphitheater years ago.

Even from halfway back, she could see the kindness in his eyes. A quality some had mistaken, to their regret, for weakness.

But there wasn't just kindness there. Armand Gamache had the personality of a sniper. He watched, and waited, and took careful aim. He almost never shot, metaphorically or literally, but when he did, he almost never missed.

But a decade ago, he'd missed. He'd hit Arnot. But not Francoeur.

And now Francoeur had assembled an army, and was planning something horrific. The question was, did Gamache have another shot in him? And would he hit the target this time?

"*Oui*, Thérèse," he said now, and as he smiled his eyes crinkled into deep lines. "All shall be well."

"Julian of Norwich," she said, recognizing the phrase. All shall be well.

Through the frosted window she could see Gilles and Nichol carrying equipment up the slope and into the woods. Superintendent Brunel returned her gaze to her companion, noting the holster and gun on his belt. Armand Gamache would do what was necessary. But not before it was necessary.

"All shall be well," she said, and went back to her reading.

Gamache had given her the documents he'd found on the Ouellet Quints while researching in the Bibliothèque nationale, with the comment that something was bothering him after watching the films the night before.

"Just one thing?" Thérèse had asked. She'd watched the DVD that morning on an old laptop Nichol had brought with her. "Those poor girls. I once envied them, you know. Every little girl wanted to be either a Quint or young Princess Elizabeth."

And so they settled in, Superintendent Brunel with the file on the girls, and Chief Inspector Gamache with the book by Dr. Bernard. Thérèse put down the dossier an hour later.

"Well?" asked Gamache, taking off his reading glasses.

"There's a lot in here to damn the parents," she said.

"And a lot in here," said Gamache, laying a large hand on the book. "Did anything strike you?"

"As a matter of fact it did. The house."

"Go on."

She could see by his face it was what bothered him too.

"The documents show Isidore Ouellet sold the family farm to the government shortly after the Quints were born, for a huge profit. Well beyond its worth."

"In effect, a payment for the girls," said the Chief.

"The Québec government would make them wards of the state, and the Ouellets would go on their merry way, unburdened by mouths they couldn't feed." Thérèse put the manila folder on the table with distaste. "They suggest the Ouellets were too poor and ignorant to care for the quintuplets and would have eventually had the girls taken away by the welfare officials anyway."

Gamache nodded. The documents failed to mention it was also the depths of the Depression, when every family struggled. An economic crisis the Ouellets did not bring on themselves. And yet, again, there was the insinuation that they, uniquely, were to blame for their plight. And the benevolent government would save them and their daughters.

"They were doing the Ouellets a favor," said Gamache. "Buying their burden. Madame Ouellet had given birth to their ticket out of the Depression. Dr. Bernard's book says much the same thing. The language is couched, of course. No one wanted to be seen to criticize the parents, but the image of the ignorant Québécois farmer wasn't a hard sell in those days."

"Except they didn't cash in at all," said Thérèse. "Not according to the film. That *bénédiction paternelle* was when the girls were almost ten, and the Ouellets were still in their old home. They hadn't sold it."

Gamache tapped the manila folder with his glasses. "This is a lie. The official documents are fabricated."

"Why?"

"To make the Ouellets look bad, in case they ever went public."

Suddenly the letters by Isidore Ouellet took on another flavor. What had appeared wheedling, demanding, whining was in fact simply stating the truth.

The government had stolen their children. And the Ouellets wanted them back. Yes, they were poor, as Ouellet stated, but they could give the girls what they needed.

Gamache remembered the old farmhouse, and Isidore lacing up his daughters' skates, and Marie-Harriette, haggard, handing them each a hat.

But not just any hat. She handed them their own hats. Each different.

And then, annoyed, she'd tossed one offscreen.

Gamache's attention had been taken by that. The angry act had overshadowed the tenderness of a moment earlier, when she'd treated them as individuals. Had knitted them their own unique tuques. To protect them against the harsh world.

"Could you excuse me?"

He got up and gave her a very small bow, then put on his coat and headed into the winter day.

From her armchair, Thérèse Brunel watched him walk briskly along the road ringing the village green and over to Gabri's B and B. He disappeared inside.

Yes, Chief," said Inspector Lacoste. "I have it here."

Gamache could hear the keys click on her computer. He'd called her on her cell and caught her at home this Sunday afternoon.

"It'll take me just a moment." Her voice was muffled and he could see her pinning the phone between her shoulder and ear, while tapping away on her laptop. Trying to find the one obscure reference.

"No rush," he said, and sat on the side of the bed. In what he considered "his" bedroom at the B and B. And it still was. He'd kept it, paid for it, and even had a few of his personal items around.

In case anyone came looking.

And whenever he needed to make a call to Montréal, or Paris, he came here. If he was right, they'd be traced. He wanted nothing traced back to the Longpré house.

"Got it," said Lacoste, and her voice became clear again as she read. "In Marguerite's room . . . let's see . . . two pairs of gloves. Some heavy mitts. Four winter scarves. And yes, here it is. Two hats. One warm and store-bought and one looked hand-knitted."

Gamache stood up. "The hand-knitted one, can you describe it?"

He held his breath. Lacoste wasn't looking at the actual inventory, that was still in the little home. She was reading from the notes she'd taken.

"It was red," she read, "and had pine trees around it. A tag was sewn into it with MM on it."

"Marie-Marguerite. Anything else?"

"About the tuque? Sorry, Chief, that's it."

"And the other bedrooms? Did Constance and Josephine also have those handmade hats?"

There was another pause and more clicking.

"Yes. Josephine's was green with snowflakes. The tag inside says MJ. The one in Constance's room had reindeer—"

"And a tag with MC."

"How'd you guess?"

Gamache gave a short laugh. Lacoste went on to describe two other tuques, found in the back of the front hall closet, with MV and MH sewn in.

All accounted for.

"Why's this important, Chief?"

"It might not be, but their mother knitted those hats. It seems the only things they kept from their childhoods. The only souvenirs."

Remembrances, thought Gamache, of their mother. Of being moth-ered. And being individuals.

"There's something else, *patron*."

"And what's that?"

He was so focused on the find that for a split second he failed to take in

210

her darkening tone. The warning pulse before the impact. He started to stand up, to meet it. To bring up his defenses.

But he was just too late.

"Inspector Beauvoir's been sent on another raid. You caught me in because I was monitoring it. This one's bad."

Chief Inspector Gamache felt his cheeks both flush and drain. The atmosphere around him seemed to disappear, as though he was suddenly in a sensory deprivation tank. All his senses seemed to fail at once, and he felt like he was suspended. Then falling.

Within a moment he started breathing again, and then his senses rushed back. Acute. Everything was suddenly stark, loud, bright.

"Tell me," he said.

He gathered himself, steadied himself. With the exception of his right hand. That he kept closed in a tight, and tightening, fist.

"It was last-minute. Martin Tessier himself is leading it. Only four agents, from what I can gather."

"What's the target?" His voice was clipped, commanding. Assessing.

"A meth lab on the South Shore. Must be Boucherville, judging by the route they took."

There was a pause.

"Inspector?" demanded Gamache.

"Sorry, Chief. Seems to be Brossard. But they took the Jacques Cartier Bridge."

"The bridge doesn't matter," he said, irritated. "Has the raid begun?"

"Just. They're meeting resistance. There's arms fire."

Gamache pressed the telephone to his ear, as though that would bring him closer.

"An ambulance has just been called. Medics going in. Officer hit."

Lacoste, used to making reports, tried to make this one simply factual. And she almost succeeded.

"Officer down," she repeated the phrase. The one she herself had shouted, over and over, as she'd seen both Beauvoir and the Chief shot down. In that factory.

Officer down.

"Christ," she heard down the telephone line. It sounded more like a plea than profanity.

Gamache saw movement out of the corner of his eye and spun around. Agent Nichol was standing in the open doorway to his room. The perpetual sneer froze when she saw his face.

The Chief looked at her for a moment, then reached out and slammed the door shut with such force the pictures shook on the walls.

"Chief?" called Lacoste down the line. "Are you all right? What was that?"

It sounded like a gunshot.

"The door," he said, and turned his back on it. Through a crack in the gauzy curtains at the window he could see diffuse light, and hear slap shots and laughter. He turned his back on that. And stared at the wall. "What's happening?"

"There seems a fair amount of chaos," she reported. "I'm trying to make sense of the communications."

Gamache held his tongue and waited. Feeling his rage rising. Feeling the almost irrepressible need to slam his fist, already made and waiting to be used, into the wall. To hit it over and over, until the wall bled.

Instead, he steadied himself.

The fools. To go on a raid unprepared.

The Chief knew what the goal was, the purpose. It was simple and sadistic. It was to unhinge Beauvoir and unbalance the Chief. To push both over the edge. And possibly worse.

Officer down.

He himself had shouted that, as he'd held Jean-Guy. Held a bandage to Beauvoir's abdomen. To staunch the blood. Seeing the pain and terror in the young man's eyes. Seeing the blood all over Beauvoir's shirt. And all over his own hands.

And now Gamache could almost feel it again, in this peaceful, pleasant room. The warm, sticky blood on his hands.

"I'm sorry, Chief, all communications have gone down."

Gamache stared at the wall for a moment. All communications down. What did that mean?

He tried not to go to the worst possible conclusion. That they were down because everyone who might communicate was down.

No. He forced his mind away from that. Stick with the simple facts. He knew how catastrophic a rampant imagination, driven by fear, could be.

He stepped away from that. Time enough to have it confirmed. And whatever had happened had happened by now.

It was over. And there was nothing he could do.

He closed his eyes and tried not to see Jean-Guy. Not the terrified, wounded man in his arms. Not the drained man of recent weeks and months.

And certainly not the Jean-Guy Beauvoir sitting in the Gamaches' living room. Drinking a beer and laughing.

That was the face Gamache tried hardest to keep away.

He opened his eyes.

"Keep monitoring, please," he said. "I'll be in the bistro or at the book-store."

"Chief?" asked Lacoste, her voice uncertain.

"It will be all right." His voice was calm and composed.

"*Oui.*" She didn't sound completely convinced, but she did sound less shaky.

All shall be well, he repeated as he walked with resolve across the village green.

But he wasn't sure he believed it.

Myrna Landers sat on the sofa in her loft and stared at the TV screen.

Frozen there was a smiling little girl, her skates being laced by her father while her sisters, their skates already on, waited.

On her head she wore a tuque with reindeer.

Myrna was caught between tears and a smile.

She smiled. "She looks radiant, doesn't she?"

Gamache and Thérèse Brunel nodded. She did.

Now that he'd figured out who was who, Gamache wanted to see this film again.

Behind little Constance, her sisters Marguerite and Josephine looked on, impatient to be outside. Each girl was now distinguishable by their tuques. The pines for Marguerite, and snowflakes for Josephine. Marie-Constance looked like she could sit there all day, being tended to by her father. Reindeer racing around her head.

Virginie and Hélène stood by the door. They also wore knitted hats, and slight scowls.

On Gamache's request, Myrna again pressed rewind and they were back at the beginning. With Isidore holding out his arms, administering the *bénédiction paternelle*.

But this time they knew which little penitent was Constance, having followed her back, back, back to the beginning. She was kneeling at the end of the row.

And Constance, thought Gamache.

"Does this help us find whoever killed Constance?" Myrna asked.

"I'm not sure," admitted the Chief. "But at least now we know which girl was which."

"Myrna," Thérèse began, "Armand told me that when you first found out who Constance was, you thought it was like having Hera as a client."

Myrna glanced at Thérèse, then back at the screen. "Yes."

"Hera," Thérèse repeated. "One of the Greek goddesses."

Myrna smiled. "Yes."

"Why?"

Myrna paused the image and turned to her guest. "Why?" She thought about that. "When Constance told me she was one of the Ouellet Quints, she might as well have said she was a Greek goddess. A myth. I was making a joke, that's all."

"I understand," said Thérèse. "But why Hera?"

"Why not?" Myrna was clearly confused. "I don't know what you're asking."

"It doesn't matter."

"What're you thinking?" asked Gamache.

"It's probably ridiculous," said Thérèse. "When I was head curator at the Musée des beaux-arts, I saw a lot of classical art. Much of it based in mythology. Victorian artists in particular liked to paint Greek goddesses. An excuse, I always suspected, to paint naked women, often battling serpents. An acceptable form of pornography."

"But you digress," suggested Gamache, and Thérèse smiled.

"I got to know the various gods and goddesses. But two goddesses in particular seemed to fascinate artists of that era."

"Let me guess," said Myrna. "Aphrodite?"

Superintendent Brunel nodded. "The goddess of love—and prostitutes, wouldn't you know. Conveniently, she didn't seem to own many clothes."

"And the other?" asked Myrna, though they all knew the answer.

"Hera."

"Also naked?" asked Myrna.

"No, the Victorian painters liked her because of her dramatic potential, and she suited their cautionary view of strong women. She was malicious and jealous."

They turned to the screen. The film was paused on the praying face of little Constance.

Myrna looked at Thérèse. "You think she was malicious and jealous?"

"I'm not the one who called her Hera."

"It's just a name, the only goddess who came to mind. I could have just as easily called her Aphrodite or Athena." Myrna was sounding testy, defensive.

"But you didn't."

Superintendent Brunel didn't back down. The two women held each other's eyes.

"I knew Constance," said Myrna. "First as a client, then as a friend. She never struck me that way."

"But you say she was closed off," said Gamache. "Do you really know what she kept hidden?"

"Are you putting the victim on trial?" asked Myrna.

"No," said Gamache. "This isn't judgmental. But the better we know Constance, the easier it might be to find out who needed her dead. And why."

Myrna thought about that. "I'm sorry. Constance was so private, I feel a need to protect her."

She pressed the play button and they watched little Constance pray, then rise, then playfully jostle with her sisters in line, to have their father put on their skates.

But now each of them wondered how playful that really was.

They saw the look of joy on Constance's face as her father kneeled at her feet, and her sisters, in pairs, stood behind. Watching.

Myrna's phone rang and Gamache tensed so forcefully both women looked at him.

Myrna answered it, then held it out for him.

"It's Isabelle Lacoste."

"*Merci*," he said, crossing the distance and taking the phone. It felt warm to the touch.

He turned away from Superintendent Brunel and Myrna, and spoke into the receiver.

"*Bonjour.*" His voice steady, his back straight. His head up.

From behind, the women watched as he listened. And they saw the broad shoulders sag a little, though the head remained high.

"*Merci*," he said, and slowly replaced the receiver. Then Gamache turned around.

And smiled with relief.

"Good news," he said. "Nothing to do with this case, though."

He rejoined them. Both women looked away and didn't say a word about the sheen in his eye.

TWENTY-SIX

———

"We have to go."

Gamache stood up abruptly, and both Myrna and Thérèse looked at him. A moment earlier he'd been relieved, almost ecstatic, then something had shifted and his joy had turned to anger.

Myrna paused the recording. Five happy girls stared at them, apparently mesmerized by what was happening in Myrna's loft.

"What is it?" Thérèse asked, as they put on their coats and walked down to the bookstore. "Who was on the phone?"

"*Merci*, Myrna." Gamache paused at the door and strained to produce a smile.

Myrna watched him closely. "What just happened?"

Gamache shook his head a little. "I'm sorry. I'll tell you one day."

"But not today?"

"I don't think so."

The door closed behind them and the cold closed around them. The sun was still up, but they were on the edge of the shortest day and there wasn't much light left.

"You'll tell me," said Thérèse as they walked rapidly across the village green. Past Ruth on the bench. Past families skating on the frozen pond. Past the three ancient white pines.

Thérèse Brunel was not asking, but commanding.

"Beauvoir was sent on another raid today."

Thérèse Brunel absorbed the news. Gamache's face, in profile, was grim.

"This must stop," said Gamache.

Up the hill they strode, Thérèse hurrying to keep pace. At the edge of the forest they found their snowshoes stuck in a snow bank where they'd left them. Strapping them on, they made their way back down the trail, though they barely needed the snowshoes anymore. The trail was hard packed and easy to find.

Too easy? Thérèse Brunel wondered. But there was no way around it now.

As they approached, they saw Gilles apparently hovering in midair, twenty feet up and five feet from the tree trunk. The woods were getting dark, but as the two senior officers got closer Thérèse could see the platform, nailed to the tree of peace.

Jérôme was standing at the base of the white pine, staring up. He glanced at them as they approached, then back up into the branches above their heads. It was then Superintendent Brunel noticed that Gilles was not alone up there. Nichol was standing on the platform, a couple feet back from Gilles as he worked to position the satellite dish on the wooden railing.

"Anything?" Gilles asked, his voice muffled by frozen lips. His red beard was white and crusty, as though his words had frozen and stuck to his face.

"Close." Nichol was studying something in her mittens.

Gilles adjusted the dish slightly.

"There. Stop," said Nichol.

Everyone, including Thérèse and Armand, stopped. And waited. And waited. Gilles slowly, slowly released the dish.

"Still?" he asked.

Then waited. Waited.

"Yes," she said.

"Let me see." He held out his gloved hand.

"It's locked onto the satellite. We're fine."

"Give it to me. I want to see for myself," snapped the woodsman, the biting cold gnawing at his patience.

Nichol handed over whatever she held and he studied it.

"Good," he said at last, and unseen below them three streams of steam were exhaled.

Once back on firm ground, Gilles smiled. His crystalline beard made him look like Father Christmas, and as he grinned some of it cracked off.

"Well done," said Jérôme. He was stomping his feet and all but blue with cold.

Yvette Nichol stood a few feet away, separated from the main body of the team by what looked like a long, black umbilical cord. The transmission cable.

Thérèse, Jérôme, Gilles, and Nichol, thought Gamache, looking at the glum young agent. And Nichol. Attached to their own quintuplet by a slender thread.

And Nichol. How easy it would be to cut her loose.

"Are we connected?" Gamache asked Gilles, who nodded.

"We've found a satellite," he replied through lips and cheeks numb with cold.

"The rest?"

He shrugged.

"What's that supposed to mean?" Thérèse demanded. "Will it do the job or not?"

Gilles turned to her. "And what is the job, madame? I still don't know why we're here, except that it probably has nothing to do with watching the last episode of *Survivor.*"

There was a stiff silence.

"Perhaps you can explain it to Gilles back at the schoolhouse," said Gamache. He spoke matter-of-factly, as though suggesting hot chocolate after an afternoon of tobogganing. "I expect you're ready to get inside."

The Chief turned to Nichol, standing alone a few feet away. "You and I can finish what was started."

They were clear, cold black-ice words.

He wants us to leave them alone, Thérèse thought. *He's cutting her from the pack.*

Seeing the slight smile on Armand's face, and hearing his hard voice, an alarm sounded inside her. A deep, dark gap had appeared between what Armand Gamache had said and what he meant. And Thérèse Brunel did not envy this young agent, who was about to discover what the Chief Inspector kept locked and hidden, deep inside.

"I should stay too," said Thérèse. "I'm not cold yet."

"No," said Gamache. "I think you should go."

Thérèse felt a chill in her marrow.

"You have a job to do," he said quietly. "And so do I."

"And what job is that, Armand? Like Gilles, I'm wondering."

"I'm simply doing my small part to make a crucial connection."

And there it was.

Thérèse Brunel stared at Gamache, then over to Agent Nichol, who was untangling a twist in the frozen telecommunications cable and seemed oblivious. Seemed. Thérèse looked at the sullen, petulant, but clever young woman. Armand had sent her to the Sûreté basement to learn how to listen.

Perhaps it had worked better than they realized.

Superintendent Brunel made a decision. She turned her back on Armand and the young agent, and ushered her husband and the woodsman away.

Gamache waited until he no longer heard the crunch, crunch, crunch of snowshoes, until silence fell on the winter woods. Then he turned on Yvette Nichol.

"What were you doing in the B and B?"

"*Bonjour* to you too," she said, not looking up. "Good job, Nichol. Well done, Nichol. Thank you for coming to this shithole, freezing your ass off to help us, Nichol."

"What were you doing in the B and B?"

She looked up and felt what little warmth she still had evaporate.

"What were you doing there?" she demanded.

He tilted his head slightly and narrowed his eyes. "Are you questioning me?" Nichol's eyes widened and the cable slipped from her hands.

"Are you working for Francoeur?" The words came out of his mouth like icicles.

Nichol couldn't speak, but managed to shake her head.

Gamache unzipped his parka and moved it behind his hip. His shirt was exposed. And so was his gun.

As she watched, he removed his warm gloves and held his right hand loose at his side.

"Are you working for Francoeur?" he repeated, his voice even quieter.

She shook her head vehemently and mouthed, "No."

"What were you doing in the B and B?"

"I was looking for you," she managed.

"Why?"

"I was at the schoolhouse getting the cable ready for here and saw you go into the B and B, so I followed you."

"Why?"

It had taken him a while to put it together. At first he thought he owed Nichol an apology, for slamming the door in her face. But then he'd begun to wonder what she was doing in the B and B.

Was she there for the same reason he'd gone, to make a quiet call? If so, who was she calling? Gamache could guess.

"Why were you in the B and B, Yvette?"

"To speak to you."

"You could've spoken to me at Emilie's home. You could have spoken to me at the schoolhouse. Why were you in the B and B, Yvette?"

"To talk to you," she repeated, her voice barely a squeak. "Privately."

"What about?"

She hesitated. "To tell you that this won't work." She gestured up toward the hunting blind and the satellite dish. "Even if you get online, you can't get into the Sûreté system."

"Who says that's our goal?"

"I'm not an idiot, Chief Inspector. You asked for untraceable satellite equipment. You're not building a robot army. If you were going in through the front door you could do that from home or your office. This is something else. You brought me here to help you break in. But it won't work."

"Why not?" Despite himself, he was interested.

"Because while all this shit might get you connected, and even hide where you are for a while, you need a code to get into the deepest files. Your own Sûreté security code will give you away. So will Superintendent Brunel's. You know that."

"How much do you know about what we're doing?"

"Not much. I knew nothing until yesterday, when you asked for my help." They stared at each other.

"You invited me here, sir. I didn't ask. But when you asked for help, I agreed. And now you treat me like your enemy?"

Gamache was having none of her mind games. He knew there was a far more likely reason she'd agreed to come down. Not loyalty to him, but to another. She was in the B and B to report to Francoeur, and had he not been distracted by his concern for Jean-Guy, he'd have caught her at it.

"I invited you because we had no choice. But that doesn't mean I trust you, Agent Nichol."

"What do I need to do to gain your trust?"

"Tell me why you were in the B and B."

"I wanted to warn you that without a security code, none of this will work."

"You're lying."

"No."

Gamache knew she was lying. She didn't need to tell him about the code privately.

"What have you told Francoeur?"

"Nothing," she pleaded. "I'd never do that."

Gamache glared at her. Once the computer was turned on. Once the satellite connection was made. Once Jérôme opened that door and stepped through, it was just a matter of time before they were found. Their only hope rested with the embittered young agent in front of him, trembling with cold and fear and indignation, real or forced.

Time was running out to save Beauvoir, and to find out what Francoeur's goal was. There was a purpose here that went well beyond hurting Gamache and Beauvoir.

Something far bigger, put in place years ago, was maturing now. Today. Tomorrow. Soon. And Gamache still didn't know what it was.

He felt slow, stupid. It was as though all sorts of clues, elements, were floating in front of him, but one piece was missing. Something that would connect them all. Something he'd either missed or hadn't yet found.

He now knew it involved Pierre Arnot. But what was their goal?

Gamache could have screamed his frustration.

What role did this pathetic young woman play in all of this? Was she the nail in their coffin, or their salvation? And why did one look so much like the other?

Gamache brought his parka forward and zipped it up with a hand so cold he could barely tell he was holding the zipper. Putting his gloves back on, he scooped up the heavy cable at her feet.

As Nichol watched, Chief Inspector Gamache put the thick black cable over his shoulder and leaned forward, lugging it through the forest, in a direct route to the schoolhouse.

After a few steps he felt it grow lighter. Agent Yvette Nichol's snowshoes plodded along in the trail he was making, picking up the slack.

She fell in behind him, puffing with the effort and relief.

He'd caught her. He might even suspect. But he hadn't gotten the truth from her.

Thérèse Brunel got Jérôme and Gilles settled in the schoolhouse, in front of the woodstove. Heat radiated from it and the men stripped off their heavy parkas, hats, mitts, and boots and sat with their feet out, as close as they could get to the fire without themselves bursting into flames.

The room smelled of wet wool and wood smoke. It was warm now, but Gilles and Jérôme were not.

After shoving more wood into the stove, Thérèse went over to Emilie's to get Henri, then to the general store, where she picked up milk, cocoa and marshmallows. The hot chocolate now simmered in a pot on top of the stove, and the scent joined that of wet wool and wood smoke. She poured it into mugs and topped each with a couple of large, soft marshmallows.

But the hot chocolate shook so badly in Gilles's hands, Thérèse had to take the mug from him.

"You asked what this is about," she said.

Gilles nodded. His teeth chattered violently as he listened, and he alternately hugged himself and held his hands out to the stove as she spoke. His beard had melted a wet stain on his sweater.

When she finished speaking, Thérèse handed him back his hot chocolate, the marshmallow melted to white foam on the top. He gripped the warm mug to his chest like a little boy, frightened by a scary story and trying to be brave.

Beside him, Jérôme had remained quiet while his wife described what they were looking for, and why. Dr. Brunel kneaded his feet, trying to get the blood flowing again. Pins and needles stabbed his toes as the circulation returned.

The sun was now barely visible over the dark forest, the forest that still contained Armand Gamache and Agent Nichol. Thérèse turned on the lights and looked at the blank monitors her husband had set up that morning.

What if this doesn't work?

They'd have made a very poor Scout troop, she thought. Not only were they unprepared for this to fail, they were using stolen equipment to hack into police files. If there were badges for deception, they'd be covered in them.

They heard heavy footsteps on the wooden porch, and Thérèse opened the door to find Armand there, puffing with exertion.

"You all right?" she asked, though they both knew she was really asking, "Are you alone?"

"Never better," he gasped. His face was red from exertion and the bitter cold. Dropping the cable on the stoop, he entered the schoolhouse, followed a moment later by Agent Nichol. Her face was no longer pallid. Now it was blotched, white and red. She looked like the Canadian flag.

Thérèse exhaled, unaware until that moment just how concerned she'd really been.

"Do I smell chocolate?" Gamache asked, through frozen lips. Henri had run over to greet him and the Chief was on one knee, hugging the shepherd. For warmth as much as affection, Thérèse suspected. And Henri was happy to give him both.

Space was made by the woodstove for the newcomers.

Thérèse poured them mugs of hot chocolate, and after Gamache and Nichol had stripped off their outerwear, the five sat silently around the woodstove. For the first couple of minutes Gamache and Nichol shuddered with cold. Their hands shook and every now and then they spasmed as the bitter winter, like a wraith, left their body.

Then the little schoolhouse grew quiet, except for the odd squeal of a chair leg on the wooden floor, the crackle of the fire, and Henri's groans as he stretched out at Gamache's feet.

Armand Gamache felt he could nod off. His socks were now dry and slightly crispy, the mug of hot chocolate warmed his hands, and the heat from the stove enveloped him. Despite the urgency of their situation, he felt his lids grow heavy.

Oh, for just a few minutes, a few moments, of rest.

But there was work to be done.

Putting down his mug, he leaned forward, hands clasped together. He looked at the circle huddled around the woodstove in the tiny one-room schoolhouse. The five of them. Quints. Thérèse, Jérôme, Gilles, Armand, and Nichol.

And Nichol, he thought again. Hanging off the end. The outlier.

"What's next?" he asked.

TWENTY-SEVEN

⌒

"Next?" asked Jérôme.

He never expected it to get this far. Looking across the room at the bank of blank monitors, he knew what had to happen.

Beneath the thick sweater he felt a trickle of perspiration, as though his round body was weeping. If Three Pines was their foxhole, he was about to raise his head. Armand had given them a weapon, but it was a pointy stick against a machine gun.

He walked away from the warmth of the fire and felt the chill again as he approached the far reaches of the room. Two old, battered computers sat side-by-side, one on the teacher's desk, the other on the table they'd dragged over. Above them, glued to the wall, was the cheerful alphabet, illustrated with bumblebees and butterflies and ducks and roses. And below that, musical notes.

He hummed it slowly, following the notes.

"Why're you singing that?" asked Gamache.

Jérôme started a little. He hadn't realized Armand was with him and he hadn't realized he was humming.

"It's that." Jérôme pointed to the notes. "Do-re-mi is the top line, and then this song is beneath it."

He hummed some more and then, to his surprise, Armand started quietly, slowly, singing.

"What do you do with a drunken sailor . . ."

Jérôme examined his friend. Gamache was staring at the music and smiling. Then he turned to Jérôme.

". . . early in the morrrr . . . ning."

Jérôme smiled in genuine amusement and felt some of his terror detach and drift away on the back of the musical notes and the silly words from his serious friend.

"An old sea shanty," Gamache explained, and returned to look at the notes on the wall. "I'd forgotten that Miss Jane Neal was the teacher here, before the school was closed and she retired."

"You knew her?"

Gamache remembered kneeling in the bright autumn leaves and closing those blue eyes. It was years ago now. Felt like a lifetime.

"I caught her killer."

Gamache gazed again at the wall, with the alphabet and music.

"*Way, hey, and up she rises . . .*" he whispered. It felt somehow comforting to be in this room where Miss Jane Neal had done what she loved, for children she adored.

"We need to get the cable in here," said Jérôme, and for the next few minutes, while Gilles drilled a hole in the wall to snake the cable through, Jérôme and Nichol crawled under the desks and sorted out the wires and boxes.

Gamache watched all this, marveling that they'd begun the day thirty-five thousand kilometers from any communication satellite and now they were just centimeters from that connection.

"Did you make your connection?" Thérèse Brunel asked as she joined him. She nodded toward the young agent.

Her husband and Nichol were squeezed under the desk, trying not to elbow each other. At least, Dr. Brunel was trying not to—it looked as though Agent Nichol was doing her best to shove her bony elbows into him whenever she could.

"I'm afraid not," Gamache whispered.

"But you both made it back, Chief Inspector. That's something."

Gamache grinned, though without amusement. "Some victory. I didn't gun down one of my own agents in cold blood."

"Well, we take our victories where we can get them," she smiled. "I'm not sure Jérôme would've passed up the chance."

By now the two under the desk were openly elbowing each other.

The hole in the schoolhouse wall was completed and Gilles shoved the cable through. Jérôme grabbed it and pulled.

"I'll take it."

Before Jérôme knew it, Nichol had grabbed the cable from him and was attaching it to the first of the metal boxes.

"Wait." He yanked it back. "You can't connect it." He gripped the cable in both hands and tried to bring his sudden panic under control.

"Of course I can." She almost swiped it from him and might have, had Superintendent Brunel not cut in.

"Agent Nichol," she commanded. "Get out from there."

"But—"

"Do as you're told," she said, as though speaking to a willful child.

Both Jérôme and Nichol crawled out from under the desk, Jérôme still gripping the black cable. Behind them they could hear the hiss as Gilles, still outside, sprayed the hole he'd made with foam insulation.

"What's the problem?" Gamache asked.

"We can't connect it," said Jérôme.

"Yes we ca—"

But the Chief raised his hand and cut Nichol off.

"Why not?" he asked Jérôme. They'd come so far. Why not the last few inches?

"Because we don't know what'll happen once we do."

"Isn't tha—"

But again, Nichol was cut off. She shut her mouth, but fumed.

"Why not?" Gamache asked again, his voice neutral, assessing the situation.

"I know it sounds overcautious, but once this is plugged in, we have the ability to connect to the world. But it also means the world can connect to us. This"—he held up the cable—"is a highway that goes in both directions."

Agent Nichol looked like she was about to wet her pants.

Chief Inspector Gamache turned to her and nodded.

"But the power isn't on." The dam broke and the words rushed from her. "That might as well be rope for all the connecting it'll do. We have to attach it to the computers and we have to turn the power on. We have to make sure it works. Why wait?"

Gamache felt a chill on his neck and turned to see Gilles walking into the tense atmosphere. He shut the door, took off his tuque and mitts and coat, and sat by the door as though guarding it.

Gamache turned to Thérèse.

"What do you think?"

"We should wait." On seeing Nichol open her mouth again, Thérèse headed off any comment. Looking directly at the young agent she spoke.

"You've just arrived, but we've been living with this for weeks, months. We've risked our careers, our friendships, our homes, perhaps even more. If my husband says we pause, then we pause. Do you understand?"

Nichol gave in with bad grace.

As they left, Gamache turned the key in the Yale lock and put it in his breast pocket. Gilles joined him for the short walk through the dark, back to Emilie's home.

"You know that young woman's right?" Gilles said, his voice low and his eyes on the snowy ground.

"We need to test it?" said Gamache, also in a whisper. "*Oui*, I know."

He watched Nichol, up ahead, and behind her Jérôme and Thérèse.

And he wondered what Jérôme was really afraid of.

After a dinner of beef stew, they took their coffees into the living room, where a fire had been laid.

Thérèse put a match to the newspaper and watched it flare and burn bright. Then she turned to the room. Gamache and Gilles sat together on one of the sofas and Jérôme sat across from them. Nichol was in the corner, working on a jigsaw puzzle.

After plugging in the lights on the Christmas tree, Thérèse joined her husband.

"Wish I'd thought to bring gifts," she said, gazing at the tree. "Armand, you look pensive."

Gamache had followed her gaze and was looking under the tree. Something had twigged, some little thought to do with trees, or Christmas, or presents. Something triggered by what Thérèse just said, but the direct question had chased it away. He furrowed his brow and continued to look at the cheerful Christmas tree in the corner of the room. Bare underneath. Barren of gifts.

"Armand?"

He shook his head and met her gaze. "Sorry, I was just thinking."

Jérôme turned to Gilles. "You must be exhausted."

Jérôme looked exhausted himself.

Gilles nodded. "Been a while since I climbed a tree."

"Do you really hear them talk?" Jérôme asked.

The woodsman studied the rotund man across from him. The man who'd stayed at the base of the white pine in the bitter cold, calling encouragement, when he could have left. He nodded.

"What do they say?" Jérôme asked.

"I don't think you want to know what they're saying," said Gilles with a smile. "Besides, mostly I just hear sounds. Whispers. Other stuff."

The Brunels looked at him, waiting for more. Gamache held his coffee, and listened. He knew the story.

"Have you always been able to hear them?" Thérèse finally asked.

In the corner, Agent Nichol looked up from the puzzle.

Gilles shook his head. "I was a lumberjack. I cut down hundreds of trees with my chain saw. One day, as I cut into an old-growth oak, I heard it cry."

Silence met the remark. Gilles stared into the fireplace, and the burning wood.

"At first I ignored it. Thought I was hearing things. Then it spread, and I could hear not just my tree, but all the trees crying."

He was quiet for a moment.

"It was horrible," he whispered.

"What did you do?" Jérôme asked.

"What could I do? I stopped cutting and I made my team stop." He looked at his huge, worn hands. "They thought I was mad, of course. I'd have thought the same thing, if I hadn't heard it myself."

Gilles looked directly at Jérôme as he spoke.

"I could live in denial for a while, but once I knew, I could never un-know. You know?"

Jérôme nodded. He did know.

"Gilles now makes the most wonderful furniture, from found wood," said Gamache. "Reine-Marie and I have a couple of pieces."

Gilles smiled. "Doesn't pay the bills, though."

"Speaking of payment—" Gamache began.

Gilles looked at the Chief Inspector. "Don't say any more."

"*Désolé*," said Gamache. "I shouldn't have said that much."

"I was glad to help. I can stay if you'd like. That way I'll be here if you need help."

"Thank you," said Gamache, getting to his feet. "We'll call if we need you."

"Well, I'll come tomorrow morning. You'll find me in the bistro if you need me."

With his coat on and his large hand on the doorknob, Gilles looked at the four of them.

"There's a reason thieves steal at night, you know."

"Are you calling us thieves?" asked Thérèse with some amusement.

"Aren't you?"

Armand closed the door and looked at his colleagues.

"We have some decisions to make, *mes amis*."

Jérôme Brunel drew the curtains and walked back to his seat by the fire.

It was almost midnight and, while bone-tired, they'd gotten their second, or third, wind. More coffee had been made, another maple log was tossed on the fire, Henri had been walked and now slept curled up by the hearth.

"*Bon*," said Gamache, leaning forward and looking into their faces. "What do we do now?"

"We're not ready to connect," said Jérôme.

"What you mean is, you're not ready," Nichol said. "What're you waiting for?"

"We won't get a second chance," Jérôme snapped. "When I operated on a patient I didn't think, *Well, if I screw up I can always try again*. No. One shot, that's it. We have to make sure we're prepared."

"We are prepared," Nichol insisted. "Nothing more's going to happen. No more equipment's going to show up. No more help. You have everything you're ever going to have. This is it."

"Why're you so impatient?" Jérôme demanded.

"Why aren't you?" she replied.

"That's enough," said Gamache. "What can we do to help, Jérôme? What do you need?"

"I need to know about all that equipment she brought." He glanced at Nichol, who was sitting with her arms across her chest. "Why do we need two computers?"

"One's for me," Nichol said. She decided to speak to them as though to Henri. "I'll be encrypting the channel we use to access the Sûreté network. If anyone picks up your signal, they'll need to break the encryption. It buys us time."

That last bit they understood, even Henri, but they needed to think about the encryption part.

"What you're saying," said Thérèse, slowly picking her way through the technical talk, "is that when Jérôme types something on the keyboard it's put into code? Then that code is scrambled?"

"Exactly," said Nichol. "All before it leaves the room." She paused and her arms closed even tighter across her body, like steel straps.

"What is it?" Gamache asked.

"They'll still find you." Her voice was soft. It held no triumph. "My programs only make it difficult for them to see you, but not impossible. They know what they're doing. They'll find us."

It didn't escape the Chief Inspector that within a breath, the "you" had become "us." There were few more significant breaths.

"Will they know who we are?" he asked.

Gamache saw the vise grip loosen around the young agent's chest. She leaned slightly forward.

"Now that's an interesting question. I've intentionally created an encryption that appears clunky, unsophisticated."

"Intentionally?" asked Jérôme, not convinced it was on purpose at all. "Why would anyone do that? We don't need 'clunky,' for God's sake. We need the best there is."

He looked at Gamache, and the Chief Inspector could see the slight lash of panic.

Nichol was silent, either because she'd finally figured out the immense power of silence, or because she was miffed. Gamache suspected the latter, but it gave him time to consider Jérôme's very good question.

Why appear unsophisticated?

"To throw them off," he said at last, turning to the petulant little face. "They might see us, but they might not take us seriously."

"*C'est ça*," Nichol said, unwinding slightly. "Exactly. They'll be looking for a sophisticated attack."

"It'll be like taking a stone to a nuclear war," said Gamache.

"Yes," said Nichol. "If found, we won't be taken seriously."

"For good reason," said Thérèse. "How much damage can a stone do?"

The David and Goliath analogy aside, the reality was a stone wasn't much of a weapon. She turned to Jérôme, expecting to see a dismissive look on his face, and was surprised to see admiration.

"We don't need to do damage," he said. "We just need to sneak past the guards."

"That's the hope," said Nichol, and gave a great sigh. "I don't think it'll work, but it's worth a try."

"Jeez," said Thérèse. "It's like living with a Greek chorus."

"My programs will make it difficult for them to see us, but we need a security code to even get in, and they'll know as soon as you log in with your own codes."

"And what could stop them from finding us?" Gamache asked.

"I told you that before. A different security code. One that won't draw any attention. But even that won't stop them for long. As soon as we break into a file they're trying to protect, they'll know it. They'll hunt us down, and they'll find us."

"How long will that take, do you think?"

Nichol's thin lips pouted as she thought. "Finesse won't matter at that stage. All that'll matter is speed. Get in, get what we need, and get out. It's unlikely we'll have more than half a day. Probably less."

"Half a day from the time we break into the first secure file?" Gamache asked.

"No," said Jérôme. He spoke to Gamache, but was looking at Nichol. "She means twelve hours from our first effort."

"Maybe less," said Nichol.

"Twelve hours should be enough, don't you think?" asked Thérèse.

"It wasn't before," said Jérôme. "We've had months and still haven't found what we need."

"But you didn't have me," said Nichol.

They looked at her, marveling at the indestructibility, and delusion, of youth.

"So when do we start?" asked Nichol.

"Tonight."

"But, Armand—" Thérèse began. Jérôme's hand had tightened over hers, to the point of hurting her.

"Gilles was right," said the Chief, his voice decisive. "There's a reason thieves work at night. Fewer witnesses. We have to get in and get out while everyone else sleeps."

"Finally," said Nichol, getting up.

"We need more time," said Thérèse.

"There is no more time." Gamache consulted his watch. It was almost one in the morning.

"Jérôme, you have an hour to get your notes together. You know where the alarm was tripped last time. If you can get there fast, we might be in and out with the information in time for breakfast."

"Right," said Jérôme. He released his grip on his wife's hand.

"You get some sleep," Gamache said to Nichol. "We'll wake you in an hour."

He went to the kitchen, and heard the door close behind him.

"What're you doing, Armand?" asked Thérèse.

"Making fresh coffee." His back was to her as he counted the spoons of coffee into the machine.

"Look at me," she demanded. Gamache's hand stopped, the heaping spoon was suspended and a few grains fell to the counter.

He lowered the spoon to the coffee can and turned.

Thérèse Brunel's eyes were steady. "Jérôme's exhausted. He's been going all day."

"We all have," said Gamache. "I'm not saying this is easy—"

"You're suggesting Jérôme and I are looking for 'easy'?"

"Then what are you looking for? You want me to say we can all go to sleep and forget what's happening? We're close, we finally have a chance. This ends now."

"My God," said Thérèse, looking at him closely. "This isn't about us. This's about Jean-Guy Beauvoir. You don't think he'll survive another raid. That's why you're pushing us, pushing Jérôme."

"This isn't about Beauvoir." Gamache reached behind him and clutched the marble countertop.

"Of course it is. You'd sacrifice all of us to save him."

"Never," Gamache raised his voice.

"That's what you're doing."

"I've been working at this for years," said Gamache, approaching her. "Long before the raid on the factory. Long before Jean-Guy got into trouble. I've given up everything to see this through. It ends tonight. Jérôme will just have to dig deeper. We all will."

"You're not being rational."

"No, you aren't," he seethed. "Can't you see Jérôme's frightened? Scared sick? That's what's draining his energy. The longer we wait, the worse it'll get."

"You're saying you're doing this to be kind to Jérôme?" demanded Thérèse, incredulous.

"I'm doing this because one more day and he'll crack," said Gamache. "And then we'll all be lost, including him. If you can't see it, I can."

"He's not the one who's falling apart," she said. "He's not the one who was in tears today."

Gamache looked as though she'd hit him with a car.

"Jérôme can and will do it tonight. He'll go back in and get us the information we need to nail Francoeur and stop whatever's planned." Gamache's voice was low and his eyes glared. "Jérôme agrees. He, at least, has a backbone."

Gamache opened the door and left, going up to his room and staring at the wall, waiting for the trembling in his hand to subside.

At two in the morning Jérôme stood up.

Armand had awoken Nichol and come downstairs. He didn't look at Thérèse and she didn't look at him.

Nichol descended, disheveled, and put on her coat.

"Ready?" Gamache asked Jérôme.

"Ready."

Gamache signaled Henri, and they quietly left the home. Like thieves in the night.

TWENTY-EIGHT

Nichol marched ahead, the only one anxious to get to the schoolhouse. But her rush was futile, Gamache knew, since he had the key.

Jérôme held Thérèse's hand. Both wore puffy black coats and puffy white mitts. They looked like Mickey and Minnie Mouse out for a stroll.

Chief Inspector Gamache brushed past Superintendent Brunel and unlocked the schoolhouse door. He held it open for them, but instead of entering himself, he let it drift shut.

He saw the light go on through the frosted window and heard the metallic clank as the top of the woodstove was lifted and logs were fed to the dying embers.

But outside, there was only a hush.

He tipped his head back and looked into the night sky. Was one of the bright specks not a star at all, but the satellite that would soon transport them from this village?

He brought his gaze back to earth. To the cottages. The B and B, the bakery. Monsieur Béliveau's general store. Myrna's bookstore. The bistro. The scene of so many great meals and discussions. He and Jean-Guy. Lacoste. Even Nichol.

Going back years.

He was about to order the final connection made, and then there'd be no turning back. As Nichol so clearly pointed out, they'd be found eventually. And traced back here.

And then no number of woodsmen, of huntsmen, of villagers, of demented poets, of glorious painters and innkeepers could stop what would happen. To Three Pines. To everyone in it.

Armand Gamache turned his back on the sleeping village, and went inside.

Jérôme Brunel had taken his seat in front of one of the monitors, and Thérèse was standing behind him. Yvette Nichol sat beside Dr. Brunel at her own keyboard and monitor, her back already slumped, like a widow's hump.

They all turned to look at him.

Gamache did not hesitate. At his nod, Yvette Nichol slid under the desk.

"OK?" she asked.

"*Oui*," he said, his voice clipped, determined.

There was silence, then they heard a click.

"Done," she called, and crawled back out.

Gamache met Jérôme's eyes, and nodded.

Jérôme reached out, surprised to see his finger wasn't trembling, and pressed the power button. Lights flashed on. There was a slight crackling and then their screens flashed alive.

Gamache reached into his pocket and brought out a neatly folded piece of paper. He smoothed it out and placed it in front of Jérôme.

Agent Nichol looked at it. At the insignia. And the line of letters and numbers. Then she looked up at the Chief.

"The national archives," she whispered. "My God, it might work."

"OK, everything's live and we're online," Jérôme reported. "All the encryption programs and sub-programs are running. Once I log in, the clock starts."

While Dr. Brunel slowly, carefully, typed in the long access code, Gamache turned away to look at the wall, and the ordnance map. So detailed. Even so, it would not have shown where they now stood had some child years ago not put that dot on the page and written, in careful, clear letters, *Home*.

Gamache stared at it. And he thought of St. Thomas's Church across the way. And the stained-glass window made after the Great War, showing bright young soldiers walking forward. Not with brave faces. They were filled with fear. But still they advanced.

Below them was the list of the young men who never made it home. And below the names the inscription *They were our children.*

Gamache heard Jérôme type in the sequence of numbers and letters. Then he heard nothing. Only silence.

The code was in place. Only one thing left to do.

Jérôme Brunel's finger hovered above the enter button.

Then he brought it down.

"*Non*," said Armand. He gripped Jérôme's wrist, stopping the finger

236

millimeters from the button. They stared at it, not daring to breathe, wondering if Jérôme had actually hit enter before Gamache had stopped him.

"What're you doing?" Jérôme demanded.

"I made a mistake," said Gamache. "You're exhausted. We all are. If this's going to work we need to be sharp. Rested. There's too much at stake."

He glanced again to the map on the wall. And the mark that was almost invisible.

"We'll come back tomorrow night and start fresh," said Gamache.

Jérôme Brunel looked like a man who'd had his execution stayed. Not sure if this was a kindness, not sure if this was a trick. After a moment his shoulders rolled forward and he sighed.

With what felt like the last of his energy, Dr. Brunel erased the code and handed the paper back to Gamache.

As he returned it to his pocket, Gamache caught Thérèse's eye. And nodded.

"Can you unplug us, please?" Jérôme asked Nichol.

She was about to argue, but decided against it, too tired herself to fight. Once again she slid off her chair and crawled under the desk.

When the cable was unplugged, they turned the lights out and Gamache relocked the door. Hoping he hadn't made a mistake. Hoping he hadn't just given Francoeur that critical twenty-four hours to complete his plan.

As they trudged back to Emilie Longpré's home, Gamache caught up with Thérèse.

"You were right. I—"

Thérèse held up her Minnie Mouse hand and Gamache fell silent.

"We were both wrong. You were afraid to stop and I was afraid to go."

"You think we'll have less fear tomorrow?" he asked.

"Not less fear," she said. "But perhaps more courage."

Once in the warm house, they went to bed, falling asleep as soon as their heads hit the pillow. Just before drifting off, Gamache heard Henri groan contentedly, and the house creak in ways that felt like home.

Gamache opened his eyes and found himself staring directly into Henri's face. How long the dog had been sitting there, his chin on the side of the bed, his wet nose within inches of Gamache's face, was impossible to say.

But as soon as Armand's eyes fluttered open, Henri's entire body began to wag.

The day had begun. He looked at the bedside clock.

Almost nine. He'd had six hours of sleep, and felt as though he'd had double that. Rested and refreshed, he was certain now he'd come close to making a disastrous decision the night before. They'd rest up today, and go back that night, no longer battling fatigue and confusion and each other.

As he dressed, Gamache could hear the scrape of shovels. He drew back the curtains and saw the whole village covered in white, and the air filled with it. Flakes drifted down and piled up on the three gigantic pines, on the forest, on the homes.

There was no wind at all, and the snow fell straight down. Gentle and relentless.

He could see Gabri and Clara, out clearing their paths. He first heard, then saw, Billy Williams's plow coming down the hill into the village. Past the small church, past the schoolhouse. And around the village green.

Parents skated on the frozen pond with shovels, clearing away the snow, while children with hockey sticks and ants in their pants waited on the makeshift benches.

He went downstairs and found he was the first one up.

While Henri ate, Gamache put on a pot of coffee and laid a new fire in the living room hearth. Then they went for a walk.

"Come on over to the bistro for breakfast," Gabri called. He wore a tuque with an immense pom-pom and was leaning on his snow shovel. "Olivier will make you blueberry crêpes with some of Monsieur Pagé's maple syrup."

"And bacon?" asked Gamache, knowing he was already lost.

"*Bien sûr,*" said Gabri. "Is there any other way to eat crêpes?"

"I'll be right back."

Gamache hurried home, wrote a note for the others, then he and Henri returned to the bistro. The Chief settled in by the fireplace and had just taken a sip of *café au lait* when Myrna joined him.

"Do you mind company?" she asked. But she was already in the armchair opposite him and had signaled for a coffee of her own.

"I was going to come over to your shop after breakfast," explained the Chief Inspector. "I'm looking for gifts."

"For Reine-Marie?"

"No, for everyone here. To say thank you."

"There's no need, you know," said Myrna.

Gabri brought her coffee, then pulled up a chair and joined them.

"What're we talking about?" he asked.

"Gifts," said Myrna.

"For me?" he asked.

"Who else?" asked Myrna. "You're all we ever think about."

"We have that in common, *ma chère*," said Gabri.

"What're we talking about?" asked Olivier, as he placed two plates of blueberry crêpes and maple-smoked bacon in front of Myrna and Gamache.

"Me," said Gabri. "Me, me, me."

"Oh, good," said Olivier, bringing over another chair. "It's been thirty seconds since we visited that subject. So much must have happened."

"Actually, there is something I want to ask you two," said Gamache. Myrna passed him the jug of maple syrup.

"*Oui?*" asked Olivier.

"Did you open Constance's gifts?" the Chief asked.

"No, we put them under the tree. Would you like us to open them?"

"No. I already know what she gave you."

"What?" asked Gabri. "A car? A pony?"

"I won't tell you, but I will say that I think it's something you can use."

"A muzzle?" asked Olivier.

"What're we talking about?" asked Clara, dragging over a chair. Her cheeks were red and her nose was running and Gamache, Gabri, Myrna and Olivier all handed her a napkin, just in time.

"Gifts," said Olivier. "From Constance."

"We're not talking about you?" Clara asked Gabri.

"I know. An abomination of nature. Though, to be fair, we have been talking about the gifts Constance gave me."

"Us," said Olivier.

"Yes, she gave me one too," said Clara, and turned to Gamache. "You dropped it off the other day."

"Did you open it?"

"I'm afraid I did," Clara admitted, and took a piece of Myrna's bacon.

"That's why I keep your presents under my tree until Christmas morning," said Myrna, moving her plate away.

"What did Constance give you?" asked Gabri.

"This."

Clara unwound the scarf from her neck and gave it to Myrna, who took it, admiring the bright and cheerful lime green.

"What're these? Hockey sticks?" Myrna pointed to a pattern at either end of the scarf.

"Paintbrushes," said Clara. "Took me a while to figure it out."

Myrna passed it back to Clara.

"Oh, let's get ours," said Gabri. He rushed off, and by the time he returned Myrna and Gamache had finished their breakfasts and were on their second *cafés au lait*. Gabri handed one of the packages to Olivier and kept the other for himself. They were identical, both wrapped in bright red paper with candy canes all over it.

Gabri ripped the wrapping off his. "Mitts," he exclaimed, as though they were a pony and a car rolled into one magnificent present.

He tried them on. "They even fit. It's so hard to find ones for hands this large. And you know what they say about big hands . . ."

No one pursued that.

Olivier tried on his mitts. They also fit.

There was a bright yellow crescent moon pattern on each mitt.

"What do you think the pattern means?" Clara asked.

They all thought.

"Did she know about your habit of mooning?" Myrna turned to Gabri.

"Who doesn't?" said Gabri. "But a half moon?"

"It's not even a half moon," said Clara. "It's a crescent moon."

Gabri laughed. "A croissant moon? My two favorite things. Croissants and mooning."

"Sadly, this is true," Olivier confirmed. "And he has such a full moon."

"Paintbrushes for Clara and croissants for the guys," said Myrna. "Perfect."

Gamache watched them admiring the gifts. Then the thought that had eluded him last night drifted into his consciousness, like a snowflake, and landed.

He turned to Myrna. "She didn't give you a present."

"Well, just coming down was more than enough," said Myrna.

Gamache shook his head. "We found these gifts in her suitcase, but nothing for you. Why not? It doesn't make sense that Constance would make gifts for everyone else, but not bring anything for you."

"I didn't expect one."

"Even so," said Gamache. "If she brought them for the others, she'd bring one for you, no?"

Myrna saw his logic. She nodded.

"Maybe that photograph she packed was for Myrna," Clara suggested. "The one with the four sisters."

"Possibly, but why not wrap it, like your gifts? Returning for Christmas wasn't part of the original plan, was it?" he asked, and Myrna shook her head. "She initially came for a few days?"

Myrna nodded.

240

"So, as far as she knew, when she first came down, she wasn't coming back," said Gamache, and they looked at him strangely. The point had already been made, why pound it home?

"Right," said Myrna.

Gamache stood up. "Can you come with me?"

He meant Myrna, but they all followed him through the door connecting the bistro to the bookstore. Ruth was already there, putting books into her oversized purse, whose bottom had long since taken on the shape of a Scotch bottle. Rosa stood beside Ruth, and looked at them as they arrived.

Henri stopped dead and lay down. Then he rolled over.

"Get up, you wretched thing," said Gamache, but Henri only looked at him upside down and swished his tail.

"God," Gabri stage-whispered. "Imagine their children. Big ears and big feet."

"What do you want?" Ruth demanded.

"It's my store," said Myrna.

"It's not a store, it's a library." She snapped her bag shut.

"Idiot," they both muttered.

Gamache walked over to the large Christmas tree.

"Can you look at them, please?" He pointed to the presents under the tree.

"But I know what's there. I wrapped them myself. They're for everyone here, and Constance."

And Constance, thought Gamache. Still that, even in death.

"Just look anyway, please."

Myrna got on her knees and sifted through the wrapped gifts.

"Now there's a full moon," said Gabri with admiration.

Myrna sat back on her heels. In her hand was a gift wrapped in bright red paper, with candy canes.

"Can you read the card?" Gamache asked.

Myrna struggled to her feet and opened the small flap. "*For Myrna*," she read. "*The key to my home. Love, Constance.*"

"What does that mean?" Gabri asked, looking from face to face and settling on Gamache's.

But the Chief only had eyes for the package.

"Open it, please," he said.

241

TWENTY-NINE

⌒

Myrna took the Christmas present to a seat by the window of her bookshop.

Everyone leaned forward as she peeled off the tape, except Ruth, who remained where she was and looked out the window at the endless snow.

"What did she give you?" Olivier craned his neck. "Let me see."

"More mitts," said Clara.

"No, I think it's a hat," said Gabri. "A tuque."

Myrna lifted it up. It was light blue and it was indeed a tuque. And on it was a design.

"What's the pattern?" asked Clara. It looked like bats to her, but that probably didn't make sense.

"They're angels," said Olivier.

They leaned closer.

"Isn't that beautiful," said Gabri, stepping back. "You were her guardian angel."

"It's wonderful." Myrna held up the hat, admiring it and trying to hide her disappointment. Myrna had let herself believe that the package would magically reveal Constance. Her most private life. That the gift would finally let Myrna enter Constance's home.

It was a lovely gesture, but it was hardly a key to anything.

"How'd you know it was there?" Clara asked Gamache.

"I didn't," he conceded, "but it seemed unlikely she'd give you a gift and not bring one for Myrna. Then I realized if she had brought one for Myrna it would have been on her first visit, since she didn't expect to return."

"Well, mystery solved," said Gabri. "I'm heading back to the bistro. You coming, Maigret?"

"Right behind you, Miss Marple," said Olivier.

Ruth got up with a grunt. She stared at the package, then at Gamache. He nodded to her, and she to him. Only then did she and Rosa leave.

"You two seem to have developed telepathy." Clara watched the old poet walk carefully down the snowy path, the duck in her arms. "Not sure I'd want her in my head."

"She's not in my head," he assured her. "But Ruth is often on my mind. Did you know that her poem 'Alas' was written for Virginie Ouellet, after she died?"

"No," admitted Myrna, her hand resting on the tuque, watching Ruth pause and give the hockey players instructions, or hell. "It made Ruth famous, didn't it?"

Gamache nodded. "I don't think she's ever recovered from that."

"The fame?" asked Clara.

"The guilt," said Gamache. "Of profiting from someone else's sorrow."

Who hurt you once, / so far beyond repair / that you would greet each overture / with curling lip?"

Myrna whispered the words as she watched Ruth and Rosa, heads bowed into the snow. Making for home.

"We all have our albatrosses," she said.

"Or ducks," said Clara, and knelt by her friend's chair. "Are you all right?"

Myrna nodded.

"Would you like to be alone?"

"Just for a few minutes."

Clara stood, kissed Myrna on the top of her head, and left.

But Armand Gamache did not leave. Instead he waited for the connecting door to close, then he sat in the chair vacated by Ruth and stared at Myrna.

"What's wrong?" he asked.

Myrna lifted the tuque and put it on. The knitted hat perched on Myrna's head like a light blue light bulb. Then she handed it to him. After examining it, Gamache lowered the hat to his knee.

"This wasn't made for you, was it?"

"No. And it's not new," she said.

Gamache could see the wool was worn, slightly pilled. And he saw something else. A tiny tag had been sewn into the inside of the tuque. Putting on his reading glasses, he brought the hat to his face so that the rough wool almost rubbed his nose.

It was difficult to read the tag, the printing was so small and the letters smudged.

He took off his glasses and handed the tuque back to Myrna. "What do you think it says?"

She examined it, squinting. "MA," she finally said.

The Chief nodded, unconsciously fiddling with his glasses.

"MA," he repeated, and looked out the window. His gaze was unfocused. Trying to see what wasn't there.

An idea, a thought. A purpose.

Why had someone sewn MA into the tuque?

It was, he knew, the same as the tag they'd found in the other tuques in Constance's home. Constance's had had a pattern of reindeer, and MC on the tag. Marie-Constance.

Marguerite's had MM inside. Marie-Marguerite.

Josephine's tuque had MJ.

He looked down at the tuque in his hand. MA.

"Maybe it belonged to their mother," said Myrna. "That must be it. She made one for each of the girls, and one for herself."

"But it's so small," said the Chief.

"People were smaller back then," said Myrna, and Gamache nodded.

It was true. Especially women. The Québécoise tended to be petite even today. He looked at the hat again. Would it fit a grown woman?

Maybe.

And it might make sense for Constance to keep this, the only memento of her mother. There wasn't a single photograph of their parents in the Quints' home. But they had something much more precious. Hats their mother had made.

One for each of them, and one for herself.

And what had she put inside? Not her initials. Of course not. She stopped being Marie-Harriette when her girls had been born, and became Mama. Ma.

Maybe this was the key to Constance after all. And maybe, in giving it to Myrna, Constance was signaling her willingness to finally let go. Of the past. Of the rancor.

Gamache wondered if Constance and her sisters ever knew that their parents hadn't sold them to the state, but that the girls had, in effect, been expropriated.

Did Constance finally realize that her mother had loved her? Was that the albatross she'd been lugging around all her life? Not some terrible wrong, but the horror that came from realizing, too late, she hadn't been wronged? That she'd been loved all along?

Who hurt you once, / so far beyond repair?

Maybe the answer, for the Quints and for Ruth, was simple.

They'd done it to themselves.

Ruth in writing the poem and taking on an unnecessary burden of guilt, and the Quints in believing a lie and not recognizing their parents' love.

He looked at the tuque again, rotated it, examining the pattern. Then he lowered it.

"How could this be a key to her home?" he asked. "Does the angel pattern mean anything to you?"

Myrna looked out the window, at the village green and the skaters, and she shook her head.

"Maybe it means nothing," said the Chief. "Why reindeer or pine trees or snowflakes? The patterns Madame Ouellet knitted into the other hats are just cheerful symbols of winter and Christmas."

Myrna nodded, kneading the hat and watching the happy children on the frozen pond. "Constance told me she and her sisters loved hockey. They'd get up a team and play the other village kids. Apparently it was Brother André's favorite sport."

"I didn't know that," said Gamache.

"I think they might have all bought into the belief that Frère André was their guardian angel. Hence," she held up the tuque, "the hat."

Gamache nodded. There were plenty of references to Brother André in the archived papers as well. Both sides had invoked the saint's potent memory.

"But why would she give me the hat?" Myrna asked. "So that she could tell me about Brother André? Was he the key to their home? I don't get it."

"Maybe she wanted to get it out of her house," said Gamache, rising to his feet. "Maybe that was the key. Breaking loose from the legend."

Maybe, maybe, maybe. It was no way to run an investigation. And time was running out. If this crime wasn't solved by the time he and the Brunels and Nichol returned to the schoolhouse, then it would not be solved.

Not by him anyway.

"I need to see the film again," said Gamache, making for the stairs up to Myrna's loft.

There," Gamache pointed at the screen. "Do you see it?"

But once again he'd hit the pause button a moment too late.

He rewound and tried again. And again. Myrna sat on the sofa beside him. Over and over he played the same twenty seconds of the recording. The old film, in the old farmhouse.

The girls laughing and teasing each other. Constance sitting on the rough bench, her father at her feet, lacing the skates. The other girls at the door, teetering on their blades and already holding hockey sticks.

Then their mother enters the frame and hands out the hats. But there's an extra hat, which she throws offscreen.

Over and over, Chief Inspector Gamache played it. The extra hat was only visible for an instant as it whirled out of the frame. Finally, he captured it, frozen in that split second between when it left Marie-Harriette's hand and when it left the screen.

They leaned closer.

The tuque was light in color, that much they could see. But in a black and white film it was impossible to say what the color was exactly. But now they could see the pattern. It was fuzzy, blurry, but clear enough.

"Angels," said Myrna. "It's this one." She looked down at the hat in her hand. "It was the mother's."

But Gamache was no longer looking at the frozen hat. He was looking at Marie-Harriette's face. Why was she so upset?

"May I use your phone?"

Myrna brought it over and he placed his call.

"I checked the death certificates, Chief," Inspector Lacoste reported in answer to his question. "They're definitely all dead. Virginie, Hélène, Josephine, Marguerite, and now Constance. All the Ouellet Quints are gone."

"Are you sure?"

It was rare for the Chief to question her findings, and it made her question herself.

"I know we thought maybe one was still alive," said Lacoste. "But I've found death certificates and burial records for all of them. All interred in the same cemetery close to their home. We have proof."

"There was proof Dr. Bernard delivered the babies," Gamache reminded her. "Proof Isidore and Marie-Harriette sold them to Québec. Proof Virginie died in an accidental fall, when we now suspect that was almost certainly not the case."

Inspector Lacoste took his point.

"They were extremely private," she said slowly, getting her head around what he was saying. "I suppose it's possible."

"They weren't just private, they were secretive. They were hiding something." The Chief thought for a moment. "If they are all dead, is it possible there was more to their deaths than we know?"

"Like Virginie's, you mean?" asked Lacoste, her own mind churning to catch up with his.

"If they lied about one death, they could lie about them all."

"But why?"

"Why does anyone lie to us?" he asked.

"To cover up a crime," she said.

"To cover up murder."

"You think they were murdered?" she asked, not succeeding in keeping the astonishment out of her voice. "All of them?"

"We know Constance was. And we know Virginie died a violent death. What do we really know about that?" asked the Chief. "The official record says she died from a fall down the stairs. Corroborated by Hélène and Constance. But the doctor's notes and the initial police reports had a different version."

"*Oui*. Suicide."

"But maybe even that was wrong."

"You think Hélène or Constance killed her?"

"I think we're getting closer to the truth."

It felt to Gamache as though they'd finally broken into the Ouellet home. He and Lacoste were stumbling around in the dark, but soon whatever that wounded family was hiding would be revealed.

"I'll go back over my notes," said Lacoste, "and dig deeper into the old files, see if there was even a hint that those deaths were anything but natural."

"Good. And I'll check the parish records."

It was where the priest kept records of births and deaths. The Chief knew he'd find, written in longhand, the record of the five births. He wondered how many deaths he'd find.

Chief Inspector Gamache drove directly to the Sûreté forensics lab and dropped the tuque off, with instructions to give him a full report by the end of the day.

"Today?" the technician asked, but he was speaking to the Chief Inspector's back.

Gamache went up to his offices and arrived in time for the briefing. Inspector Lacoste was leading it, but only a few officers had bothered to show up. She rose as the Chief Inspector entered. The others did not, at first. But on seeing his stern face, they got up.

"Where're the others?" Gamache asked brusquely.

"On assignment," replied one of the officers. "Sir."

"My question was for Inspector Lacoste." He turned to her.

"They were told of the meeting, but chose not to come."

"I'll need their names, please," said Gamache, and was about to leave when he stopped and looked at the agents, still standing. He considered them for a moment and seemed to sag.

"Go home," he finally said.

This they hadn't expected, and they stood there surprised and uncertain. As was Lacoste, though she struggled not to show it.

"Home?" one of them asked.

"Leave," said the Chief. "Make of it what you will, but just go."

The agents looked at each other and grinned.

He turned his back on them and made for the door.

"Our cases?"

Gamache stopped and turned back to see the young officer he'd tried to help a few days ago.

"Will your cases really be further along if you stay?"

It was a rhetorical question.

He knew these agents, looking at him so triumphantly, were spreading the word throughout the Sûreté that Chief Inspector Gamache was finished. Had given up.

And now he'd done them the very great favor of confirming it. By in effect closing his department.

"Consider this a Christmas gift."

They no longer tried to hide their satisfaction. The coup was complete. They'd brought the great Chief Inspector Gamache to his knees.

"Go home," he said, his voice weary. "I intend to, soon."

He left the room, his back straight, his head up. But he walked slowly. A wounded lion just trying to survive the day.

"Chief?" said Inspector Lacoste, catching up.

"My office, please."

They went in and he closed the door, then motioned her to take a seat.

"Anything more on the Ouellet case?" he asked.

"I spoke to the neighbor again, to find out if the sisters ever had any visitors. She told me what she first told the investigators. No one ever went to the house."

"Except her, as I recall."

"Once," said Lacoste, "for lemonade."

"Did she think it was strange that she was never invited inside?"

"No. She said after a few years you get used to different eccentricities. Some neighbors are nosy, some like parties, some are very quiet. It's an old, established neighborhood and the sisters had been there for many years. No one seemed to question."

Gamache nodded and was quiet for a moment, playing with the pen on his desk.

"You need to know that I've decided to retire."

"Retire? Are you sure?"

She tried to read his expression. His tone. Was he saying what she thought he was?

"I'll write my letter of resignation and deliver it tonight or tomorrow. It'll be effective immediately." He sat forward at his desk and examined his hands for a moment, noticing that the tremor was gone. "You've been with me for a long time, Inspector."

"Yes, sir. You found me on the garbage pile, as I remember."

"Dumpster diving." He smiled.

It wasn't totally inaccurate. Chief Inspector Gamache had hired her away from the Serious Crimes division on the day she was to quit. Not because she couldn't do the job. Not because she'd screwed up. But because she was different. Because her colleagues had caught her at the scene of a particularly vicious crime against a child with her eyes closed and her head bowed.

Isabelle Lacoste's error was in telling the truth when asked what she was doing.

She'd been meditating, sending thoughts to the victim, reassuring her that she wouldn't be forgotten. From then on the other agents had made Isabelle Lacoste's life one long hell, until she couldn't take it anymore. She knew it was time to go.

And she was right. She simply hadn't realized where she'd be going.

Chief Inspector Gamache had heard about the meditation and wanted to meet the young agent who'd become the laughingstock of the Sûreté. When she was finally called in to her boss's office, letter of resignation in hand, she'd expected it to be just the two of them. Instead, another man rose from the large chair. She'd recognized him immediately. She'd seen Chief Inspector Gamache at the academy. Seen him on television and read about him in the newspaper. She'd once ridden with him in an elevator, and been so close she could smell his cologne. So attractive had been that aroma, and so powerful had been the pull of the man, she'd almost followed him from the elevator.

Chief Inspector Gamache had risen from his seat when she'd entered her boss's office, and bowed slightly. To her. There was something old-worldly about him. Something otherworldly about him.

He extended his hand. "Armand Gamache," he'd said.

She'd taken it, feeling light-headed. Not at all sure what was happening. She hadn't left his side since.

Not literally, of course. But professionally, emotionally. She would follow wherever he went.

And now he was telling her he was resigning.

She couldn't say this was a complete surprise. She'd, in fact, been expecting it for some time. Since the department had begun to be dismantled and the agents spread among the other departments. Since the atmosphere at Sûreté headquarters had grown dank and sour with the smell of rot.

"Thank you for all you've done for me," he said. He got up and smiled. "I'll email you a copy of my resignation letter. Perhaps you can circulate it."

"Yessir."

"As soon as you get it, please."

"I'll do that."

She walked with him to the door to his office. He offered her his hand, as he had in their first meeting.

"Not a day goes by when I'm not proud of you, Inspector Lacoste."

She felt his hand, strong. None of the weariness he'd shown the other agents. No defeat, or resignation. He was resolute. He held her hand and looked at her with complete focus.

"Trust your instincts. You understand?"

She nodded.

He opened the door and left without a backward glance. Walking slowly but without hesitation from the department he'd created and this day destroyed.

THIRTY

～

"I think you'll want to see this, sir."

Tessier caught up with Chief Superintendent Francoeur, and ordered everyone else out of the elevator. The doors closed and Tessier handed him a sheet of paper.

Francoeur quickly scanned it.

"When was this recorded?"

"An hour ago."

"And he sent everyone home?" Francoeur began to hand the paper back to Tessier, but changed his mind. Instead, he folded it and put it in his pocket.

"Inspector Lacoste is still there. They seem focused on the Ouellet case, but everyone else has gone."

Francoeur looked straight ahead and saw his imperfect reflection in the scuffed and pocked metal door of the elevator.

"He's had it," said Tessier.

"Don't be a fool," snapped Francoeur. "According to the files you picked off the therapist's computer, Gamache still thinks we have him under surveillance."

"But no one believes him."

"He believes it, and he's right. Don't you think this might be for our benefit?" Francoeur tapped his breast pocket, where the transcription now sat. "He wants us to know he's resigning."

Tessier thought about that. "Why?"

Francoeur stared ahead. At the door. He remembered when it had been new. When the stainless steel gleamed, and the reflection was perfect. He took a deep breath and tipped his head back, closing his eyes.

What was Gamache about? What was he doing?

Francoeur should have been pleased, but alarms were sounding. They were so close. And now this.

What're you up to, Armand?

The parish priest met him with keys to the old stone church.

Long gone were the days when churches were unlocked. Those days disappeared along with the chalices and crucifixes and anything else that could be stolen or defaced. Now the churches were cold and empty. Though not all of that could be laid at the feet of the vandals.

Gamache brushed the snow from his coat, took off his hat, and followed the priest. Father Antoine's Roman collar was hidden beneath a worn scarf and heavy coat. He hurried, not happy to be taken from his lunch and his hearth on this snowy day.

He was elderly, stooped. Closing in on eighty, Gamache guessed. His face was soft, the veins in his nose and cheeks purple and protruding. His eyes were tired. Exhausted from looking for miracles in this hardscrabble land. Though it had produced one miracle within living memory. The Ouellet Quints. But perhaps, thought Gamache, one was worse than none. God had visited once. And then not returned.

Father Antoine knew what was possible, and what was passing him by.

"Which one do you want?" Father Antoine asked when they were in his office at the back of the church.

"The 1930s forward, please," said the Chief. He'd called ahead and spoken to Father Antoine, but still the priest seemed put out.

He looked around the room, as did Gamache. Books and files were everywhere. Gamache could see that it had once been a comfortable, even inviting, room. There were two easy chairs, a hearth, bookcases. But now it felt neglected. Filled, but empty.

"It'll be over there." The priest pointed to a bookcase by the window, dropped the keys on the desk, and left.

"*Merci, mon père*," the Chief called after him, then closed the door, turned on the lamp on the desk, took off his coat, and got to work.

Chief Superintendent Francoeur handed the paper to his lunch companion and watched as he read, folded it back up, and placed it on the table beside the bone china plate with the warm whole-grain roll. A curl of shaved butter sat beside a sterling silver knife.

254

"What do you think it means?" his companion asked. His voice, as always, was warm, friendly, steady. Never flustered, rarely angry.

Francoeur didn't smile, but he felt like it. Unlike Tessier, this man wasn't fooled by Gamache's plodding attempt to throw them off.

"He suspects we've bugged his office," said Francoeur. He was hungry, but he didn't dare appear distracted in front of this man. "That"—he nodded toward the paper on the linen tablecloth—"was meant for us."

"I agree. But what does it mean? Is he resigning or not? What message is he sending us? Is this"—he tapped the paper—"a surrender, or a trick?"

"To be honest, sir, I don't think it matters."

Now Francoeur's companion looked interested. Curious.

"Go on."

"We're so close. Having to deal with that woman at first seemed a problem—"

"By 'deal with,' you mean throwing Audrey Villeneuve off the Champlain Bridge," the man said. "A problem you and Tessier created."

Francoeur gave him a thin smile and composed himself. "No, sir. She created it by exceeding her mandate."

He didn't say that she should never have been able to find the information. But she had. Knowledge might be power, but it was also an explosive.

"We contained it," said Francoeur. "Before she could say anything."

"But she did say something," his companion pointed out. "It was only good luck that she went to her supervisor, who then came to us. It was very nearly a catastrophe."

The use of that word struck Francoeur as interesting, and ironic, considering what was about to happen.

"And we're sure she didn't tell anyone else?"

"It would've come out by now," said Francoeur.

"That's not very reassuring."

"She didn't really know what she'd found," said Francoeur.

"No, Sylvain. She knew, but she couldn't quite believe it."

Instead of anger in his companion's face, Francoeur saw satisfaction. And felt a frisson of that himself.

They'd counted on two things. Their ability to conceal what was happening and, if found, that it would be dismissed as inconceivable. Unbelievable.

"Audrey Villeneuve's files were immediately overwritten, her car cleaned out, her home searched," said Francoeur. "Anything even remotely incriminating has disappeared."

"Except her. She was found. Tessier and his people missed the water.

Hard to do, wouldn't you say, given it's such a large target? Makes me wonder how good their aim must be."

Francoeur looked around. They were alone in the dining room, except for a cluster of bodyguards by the door. No one could see them. No one could record them. No one could overhear them. But still, Francoeur lowered his voice. Not to a whisper. That felt too much like plotting. But he dropped his voice to a discreet level.

"That turned out to be the best possible outcome," said Francoeur. "It's still listed as a suicide, but the fact that her body was found under the bridge allowed Tessier and his people to get under there too. Without questions being asked. It was a godsend."

Francoeur's companion raised his brows and smiled.

It was an attractive, almost boyish expression. His face held just enough character, just enough flaws, to appear genuine. His voice held a hint of roughness, so that his words never came across as glib. His suits, while tailored, were just that little bit off, so that he looked like both an executive and a man of the people.

One of us, to everyone.

There were few people Sylvain Francoeur admired. Few men he met he didn't immediately want to piss on. But this man was one. More than thirty years they'd known each other. They'd met as young men and each had risen in his respective profession.

Francoeur's lunch companion ripped the warm bun in half and buttered it.

He'd come up the hard way, Francoeur knew. But he'd come up. From a worker on the James Bay hydro dams to one of the most powerful men in Québec.

It was all about power. Creating it. Using it. Taking it from others.

"Are you saying God is on our side?" his companion asked, clearly amused.

"And luck," said Francoeur. "Hard work, patience, a plan. And luck."

"And was it luck that tipped Gamache to what we were doing? Was it luck that he stopped the dam collapse last year?"

The conversation had taken a turn. The voice, so warm, had solidified.

"Years we worked on that, Sylvain. Decades. Only to have you bungle it."

Francoeur knew the next few moments were critical. He couldn't look weak, but neither could he confront. So he smiled, picked up his own roll, and tore it in half.

"You're right, of course. But I think that'll prove a godsend too. The dam was always problematic. We didn't know for sure it would actually

256

come down. And it would've caused so much damage to the power grid it would've taken years to recover. This is much better."

He looked out the floor-to-ceiling windows, through the falling snow.

"I'm convinced it's even better than the original plan. It has the very great advantage of being visible. Not happening in the middle of nowhere, but right here, in the center of one of the biggest cities in North America. Think of the visuals."

Both men paused. Imagining it.

It wasn't an act of destruction they were contemplating, but creation. They would manufacture rage, an outrage so great it would become a crucible. A cauldron. And that would produce a cry for action. And that would need a leader.

"And Gamache?"

"He's no longer a factor," said Francoeur.

"Don't lie to me, Sylvain."

"He's isolated. His division's a shambles. He all but destroyed it himself today. He has no more allies, and his friends have turned away."

"Gamache is alive." Francoeur's companion leaned forward and lowered his voice. Not to conceal what he was about to say. But to drive home a point. "You've killed so many, Sylvain. Why hesitate with Gamache?"

"I'm not hesitating. Believe me, I'd like nothing better than to get rid of him. But even people no longer loyal to him would ask questions if he suddenly turned up in the St. Lawrence or was a hit-and-run. We don't need that now. We've killed his career, his department. We've killed his credibility and broken his spirit. No need to kill the man, just yet. Not unless he gets too close. But he won't. I have him distracted."

"How?"

"By dangling someone he cares about over the edge. Gamache is desperate to save this man—"

"Jean-Guy Beauvoir?"

Francoeur paused a moment, surprised his companion knew that. But then another thought occurred to him. While he was spying on Gamache, was this man spying on him?

It doesn't matter, thought Francoeur. *I've nothing to hide.*

But still, he felt a sentry rise inside him. A guard went up. He knew what he himself was capable of. He took pride in it even. Thought of himself as a wartime commander, not shrinking from difficult decisions. From sending men to their deaths. Or ordering the deaths of others. It was unpleasant but necessary.

Like Churchill, allowing the bombing of Coventry. Sacrificing a few for the many. Francoeur slept at night knowing he was far from the first commander to walk this road. For the greater good.

The man across the table took a sip of red wine and watched him over the rim. Francoeur knew what he himself was capable of. And he knew what his companion was capable of, and had already done.

Sylvain Francoeur doubled his guard.

Armand Gamache found the parish registers, in thick leather-bound volumes, exactly where the priest thought they'd be. He pulled a couple from the dusty stacks, taking the one from the 1930s with him to the desk.

He put his coat back on. It was cold and damp in the office. And he was hungry. Ignoring the grumbling in his stomach, he put on his reading glasses and bent over the old book listing births and deaths.

Francoeur cut through the puff pastry of his salmon en croute and saw the flaky pink fish, with watercress on top. Lemon and tarragon butter dripped out of the pastry.

He took a forkful as his companion ate his braised lamb shank with garlic and rosemary. Silver salvers of baby green beans and spinach sat between them on the table.

"You didn't answer my question, Sylvain."

"Which one?"

"Is the Chief Inspector really resigning? Is he signaling his surrender, or trying to lead us astray?"

Francoeur's eyes went again to the paper, neatly folded on the table. The transcription of the conversation in Gamache's office earlier that day.

"I began to say that, in my opinion, it doesn't matter."

His companion put down his fork and touched the linen napkin to his lips. He managed to make an effete mannerism look quite masculine.

"But you didn't explain what you meant by that."

"I mean, he's too late. It's all in place from our end. All we need is for you to say the word."

Francoeur's fork hovered just above his plate, as he looked across the table.

If the word was given now, they were just minutes from finishing what began decades ago. What started as two idealistic young men, and a whispered conversation, would end here. Thirty years later. With gray in their hair, and liver spots on their hands, and lines on their faces. With crisp linen and polished silver, red wine and fine food. Not with a whisper, but a bang.

"Soon, Sylvain. We're within hours, perhaps a day. We stick to the plan."

Like his companion, Chief Superintendent Francoeur knew patience was power. He'd need just a little more of one to achieve the other.

They were all there.

Marie-Virginie.

Marie-Hélène.

Marie-Josephine.

Marie-Marguerite.

And Marie-Constance.

He'd found the register of their birth. A long list of names, under Ouellet. And he'd found their deaths. Isidore, Marie-Harriette, and their children. Constance's, of course, hadn't yet been entered, but soon would be. Then the register would be complete. Birth, then death. And the book could be closed.

Gamache sat back in the chair. Despite the disorder, this room was calming. He knew it was almost certainly the quiet and the scent of old books.

He replaced the long, heavy books and left the church. As he walked across to the rectory, he passed the graveyard. The field of old gray stones was partly buried under snow, giving it a tranquil feel. More snow was falling, as it had all day. Not heavily, but steadily. Straight down, in large, soft flakes.

"Oh, what the hell," he said out loud to himself, and stepped off the path. He immediately sank to mid-shin and felt snow tumble down his boots. He trudged forward, occasionally sinking up to his knees as he moved from stone to stone. Until he found them.

Isidore and Marie-Harriette. Side by side, their names written in stone for eternity. Marie-Harriette had died so young, at least by today's standards. Shy of forty. Isidore had died so old. Just shy of ninety. Fifteen years ago.

The Chief tried to clear the snow from the front of the tombstone, to read the other names and dates, but there was too much of it. He looked around, then retraced his steps.

He saw the priest approaching and greeted him.

"Did you find what you were looking for?" asked Father Antoine.

He sounded friendlier now. Perhaps, Gamache thought, he suffered more from low blood sugar than ill temper or chronic disappointment in a God who had dropped him here, then forgotten about him.

"Sort of," said Gamache. "I tried to look at the graves but there's too much snow."

"I'll get a shovel."

Father Antoine returned a few minutes later and Gamache cleared a path to the monument, then dug out the stone itself.

Marie-Virginie.

Marie-Hélène.

Marie-Josephine.

Marie-Marguerite.

And Marie-Constance. Her birthdate was there, just not yet her death. There was a presumption that she'd be buried with her siblings. In death as in life.

"Let me ask you this, *mon père*," said Gamache.

"*Oui?*"

"Would it be possible to fake a funeral? And fake the registry?"

Father Antoine was taken aback by the question. "Fake it? Why?"

"I'm not sure why, but is it possible?"

The priest thought about that. "We don't enter a death in the registry without seeing the death certificate. If that's not accurate, then yes, I suppose the registry would be wrong too. But the funeral? That would be more difficult, *non?* I mean, we'd have to bury someone."

"Could it be an empty casket?"

"Well, that's not likely. The funeral home hardly ever delivers empty caskets for burial."

Gamache smiled. "I suppose not. But they wouldn't necessarily know who was in it. And if you didn't know the parishioner, you could be fooled too."

"Now you're suggesting there was someone in the casket, but the wrong person?"

Father Antoine was looking skeptical. And well he should be, thought the Chief.

Still, so much of the Ouellet Quintuplets' lives had been faked, why not their deaths too? But to what end? And which one might still be alive?

He shook his head. By far the most reasonable answer was the simplest. They were all dead. And the question he should be asking himself was not if they were dead, but if they were murdered.

He looked at the neighboring gravestones. To the left, more Ouellets.

Isidore's family. To the right, the Pineaults. Marie-Harriette's family. All the Pineault boys' names began with Marc. Gamache leaned closer and wasn't surprised to see that all the girls' names started with Marie.

His gaze was drawn back to Marie-Harriette.

Long dead and buried in another town, / my mother hasn't finished with me yet.

Gamache wondered what the unfinished business was, between mother and daughters. Mama. Ma.

"Has anyone been by lately asking about the Quints?" Gamache asked as they walked single-file back down the narrow path he'd cleared.

"No. Most people have long ago forgotten them."

"Have you been priest here long?"

"About twenty years. Long after the Quints had moved away."

So this tired priest never even got the benefit of the miracle. Just the bodies.

"Did the girls ever come back for a visit?"

"No."

"And yet they're buried here."

"Well, where else would they be buried? In the end, most people come home."

Gamache thought it was probably true.

"The parents? Did you know them?"

"I knew Isidore. He lived a long time. Never remarried. Always hoped the girls would come back, to look after him in his old age."

"But they never did."

"Only for his funeral. And then to be buried themselves."

The priest accepted the old keys from Gamache and they parted. But he had one more stop to make before returning to Montréal.

A few minutes later Chief Inspector Gamache pulled into a parking spot and turned the car off. He looked at the high walls, with the spikes and curls of barbed wire on top. Guards in their towers watched him, their rifles across their chests.

They needn't have worried. The Chief had no intention of getting out, though he was tempted.

The church was just a few kilometers from the SHU, the penitentiary where Pierre Arnot now lived. Where Gamache had put him.

His intention, after he'd spoken to the priest and looked at the register, had been to drive straight back to Montréal. Instead, he found himself tempted here. Drawn here. By Pierre Arnot.

They were just a few hundred meters apart, and with Arnot were all the answers.

Gamache was more and more convinced that whatever was coming to a head, Arnot had started it. But Gamache also knew that Arnot would not stop it. That was up to Gamache and the others.

While tempted to confront Arnot, he would not betray his promise to Thérèse. He started his car, put it in gear and drove away. But instead of heading back to Montréal, he turned in the other direction, back to the church. Once there, he parked by the rectory and knocked on the door.

"You again," said the priest, but he didn't seem unhappy.

"*Désolé, mon père,*" said Gamache, "but did Isidore live in his own home until his death?"

"He did."

"He cooked and cleaned and cut firewood himself?"

"The old generation," smiled the priest. "Self-sufficient. Took pride in that. Never asked for help."

"But the older generation often had help," said Gamache. "At least in years past. The family looked after the parents and grandparents."

"True."

"So who looked after Isidore if not his children?"

"He had help from one of his brothers-in-law."

"Is he still here? Can I speak with him?"

"No. He moved away after Isidore died. Old Monsieur Ouellet left him the farm, as thanks I guess. Who else was he going to give it to?"

"But he's not living at the farm now?"

"No. Pineault sold it and moved to Montréal, I think."

"Do you have his address? I'd like to talk with him about Isidore and Marie-Harriette and the girls. He'd have known them all, right? Even their mother."

Gamache held his breath.

"Oh yes. She was his sister. He was the girls' uncle. I don't have his address," said Father Antoine, "but his name's André. André Pineault. He'd be an old man now himself."

"How old would he be?"

Père Antoine thought. "I'm not sure. We can check the parish records if you like, but I'd say he'd be well into his seventies. He was the youngest of that generation, quite a few years younger than his sister. The Pineaults were a huge family. Good Catholics."

262

"Are you sure he's alive?"

"Not sure, but he isn't here." The priest looked past Gamache, toward the graveyard. "And where else would he go?"

Home. No longer the farmhouse but the grave.

THIRTY-ONE

⁓

The technician handed Gamache the report and the tuque. "Done."

"Anything?"

"Well, there were three significant contacts on that hat. Besides your own DNA, of course." He looked at Gamache with disapproval, having contaminated the evidence.

"Who're the others?"

"Well, let me just say that more than three people have handled it. I found traces of DNA from a bunch of people and at least one animal. Probably incidental contact years ago. They picked it up, might've even worn it, but not for long. It belonged to someone else."

"Who?"

"I'm getting to that."

The technician gave Gamache an annoyed look. The Chief held out his hand, inviting the man to get on with it.

"Well, as I said, there were three significant contacts. Now, one's an outlier, but the other two are related."

The outlier, Gamache suspected, was Myrna, who'd held the hat, and even tried to put it on her head.

"One of the matches came from the victim."

"Constance Ouellet," said Gamache. This was no surprise, but best to have it confirmed. "And the other?"

"Well, that's where it gets interesting, and difficult."

"You said they were related," said Gamache, hoping to head off any long, and no doubt fascinating, lecture.

"And they are, but the other DNA is old."

"How old?"

"Decades, I'd say. It's difficult to get an accurate reading, but they're definitely related. Siblings, maybe."

Gamache stared at the angels. "Siblings? But could it be parent and child?"

The technician thought and nodded. "Possible."

"Mother and daughter," said Gamache, almost to himself. So they were right. The MA stood for Ma. Marie-Harriette had knitted six hats. One for each of her daughters and herself.

"No," said the technician. "Not mother and daughter. Father and daughter. The old DNA is almost certainly male."

"Pardon?"

"I can't be one hundred percent sure, of course," said the technician. "It's there in the report. The DNA was from hair. I'd say that hat belonged to a man, years ago."

Gamache returned to his office.

The department was deserted. Even Lacoste had gone. He'd called her from his parked car outside the rectory and asked her to find André Pineault. Now, more than ever, Gamache wanted to speak with the man who'd known Marie-Harriette. But, more than that, Pineault had known Isidore and the girls.

Father and daughter, the technician had said.

Gamache could see Isidore with his arms out, blessing his children. The look of surrender on his face. Was it possible he wasn't blessing them, but asking for forgiveness?

Then shall forgiven and forgiving meet again.

Is that why none had married? Is that why none had returned, except to make sure he was really dead?

Is that why Virginie had killed herself?

Is that why they hated their mother? Not for what she'd done, but what she'd failed to do? And was it possible that the state, so arrogant and high-handed, had in fact saved the girls by taking them from that grim farm-house?

Gamache remembered the joy on Constance's face as her father laced up her skates. Gamache had taken it at face value, but now he wondered. He'd investigated enough cases of child abuse to know the child, when put in a room with both parents, would almost always embrace the abuser.

A child's effort to curry favor. Was that what was on little Constance's face? Not real joy, but the one plastered there by desperation and practice?

266

He looked down at the hat. The key to their home. It was best not to leap to a conclusion that might be far from the truth, Gamache cautioned himself, even as he wondered if that was the secret Constance had locked away. The one she was finally willing to drag into the light.

But that didn't explain her murder. Or perhaps it did. Had he failed to see the significance of something, or make a vital connection?

More and more he felt it was essential to speak with their uncle.

Lacoste had emailed to say she'd found him, she thought. Might not be the correct Pineault, it was a common name, but his age checked out and he'd moved into the small apartment fourteen years ago. So the timing fit with Isidore's death and the sale of the farm. She'd asked if the Chief wanted her to interview Pineault, but Gamache had told her to go home herself now. Get some rest. He'd do it, on his way back to Three Pines.

On his desk he found the dossier Lacoste had left, including an address for Monsieur Pineault in east-end Montréal.

Gamache slowly swung his chair around until his back was to the dark and empty office, and looked out the window. The sun was setting. He looked at his watch. 4:17. The time the sun should be going down. Still, it always seemed too soon.

He rocked himself gently in the chair, staring out at Montréal. Such a chaotic city. Always was. But a vibrant city too. Alive and messy.

It gave him pleasure to look at Montréal.

He was contemplating doing something that might prove monumentally foolish. It was certainly not rational, but then this thought hadn't come from his brain.

The Chief Inspector gathered his papers and left, without a backward glance. He didn't bother locking his office door, didn't even bother closing it. No need. He doubted he'd be back.

In the elevator he pressed up, not down. Once there, he exited and walked decisively down the corridor. Unlike the homicide department, this one wasn't empty. And as he walked by, agents looked up from their desks. A few reached for their phones.

But the Chief paid no attention. He walked straight toward his goal. Once there, he didn't knock, but opened the door then closed it firmly behind him.

"Jean-Guy."

Beauvoir looked up from the desk and Gamache felt his heart constrict. Jean-Guy was going down. Setting.

"Come with me," Gamache said. He'd expected his voice to be normal, and was surprised to hear just a whisper, the words barely audible.

"Get out." Beauvoir's voice, too, was low. He turned his back on the Chief.

"Come with me," Gamache repeated. "Please, Jean-Guy. It's not too late."

"What for? So you can fuck with me some more?" Beauvoir turned to glare at Gamache. "To humiliate me even more? Well, fuck you."

"They stole the therapist's records," said Gamache, approaching the younger man, who looked so much older. "They know how to get into our heads. Yours, mine. Lacoste's. Everyone's."

"They? Who're 'they'? Wait, don't tell me. 'They' aren't 'you.' That's all that matters, isn't it? The great Armand Gamache is blameless. It's 'their' fault. It always is. Well, take your fucking perfect life, your perfect record and get the fuck out. I'm just a piece of shit to you, something stuck to your shoe. Not good enough for your department, not good enough for your daughter. Not good enough to save."

The last words barely made it from Beauvoir's mouth. His throat had constricted and they just scraped by. Beauvoir stood up, his thin body shaking.

"I tried . . ." Gamache began.

"You left me. You left me to die in that factory."

Gamache opened his mouth to speak. But what could he say? That he'd saved Beauvoir? Dragged him to safety. Staunched his wound. Called for help.

That it wasn't his fault?

As long as Armand Gamache lived he'd see not Jean-Guy's wound, but his face. The terror in those eyes. So afraid of dying. So suddenly. So unexpectedly. Pleading with Gamache to at least not let him die alone. Begging him to stay.

He'd clung to Gamache's hands, and to this day Gamache could feel them, sticky and warm. Jean-Guy had said nothing, but his eyes had shrieked.

Armand had kissed Jean-Guy on the forehead, and smoothed his bedraggled hair. And whispered in his ear. And left. To help the others. He was their leader. Had led them into what proved to be an ambush. He couldn't stay behind with one fallen agent, no matter how beloved.

He'd been shot down himself. Almost died. Had looked up to see Isabelle Lacoste. She'd held his eyes, and his hand, and heard him whisper. Reine-Marie.

She hadn't left him. He'd known the unspeakable comfort of not being alone in the final moments. And he'd known then the unspeakable loneliness Beauvoir must have felt.

Armand Gamache knew he'd changed. A different man was lifted from the concrete floor than had hit it. But he also knew that Jean-Guy Beauvoir had never really gotten up. He was tethered to that bloody factory floor, by pain and painkillers, by addiction and cruelty and the bondage of despair.

Gamache looked into those eyes again.

They were empty now. Even the anger seemed just an exercise, an echo. Not really felt anymore. Twilight eyes.

"Come with me now," said Gamache. "Let me get you help. It's not too late. Please."

"Annie kicked me out because you told her to."

"You know her, Jean-Guy. Better than I ever will or could. You know she can't be made to do anything. It almost killed her, but what she did was an act of love. She sent you away because she wanted you to get help for your addiction."

"They're painkillers," Beauvoir snapped. This too was an old argument. A grim dance between the men. "Prescription."

"And these?" Gamache leaned forward and took the anti-anxiety pills from Beauvoir's desk.

"They're mine." Beauvoir slapped the bottle out of Gamache's hand and the pills fell to the desk, scattering. "You've taken everything from me and left me with these." In one fluid gesture, Jean-Guy picked up the pill bottle and threw it at the Chief. "That's it. All I have left. And now you want to take them too."

Beauvoir was emaciated, trembling. But he faced the larger man.

"Did you know the other agents used to call me your bitch, because I scurried around after you?"

"They never called you that. You had their complete respect."

"Had. Had. But not anymore?" Beauvoir demanded. "I was your bitch. I kissed your ass and your ring. I was a laughingstock. And after the raid, you told everyone I was a coward—"

"Never!"

"—told them I was broken. Was useless—"

"Never!"

"Sent me to a shrink, then to rehab, like I was some fucking weakling. You humiliated me."

As he spoke, he shoved Gamache back. With each statement he pushed.

Then pushed again. Until the Chief Inspector's back hit the thin wall of Beauvoir's office.

And when there was nowhere else to go, not forward, not back, Jean-Guy Beauvoir reached under the Chief's jacket and took his gun.

And the Chief Inspector, though he could have stopped him, did nothing.

"You left me to die, then made me a joke."

Gamache felt the muzzle of the Glock in his abdomen and took a sharp breath as it pressed deeper.

"I suspended you." His voice was strangled. "I ordered you back to rehab, to help you."

"Annie left me," said Beauvoir, his eyes watering now.

"She loves you, but couldn't live with an addict. You're an addict, Jean-Guy."

As the Chief spoke, Jean-Guy leaned in further, shoving the gun deeper into Gamache's abdomen, so that he could barely breathe. But still he didn't fight back.

"She loves you," he repeated, his voice a rasp. "You have to get help."

"You left me to die," Beauvoir said, gasping for breath. "On the floor. On the fucking dirty floor."

He was crying now, leaning into Gamache, their bodies pressed together. Beauvoir felt the fabric of Gamache's jacket against his unshaven face and smelled sandalwood. And a hint of roses.

"I've come back for you now, Jean-Guy." Gamache's mouth was against Beauvoir's ear, his words barely audible. "Come with me."

He felt Beauvoir's hand shift and the finger on the trigger tighten. But still he didn't fight back. Didn't struggle.

Then shall forgiven and forgiving meet again.

"I'm sorry," said Gamache. "I'd give my life to save you."

Or will it be, as always was, / too late?

"Too late." Beauvoir's words were muffled, spoken into Gamache's shoulder.

"I love you," Armand whispered.

Jean-Guy Beauvoir leapt back and swung the gun, catching Gamache on the side of the face. He stumbled sideways against a filing cabinet, putting his arm out against the wall to stop himself from falling. Gamache turned to see Beauvoir pointing the Glock at him, his hand wavering madly.

Gamache knew there were agents on the other side of the door who could have come in. Who could have stopped this. Could stop it still. But didn't.

He straightened and held out his hand, now covered with his own blood.

"I could kill you," said Beauvoir.

"*Oui*. And maybe I deserve it."

"No one would blame me. No one would arrest me."

And Gamache knew that was true. He'd thought if he was ever gunned down, it wouldn't be in Sûreté headquarters, or at the hands of Jean-Guy Beauvoir.

"I know," the Chief said, his voice low and soft. He took a step closer to Beauvoir, who didn't retreat. "How lonely you must be."

He held Jean-Guy's eyes and his heart broke for this boy he'd left behind.

"I could kill you," Beauvoir repeated, his voice weaker.

"Yes."

Armand Gamache was face to face with Jean-Guy. The gun almost touching his white shirt, now flecked with blood.

He held out his right hand, a hand that no longer trembled, and he felt the metal.

Gamache closed his hand over Jean-Guy's hand. It felt cold. Like the gun. The two men stared at each other for a moment, before Jean-Guy released the gun.

"Leave me," Beauvoir said, all fight and most of the life gone from him.

"Come with me."

"Go."

Gamache put the gun back in his holster and walked to the door. There he hesitated.

"I'm sorry."

Beauvoir stood in the center of his office, too tired to even turn away.

Chief Inspector Gamache left, walking into a cluster of Sûreté agents, some of whom he'd taught at the academy.

Armand Gamache had always held unfashionable beliefs. He believed that light would banish the shadows. That kindness was more powerful than cruelty, and that goodness existed, even in the most desperate places. He believed that evil had its limits. But looking at the young men and women staring at him now, who'd seen something terrible about to happen and had done nothing, Chief Inspector Gamache wondered if he could have been wrong all this time.

Maybe the darkness sometimes won. Maybe evil had no limits.

He walked alone back down the corridor, pressed the down button, and in the privacy of the elevator he covered his face with his hands.

You sure you don't need a doctor?"

André Pineault stood at the door to the washroom, arms folded across his broad chest.

"No, I'll be fine." Gamache splashed more water on his face, feeling the sting as it hit the wound. Pink liquid swirled around the drain, then disappeared. He lifted his head and saw his reflection, with the jagged cut on his cheekbone, and the bruise just beginning to show.

But it would heal.

"Slipped on the ice, you say?" Monsieur Pineault handed Gamache a clean towel, which the Chief pressed to the side of his face. "I've slipped like that. Mostly in bars, after a few drinks. Other guys were slipping too. All over the place. Sometimes we're arrested for slipping."

Gamache smiled, then winced. Then smiled again.

"That ice is pretty treacherous," agreed the Chief.

"*Maudit tabarnac*, you speak the truth," said Pineault, leading the way down the hall into the kitchen. "Beer?"

"*Non, merci.*"

"Coffee?" It was offered without enthusiasm.

"Perhaps some water."

Had Gamache asked for piss, Pineault could not have been less enthusiastic. But he poured a glass and got out ice cubes. He plopped one in the water and wrapped the rest in a tea towel. He gave both to the Chief.

Gamache traded the hand towel for the ice, and pressed that to his face. It felt immediately better. Clearly André Pineault had done this before.

The older man popped a beer open, pulled out a chair, and joined Gamache at the laminate table.

"So, *patron*," he said, "you wanted to talk about Isidore and Marie-Harriette? Or the girls?"

When Gamache had rung the doorbell, he'd introduced himself and explained he wanted to ask some questions about Monsieur et Madame Ouellet. His authority, however, was undermined by the fact he looked like he'd just lost a bar brawl.

But André Pineault didn't seem to find that at all unusual. Gamache had tried to clean himself up in the car, but hadn't done a very good job of it. Normally he'd have gone home to change, but time was short.

Now, sitting in the kitchen, sipping cool water, with half his face numb, he was beginning to feel human, and competent, again.

Monsieur Pineault sat back in his chair, his chest and belly protruding. Strong, vigorous, weathered. He might be over seventy by the calendar, but he seemed ageless, almost immortal. Gamache couldn't imagine anyone or anything felling this man.

Gamache had met many Québécois like this. Sturdy men and women, raised to look after farms and forests and animals, and themselves. Robust, rugged, self-sufficient. A breed now looked down upon by more refined city types.

Fortunately men like André Pineault didn't much care. Or, if they did, they simply slipped on ice, and took the city man down with them.

"You remember the Quints?" Gamache asked, and lowered the ice pack to the kitchen table.

"Hard to forget, but I didn't see much of them. They lived in that theme park place the government built for them in Montréal, but they came back for Christmas and for a week or so in the summer."

"Must've been exciting, having local celebrities."

"I guess. No one really thought of them as local, though. The town sold souvenirs of the Ouellet Quints and named their motels and cafés after them. The Quint Diner, that sort of thing. But they weren't local. Not really."

"Did they have any friends close by? Local kids they hung out with?"

"Hung out?" asked Pineault with a snort. "Those girls didn't 'hang out.' Everything they did was planned. You'd have thought they were the queens of England."

"So no friends?"

"Only the ones the film people paid to play with them."

"Did the girls know that?"

"That the kids were bribed? Probably."

Gamache remembered what Myrna had said about Constance. How she ached for company. Not her ever-present sisters, but just one friend, who didn't have to be paid. Even Myrna had been paid to listen. But then Constance had stopped paying Myrna. And Myrna hadn't left her.

"What were they like?"

"OK, I guess. Stuck to themselves."

"Stuck up?" Gamache asked.

Pineault shifted in his chair. "Can't say."

"Did you like them?"

Pineault seemed flummoxed by the question.

"You must've been about their age . . ." Gamache tried again.

"A little younger." He grinned. "I'm not that old, though I might look it."

"Did you play with them?"

"Hockey, sometimes. Isidore would get up a team when the girls were home for Christmas. Everyone wanted to be Rocket Richard," said Pineault. "Even the girls."

Gamache saw the slight change in the man.

"You liked Isidore, didn't you?"

André grunted. "He was a brute. You'd have thought he was pulled from the ground, like a big dirty old stump. Had huge hands."

Pineault spread his own considerable hands on the kitchen table and looked down, smiling. Like Isidore, André's smile was missing some teeth, but none of the sincerity.

He shook his head. "Not one for conversation. If I got five words out of him the last ten years of his life, I'd be surprised."

"You lived with him, I understand."

"Who told you that?"

"The parish priest."

"Antoine? Fucking old lady, always gossiping, just like when he was a kid. Played goalie, you know. Too lazy to move. Just sat there like a spider in a web. Gave us the willies. And now he lords it over that church and practically charges to show tourists where the Quints were baptized. Even shows them the Ouellet grave. 'Course, nobody much cares anymore."

"After they were grown up they never came back to visit their father?"

"Antoine tell you that as well?"

Gamache nodded.

"Well, he's right. But that was OK. Isidore and I were just fine. He milked the cows the day he died, you know. Almost ninety and practically dropped dead in the milk bucket." He laughed, realizing what he'd said. "Kicked the bucket."

Pineault took a swig of beer and smiled. "Hope it runs in the family. It's how I'd like to die." He looked around the small, neat kitchen and remembered where he was. And how he was likely to die. Though Gamache suspected facedown in a bucket of milk was probably not as much fun as it sounded.

"You helped around the farm?" Gamache asked.

Pineault nodded. "Also did the cleaning and cooking. Isidore was pretty good with the outdoor stuff, but hated the inside stuff. But he liked an orderly home."

Gamache didn't have to look around to know André Pineault also liked one. He wondered if years with the exacting Isidore had rubbed off, or if it came naturally to the man.

"Luckily for me his favorite meal was that spaghetti in a can. The alphabets one. And hot dogs. At night we played cribbage or sat on the porch."

"But you wouldn't talk?"

"Not a word. He'd stare across the fields and so would I. Sometimes I'd go into town, to the bar, and when I got back he'd still be there."

"What did he think about?"

Pineault pursed his lips, and looked out the window. There was nothing to see. Just the brick wall of the building next door.

"He thought about the girls." André brought his eyes back to Gamache. "The happiest moment of his life was when they were born, but I don't think he ever really got over the shock."

Gamache remembered the photograph of young Isidore Ouellet looking wild-eyed at his five daughters wrapped in sheets and dirty towels and dish rags.

Yes, it had been a bit of a shock.

But a few days later there was Isidore, cleaned up like his daughters. Scrubbed for the newsreels. He held one of his girls, a little awkwardly, a little unsure, but so tenderly. So protectively. Deep in those tanned, strapping arms. Here was a rough farmer not schooled, yet, in pretense.

Isidore Ouellet had loved his daughters.

"Why didn't the girls visit him when they got older?" Gamache asked.

"How'm I supposed to know? You'll have to ask them."

Them? thought Gamache.

"I can't."

"Well, if you've come to me for their address, I don't have it. Haven't seen or heard from them in years."

Then André Pineault seemed to twig. His chair gave a long, slow scrape on the linoleum as he pushed back from the table. Away from the Chief Inspector.

"Why're you here?"

"Constance died a few days ago." He watched Pineault as he spoke. So far there was no reaction. The large man was simply taking it in.

"I'm sorry to hear it."

But Gamache doubted that. He might not be happy about the news, but neither was he unhappy. As far as the Chief could tell, André Pineault didn't care either way.

"So how many are left?" Pineault asked.

"None."

"None?" That did seem to surprise him. He sat back and grabbed his beer. "Well, that's it then."

"It?"

"The last of them. No more Quints."

"You don't seem upset."

"Look, I'm sure they were very nice girls, but as far as I could see a pile of *merde* dropped on Isidore and Marie-Harriette the moment they were born."

"It was what their mother prayed for," Gamache reminded him. "The whole Brother André story."

"What do you know about that?" Pineault demanded.

"Well, it's hardly a secret, is it?" asked Gamache. "Your sister visited Brother André at the Oratory. She climbed the steps on her knees to pray for children and ask for his intercession. The girls were born the day after Frère André died. It was a big part of their story."

"Oh, I know," said Pineault. "The Miracle Babies. You'd have thought Jesus Christ had delivered them himself. Marie-Harriette was just a poor farmer's wife who wanted a family. But I'll tell you something." Pineault leaned his thick body closer to Gamache. "If God did that, he must'a hated her."

"Did you read the book by Dr. Bernard?" Gamache asked.

He'd expected Pineault to get angry, but instead he grew quiet and shook his head.

"Heard about it. Everyone did. It was a bunch of lies. Made Isidore and Marie-Harriette out to be dumb farmers, too stupid to raise their own children. Bernard heard about the visit to Brother André and turned it into some Hollywood crap. Told the newsreels, the reporters. Wrote about it in his book. Marie-Harriette wasn't the only one to go to the Oratory for Brother André's blessing. People still do. No one talks about all the others climbing those stairs on their Goddamned knees."

"The others didn't give birth to quintuplets."

"Lucky them."

"You didn't like the girls?"

"I didn't know them. Every time they came home, there were cameras and nannies and that doctor and all sorts of people. At first it was fun, but then it became . . ." he looked for the word. "*Merde*. And it turned every-one's lives into *merde*."

"Did Marie-Harriette and Isidore see it that way?"

"How would I know? I was a kid. What I do know is that Isidore and Marie-Harriette were good, decent people just trying to get by. Marie-Harriette wanted to be a mother more than anything, and they didn't let her. They took that from her, and from Isidore. That Bernard book said they'd sold the girls to the government. It was bullshit, but people believed it. Killed her, you know. My sister. Died of shame."

"And Isidore?"

"Got even quieter. Didn't smile much anymore. Everyone whispering be-hind his back. Pointing him out. He stayed pretty close to home after that."

"Why didn't the girls visit the farm once they grew up?" Gamache asked. He'd asked before and been rebuffed, but it was worth another try.

"They weren't welcome and they knew it."

"But Isidore wanted them to come, to look after him," said Gamache.

Pineault grunted with laughter. "Who told you that?"

"The priest, Father Antoine."

"What does he know? Isidore wanted nothing more to do with the girls. Not after Marie-Harriette died. He blamed them."

"And you didn't keep in touch with your nieces?"

"I wrote to tell them their father was dead. They showed up for the fu-neral. That was fifteen years ago. Haven't seen them since."

"Isidore left the farm to you," said Gamache. "Not to the girls."

"True. He'd washed his hands of them."

Gamache brought the tuque from his pocket and put it on the table. For the first time in quite a few minutes, he saw a genuine smile on André's face.

"You recognize it."

He picked it up. "Where'd you find it?"

"Constance gave it to a friend, for Christmas."

"Funny kind of present. Someone else's tuque."

"She described it as the key to her home. Do you know what she might've meant by that?"

Pineault examined the hat, then returned it to the table. "My sister made a tuque for all the kids. I don't know whose this is. If Constance was giving it away it probably belonged to her, don't you think?"

"And why would she call it the key to her home?"

"*Câlice*, I don't know."

"This tuque didn't belong to Constance." Gamache tapped it.

"Then one of the others, I guess."

"Did you ever see Isidore wearing it?"

"You must've fallen harder on the ice than you think," he said with a snort. "That was sixty years ago. I can't remember what I wore, never mind him, except that he wore plaid shirts summer and winter, and they stank. Any other questions?"

"What did the girls call their mother?" Gamache asked, as he got up.

"*Tabarnac*," Pineault swore. "Are you sure you're all right?"

"Why do you ask?"

"You've started asking stupid questions. What did the girls call their mother?"

"Well?"

"How the fuck should I know? What does anyone call their mother?"

Gamache waited for the answer.

"Mama, of course," said André.

They hadn't gone two paces before Pineault stopped.

"Wait a minute. You said Constance died, but that doesn't explain the questions. Why're you asking all this?"

Gamache was wondering when Pineault would get around to asking. It had taken the older man quite a while, but then he was probably distracted by the stupid questions.

"Constance didn't die a natural death."

"How did she die?" He was watching Gamache with sharp eyes.

"She was murdered. I'm with homicide."

"*Maudit tabarnac*," muttered Pineault.

"Can you think of anyone who might have killed her?" Gamache asked.

André Pineault thought about that and slowly shook his head.

Before he left the kitchen, Gamache noticed Pineault's dinner waiting on the counter.

A can of Alphagetti and hot dogs.

THIRTY-TWO

⁓

The snow plows were out, with their flashing lights, as Gamache drove over the Champlain Bridge, off the island of Montréal.

The rush hour traffic was bumper to icy bumper and Gamache could see a massive plow in his rearview mirror, also trapped in traffic.

There was nothing to do but crawl along. His face had begun to throb but he tried to ignore it. Harder to ignore was how it had happened. But, with effort, he shifted his thoughts to his interview with André Pineault, the only person alive who knew the Quints, and their parents. He'd created in Gamache's mind an image of bitterness, of loss, of poverty beyond economics.

The Ouellet home should have been filled with screaming kids. Instead, there were just Marie-Harriette and Isidore. And a home stuffed with innuendo and legend. Of a miracle granted. Then sold. Of girls saved from grinding poverty and greedy parents.

A myth had been created. To sell tickets and films and meals at the Quint Diner. To sell books and postcards. To sell the image of Québec as an enlightened, progressive, God-fearing, God-pleasing country.

A place where the deity strolled among them, granting wishes to those on bended, bloody knee.

The thought stirred something in Gamache's mind, as he watched impatient drivers try to cut between lanes, thinking they could get through the bumper-to-bumper traffic faster. That a miracle, reserved for the other lane, would suddenly occur and all the cars ahead would disappear.

Gamache watched the road, and thought of miracles and myths. And how Myrna described that moment when Constance had first admitted she wasn't a Pineault at all, but one of the Ouellet Quints.

Myrna had said it was as though one of the Greek gods had materialized.

279

Hera. And later, Thérèse Brunel had pointed out that Hera wasn't just any goddess, but the chief female. Powerful and jealous.

Myrna had protested, saying it was just a name she'd pulled out of the air. She could have said Athena or Aphrodite. Except she hadn't. Myrna had named solemn and vengeful Hera.

The question that Gamache turned over and over in his mind was whether Constance wanted to tell Myrna about something done to her. Possibly by her father. Or something she'd done, or they'd all done, to someone else.

Constance had a secret. That much was obvious. And Gamache was all but certain she was finally ready to tell it, to drop the albatross at Myrna's feet.

Suppose Constance Ouellet had gone to someone else first? Someone she knew she could trust. Who could that be? Was there anyone, besides Myrna, Constance might consider a confidant?

The fact was there really wasn't anyone else. The uncle, André, hadn't seen them in years and hardly seemed a fan. There were the neighbors, who were all kept at a polite distance. The priest, Père Antoine, if Constance was inclined to a confession or an intimate chat to save her soul, seemed to consider them as commodities and nothing more. Neither human nor divine.

Gamache went back over the case. Over and over. And what kept coming to him was the question of whether Marie-Constance Ouellet was really the last of her kind. Or had one of them escaped. Faked her death, changed her name. Made a life for herself.

It would have been far easier back in the fifties and sixties. Even the seventies. Before computers, before the need for so much documentation.

And if one of the Quints still lived, could she have killed her sibling to keep her quiet? To keep her secret?

But what was that secret? That one sister still lived? That she'd faked her death?

Gamache stared at the brake lights ahead, his face bathed in the glowing red lights, and he remembered what Father Antoine had said. They'd have to have buried someone.

Was that the secret? Not that one of the sisters lived, but that someone else must have died, and been buried.

He completely forgot he was on the bridge, meters from the long drop to the slushy river. His mind was now occupied by this puzzle. Again he went back over the case, looking for some elderly woman. Almost eighty. There were a few elderly men. The priest, Father Antoine. The uncle, André Pineault. But no women, except Ruth.

For a moment Gamache toyed with the thought that Ruth was indeed a missing Quint. Not an imaginary sister, as Ruth had claimed, but a real one. And maybe that explained why Constance had visited Ruth, had formed a bond with the embittered old poet who'd written a seminal poem about the death of whom? Virginie Ouellet.

Was it possible? Could Ruth Zardo be Virginie? Who hadn't thrown herself down the stairs, but down a rabbit hole, and popped up in Three Pines?

As much as he liked the idea, he was forced to dismiss it. Ruth Zardo, for all her snarling demands for privacy, was actually fairly transparent in her life. Her family had moved to Three Pines when Ruth was a child. As much fun as it would be to arrest Ruth for murder, he had to grudgingly give up that idea.

But then another thought settled. There was one other elderly woman on the periphery of the case. The neighbor. The one who lived with her husband, next door, and who'd been invited onto the porch for lemonade. Who'd befriended, as much as that was possible, the very private sisters.

Could she be Virginie? Or even Hélène? Escaping the life of a Ouellet Quint? Tunneling out through the grave?

And he realized they only had the neighbor's word for it that she hadn't been invited further into the home. Perhaps she was more than a neighbor. Perhaps it was no coincidence the sisters had moved into that home.

Gamache was finally off the bridge. He took the first exit and pulled off the road to call Lacoste.

"The medical records check out, Chief," she said from her home. "It's possible they were forged, but we both know that's a lot more difficult than it sounds."

"Dr. Bernard could have arranged for it," said Gamache. "And we know the weight of the government was behind the Ouellet Quints. And that might explain why the death certificate was so vague, saying it was an accident, but hinting at possible suicide."

"But why would they agree to such a thing?"

It was, Gamache knew, a good question. He looked at the dry cheese sandwich on the seat next to him. The white bread curled up slightly on the cellophane. The snow was piling up on the windshield and he watched the wipers swish it away.

Why would Virginie want to fake her death, and why would Bernard and the government help?

"I think we know why Virginie would want to do it," said Gamache. "She seemed the most damaged by the public life."

Lacoste was quiet, thinking. "And the neighbor, if she really is Virginie, is married. Maybe Virginie knew the only hope for a normal life was to start again, fresh. As someone else."

"What's her name?"

He heard clicking as Lacoste brought up the file. "Annette Michaud."

"If she is Virginie, then Bernard and the government must have helped her," said Gamache, musing out loud. "Why? They probably wouldn't have done it willingly. Virginie must have had something on them. Something she was threatening to tell."

He thought again of that little girl, locked out of her home. Turning a wretched face to the newsreel camera, begging for help.

If he was right, that meant Virginie Ouellet, one of the miracles, was also a murderer. Perhaps a double murderer. One years ago that let her escape, and one days ago, to keep her secret.

"I'll interview her again tonight, *patron*," said Lacoste.

In the background Gamache could hear shrieks of laughter from Lacoste's young children and he looked at his dashboard clock. Six thirty. A week before Christmas. Through the half moon of cleared snow on his windshield he saw an illuminated plastic snowman and icicle lights out in front of the service station.

"I'll go," he said. "Besides, it's closer for me. I'm just across the bridge."

"It'll already be a long night, Chief," said Lacoste. "Let me go."

"It'll be a long night for both of us, I think," said Gamache. "I'll let you know what I find. In the meantime, try to find out as much as you can about Madame Michaud and her husband."

He hung up and turned his car back toward Montréal. Toward the congested bridge. As he slowly made his way back into the city he thought about Virginie. Who might have escaped, but just to the house next door.

Gamache exited the bridge and negotiated the smaller back roads until he arrived at the Ouellet home. Dark. A hole in the cheerful Christmas neighborhood.

He parked his car and looked at the Michaud house. The walk had been shoveled, and one of the trees in the front yard was decked out in bright Christmas bulbs. Lights were on, though the curtains were drawn. The house looked warm, inviting.

A home like any other on the street. One among equals.

Is that what the famous Quints had yearned for? Not celebrity, but company? To be normal? If so, and if this was a long-lost Quint, she'd achieved it. Unless she'd killed to do it.

Gamache rang the doorbell, and it was answered by a man in his early eighties, Gamache guessed. He opened the door without hesitation, without worry that whoever was on the other side might wish him wrong.

"*Oui?*"

Monsieur Michaud wore a cardigan and gray flannels. He was neat and comfortable. His moustache was white and trimmed and his eyes were without suspicion. In fact, he looked at Gamache as though expecting the best, not the worst.

"Monsieur Michaud?"

"*Oui?*"

"I'm one of the officers investigating what happened next door," said Gamache, bringing out his Sûreté ID. "May I come in?"

"But you've been hurt."

The voice came from behind Michaud and now the elderly man stepped back and his wife stepped forward.

"Come in," said Annette Michaud, reaching out to Gamache.

The Chief had forgotten about his face and bloody shirt and now he felt badly. The two elderly people were looking at him with concern. Not for themselves, but for him.

"What can we do?" Monsieur Michaud asked, as his wife led them into the living room. A Christmas tree was decorated, its lights on. Beneath it some gifts were wrapped, and two stockings hung off the mantel. "Would you like a bandage?"

"No, no, I'm fine. *Merci*," Gamache assured them. At Madame Michaud's prompting he gave her his heavy coat.

She was small and plump and wore a housedress with thick stockings and slippers.

The home smelled of dinner, and Gamache thought of the dry cheese sandwich, still uneaten, in the cold car.

The Michauds sat on the sofa, side by side, and looked at him. Waiting.

Two less likely murderers would be hard to find. But Gamache, in his long career, had arrested more unlikely killers than obvious ones. And he knew the strong, wretched emotions that drove the final blow could live anywhere. Even in these nice people. Even in this quiet home with the scent of pot roast.

"How long have you lived in this neighborhood?" he asked.

"Oh, fifty years," said Monsieur Michaud. "We bought the home when we married in 1958."

"1959, Albert," said Madame.

Virginie Ouellet had died July 25, 1958. And Annette Michaud arrived here in 1959.

"No children?"

"None," said Monsieur.

Gamache nodded. "And when did your neighbors move in, the Pineault sisters?"

"That would've been twenty-three years ago," said Monsieur Michaud.

"So accurate," said Gamache with a smile.

"We've been thinking about them, of course," said Madame. "Remembering them."

"And what do you remember?"

"They were perfect neighbors," she said. "Quiet. Private. Like us."

Like us, thought Gamache, watching her. She was indeed about the right age and right body type. He didn't ask if she had the right temperament to kill. It wasn't about that. Most murderers were themselves surprised by the crime. Surprised by the sudden passion, the sudden blow. The sudden shift that took them from good, kindly people to killers.

Had she planned it, or was it a surprise to both her and Constance? Had she gone over there, only to discover Constance's intention to return to the village, to tell Myrna everything, not out of spite, not to hurt her sister, but to finally free herself.

Virginie had been freed by a crime, Constance would be freed by the truth.

"You were friends?" Gamache asked.

"Well, friendly. Cordial," said Madame Michaud.

"But they invited you over for drinks, I understand."

"A lemonade, once. That hardly makes a friendship." Her eyes, while still warm, were also sharp. As was her brain.

Gamache leaned forward and concentrated fully on Madame Michaud.

"Did you know that they were the Ouellet Quints?"

Both Michauds sat back. Monsieur Michaud's brows shot up, surprised. But Madame Michaud's brows descended. He was feeling, she was thinking.

"The Ouellet Quints?" she repeated. "The Ouellet Quints?" This time with the emphasis on "the."

Gamache nodded.

"But that's not possible," said Albert.

"Why not?" asked Gamache.

Michaud sputtered, his brain tripping over his words. He turned to his wife. "Did you know this?"

"Of course not. I'd have told you."

Gamache sat back and watched them try to absorb this information. They seemed genuinely shocked, but were they shocked at the news, or the news that he knew?

"You never suspected?" he asked.

They shook their heads, still apparently unable to speak. For this generation it really would have been akin to hearing their neighbors were Martians. Something both familiar and alien.

"I saw them once," said Monsieur Michaud. "My mother took us to their home. They came out every hour on the hour and walked around the fence, waving to the crowds. It was thrilling. Show him what you've got, Annette."

Madame Michaud got to her feet, and both men rose as well. She returned a minute later.

"Here. My parents bought this for me in a souvenir shop."

She held out a paperweight, with a photo of the pretty little cottage and the five sisters in front.

"My parents took me to see them too, right after the war. I think my father had seen some terrible things and he wanted to see something hopeful."

Gamache looked at the paperweight, then handed it back.

"They really did live next door?" asked Monsieur Michaud, finally grasping what Gamache had said. "We knew the Quints?"

He turned to his wife. She didn't seem pleased. Unlike her husband, she seemed to remember why Gamache was there.

"Her death couldn't have been because she was a Quint, could it?" she asked.

"We don't know."

"But it was so long ago," she said, holding his eyes.

"What was?" Gamache asked. "They might have grown up, might have changed their name, but they would always be the Quints. Nothing could change that."

They stared at each other while Monsieur Michaud muttered, "I can't believe it. The Quints."

Armand Gamache left the warmth of their home. The aroma of pot roast was embedded in his coat and followed him out the door and into his car.

He drove back across the Champlain Bridge, the traffic now thinned as the worst of the rush hour ended. He wasn't sure he'd gotten any closer to the answer. Was he creating his own myth? The missing Quint? The one who rose from the dead? Another miracle.

W here is he now?" Francoeur asked.

"He's over the Champlain Bridge," said Tessier. "And heading south. I think he's heading back down to that village."

Francoeur leaned back in his chair and regarded Tessier, but the Inspector knew that look. He wasn't really seeing him; the Chief Superintendent was mulling something over.

"Why does Gamache keep going back to that village? What's in that place?"

"According to his case file, the Quint, the one who was killed, had friends there."

Francoeur nodded, but in an abstract way. Thinking.

"Are we sure it's Gamache?" Francoeur asked.

"It's him. We're tracking his cell phone and car. When he left here he went to see some fellow named"—Tessier consulted his notes—"André Pineault. Then he called Isabelle Lacoste, I have the transcript here. He then returned to the home where the murder happened and spoke to the neighbor. He just left. He seems focused on the case."

Francoeur pursed his lips and nodded. They were in his office, the door closed. It was almost eight in the evening, but Francoeur wasn't ready to go home. He had to make sure everything was set. Every detail was taken care of. Every contingency thought of. The only blip on an otherwise clear horizon was Armand Gamache. But now Tessier was saying that blip had disappeared into that village, into the void.

Francoeur knew he should be relieved, but a sick feeling had settled into his stomach. Maybe he was so used to being locked together with Gamache, so used to the struggle, he couldn't see that the fight was over.

Francoeur wanted to believe it. But Sylvain Francoeur was a cautious man, and while the evidence said one thing, his insides told him something else.

If Armand Gamache went over the edge, it wouldn't be willingly. There'd be claw marks all the way over. This was a trick, somehow. He just didn't know how.

It's too late, he reminded himself. But the worry remained.

"When he was here at headquarters, he went to see Jean-Guy Beauvoir," said Tessier.

Francoeur sat forward. "And?"

As Tessier described what happened, Francoeur felt himself relax.

There were the claw marks. How perfect this was. Gamache had pushed Beauvoir and Beauvoir had pushed Gamache.

And both men had finally fallen.

"Beauvoir won't be any trouble," said Tessier. "He'll do anything we say now."

"Good."

There was one more thing Francoeur needed Beauvoir to do.

"There's something else, sir."

"What?"

"Gamache went to the SHU," said Tessier.

Francoeur's face went ashen. "Why the hell didn't you tell me that first?"

"Nothing happened," Tessier rapidly assured him. "He stayed in his car."

"Are you sure?" Francoeur's eyes drilled into Tessier.

"Absolutely certain. We have the security tapes. He just sat there and stared. The Ouellets are buried nearby," Tessier explained. "He was in the area. That's why he went."

"He went to the SHU because he knows," said Francoeur. His eyes, no longer on Tessier, were flicking around, as though moving from thought to thought. Trying to follow a fast-moving foe.

"*Merde*," he whispered, then his eyes focused back on Tessier. "Who else knows about this?"

"No one."

"Tell me the truth, Tessier. No bullshit. Who else did you tell?"

"No one. Look, it doesn't matter. He didn't even get out of the car. Didn't call the warden. Didn't call anyone. He just sat there. How much could he know?"

"He knows Arnot's involved," shouted Francouer, then reined himself in and took a deep breath. "He's made that connection. I don't know how, but he has."

"He might suspect," said Tessier, "but even if he knows about Arnot, he can't know it all."

Francoeur again shifted his eyes from Tessier and looked into the distance. Scanning.

Where are you, Armand? You haven't given up at all, have you? What's going on in that head of yours?

But then another thought occurred to Francoeur. Maybe like the failure of the dam plan, and the death of Audrey Villeneuve, and even Tessier's people missing the river with her body, maybe this was a godsend too.

It meant that while Gamache had figured out the Arnot connection, that was as far as he'd gotten. Tessier was right. Arnot was not enough. Gamache might suspect Arnot was involved, but he didn't know the full picture.

Gamache was standing in front of the right door, but he hadn't yet found the key. Time was now on their side. It was Gamache who'd run out of it.

"Find him," said Francoeur.

When Tessier didn't answer, Francoeur looked at him. Tessier glanced up from his BlackBerry.

"We can't."

"What do you mean?" Francoeur's voice was now low, completely in control. The panic gone.

"We followed him," Tessier assured his boss. "But then the signal disappeared. I think that's a good thing," he hurriedly said.

"How can losing Chief Inspector Gamache with only hours to go, after he's clearly connected Arnot to the plan, be a good thing?"

"The signal didn't die, it just disappeared, which means he's in an area without satellite coverage. That village."

So he hadn't doubled back.

"What's the village called?" he asked.

"Three Pines."

"You're sure Gamache is there?"

Tessier nodded.

"Good. Keep monitoring."

If he's there, thought Francoeur, he's as good as dead. Dead and buried in a village that didn't even register. Gamache was no threat to them there.

"If he leaves, I need to know immediately."

"Yessir."

"And tell no one about the SHU."

"Yessir."

Francoeur watched Tessier leave. Gamache had been close. So close. Within meters of finding out the truth. But had stopped short. And now they had Gamache cornered, in some forgotten little village.

That must've smarted," said Jérôme Brunel, stepping back from an examination of Gamache's face and eyes. "There's no concussion."

"Shame," said Thérèse, sitting at the kitchen table watching. "Might've knocked some sense into him. Why in the world would you confront Inspector Beauvoir? Especially now?"

"It's difficult to explain."

"Try."

"Honestly, Thérèse, can it matter at this stage?"

"Does he know what you're doing? What we're doing?"

"He doesn't even know what he's doing," Gamache said. "He's no threat."

Thérèse Brunel was about to say something, but seeing his face, the bruise and the expression, she decided not to.

Nichol was upstairs, sleeping. They'd already eaten, but saved some for Gamache. He carried a tray with soup and a fresh baguette, pâté and cheeses into the living room and set it in front of the fire. Jérôme and Thérèse joined him there.

"Should we wake her up?" Gamache asked.

"Agent Nichol?" asked Jérôme, with some alarm. "We only just got her down. Let's enjoy the peace."

It was odd, thought Gamache as he ate the lentil soup, that no one thought to call Nichol by her first name. Yvette. She was Nichol or Agent Nichol.

Not a person, certainly not a woman. An agent, and that was all.

When dinner and the dishes were done, they took their tea back to the living room. Where normally they'd have had a glass of wine with their dinner, or a cognac after, none of them considered it.

Not that night.

Jérôme looked at his watch. "Almost nine. I think I'll try to get some sleep. Thérèse?"

"I'll be up in a moment."

They watched Jérôme haul himself up the stairs, then Thérèse turned to Armand.

"Why did you go to Beauvoir?"

Gamache sighed. "I had to try, one more time."

She looked at him for a long moment. "You mean one last time. You think you won't get another chance."

They sat quietly for a moment. Thérèse kneaded Henri's ears while the shepherd moaned and grinned.

"You did the right thing," she said. "No regrets."

"And you? Any regrets?"

"I regret bringing Jérôme into this."

"I brought him in," said Gamache. "Not you."

"But I could've said no."

"I don't think any of us believed it would come to this."

Superintendent Brunel looked around the living room, with its faded slipcovers and comfortable armchairs and sofas. The books and vinyl records and old magazines. The fireplace, and the windows looking to the dark back garden in one direction and the village green in the other.

She could see the three huge pine trees, Christmas lights bobbing in the slight breeze.

"If it had to come to this, this's a pretty good place to wait for it."

Gamache smiled. "True. But of course, we're not waiting. We're taking the fight to them. Or Jérôme is. I'm just the muscle."

"Of course you are, *mon beau*," she said in her most patronizing tone.

Gamache watched her for a moment. "Is Jérôme all right?"

"You mean, is he ready?" asked Thérèse.

"*Oui.*"

"He won't let us down. He knows it all depends on him."

"And on Agent Nichol," Gamache pointed out.

"*Oui.*" But it was said without conviction.

Even drowning people, Gamache realized, when tossed a life preserver by Nichol, hesitated. He couldn't blame them. He did too.

He hadn't forgotten seeing her in the B and B when she had no business being there. No business, that is, of theirs. But there was clearly another agenda she was following.

No. Armand Gamache had not forgotten that.

After Thérèse Brunel had gone upstairs, Gamache put another log on the fire, made a fresh pot of coffee, and took Henri for a walk.

Henri bounced ahead, trying to catch the snowballs Gamache was throwing to him. It was a perfect winter night. Not too cold. No wind. The snow was still falling, but more gently now. It would stop before midnight, Gamache thought.

He tipped his head back, opened his mouth, and felt the huge flakes hit his tongue. Not too hard. Not too soft.

Just right.

He closed his eyes and felt them hit his nose, his eyelids, his wounded cheek. Like tiny kisses. Like the ones Annie and Daniel used to give him, when they were babies. And the ones he gave them.

He opened his eyes and continued his walk slowly around and around the pretty little village. As he passed homes, he looked through the windows throwing honey light onto the snow. He saw Ruth bent over a white plastic table. Writing. Rosa sat on the table, watching. Maybe even dictating.

He walked around the curve of the green and saw Clara reading by her fireplace. Curled into a corner of her sofa, a blanket over her legs.

He saw Myrna, moving back and forth in front of her window in the loft, pouring herself a cup of tea.

From the bistro he heard laughter and could see the Christmas tree, lit and cheerful in the corner, and patrons finishing late dinners, enjoying drinks. Talking about their days.

He saw Gabri in the B and B, wrapping Christmas gifts. The window must have been open slightly, because he heard Gabri's clear tenor singing "The Huron Carol." Rehearsing for the Christmas Eve service in the little church.

As Gamache walked, he hummed it to himself.

Every now and then a thought about the Ouellet murder entered his head. But he chased it out. Ideas came to mind about Arnot, and Francoeur. But he chased those away too.

Instead he thought about Reine-Marie. And Annie. And Daniel. And his grandchildren. About what a very fortunate man he was.

And then he and Henri returned to Emilie's home.

While everyone slept, Armand stared into the fire, thinking. Going over and over the Ouellet case in his mind.

Then, just before eleven, he started making notes. Pages and pages.

The fire died in the hearth, but he didn't notice.

Finally, he placed what he'd written into envelopes and put on his coat and boots and hat and mitts. He tried to wake Henri, but the shepherd was snoring and muttering and catching snowballs in his dreams.

And so he'd gone out alone. The homes of Three Pines were dark now. Everyone sound asleep. The lights on the huge trees were off and the snow had stopped. The sky was again filled with stars. He dropped two envelopes through a mail slot and returned to Emilie's home with one regret. That he hadn't had the chance to get Christmas gifts for the villagers. But he thought they'd understand.

An hour later, when Jérôme and Thérèse came downstairs, they found Gamache asleep in the armchair, Henri snoring at his feet. A pen in his hand and an envelope, addressed to Reine-Marie, on the floor where it had slid off the arm of the chair.

"Armand?" Thérèse touched his arm. "Wake up."

Gamache snapped awake, almost hitting Thérèse with his head as he sat up straight. It took him just a moment to gather his wits.

Nichol came clomping down the stairs, not really disheveled since she was rarely "sheveled."

"It's time," said Thérèse. She seemed almost jubilant. Certainly relieved. The wait was over.

THIRTY-THREE

Agent Nichol crawled under the desk, her hands and knees on the dusty floor. Picking up the cable, she guided it to the metal box.

"Ready?"

Up above, Thérèse Brunel looked at Armand Gamache. Armand Gamache looked at Jérôme Brunel. And Dr. Brunel did not hesitate.

"Ready," he said.

"Are you sure this time?" came the petulant voice. "Maybe you want to think about it over a nice hot chocolate."

"Just do it, for chrissake," snapped Jérôme.

And she did. There was a click, then her head appeared from beneath the desk. "Done."

She crawled out and took her seat beside Dr. Brunel. In front of them was equipment Jane Neal, the last teacher to sit at that desk, could not have imagined. Monitors, terminals, keyboards.

Once again Gamache gave Jérôme the access code, and he typed, and typed until there was just one more key to hit.

"There's no going back after this, Armand."

"I know. Do it."

And Jérôme Brunel did. He hit enter.

And . . . nothing happened.

"This's an old setup," said Nichol, a little nervously. "It might take a moment."

"I thought you said it would be ultra fast," said Jérôme, a touch of panic creeping around the edges of his words. "It needs to be fast."

"It will be." Nichol was rapidly hitting keys on her terminal. Like clog dancing on the computer.

"It's not working," said Jérôme.

"Fuck," said Nichol, pushing herself away from the desk. "Piece of crap."

"You brought it," said Jérôme.

"Yeah, and you refused to test it last night."

"Stop," said Gamache, holding up his hand. "Just think. Why isn't it working?"

Ducking under the desk again, Nichol removed and reattached the satellite cable.

"Anything?" she called.

"Nothing," Jérôme replied, and Nichol returned to her chair. They both stared at their screens.

"What could be the problem?" Gamache repeated.

"*Tabarnac,*" said Nichol, "it could be anything. This isn't a potato peeler, you know."

"Calm down and walk me through this."

"All right." She tossed her pen onto the desk. "It could be a bad connection. Some fault in the cable. A squirrel could've chewed through a wire—"

"The likely reasons," said Gamache. He turned to Jérôme. "What do you think?"

"I think it's probably the satellite dish. Everything else is working fine. If you want to play FreeCell, knock yourself out. The problem only occurs when we try to connect."

Gamache nodded. "Do we need a new dish?"

He hoped, prayed, the answer was . . .

"No. I don't think so," said Jérôme. "I think it has snow on it."

"You're kidding, right?" said Thérèse.

"He might be right," Nichol conceded. "A blizzard could pack snow into the dish and screw up the reception."

"But the snow we had yesterday wasn't a blizzard," said the Chief.

"True," said Jérôme. "But there was a lot of it, and if Gilles tilted the dish almost straight up, it would be a perfect bowl, to catch what fell."

Gamache shook his head. It would be poetic, that state-of-the-art technology could be paralyzed by snowflakes, if it wasn't so serious.

"Call Gilles," he said to Thérèse. "Have him meet me at the dish."

He threw on his outdoor gear, grabbed a flashlight, and headed into the darkness.

It was more difficult to find the path through the woods than he'd expected—it was dark and the trail had all but filled in with snow. He pointed his flashlight here and there, hoping he was at the right spot.

Eventually he found what were now simply soft contours in an otherwise flat blanket of snow. The trail. He hoped. He plunged in.

Yet again he felt snow tumble down his boots and begin to soak his socks. He shoved his legs forward through the deep snow, the light he carried bouncing off trees and lumps that would be bushes in the spring.

He finally reached the sturdy old white pine, with the wooden rungs nailed into her trunk. He caught his breath, but only for a moment. Each minute counted now.

Being thieves in the night depended on the night. And it was slipping away. In just a few hours people would wake up. Go in to work. Sit at monitors. Turn them on. There'd be more eyes to see what they were doing.

The Chief looked up. The platform seemed to twirl away from him, lifting higher and higher into the tree. He looked down at the snow and steadied himself against the rough bark.

Turning the flashlight off, he stuck it in his pocket, and with one last deep breath he grabbed the first rung. Up, up he climbed. Quickly. Trying to outrun his thoughts. Faster, faster, before he lost his nerve and the fear he'd exhaled found him again in the cold, dark night.

He'd climbed this tree once before, a few years earlier. It had horrified him even then, and that had been on a sunny autumn day. Never would he have dreamed he'd have to go back up those rickety rungs, when they were covered in ice and snow. At night.

Grip, pull up, step up. Grab the next rung. Pull himself up.

But the fear had found him and was clawing at his back. At his brain.

Breathe, breathe, he commanded himself. And he gasped in a deep breath.

He didn't dare stop. He didn't dare look up. But finally he knew he had to. Surely he was almost there. He paused for a moment and tilted his head back.

The wooden platform was still a half dozen rungs away. He almost sobbed. He could feel himself growing light-headed, and the blood draining from his feet and hands.

"Keep going, keep going," he whispered into the rough bark.

The sound of his own voice comforted him, and he reached for the next wooden slat, barely believing he was doing it. He began to hum to himself, the last song he'd heard. "The Huron Carol."

He began to sing it, softly.

"*Twas in the moon of wintertime,*" he exhaled into the tree, "*when all the birds had fled.*"

The carol was more spoken than sung, but it calmed his frantic mind just enough.

"*That mighty Gitchi Manitou sent angel choirs instead.*"

His hand banged against the old wooden platform, and without hesitation he scrambled through the hole and lay flat on his stomach, his cheek buried in the snow, his right arm around the tree trunk. His heavy breath propelled snowflakes away, in a tiny blizzard. He slowed his breathing, afraid of hyperventilating, then crept to his knees and crouched low as though something just over the edge might reach up and yank him over.

But Gamache knew the enemy wasn't just over the edge. It was on the platform with him.

Pulling the flashlight from his pocket, he turned it on. The dish was locked on a small tripod, which Gilles had screwed to the railing of the hunting blind.

It was pointing up.

"Oh, Christ," said Gamache, and briefly wondered how bad Francoeur's plan could really be. Maybe they didn't have to stop it. Maybe they could go back to bed and pull the covers up.

"*Twas in the moon of wintertime,*" he mumbled as he moved forward, on his knees. The platform felt like it was tilting and Gamache felt himself pitching forward, but he shut his eyes, and steadied himself.

"*Twas in the moon of wintertime,*" he repeated. Get the snow off the dish, and get down.

"Armand."

It was Thérèse, standing at the foot of the tree.

"*Oui,*" he called down, and turned the flashlight in that direction.

"Are you all right?"

"Fine," he said, and scrambled as far from the edge as possible, his boots scraping at the snow. His back banged against the tree and he grabbed at it. Not for fear he'd fall, but the fear that had been clawing at him as he climbed had finally wrapped itself around him. And was dragging him to the edge.

Gamache was afraid he'd throw himself over.

He pressed his back harder against the trunk.

"I called Gilles, but he can't be here for half an hour." Her voice came to him out of the darkness.

The Chief cursed himself. He should have asked Gilles to stay with them, in case this very thing happened. Gilles had offered the night before and he'd told him to go home. And now the man was half an hour away, when every moment counted.

Every moment counted.

The words cut through the shriek in his head. Cut through the fear, cut through the comforting carol.

Every moment counts.

Letting go of the tree, he jammed the flashlight into the snow, pointed at the satellite dish, and moved forward on his hands and knees, as fast as he could.

At the wooden railing, he stood up and looked into the satellite dish. It was filled with snow. He dropped his gloves to the platform and carefully, rapidly, scooped the snow out of it. Trying not to knock it off its beam. Trying not to dislodge the receptor at the very center of the dish.

Finally, it was done and he lunged away from the edge, and back to the tree, putting his arms around it, grateful there was no one to see him doing it. But honestly, at that stage Chief Inspector Gamache didn't care if the image went viral. He wasn't going to let go of that tree.

"Thérèse," he called, and heard the fear in his voice.

"Here. Are you sure you're all right?"

"The snow's off the dish."

"Agent Nichol's on the road," said Thérèse. "When Jérôme connects she'll turn her flashlight on and off."

Gamache, still gripping the tree, turned his head and stared across the treetops toward the road. All he saw was darkness.

"*Twas in the moon of wintertime*," he whispered to himself. "*When all the birds had fled.*"

Please, Lord, please.

"*Twas in the moon of winter—*"

And then he saw it.

A light. Then the darkness. Then a light.

They were connected. It had begun.

Is it working?" Thérèse asked as soon as they opened the door of the old schoolhouse.

"Perfectly," said Jérôme, his voice almost giddy. He typed in a few instructions and images popped up and disappeared, and new ones came on. "Better than I'd imagined."

Gamache looked at his watch. One twenty.

The countdown had begun.

"Holy shit," said Nichol, her eyes round and bright. "It works."

Chief Inspector Gamache tried to ignore the surprise in her voice.

"What now?" Thérèse asked.

"We're in the national archives," Jérôme reported. "Agent Nichol and I talked about it and decided to split up. Double our chances of finding something."

"I'm going in through a terminal in a school library in Baie-des-Chaleurs," said Nichol. On seeing the surprise in their faces, she lowered her eyes and mumbled, "I've done this before. Best way to snoop."

While Jérôme and Thérèse seemed surprised, Gamache was not. Agent Nichol was born to the shadows. To the margins. She was a natural snooper.

"And I'm going in through the Sûreté evidence room in Schefferville," said Jérôme.

"The Sûreté?" asked Thérèse, looking over his shoulder. "Are you sure?"

"No," he admitted. "But our only advantage is to be bold. If they trace us back to some Sûreté outpost, it might just confuse them long enough for us to disappear."

"You think so?" asked Gamache.

"It confused you."

Gamache smiled. "True."

Thérèse also smiled. "Off you go then, and don't forget to play dirty."

Thérèse and Gamache had brought Hudson's Bay blankets from Emilie's home, and the two made themselves useful by putting them up at the windows. It would still be obvious that someone was in the schoolhouse, but it would not be obvious what they were doing.

Gilles arrived and brought in more firewood. He fed chopped logs into the stove, which began pouring out good heat.

For the next couple of hours, Jérôme and Nichol worked almost in silence. Every now and then they'd exchange words and phrases like 418s. Firewalls. Symmetric keys.

But for the most part they worked quietly, the only sounds in the schoolhouse the familiar tapping of keys, and the muttering of the woodstove.

Gamache, Gilles, and Henri had returned to Emilie's home and brought back bacon and eggs, bread and coffee. They cooked on the woodstove, filling the room with the aroma of bacon, wood smoke and coffee.

But so great was Jérôme's concentration that he didn't seem to notice. He and Nichol talked about packets and encryption. Ports and layers.

298

When breakfast was put beside them the two barely looked up. Both were immersed in their own world of NIPS and countermeasures.

Gamache poured himself a coffee and leaned against the old map by the window, watching. Resisting the temptation to hover.

It reminded him a little of the rooms of his tutors at Cambridge. Papers piled high. Notepads, scribbled thoughts, mugs of cold tea and half-eaten crumpets. A stove for heat, and the scent of drying wool.

Gilles sat in what they'd begun to call his chair, at the door of the school-house. He ate his breakfast and, when he was finished, poured himself an-other mug of coffee and tipped his chair back against the door. He was their deadbolt.

Gamache looked at his watch. It was twenty-five past four. He felt like pacing, but knew that would be annoying. He was dying to ask how it was going, but knew that would simply break their concentration. Instead, he called Henri and put on his coat, thrusting his hands deep in his pockets. In his panic, he'd left his gloves on the platform with the satellite dish and he sure as hell wasn't going back for them.

Thérèse and Gilles joined them, and they went for a stroll.

"It's going well," said Thérèse.

"Yes," said Gamache. It was cold, and clear, and crisp, and dark. And quiet.

"Like thieves in the night, eh?" he said to Gilles.

The woodsman laughed. "I hope I didn't insult you with that."

"Far from it," said Thérèse. "It's a natural career progression. Sorbonne, chief curator at the Musée des beaux-arts, Superintendent of the Sûreté, and finally, the pinnacle. A thief in the night." She turned to Gamache. "And all thanks to you."

"You're welcome, madame." Gamache bowed solemnly.

They sat on a bench and looked across to the schoolhouse, with its light muffled by the blankets. The Chief wondered if the quiet woodsman be-side him knew what would happen if they failed. And what would happen if they succeeded.

In either case, all hell was about to break loose. And come here.

But at this moment there was peace and quiet.

They walked back to the schoolhouse, Henri leaping and catching the snowballs, only to have them disappear in his mouth. But he never stopped trying, never gave up.

An hour later Jérôme and Nichol tripped their first alarm.

THIRTY-FOUR

The phone woke Sylvain Francoeur and he grabbed the receiver before the second ring.

"What is it?" he said, instantly alert.

"Sir, it's Charpentier here. There's been a breach."

Francoeur got up on one elbow and waved his wife to go back to sleep.

"What's that mean?"

"I'm monitoring network activity, and someone's accessed one of the restricted files."

Francoeur turned on the light, put on his glasses, and looked at the clock on the bedside table. The bright red numbers said 5:43 A.M. He sat up.

"How serious?"

"I don't know. It might not be anything. As instructed, I called Inspector Tessier and he told me to call you."

"Good. Now explain what you saw."

"Well, it's complicated."

"Try."

Charpentier was surprised that so much menace could be contained in such a small word. He tried. His best. "Well, the firewall's not showing that an unauthorized connection's been made, but . . ."

"But what?"

"It's just that someone opened the file and I'm not sure who it was. It was within the network, so the person had access codes. It's probably someone within the department, but we can't be sure."

"Are you telling me you don't know if there has been a breach?"

"I'm saying there has, but we don't know if it's someone from the outside, or one of our own. Like a house alarm. At first it's hard to tell if it's an intruder or a raccoon."

"A raccoon? You're not seriously comparing the Sûreté's state-of-the-art, multimillion-dollar security system with a house alarm?"

"I'm sorry, sir, but it's only because it's state-of-the-art that we found it at all. Most systems and programs would've missed it. But it's so sensitive, sometimes we find things that don't need to be found. That aren't threats."

"Like a raccoon?"

"Exactly," said the agent, obviously regretting the analogy. It had worked with Tessier, but Chief Superintendent Francoeur was a whole other beast. "And if there is an intruder, we can't yet tell if there's a purpose, or if it's just some hacker out to make trouble, or even someone who wandered in by mistake. We're working on it."

"By mistake?" They'd installed this system last year. Brought in the finest software designers and Internet architects to create something that couldn't be breached. And now this agent was saying some idiot might have wandered in by mistake?

"It happens more often than people realize," said Charpentier unhappily. "I don't think it's serious, but we're treating it as though it is, just in case. And the file they've accessed doesn't appear all that important."

"Which file?" Francoeur asked.

"Something about the construction schedule for Autoroute 20."

Francoeur stared at the curtains drawn in front of the bedroom window. There was a slight flutter as the cold air came into his home.

The file seemed so trivial, so far from anything that could threaten their plan, but Francoeur knew that file for what it was. For what it contained. And now someone was sniffing around.

"Check it out," he said, "and call me back."

"Yessir."

"What is it?" asked Madame Francoeur, watching her husband head to the bathroom.

"Nothing, just a little trouble at work. Go back to sleep."

"Are you getting up?"

"Might as well," he said. "I'm awake now, and the alarm'll go off soon anyway."

But alarms were already going off for Chief Superintendent Francoeur.

They've seen us," said Jérôme. "I tripped the alarm here."

"Where?" asked Gamache, pulling up a chair.

Jérôme showed him.

302

"Construction files?" asked Gamache, and turned to Thérèse. "Why would the Sûreté have any files on road construction, never mind ones that are secure?"

"No reason. It isn't our jurisdiction. The roads, yes, but not repairing them. And it certainly wouldn't be confidential."

"They must be looking for us," said Nichol. Her voice was calm. Just reporting facts.

"To be expected," said Jérôme, his voice also calm.

On his monitor they saw files open and close. Appear and disappear.

"Stop typing," said Nichol.

Jérôme lifted his hands off the keyboard and they hovered in midair.

Gamache stared at the monitor. He could almost see lines of code appear, grow, then contract.

"Have they found you?" Jérôme asked Nichol.

"No. I'm over in another file. It's also about construction, but it's old. Can't be important."

"Wait," said Gamache, dragging his chair over to her monitor. "Show me."

Sir, it's Charpentier again."

"*Oui*," said Francoeur. He'd showered and dressed and was about to head in. It was now just after six.

"It was nothing."

"Are you sure?"

"Certain. I had a good look around. Ran all sorts of scans and couldn't find any unauthorized access to our network. It happens fairly often, as I said. A ghost in the machine. I'm sorry to disturb you with this."

"You did the right thing." While relieved, Francoeur still didn't relax. "Put more agents on to monitor."

"Another shift starts at eight—"

"I mean now." The voice was sharp, and Charpentier responded immediately.

"Yessir."

Francoeur hung up, then punched in Tessier's number.

These are shift reports," said Gamache. "From a company called Aqueduct. They're thirty years old. Why're you looking at them?"

"I was following a trail. A name popped up in another file and I followed it here."

"What name?" Gamache asked.

"Pierre Arnot."

"Show me." Gamache leaned in and Nichol scrolled down. Gamache put on his glasses and scanned the pages. There were lots of names. It appeared to be work schedules and soil reports and things called loads. "I don't see it."

"Neither did I," admitted Nichol. "But it's associated with this file."

"Maybe it's another Pierre Arnot," said Jérôme from his desk. "It's not an uncommon name."

Gamache hummed to show he'd heard, but his attention was taken by the file. There was no actual mention of any Arnot.

"How could his name be attached to this file, but not appear in it?" Gamache asked.

"It could be hidden," said Nichol. "Or an outside reference. Like your name might be attached to a file on balding, or licorice pipes."

Gamache glanced at Jérôme, who'd given a snort.

Still, he understood. Arnot's name didn't need to appear in the file to be somehow associated with it. Somewhere down the line, there was a connection.

"Keep going," said the Chief, and got up.

Charpentier's very good at what he does," Tessier reassured Francoeur over the phone. He too was dressed and ready for work. As he'd put on his socks he'd realized that when he took them off that night, everything would have changed. His world. The world. Certainly Québec. "If he says it's nothing, then that's what it was."

"No." The Chief Superintendent wanted to be convinced, to be reassured. But he wasn't. "There's something wrong. Call Lambert. Get her in."

"Yessir." Tessier hung up and dialed Chief Inspector Lambert, the head of Cyber Crimes.

Gamache stirred the embers with a fresh log, making more room, then he shoved it in and put the cast-iron cap back on.

"Agent Nichol," he said after a few moments. "Can you look up that company?"

"What company?"

"Aqueduct." He walked across to her. "Where you followed Pierre Arnot."

"But he never showed up. It must've been another Arnot or a coinciden-tal contact. Something not very significant."

"Maybe, but please find out what you can about Aqueduct." He was leaning over her, one hand on the desk, the other on the back of her chair.

She huffed, and the screen she was looking at flew away. A few clicks later and images of old Roman bridges and water systems leapt onto the monitor. Aqueducts.

"Satisfied?" she demanded.

"Scroll down," he said, and he studied the list of references to "Aque-duct."

There was a company that studied sustainability. There was a band by that name.

They went through a few pages, but the information became less and less relevant.

"Can I go back now?" asked Nichol, weary of amateurs.

Gamache stared at the screen, still feeling uneasy. But he nodded.

The full shift was called in and every desk and monitor in the Cyber Crimes division had an agent at it.

"But, ma'am," Charpentier was appealing to his boss, "it was a ghost. I've seen thousands of them—so have you. I took a good look, just to be sure. Ran all the security scans. Nothing."

Lambert turned from her shift commander to the Chief Superintendent.

Unlike Charpentier, Chief Inspector Lambert knew how critical the next few hours would be. The firewalls, the defenses, the software programs she herself had helped design needed to be impenetrable. And they were.

But Francoeur's concern had transferred itself to her. And now she won-dered.

"I'll make sure myself, sir," she said to Francoeur. He held her eyes, staring at her for so long, and so intently, that both Tessier and Charpen-tier exchanged glances.

Finally Francoeur nodded.

"I want your people to not just guard, do you understand? I want them to go looking."

"For what?" Charpentier asked, exasperated.

"For intruders," snapped Francoeur. "I want you to hunt down whoever might be out there. If there's someone trying to get in, I want you to find them, whether they're a raccoon or a ghost or an army of the undead. Got it?"

"Got it, sir," said Charpentier.

Gamache reappeared at Nichol's elbow.

"I made a mistake," he said right into her ear.

"How?" She didn't look at him but continued to concentrate on what she was doing.

"You said it yourself, the file was old. That means Aqueduct was an old company. It might not exist anymore. Can you find it in archives?"

"But if it doesn't exist how can it matter?" asked Nichol. "Old file, old company, old news."

"Old sins have long shadows," said Gamache. "And this is an old sin."

"More fucking quotes," mumbled Nichol under her breath. "What does it even mean?"

"It means, what started small three decades ago might have grown," said the Chief, not looking at Agent Nichol, but reading her screen. "Into something . . ."

He looked at Nichol's face, so flat, so repressed.

". . . big," he finally said. But the word that had actually come to mind was "monstrous."

"We've found the shadow." Gamache turned back to the screen. "Now it's time to find the sin."

"I still don't understand," she muttered, but Gamache suspected that wasn't true. Agent Yvette Nichol knew a great deal about old sins. And long shadows.

"This'll take a few minutes," she said.

Gamache joined Superintendent Brunel, who was standing by the window looking at her husband, clearly longing to watch over his shoulder.

"How's Jérôme doing?"

"Fine, I suppose," she said. "I think tripping that alarm shook him. It came earlier than he expected. But he recovered."

Gamache looked at the two people seated at their desks. It was almost seven thirty in the morning. Six hours since they'd begun.

He walked over to Jérôme. "Would you like to stretch your legs?"

Dr. Brunel didn't answer at once. He stared at the screen, his eyes following a line of code.

"*Merci*, Armand. In a few minutes," Jérôme said, his voice distant, distracted.

"Got it," said Nichol. "Les Services Aqueduct," she read, and Gamache and Thérèse leaned over her shoulder to look. "You were right. It's an old company. Looks like it went bankrupt."

"What did it do?"

"Engineering mostly, I think," she said.

"Roads?" asked Thérèse, thinking of the alarm Jérôme had tripped. The road construction schedule.

There was a pause while Nichol searched some more. "No. Looks like it's sewage systems, mostly in outlying areas. This was in the days when there was government money to clean up the waste dumped into rivers."

"Treatment plants," said Gamache.

"That sort of thing," said Nichol, concentrating on the screen. "But see here," she pointed to a report. "Change of government. Contracts dried up, and the company went under. End of story."

"Wait," said Jérôme sharply, from the next desk. "Stop what you're doing."

Gamache and Thérèse froze, as though their own movement would somehow betray them. Then Gamache stepped over to Jérôme.

"What is it?"

"They're out looking," he said. "Not just guarding the files, but now they're looking for us."

"Did we trip another alarm?" Thérèse asked.

"Not that I know of," said Jérôme, and glanced over at Nichol, who checked her equipment and shook her head.

Dr. Brunel turned back to his monitor and stared. His pudgy hands were raised over his keyboard, ready to leap into action if need be. "They're using a new program, one I haven't seen before."

No one moved.

Gamache stared at the screen and half expected to see a specter crawl out from the corner of the monitor. Picking up pieces of text, files, documents, and looking beneath. For them.

He held his breath, not daring to move. In case. He knew it was irrational, but he didn't want to risk it.

"They won't find us," said Nichol, and Gamache admired her bravado. She'd spoken in a whisper and Gamache was glad of it. Bravado was one thing, but silence and stillness were the first rules of hiding. And he was under no illusions. That's what they were doing.

Gilles seemed to sense it too. He tipped his chair forward quietly and put his feet on the ground, but stayed where he was, guarding the door, as though their pursuers would come through there.

"Do they know we've hacked them?" asked Thérèse.

Jérôme didn't answer her.

"Jérôme," Thérèse repeated. She too had lowered her voice to an urgent hiss. "Answer me."

"I'm sure they've seen our signature."

"What does that mean?" asked Gamache.

"It means they probably know something's up," said Nichol. "The encryption will hold." But for the first time she sounded unsure, like she was talking to herself. Convincing herself.

And now Gamache understood. The hunter and his hounds were sniffing around. They'd picked up a scent, and now were trying to decide what they'd found. If anything.

"Whoever's on the other end isn't some hack," said Jérôme. "This isn't some impatient kid, this's a seasoned investigator."

"What do we do now?" asked Thérèse Brunel.

"Well, we can't just sit here," said Jérôme. He turned to Nichol. "Do you really think your encryption is hiding us?"

She opened her mouth but he cut her off. He'd had too much experience with arrogant young residents during grand rounds at the hospital not to recognize someone who would rather eat a juicy lie than an unpalatable truth.

"For real," he cautioned, and held her pasty gaze.

"I don't know," she admitted. "But we might as well believe it."

Jérôme laughed and got up. He turned to his wife. "Then the answer to your question is that the encryption held and we're just fine."

"She didn't say that," said Thérèse, following him to the coffeepot on the woodstove.

"No," he admitted, pouring himself a cup. "But she's right. We might as well believe it. It changes nothing. And for what it's worth, I think they haven't a clue what we're about, even if they know we're here. We're safe."

Gamache stood behind Nichol's chair. "You must be tired. Why don't you take a break too? Splash some water on your face."

When she didn't respond, he looked at her more closely.

Her eyes were wide.

"What is it?" he asked.

"Oh, *merde*," she said under her breath. "Oh, *merde*."

"What?" Gamache looked at the monitor. UNAUTHORIZED ACCESS filled the screen.

"They found us."

THIRTY-FIVE

⁓

"I found something," Chief Inspector Lambert said into the phone. "Better come down."

Chief Superintendent Francoeur and Inspector Tessier arrived within minutes. Agents were crowded around Lambert's monitor, watching, though they scattered when they saw who'd entered the room.

"Leave," said Tessier, and they did. He closed the door and stood in front of it.

Charpentier was at another terminal in the office, his back to his boss, typing at lightning speed.

Francoeur leaned over Chief Inspector Lambert.

"Show me."

Jérôme!" Thérèse Brunel called, and joined Chief Inspector Gamache and Nichol.

"Show me," said Gamache.

"When I brought up the old Aqueduct file, I must've set off an alarm," said Nichol, her face white.

Jérôme arrived and scanned the monitor, then he reached in front of her.

"Hurry up," he said, swiftly typing in a few short commands. "Get out of that file." The error message disappeared.

"You didn't just set off an alarm, you stepped on a landmine. Jesus."

"Maybe they didn't see the message," said Nichol slowly, watching the screen.

They waited, and waited, staring at the static screen. Despite himself, Gamache realized he was looking for some being to actually appear. A shadow, a form.

"We have to go back into the Aqueduct file," he said.

"You're insane," said Jérôme. "That's where the alarm was tripped. It's the one place we need to avoid."

Gamache pulled a chair over and sat close to the elderly doctor. He looked him in the eyes.

"I know. That's why we need to go back. Whatever they're trying to hide is in that file."

Jérôme opened his mouth, then closed it again. Trying to marshal a rational argument against the inconceivable. To knowingly walk back into a trap.

"I'm sorry, Jérôme, but it's what we've been looking for. Their vulnerability. And we found it in Aqueduct. It's in there somewhere."

"But it's a thirty-year-old document," said Thérèse. "A company that doesn't even exist anymore. What could possibly be in there?"

All four of them stared at the screen. The cursor pulsed there, like a heartbeat. Like something alive. And waiting.

Then Jérôme Brunel leaned forward and started typing.

Aqueduct?" said Francoeur, stepping back as though slapped. "Erase the files."

Chief Inspector Lambert looked at him, but one glance at the Chief Superintendent's face was enough. She started erasing.

"Who is it?" Francoeur asked. "Do you know?"

"Look, I can either erase the files or chase the intruder, but I can't do both," said Lambert, her fingers flying over the keys.

"I'll take the intruder," said Charpentier, from across the office.

"Do it," said Francoeur. "We need to know."

"It's Gamache," said Tessier. "Has to be."

"Chief Inspector Gamache can't do this," said Lambert as she worked. "Like all senior officers, he knows computers, but he's not an expert. This isn't him."

"Besides," said Tessier, watching the activity. "He's in some village in the Townships. No Internet."

"Whoever this is has high-speed and huge bandwidth."

"Christ." Francoeur turned to Tessier. "Gamache was a decoy."

"So who is it?" asked Tessier.

Shit," said Nichol. "The files are being erased."

She looked at Jérôme, who looked at Thérèse, who looked at Gamache.

"We need those files," said Gamache. "Get them."

"He'll find us," said Jérôme.

"He's found us already," said Gamache. "Get them."

"She," said Nichol, also reacting swiftly. "I know who that is. It's Chief Inspector Lambert. Has to be."

"Why do you say that?" asked Thérèse.

"Because she's the best. She trained me."

"The whole entry's disappearing, Armand," said Jérôme. "You lead them away."

"Right," said Nichol. "The encryption's holding. I can see she's confused. No, wait. Something's changed. This isn't Lambert anymore. It's someone else. They've split up."

Gamache moved to Jérôme.

"Can you save some files?"

"Maybe, but I don't know which ones are important."

Gamache thought for a moment, his hand clutching the back of Jérôme's wooden chair.

"Forget the files. It all started with Aqueduct thirty years ago or more. Somehow Arnot was involved. The company went under, but maybe it didn't disappear. Maybe it just changed its name."

Jérôme looked up at him. "If I leave, there's no saving Aqueduct. They'll dismantle it all until there's no trace."

"Go. Get out. Find out what became of Aqueduct."

They're trying to save the files," said Lambert. "They know what we're doing."

"This isn't some outside hacker," said Francoeur.

"I don't know who it is," said Lambert. "Charpentier?"

There was a pause before Charpentier spoke. "I can't tell. It's not registering properly. It's like a ghost."

"Stop saying that," said Francoeur. "It's not a ghost, it's a person at a terminal somewhere."

The Chief Superintendent took Tessier aside.

"I want you to find out who's doing this." He'd dropped his voice, but the words and ferocity were clear. "Find out where they are. If not Gamache, then who? Find them, stop them, and erase the evidence."

Tessier left, in no doubt about what Francoeur had just ordered him to do.

You OK?" Gamache asked Nichol.

Her face was strained, but she gave him a curt nod. For twenty minutes she'd led the hunter astray, dropping one false trail after another.

Gamache watched her for a moment, then returned to the other desk.

Aqueduct had gone bankrupt, but as so often happened, it was reborn under another name. One company morphed into another. From sewers and waterways, to roads, to construction materials.

The Chief Inspector took a seat and continued to read the screen, trying to figure out why the Chief Superintendent of the Sûreté was desperate to keep these files secret. So far they seemed not simply benign, but dull. All about construction materials, and soil samples, and rebar and stress tests.

And then he had an idea. A suspicion.

"Can you go back to where we tripped the first alarm?"

"But that's nothing to do with this company," Jérôme explained. "It was a schedule of repairs on Autoroute 20."

But Gamache was staring at the screen, waiting for Dr. Brunel to comply. And he did. Or tried to.

"It's gone, Armand. Not there anymore."

"I have to get out, sir," said Nichol, rattled into courtesy. "I've stayed too long. They'll find me soon."

Almost there," Charpentier reported. "Another few seconds. Come on, come on." His fingers flew over the keys. "I've got you, you little shit."

"Ninety percent of the files are destroyed," said Lambert from across her office. "Not many places he can go. Do you have him?"

There was silence, except for the rapid clicking of keys.

"Do you have him, Charpentier?"

"Fuck."

The clicking stopped. Lambert had her answer.

I'm out," said Nichol, and sat back in her chair for the first time in hours. "That was too close. They almost got me."

"Are you sure they didn't?" asked Jérôme.

Nichol lugged herself forward and hit a few keys, then took a deep breath. "No. Just missed. Christ."

Dr. Brunel looked from his wife to Gamache to Nichol. Then back to Thérèse.

"Now what?"

Now what?" Charpentier asked. He was pissed off. He hated being bested, and whoever was on the other end had done just that.

It'd been close. So close that for an instant Charpentier had thought he had him. But at the last moment, poof. Gone.

"Now we call in the others and look again," said Chief Inspector Lambert.

"You think he's still in the system?"

"He didn't get what he came for." She turned back to her monitor. "So yes, I think he's still there."

Charpentier got up to go into the main room. To tell the other agents, all specialists in cyber searches, to go back in. To find the person who'd hacked into their own system. Who'd violated their home.

As he closed the door, he wondered how Inspector Lambert knew what the intruder was looking for. And he wondered what could be so important to the intruder that he'd risk everything to find it.

Now we take a break," said Gamache, getting up. His muscles were sore and he realized he'd been tensing them for hours.

"But they'll be searching for us even harder now," said Nichol.

"Let them. You need a break. Go for a walk, clear your head."

Both Nichol and Jérôme looked unconvinced. Gamache glanced at Gilles, then back at them.

"You're forcing me to do something I don't want to do. Gilles here teaches yoga in his spare time. If you're not up and headed for the door in thirty seconds, I'll order you to take a class from him. His downward dog is spectacular, I hear."

Gilles stood up, stretched, and walked forward.

"I could use some chakra work," he admitted.

Jérôme and Nichol got up and made for their parkas and the door. Gilles joined Gamache by the woodstove.

"Thanks for playing along," the Chief said.

315

"What 'playing along'? I actually teach a yoga class. Want to see?"

Gilles stood on one foot and slowly moved his other leg around, lifting his arms.

Gamache raised his brows and approached Thérèse, who was also watching.

"I'm waiting for the downward dog," she confided as she put on her coat. "You coming?"

"No. I'd like to read some more."

Superintendent Brunel followed his gaze to the terminals.

"Be careful, Armand."

He smiled. "Don't worry. I'll try not to spill coffee into it. I just want to go back over some of what Jérôme found."

She left, taking Henri with her, while Gamache pulled his chair up to the computer and started reading. Ten minutes later Gamache felt a hand on his shoulder. It was Jérôme.

"Can I get in?"

"You're back."

"We've been back for a few minutes, but didn't want to disturb you. Find anything?"

"Why did they erase that file, Jérôme? Not Aqueduct, though that's an interesting question too. But the first one you found. The construction schedule on the highway. It doesn't make sense."

"Maybe they're just erasing everything we looked at," suggested Nichol.

"Why would they take the time to do that?" asked Thérèse.

Nichol shrugged. "Dunno."

"You need to go back in," Jérôme said to Nichol. "How close did they get to you? Did they get your address?"

"The school in Baie-des-Chaleurs?" Nichol asked. "I don't think so, but I should change it anyway. There's a zoo in Granby with a big archive. I'll use that."

"*Bon*," said the Chief Inspector. "Ready?"

"Ready," said Jérôme.

Nichol turned her attention to her terminal, and Gamache turned to Superintendent Brunel.

"I think that first file was important," he said. "Maybe even vital, and when Jérôme found it, they panicked."

"But it doesn't make sense," said Superintendent Brunel. "I know the mandate of the Sûreté. So do you. We patrol the roads and bridges, even the federal ones. But we don't repair them. There's no reason for a repair dossier to be in Sûreté files, and certainly not hidden."

"And that makes it all the more likely the file had nothing to do with official, sanctioned Sûreté business." Gamache had her attention now. "What happens when an autoroute needs to be repaired?"

"It goes to tender, I expect," said Thérèse.

"And then what?"

"Companies bid," said Thérèse. "Where're you going with this, Armand?"

"You're right," said Gamache. "The Sûreté doesn't repair roads, but it does do investigations into, among other things, bid rigging."

The two senior Sûreté officers looked at each other.

The Sûreté du Québec investigated corruption. And there was no bigger target than the construction industry.

Just about every department of the Sûreté had been involved in investigating the Québec construction industry at one time or another. From allegations of kickbacks to bid rigging to organized crime involvement, from intimidation to homicide. Gamache himself had led investigations into the disappearance and presumed murder of a senior union official and a construction executive.

"Is that what this's about?" Thérèse asked, still holding Gamache's eyes. "Has Francoeur gotten himself involved with that filth?"

"Not just himself," said Gamache. "But the Sûreté."

The industry was huge, powerful, corrupt. And now, with the collusion of the Sûreté, unpoliced. Unstoppable.

Contracts worth billions were at stake. They stopped at nothing to win the contracts, to hold them, and to intimidate anyone who challenged them.

If there was an old sin and a long, dark shadow in Québec, it was the construction industry.

"*Merde*," said Superintendent Brunel under her breath. She knew it wasn't just a piece of shit they'd stepped on, but an empire of it.

"Go back in, please, Jérôme," said Gamache, quietly. He sat forward, his elbows on his knees. They finally had an idea what they were looking for.

"Where to?"

"Construction contracts. Big ones, recently awarded."

"Right." Dr. Brunel swung around and began typing. Beside him, at the other terminal, Nichol was also typing away.

"No, wait," said Gamache, putting a hand on Jérôme's arm. "Not new construction." He thought for a moment before speaking. "Look for repair contracts."

"*D'accord*," said Jérôme, and began to search.

Hello, I'm sorry to disturb you. Have I woken you up?"

"Who is this?" asked the groggy voice at the other end of the phone.

"My name's Martin Tessier, I'm with the Sûreté du Québec."

"Is this about my mother?" The woman's voice was suddenly alert. "It's five in the morning here. What's happened?"

"You think this might be about your mother?" Tessier asked, his voice friendly and reasonable.

"Well, she does work for the Sûreté," said the woman, fully awake. "When she arrived she said someone might call."

"So Superintendent Brunel's there with you, in Vancouver?" asked Tessier.

"Isn't that why you're calling? Do you work with Chief Inspector Gamache?"

Tessier didn't quite know how to answer that, didn't know what Superintendent Brunel might have told her daughter.

"Yes. He asked me to call. May I speak with her, please?"

"She said she didn't want to talk to him. Leave us alone. They were exhausted when they arrived. Tell your boss to stop bothering them."

Monique Brunel hung up, but continued to clutch the phone.

Martin Tessier looked at the receiver in his hand.

What to make of that? He needed to know if the Brunels had in fact traveled to Vancouver. Their cell phones had.

He'd had their phones monitored and traced. They'd flown to Vancouver and gone to their daughter's home. In the last couple days they'd driven around Vancouver to shops and restaurants. To the symphony.

But was it the people, or just their phones?

Tessier had been convinced they were in Vancouver, but now he wasn't so sure.

The Brunels had parted ways with their former friend and colleague, calling Gamache delusional. But someone had picked up the cyber search where Jérôme Brunel had left off. Or maybe he hadn't left off at all.

When the Brunel daughter had first answered the phone, he could hear the concern in her voice.

"Is this about my mother?" she'd asked.

Not "What's this about?" Not "Do you need to speak to my mother?"

No. They were the words of someone worried that something had happened to her mother. And you don't ask that when your parents are asleep a few feet away.

Tessier called his counterpart in Vancouver.

Wait," said Gamache. He was leaning forward, his reading glasses on, looking at the screen. "Go back, please."

Jérôme did.

"What is it, Armand?" Thérèse Brunel asked.

He looked white. She'd never seen him like that. She'd seen him angry, hurt, surprised. But never, in the years they'd worked together, had she ever seen him so shocked.

"Jesus," Gamache whispered. "It's not possible."

He had Jérôme bring up other files, apparently unrelated. Some very old, some very recent. Some based in the far north, some in downtown Montréal.

But all to do with construction of some sort. Repair work. On roads and bridges and tunnels.

Finally the Chief Inspector sat back and stared ahead of him. On the screen was a report on recent road repair contracts, but he seemed to be staring right through the words. Trying to grasp a deeper meaning.

"There was a woman," he finally said. "She killed herself a few days ago. Jumped from the Champlain Bridge. Can you find her? Marc Brault was investigating for the Montréal police."

Jérôme didn't ask why Gamache wanted to know. He went to work and found it quickly in the Montréal police files.

"Her name's Audrey Villeneuve. Age thirty-eight. Body found below the bridge. Dossier closed two days ago. Suicide."

"Personal information?" asked Gamache, searching the screen.

"Husband's a teacher. Two daughters. They live on Papineau, in east-end Montréal."

"And where did she work?"

Jérôme scrolled down, then up. "It doesn't say."

"It must," said Gamache, pushing forward, nudging Jérôme out of the way. He scrolled up and down. Scanning the police report.

"Maybe she didn't work," said Jérôme.

"It would say that," said Thérèse, leaning in herself, searching the report.

"She worked in transportation," said Gamache. "Marc Brault told me that. It was in the report and now it's gone. Someone erased it."

"She jumped from the bridge?" asked Thérèse.

"Suppose Audrey Villeneuve didn't jump." Gamache turned from the screen to look at them. "Suppose she was pushed."

"Why?"

"Why was her job erased from her file?" he asked. "She found something out."

"What?" asked Jérôme. "That's a bit of a stretch, isn't it? From some despondent woman to murder?"

"Can you go back?" Gamache ignored his comment. "To what we were looking at before?"

The construction contract files came up. Hundreds of millions of dollars in repair work for that year alone.

"Suppose this is all a lie?" he asked. "Suppose what we're looking at was never done?"

"You mean the companies took the money but never did the repairs?" asked Thérèse. "You think Audrey Villeneuve worked for one of these companies, and realized what was happening? Maybe she was blackmailing them."

"It's worse than that," said Gamache. His face was ashen. "The repair work hasn't been done." He paused to let that sink in. There materialized, in midair in the old schoolhouse, images. Of overpasses over the city, of tunnels under the city. Of the bridges. Huge great spans, carrying tens of thousands of cars every day.

None of it repaired, perhaps in decades. Instead, the money went into the pockets of the owners, of the union, of organized crime, and those who were entrusted to stop it. The Sûreté. Billions of dollars. Leaving kilometer after kilometer of roads and tunnels and bridges about to collapse.

Got 'em," said Lambert.

"Who are they?" Francoeur demanded. He'd returned to his office and was connected to the search on his own computer.

"I don't know yet, but they got in through the Sûreté detachment in Schefferville."

"They're in Schefferville?"

"No. *Tabarnac.* They're using the archives. The library grid."

"Which means?"

"They could be anywhere in the province. But we have them now. It's just a matter of time."

"We have no more time," said Francoeur.

"Well, you'll have to find it."

Can we lose them?" Thérèse asked, and her husband shook his head.

"Then ignore them," said Gamache. "We have to move forward. Get into the construction files. Dig as deep as you can. There's something planned. Not just ongoing corruption, but a specific event."

Jérôme threw away all caution and plunged into the files.

Stop him," yelled Francoeur into the phone.

On his computer a name had appeared, then in a flash it disappeared. But he'd seen it. And so had they.

Audrey Villeneuve.

He watched, aghast, as his screen filled with file after file. On construction. On repair contracts.

"I can't stop him," said Lambert. "Not until I find out where he is, where he's coming from."

Francoeur watched, powerless, as file after file was opened, tossed aside, and the intruder moved on. Ransacking, then racing ahead.

He looked at the clock. Almost ten in the morning. Almost there.

But so was the intruder.

And then, suddenly, the frantic online search stopped. The cursor throbbed on the screen, as though frozen there.

"Christ," said Francoeur, his eyes wide.

Gamache and Thérèse stared at the screen. At the name that had come up. Buried at the deepest level. Below the legitimate dossiers. Below the doctored documents. Below the fixed and the fraud. Below the thick layer of *merde.* There was a name.

Chief Inspector Gamache turned to Jérôme Brunel, who also stared at the screen. Not with the astonishment his wife and his friend felt. But with another overwhelming emotion.

Guilt.

"You knew," whispered Gamache, barely able to speak.

The blood had gone from Jérôme's face and his breathing was shallow. His lips were almost white.

He knew. Had known for days. Since he'd tripped the alarm that had sent them into hiding. He'd brought this secret with him to Three Pines. Lugged the name around with him, from the schoolhouse to the bistro to bed.

"I knew." The words were barely audible, but they filled the room.

"Jérôme?" asked Thérèse, not sure what was the greater shock. What they'd found, or what they'd found out about her husband.

"I'm sorry," he said. With an effort he pushed his chair back and it squealed on the wooden floor, like chalk on a blackboard. "I should've told you."

He looked into their faces and knew those words didn't come close to describing what he should have done. And hadn't. But their gaze had shifted from him back to the terminal, and the cursor blinking in front of the name.

Georges Renard. The Premier of Québec.

They know," said Francoeur. He was on the phone to his boss and had told him everything. "We have to move ahead with the plan. Now."

There was a pause before Georges Renard spoke.

"We can't move ahead," he said at last. His voice was calm. "Your part isn't the only element, you know. If Gamache is that close, then stop him."

"We're still working to find the intruder," said Francoeur, trying to bring his own voice, and breathing, under control. To sound both persuasive and reasonable.

"The intruder isn't critical anymore, Sylvain. He's obviously working with Gamache. Feeding him the information. If the Chief Inspector's the only one who can put it all together, then ignore the intruder and go after him. Plenty of time later to deal with the others. You said he's in some village in the Eastern Townships?"

"Three Pines, yes."

"Get him."

How long before they find us?" Gamache asked as he walked toward the door. Gilles brought his chair down as the Chief approached, so that the front legs thumped onto the floor. He stood up and pulled the chair aside.

"An hour, maybe two," said Jérôme. "Armand . . ."

"I know, Jérôme." Gamache took his coat off the peg by the door. "None of us is blameless in this. I doubt it would have mattered. We have to focus now, and move forward."

"Should we leave?" Thérèse asked, watching as Gamache put on his coat.

"There's nowhere to go."

He spoke gently, but firmly, so that they could harbor no false hope. If there was a stand to be taken, it would have to be here.

"We now know who's involved," said the Chief. "But we still don't know what they have planned."

"You think it's more than covering up hundreds of millions of dollars in graft?" asked Thérèse.

"I do," said Gamache. "That's a happy by-product. Something to keep their partners quiet. But the real goal is something else. Something they've been working on for years. It started with Pierre Arnot and ends with the Premier."

"We'll see what we can find on Renard," said Jérôme.

"No. Leave Renard," said Gamache. "The key now is Audrey Villeneuve. She found something and was killed. Find out everything you can about her. Where she worked, what she was working on. What she might've found."

"Can't we just call Marc Brault?" asked Jérôme. "He investigated her death. He'd have it in his notes."

"And someone edited his report," said Thérèse, shaking her head. "We don't know who to trust."

Gamache pulled his car keys out of his coat pocket.

"Where're you going?" Thérèse asked. "You're not leaving us?"

Gamache saw the look in her eyes. Much the same look he'd seen in Beauvoir's eyes that day in the factory. When Gamache had left him.

"I need to go."

He reached under his jacket and brought out his gun, holding it out to them.

Thérèse Brunel shook her head. "I brought my own weapon—"

"You did?" asked Jérôme.

"Did you think I worked in the cafeteria at the Sûreté?" asked Thérèse. "I've never used it, and I hope not to, but I will if I have to."

Gamache looked at the far end of the room, and Agent Nichol working on her terminal.

"Agent Nichol, walk with me to the car, please."

Her back remained turned to them.

"Agent Nichol."

Far from raising his voice, Chief Inspector Gamache had lowered it. It moved across the schoolroom, and lodged in that small back. They could see her tense.

And then she got up.

Gamache rubbed Henri's ears, then opened the door.

"Wait, Armand," said Thérèse. "Where're you going?"

"To the SHU. To speak to Pierre Arnot."

Thérèse opened her mouth to object, but realized it didn't matter. They were out in the open now. All that mattered was speed.

Gamache waited for Nichol outside, standing on the stoop of the schoolhouse.

Gabri walked across to the bistro and waved, but didn't approach. It was almost eleven in the morning, and the sun was gleaming on the snow. It looked as though the village was covered in jewels.

"What do you want?" asked Nichol, when she finally came out and the door was closed behind her.

She looked to Gamache not unlike the first Quint, shoved into the world against her will. He walked down the steps and along the path to his car and didn't look at her as he spoke.

"I want to know what you were doing in the B and B the other day."

"I told you."

"You lied to me. We haven't much time." Now he did look at her. "I made a choice that day in the woods to trust you, even though I knew you'd lied. Do you know why?"

She glared at him, her tiny face turning red. "Because you had no choice?"

"Because despite your behavior I think you have a good heart. A strange head," he smiled, "but a good heart. But I need to know now. Why were you there?"

She walked beside him, her head down, watching her boots on the snow.

They stopped beside his car.

"I followed you there to tell you something. But then you were so angry. You slammed the door in my face, and I couldn't."

"Tell me now," he asked, his voice quiet.

"I leaked the video."

The puffs of her words were barely visible before they disappeared.

The Chief's eyes widened and he took a moment to absorb the information.

"Why?" he finally asked.

Tears made warm tracks down her face, and the more she tried to stop them the more they came. "I'm sorry. I didn't do it to hurt. I felt so bad . . ."

She couldn't talk. Her throat closed around the words.

". . . my fault . . ." she managed. ". . . I told you there were six. I only heard . . ."

And now she sobbed.

Armand Gamache took her in his arms and held her. She heaved, and shook. And sobbed. She cried and cried, until there was nothing left. No sound, no tears, no words. Until she could barely stand. And still he held her and held her up.

When she pulled away, her face was streaked and her nose thick with slime. Gamache opened his parka and handed her his handkerchief.

"I told you there were only six gunmen in the factory," she finally managed, the words coming in hiccups and gasps. "I only heard four, but I added some. In case. You taught me that. To be careful. I thought I was. But there were . . ." The tears began again, but this time they flowed freely, with no effort to stop them. ". . . more."

"It wasn't your fault, Yvette," said Gamache. "You weren't to blame for what happened."

And he knew that was true. He remembered the moments in that factory. But not anything any video could capture. Armand Gamache remembered not the sights, nor the sounds. But how it felt. Seeing his young agents gunned down.

Holding Jean-Guy. Calling for the medics. Kissing him good-bye.

I love you, he'd whispered in Jean-Guy's ear, before leaving him on the cold, bloody concrete floor.

The images might one day fade, but the feelings would live forever.

"It wasn't your fault," he repeated.

"And it wasn't yours, sir," she said. "I wanted people to know. But I never stopped to think . . . The families . . . the other officers. I wanted to do it . . ."

She looked at him, her eyes begging him to understand.

"For me?" asked the Chief.

She nodded. "I was afraid you'd be blamed. I wanted them to know it wasn't your fault. I'm sorry."

He took her slimy hands and looked at her little face, blotched and wet with tears and mucus.

"It's all right," he whispered. "We all make mistakes. And yours might not have been a mistake at all."

"What do you mean?"

"If you hadn't released that video we never would've found out what Superintendent Francoeur was doing. It might turn out to be a blessing."

"Some fucking blessing," she said. "Sir."

"Yes." He smiled and got into his car. "While I'm gone I want you to research Premier Renard. His background, his history. See if you can find anything linking him with Pierre Arnot or Chief Superintendent Francoeur."

"Yessir. You know they're probably tracking your car and your cell. Shouldn't you leave your phone here and use someone else's car?"

"I'll be fine," he said. "Let me know what you find."

"If you get a message from the zoo, you'll know who it is."

It seemed about right to the Chief. He drove out of the village, aware that he'd be detected as soon as he left, and counting on it.

THIRTY-SIX

For the second time in two days, Armand Gamache pulled into the parking lot of the penitentiary, but this time he got out, slamming the car door. He wanted there to be no question that he was there. He meant to be seen and he meant to get inside. At the gate he showed his credentials.

"I need to see one of your prisoners."

A buzzer sounded and the Chief Inspector was admitted but shown no further than the waiting room. The officer on duty came out of a side room.

"Chief Inspector? I'm Captain Monette, the head guard. I wasn't told you'd be coming."

"I didn't know until half an hour ago myself," said Gamache, his voice friendly, examining the surprisingly young man standing in front of him. Monette could not have been thirty yet, and was solidly built. A linebacker.

"Something's come up in a case I'm investigating," Gamache explained, "and I need to see one of your high-security prisoners. He's in the Special Handling Unit, I believe."

Monette's brow rose. "You'll have to leave your weapon here."

Gamache had expected that, though he'd hoped his seniority would give him a pass. Apparently not. The Chief took out his Glock and glanced around. Cameras were trained on him from every corner of the sterile room.

Could the alarm have already been raised? If so, he'd know in a moment.

Gamache placed the gun on the counter. The guard signed for it and gave the slip to the Chief.

Captain Monette gestured for Gamache to follow him down the corridor.

"Which prisoner do you want to see?"

"Pierre Arnot."

The head guard stopped. "He's a special case, as you know."

Gamache smiled. "Yes, I know. I'm sorry, sir, but I really have very little time."

"I need to speak with the warden about this."

"No, you don't," said Gamache. "You're welcome to if you feel it necessary, but most head guards have the authority to grant interviews, especially to investigating officers. Unless"—Gamache examined the young man in front of him—"you haven't been given that authority?"

Monette's face hardened. "I can do it, if I choose."

"And why wouldn't you choose?" asked Gamache. His face was curious, but there was a sharpening of the eyes and tone.

The man now looked insecure. Not afraid, but unsure what to do and Gamache realized he probably hadn't been on the job for long.

"It really is very common," said the Chief, his voice softening just a little. Not a patronizing tone, but a reassuring one, he hoped.

Come on, come on, thought Gamache, mentally counting the minutes. Not long before the alarm would be raised. He'd wanted to be followed to the SHU, but not caught there.

Monette examined him, then nodded. He turned back down the hall without a word.

Doors opened then clanged behind them as they moved deeper and deeper into the high-security pen. And as they walked, Chief Inspector Gamache wondered what had happened to Monette's predecessor, and why they'd given the job of guarding some of the most dangerous criminals in Canada to someone so young and inexperienced.

Finally they entered an interview room, and Monette left Gamache alone.

He glanced around. Once again cameras were trained on him. Far from being disconcerting, his plan depended on those cameras.

He placed himself in front of the door and prepared to come face to face with Pierre Arnot for the first time in years.

Finally the door opened. Captain Monette entered first, then another guard came in escorting an older man in an orange prison uniform.

Chief Inspector Gamache looked at him. Then at the head guard.

"Who's this?"

"Pierre Arnot."

"But this isn't Arnot." Gamache walked up to the prisoner. "Who are you?"

"He's Pierre Arnot," said Monette firmly. "People change in prison. He's been here for ten years. It's him."

"I tell you," said Gamache, fighting, not totally successfully, to keep his temper in check. "This is not Pierre Arnot. I worked with him for years. I arrested the man and testified at his trial. Who are you?"

"Pierre Arnot," said the prisoner. He kept his eyes forward. His chin was covered in gray bristles and his hair was unkempt. He'd be, Gamache guessed, about seventy-five. The right age, even, roughly, the right build.

But not the right man.

"How long have you been here?" Gamache asked the head guard.

"Six months."

"And you?" He turned to the other guard, who looked surprised by the question.

"Four months, sir. I was one of your students at the Sûreté academy, but I flunked out. Got a job here."

"Come with me," Gamache said to the younger guard. "Walk me out."

"You're leaving?" asked the head guard.

Gamache looked back. "Go to your warden. Tell him I was here. Tell him I know."

"Know what?"

"He'll understand. And if you don't understand what I'm saying, if you're not in on it"—Gamache examined the head guard—"then my advice is to get up to the warden's office fast and arrest him."

The head guard stared at Gamache, uncomprehending.

"Go," Gamache shouted, and the head guard turned and left.

"Not you." Gamache grabbed the younger guard by the arm. "Lock him in here"—he gestured to the prisoner—"and come with me."

The young guard did as he was told, and followed Gamache as he strode back down the corridor.

"What's happening, sir?" the guard asked, working to keep up with the Chief Inspector.

"You've been here four months, the head guard for six. The other guards?"

"Most of us have come in the last six months."

"So Captain Monette might not be in on it," said Gamache quietly. Thinking as he walked rapidly toward the front gate.

At the final door, Gamache turned to the young guard, who now looked anxious.

"Strange things are about to happen, son. If Monette's in on it, or if he can't arrest the warden, you'll be given orders that won't seem right, and won't be."

"What should I do?"

"Guard that man they say is Arnot. Keep him alive."

"Yessir."

"Good. Speak with authority, carry yourself as though you know what you're doing. And don't do anything you know in your heart to be wrong."

The young man straightened up.

"What's your name?"

"Cohen, sir. Adam Cohen."

"Well, Monsieur Cohen, this is an unexpected day for all of us. Why did you fail out of the Sûreté academy? What happened?"

"I flunked my science exams." He paused. "Twice."

Gamache smiled reassuringly. "Fortunately, you won't be asked to do science today. Just use your judgment. No matter what orders are issued, you must only do what you know to be right. You understand?"

The boy nodded, his eyes wide.

"When this is over, I'll be back to talk to you about the Sûreté and the academy."

"Yessir."

"You'll be fine," said Gamache.

"Yessir."

But neither of them totally believed it.

At the door there was a moment's anxiety when Chief Inspector Gamache handed the slip over and waited for his gun. But finally the Glock was handed back and Gamache walked quickly to his car. No more could be learned here.

Pierre Arnot was almost certainly dead. Killed six months ago, so that that man could take his place. Arnot couldn't talk, because he was dead. His replacement couldn't talk because he knew nothing. And any guard who would recognize Arnot had been transferred out.

Arnot's disappearance told the Chief a great deal. It said that Pierre Arnot was once at the center of whatever was happening, but was no longer necessary.

Someone else had taken over. And Gamache knew who that was.

He got in the car and checked emails. There was a message from the zoo.

Georges Renard, now the Premier of Québec, had studied civil engineering at the École Polytechnique in the 1970s. His first job was with Les Services Aqueduct in the far north of Québec.

There it was. The link between Aqueduct and Renard. But why had Arnot's name been connected to Aqueduct?

Gamache read on. Renard's first job had been in La Grande, on the biggest engineering project in the world at that time. The construction of the massive hydroelectric dam.

And there it was. The link between Pierre Arnot and Georges Renard. As young men they'd worked in the same area. One policing the Cree reserve, the other building the dam that would destroy the reserve.

Is that where they'd first met? Is it possible this plan had started then? Was it forty years in gestation? A year ago a plot to bring down that same hydroelectric dam had almost succeeded. But Gamache had stopped it. It had taken him and Beauvoir and so many others into that factory.

And now the pieces were beginning to come together. How the bombers had known exactly where to hit the huge dam. It had always bothered the Chief Inspector that those young men, with their trucks filled with explosives, were able to get so far, and find the one soft spot in a monolithic structure.

This was how.

Georges Renard. The Premier of Québec now, but then a young engineer. If Renard knew how to put the dam up, he also knew how to bring it down.

Pierre Arnot, an officer on the Cree reserve then but on track to become the Chief Superintendent of the Sûreté, had created the rage and despair necessary to drive two young Cree to an act of terrible domestic terrorism. And Renard had given them the vital information.

They'd almost succeeded.

But to what end? Why would the elected leader of the province not only destroy the dam that provided power, but in doing so wipe out towns and villages downriver, killing thousands.

To what end?

Gamache had hoped Arnot could tell him. But more than the why, Gamache needed to know what the next target was. What was their Plan B? Gamache knew two things. It was soon, and it was big.

Armand Gamache had a sick feeling in the pit of his stomach.

The construction contracts to repair the tunnels, bridges, and overpasses hadn't been done. In years and years. Billions of dollars in contracts

331

had been awarded and put in pockets as the road system deteriorated, to the point of collapse.

Chief Inspector Gamache was almost certain the plan was to hurry that collapse. To bring down a tunnel. A bridge. A massive cloverleaf.

But to what end?

Again Gamache had to remind himself that the reason was far less important at the moment than the target. The attack was imminent, he knew. Within hours, almost certainly. He'd presumed the target was in Montréal, but it could also be in Quebec City. The capital. In fact, it could be anywhere in Québec.

There was one more message from the zoo, this one from Jérôme Brunel.

Audrey Villeneuve worked for the Ministry of Transportation in Montréal. Clerical.

He thought for a moment before writing the reply. Just two words. He hit send, started the car, and left the penitentiary behind.

The Granby Zoo?" asked Lambert. "They're getting in through the archives of the zoo. We've got them."

Over the speakerphone in his office Sylvain Francoeur could hear the tap, tap, tap as Chief Inspector Lambert hit keys. Rapid footsteps chasing the intruder.

He punched the speakerphone off when Tessier entered his office.

"I was on my way to that village when we picked up Gamache's vehicle and cell phone."

"He's left the village?"

Tessier nodded. "He went to the SHU. We got there a few minutes ago, but missed him."

Francoeur shot out of his chair. "He went inside?"

He was shrieking at Tessier so loudly he could feel the skin of his throat rip away. He half expected to spew flesh all over the imbecile in front of him.

"We didn't expect him to leave the village," said Tessier. "We actually thought he'd given his car and cell phone to someone else, as a decoy, to draw us away, but then we realized the car was at the SHU. We accessed the security cameras and saw it was Gamache."

"You're a fucking moron." Francoeur leaned across his desk. "Does he know?"

Francoeur was glaring at him and Tessier felt his heart stop for a moment.

Tessier nodded. "He knows the man in the SHU isn't Arnot. But that doesn't get him any closer."

Tessier himself had taken care of Arnot, as Arnot should have taken care of himself years before. A bullet to the brain.

"And where's Gamache now?" Francoeur demanded.

"Coming toward Montréal, sir. Heading for the Jacques Cartier Bridge. We're on him now. We won't lose him."

"Of course you won't fucking lose him," snapped Francoeur. "He doesn't want to be lost. He wants us to follow him."

He's heading to the Jacques Cartier Bridge into east-end Montréal, thought Francoeur, his mind racing. *Which means he's probably coming here. Are you that bold, Armand? Or that stupid?*

"There's something else, sir," said Tessier, looking down at his notebook, not daring to look into those heart-stopping eyes. "The Brunels aren't in Vancouver."

"Of course they aren't." Francoeur punched the speakerphone back on. "Lambert? Francoeur. Dr. Jérôme Brunel's the one who's hacked us."

Lambert's tinny voice came through. "No, sir. Not Brunel. He tripped the alarm a few days ago, right?"

"Right," said Francoeur.

"Well, the person I'm chasing is far more clever. Brunel might be one of the hackers, but I think I know who the other one is."

"Who?"

"Agent Yvette Nichol."

"Who?"

"She worked with Gamache for a while, but he fired her. Put her in the basement."

"Wait, I know her," said Tessier. "In that monitoring room. Awful little shithead."

"That's her," said Lambert. As she spoke they could still hear her fingers on the keyboard. Running Agent Nichol to ground. "I brought her to Cyber Crimes but she didn't work out. Too damaged. I sent her back."

"It's her?" asked Francoeur.

"I think so."

"Meet me in the sub-basement."

"Yessir."

"You find out where Gamache is going," he said to Tessier, and headed out the door. Was it possible Gamache's people had been working out of

Sûreté headquarters? They'd been here all along, right under their noses? In the sub-basement? That would explain the ultra high-speed.

And Gamache, hiding away in that village, was a decoy.

Yes, thought Francoeur as he descended to the sub-basement, it was the sort of bold move that would appeal to Gamache's ego.

Inspector Lambert was already outside the locked door in the basement when Chief Superintendent Francoeur and two other massive agents arrived.

Francoeur took Lambert a few paces down the corridor and whispered, "Could they be inside?"

"It's possible," said Lambert.

Francoeur turned to the two agents. "Knock it down."

One drew his weapon while the other kicked. There was a bang as the door flew open, to reveal a tiny room, with banks of monitors, keyboards, terminals, candy wrappers, moldy orange peels, empty soft drink cans. But otherwise empty.

Lambert sat at the desk and hit some keys.

"Nothing. She wasn't working from here. But let me check something."

She walked rapidly down the corridor to another door, unlocked it and called them over.

"What am I supposed to be seeing?" Francoeur asked.

"Old equipment confiscated from hackers. The room should be full."

It wasn't.

"What's missing?"

"Satellite dishes, cables, terminals, monitors," said Lambert, studying the near-empty storage room. "Clever little shit."

"She could be anywhere, is that what you're saying?" asked Francoeur.

"Anywhere, but probably somewhere that needs a satellite dish to connect to the Internet. She took one," said Lambert.

Francoeur knew where that was.

Dr. Brunel and Agent Nichol copied the files onto a USB flash drive and packed up all the documents.

"Come on, Agent Nichol," Superintendent Brunel called from the open door.

"Just a moment."

"Now," Thérèse Brunel snapped.

Nichol perched in her chair, ready to leave. But there was one last thing to do. She knew they'd be coming, searching her computer. And when they did, they'd find her little present. With a few final keystrokes she planted her logic bomb.

"Eat that, dickhead," she said, and logged out. It wouldn't keep the hounds away, but would give them a nasty surprise when they arrived.

"Hurry up," Superintendent Brunel called from the door. Her voice held no trace of panic, just imperative.

Dr. Brunel and Gilles had already gone, and the old schoolhouse was empty. Except for Nichol. She turned the computers off and gave them one last look. They were as close as she came to family these days. Her father, while proud of her, didn't understand her. Her relatives thought she was just weird, a sort of embarrassment.

And, to be fair, she thought the same of them. Of everyone.

But computers she understood. And they understood her. Life was simple around them. No debates, no arguments. They listened to her and did as she asked.

And these old ones, abandoned by others, considered useless, had done her proud. But now it was time to leave and to leave them behind. Superintendent Brunel held the door open, and Nichol hurried through it. Behind her Thérèse Brunel locked up. It was ridiculous to suppose an old Yale lock would stop what was coming for them, but it was a comforting conceit.

They walked back down the slope to Emilie Longpré's home. That had been Gamache's short email message.

See Emilie. And they knew what it meant.

Leave. Get out. There was nowhere safe, but there was someplace comfortable to sit and wait.

They were coming. Thérèse Brunel knew it. They all knew it.

They were coming here.

An electronic bleep sounded and Lambert checked her text message.

Charpentier lost her.

Lambert expected the Chief Superintendent to explode and was surprised when he just nodded.

"It doesn't matter."

Francoeur walked quickly back down the corridor toward the elevator.

Where's Gamache? he texted Tessier.

Jacques Cartier Bridge. Keep monitoring him?

No. That's what he wants. He wants to draw us away. He's a decoy.

He gave Tessier instructions, then returned, briefly, to his office. If Gamache was heading to Sûreté headquarters, he wouldn't find them waiting for him. It was almost certainly what Gamache wanted. He knew he was being followed, and he wanted their eyes on him. And not turning south. To that little village, so well hidden.

And now found.

I think you'd better not, Jérôme," said Thérèse, when her husband went to lay a fire in the hearth.

He stopped and nodded, then joined her on the sofa and together they watched the door. The front curtains were drawn and the lamps were turned on. Nichol sat in an armchair, also watching the door.

"What were you doing at the end there?" Thérèse asked Nichol.

"Huh?"

"On your computer, when I was trying to get you to leave. What were you doing?"

"Oh, nothing."

Now Jérôme focused on the young woman. "You were doing something on the computer?"

"I was setting a bomb," she said defiantly.

"A bomb?" Thérèse demanded, and turned to see Jérôme smiling and studying Agent Nichol.

"She means a logic bomb, don't you?"

Nichol nodded.

"It's a sort of cross between a super virus and a time bomb," he explained to his wife. "Programmed to do what?" he asked Nichol.

"Nothing good," she said, and challenged him to chastise her. But Jérôme Brunel only smiled and shook his head.

"Wish I'd thought of that."

Silence descended again as the three of them returned to staring at the closed curtains and the closed door.

Only Gilles had his back to the door. He gazed out the rear windows. Those curtains were open and Gilles could see the snow-covered garden and the woods. And the tall trees that whispered to him. Comforted him. Forgave him.

He continued to look into the forest even as the first footsteps sounded on the front verandah. The squeal of boots on hard snow.

They saw a shadow pass the curtains.

Then the footsteps stopped at the door.

And there was a knock.

THIRTY-SEVEN

—

Armand Gamache pulled into the driveway of the little home. Christmas lights hung off the eaves, a wreath was on the front door. All the seasonal decorations were in place. Except comfort and joy. Gamache wondered if the pall was obvious even to someone who didn't know what grief this home held.

He rang the doorbell.

And waited.

Superintendent Thérèse Brunel walked to the door. Her back was straight and her eyes determined. She held her gun behind her back and opened the door.

Myrna Landers stood on the verandah.

"You have to come to my place," she said quickly, looking from Thérèse to the people grouped behind her. "Hurry. We don't know when they'll arrive."

"Who?" asked Jérôme. He was stooped over, holding on to Henri's collar.

"Whoever you're hiding from. They'll find you here, but they might not look in my place."

"What makes you think we're hiding?" Nichol asked.

"Why else would you have come here?" asked Myrna, getting more and more antsy. "You didn't seem on vacation, and it wasn't for the outlet stores. When we saw you working all last night in the schoolhouse, then bringing document boxes back here, we guessed that something had gone wrong."

She studied the faces in front of her. "We're right, aren't we? They've found out where you are."

"Do you know what you're offering?" Thérèse asked.

339

"A safe place," said Myrna. "Who doesn't need that at least once in their lives?"

"The people who're looking for us don't want a simple chat," said Thérèse, holding Myrna's eyes. "They don't want to negotiate, they don't even want to threaten us. They want to kill us. And they'll kill you too, if we're found in your home. There is no safe place, I'm afraid."

She needed Myrna to understand. Myrna stood before her, clearly frightened, but determined. Like one of the Burghers of Calais, thought Thérèse, or those boys in the stained-glass window.

Myrna gave one decisive nod. "Armand wouldn't have brought you here if he didn't think we'd protect you. Where is he?" She peered into the room.

"He's leading them away," said Nichol, finally understanding why the Chief had chosen to take a car and a cell phone that would obviously be followed.

"Will it work?" Myrna asked.

"For a while, perhaps," said Thérèse. "But they'll still come looking for us."

"We thought so."

"We?"

Myrna turned to look at the road and Thérèse followed her glance. Standing on the snow-covered path were Clara, Gabri, Olivier, and Ruth and Rosa.

The end of the road.

"Come," said Myrna.

And they did.

Bonjour. My name's Armand Gamache. I'm with the Sûreté du Québec."

He spoke softly. Not in a whisper, but his voice low enough so that the girls he could see staring at him from down the corridor, behind their father, didn't hear.

Gaétan Villeneuve looked done in. Standing up only because if he fell he'd land on his children. The girls weren't yet in their teens and they watched him wide-eyed. Gamache wondered if the news he was about to bring them would help, or hurt. Or make barely a ripple in their ocean of grief.

"What do you want?" Monsieur Villeneuve asked. It wasn't a challenge. There wasn't enough energy there for a challenge. But neither was he letting the Chief Inspector across the threshold.

Gamache leaned in a few inches, toward Villeneuve. "I'm the head of homicide."

Now Villeneuve's weary eyes widened. He examined Gamache, then stepped aside.

"These are our daughters, Megan and Christianne."

Gamache noticed that Villeneuve had not yet moved to the singular.

"*Bonjour,*" he said to the girls, and smiled. Not a beam, but a warm smile before turning back to their father. "I wonder if we could speak privately."

"Go outside and play, girls," said Monsieur Villeneuve. He asked them kindly. Not an order, but a request, and they obeyed. He closed the door and walked Gamache to a small but cheerful kitchen at the back of the house.

It was tidy, all the dishes clean, and Gamache wondered if Villeneuve had done it, to keep order in the house for the girls, or if the girls had done it, to keep order for their grieving and lost father.

"Coffee?" Monsieur Villeneuve asked. Gamache accepted the offer, and while it was being poured he looked around the kitchen.

Audrey Villeneuve was everywhere. In the aroma of cinnamon and nutmeg for the Christmas cookies she must have baked, and the photos on the fridge, showing a grinning family camping, at a birthday party, at Disney World.

Crayon drawings were framed. Drawings only a parent knew were works of art.

This had been a happy home until a few days ago, when Audrey Villeneuve had left for work, and hadn't returned.

Villeneuve put the coffees on the table and the two men sat.

"I have some news for you, and some questions," said Gamache.

"Audrey didn't kill herself."

Gamache nodded. "It's not official, and I might be wrong—"

"But you don't think so, do you? You think Audrey was killed. Someone did this to her. So do I."

"Can you think who?" Gamache saw life and purpose creep back to this man. Villeneuve paused for a moment, thinking. Then shook his head.

"Had anything changed? Visitors, phone calls?"

Again Villeneuve shook his head. "Nothing like that. She'd been shorttempered for weeks. She wasn't normally like that. Something was bothering her, but that last morning she seemed better."

"Do you know why she was upset?" Gamache asked.

"I was afraid to ask . . ." He paused and looked down at his coffee. ". . . in case it was me."

"Did she keep an office or a desk here at home?"

"Over there." He nodded to a small desk in the kitchen. "But the other officers took all her papers."

"Everything?" Gamache asked, getting up and walking over to the desk. "You didn't find anything she might've hidden? May I?"

He motioned to the desk and Villeneuve nodded.

"I looked after they left. They searched the whole house." He watched as Gamache expertly, swiftly rifled the desk, and came up empty-handed.

"Computer?" asked Gamache.

"They took it. Said they'd bring it back, but they haven't. It didn't seem normal, for a . . ." He took a breath. "Suicide."

"It's not," said Gamache, returning to sit at the kitchen table. "She worked with the Ministry of Transport, right? What did she do?"

"She put reports onto the computer. Said it was actually quite interesting. Audrey likes things to be orderly. Organized. When we travel she has plans and backup plans. We used to kid her."

"Which department was she in?"

"Contracts."

Gamache said a quiet prayer before asking the next question. "What sort of contracts?"

"Specifications. When a contract was awarded the company had to report progress. Audrey entered that in the files."

"Was there a geographic area she looked after?"

He nodded. "Because she's so senior, Audrey looked after repair work in Montréal. The heavy volume area. It always struck me as ironic. I'd kid her all the time."

"About what?"

"That she worked at Transport, but hated using the highways, especially the tunnel."

Gamache grew still. "Which tunnel?"

"The Ville-Marie. She had to take it to get to work."

Gamache felt his heart begin to race. That was it. Audrey Villeneuve was afraid because she knew the repairs on the tunnel hadn't been done. The Ville-Marie ran under much of Montréal. If it collapsed, it would start a chain reaction in the métro, in the whole underground city. It would take the downtown core with it.

He got up, but was restrained by Gaétan Villeneuve's hand on his forearm.

"Wait. Who killed her?"

"I can't tell you that yet."

"Can you at least tell me why?"

Gamache shook his head. "You might be visited soon by other agents, wondering about my being here."

"I'll tell them you weren't here."

"No, don't do that. They already know. If they ask, tell them everything. What I asked, and what you answered."

"Are you sure?"

"Yes."

The two men walked to the door.

"I can tell you that your wife died trying to stop something horrible from happening. I want you and your girls to know that." He paused. "Stay home today. You and the girls. Don't go into downtown Montréal."

"Why? What's going to happen?" Now the blood drained from Villeneuve's face.

"Just stay here," said Gamache firmly.

Villeneuve searched Gamache's face. "My God, you don't think you can stop it, do you?"

"I really have to go, Monsieur Villeneuve."

Gamache put on his coat, but remembered something Villeneuve had said, about Audrey.

"You say your wife was happy on that last morning. Do you know why?"

"I'd assumed it was because she was going to the office Christmas party. She'd made a new dress specially for it."

"Were you going?"

"No. We had an agreement. She didn't come to my office Christmas parties and I didn't go to hers. But she seemed to be looking forward to it."

Villeneuve looked uneasy.

"What is it?" Gamache asked.

"Nothing. It's personal. Nothing to do with what happened."

"Tell me."

Villeneuve studied Gamache and seemed to realize there was nothing left to lose. "I just wondered if she was having an affair. It's not true, she'd never have done it, but with the new dress and all. She hadn't made herself a dress in a long time. And she seemed so happy. Happier than she'd been with me for a while."

"Tell me about this party. Was it only for the office staff?"

"Mostly. The Minister of Transport always showed up, but not for long. And this year there were rumors of a special guest."

"Who?"

"The Premier. Didn't seem such a big deal to me, but Audrey was excited."

"Georges Renard?"

"*Oui.* Maybe that's why she made the dress. She wanted to impress him."

Villeneuve looked at his daughters, building a snowman on the small front yard. Armand shook Gaétan Villeneuve's hand, waved to the girls, and got in his car.

He sat there for a moment, putting it together. The target, he suspected, was the Ville-Marie Tunnel.

Audrey Villeneuve had almost certainly realized something was wrong, as she'd entered the reports. After years and years of working on repair files, she knew the difference between work genuinely done, or badly done. Or not done at all.

It was possible she'd even turned a blind eye, like so many of her colleagues. Until finally she couldn't anymore. Then what would Audrey Villeneuve have done? She was organized, disciplined. She'd have gathered proof before saying anything.

And in doing that, she'd have found things she shouldn't have. Worse things than willful neglect, than corruption, than desperately needed repairs not done.

She'd have found suggestions of a plan to hurry the collapse.

And then what? Gamache's mind raced as he put it together. What would any midlevel worker do upon finding massive corruption and conspiracy? She'd have gone to her boss. And when he didn't believe her, her boss's boss.

But still, no one acted.

That would explain her stress. Her short temper.

And her happiness, finally?

Audrey Villeneuve, the organizer, had a Plan B. She'd make herself a new dress for the Christmas party, something an aging politician might notice. She'd wander up to him, casually. Perhaps flirt a little, perhaps try to get him on his own.

And then she would tell him what she'd found.

Premier Renard would believe her. She was sure of it.

Yes, thought Gamache as he started his car and headed toward downtown Montréal, Renard would have known she was telling the truth.

After a few blocks he stopped to use a public phone.

"Lacoste residence," came the little voice. "Mélanie speaking."

"Is your mother home, please?"

Please, Gamache begged. *Please.*

"One moment, *s'il vous plaît*." He heard a scream, "Mama. Mama. *Télé-phone*."

A few seconds later he heard Inspector Lacoste's voice. *"Oui?"*

"Isabelle, I can't talk long. The target's the Ville-Marie Tunnel."

"Oh my God," came the hushed response.

"We need to close it down, now."

"Got it."

"And Isabelle. I've handed in my resignation."

"Yes sir. I'll tell the others. They'll want to know."

"Good luck," he said.

"And you? Where're you going?"

"Back to Three Pines. I left something there." He paused before he spoke again. "Can you find Jean-Guy, Isabelle? Make sure he's all right today?"

"I'll make sure he's far away from what's about to happen."

"Merci."

He hung up, called Annie to warn her to stay away from downtown, then got back in his car.

Sylvain Francoeur sat in the backseat of the black SUV. Tessier sat beside him, and in the rearview mirror Francoeur could see the unmarked van, carrying two more agents and the equipment they'd need.

Francoeur had been happy to get out of the city, given what was about to happen. Far from the trouble and far from any possible blame. None of it would stick to him, as long as he got to the village in time.

It was coming down to the wire.

"Gamache didn't go to headquarters," Tessier whispered, checking his device. "He was tracked to east-end Montréal. The Villeneuve place. Should we pick him up?"

"Why bother?" Francoeur had a smile on his face. This was perfect. "We searched it. He won't find anything there. He's wasting what little time's left. He thinks we'll follow him. Let him think that."

Tessier hadn't been able to find Three Pines on any map, but it didn't matter. They knew approximately where it was, from where Gamache's signal always disappeared. But "approximately" wasn't good enough for the careful Francoeur. He needed no delays, no unknowns. So he'd found a certainty. Someone who did know where the village could be found.

Francoeur looked over at the haggard man behind the wheel.

345

Jean-Guy Beauvoir held tight to the steering wheel, his face blank, as he drove them straight to Three Pines.

Olivier looked out the window. From Myrna's loft they had a panoramic view over the village, past the three huge pine trees and up the main road out of Three Pines.

"Nothing," he said, and returned to sit beside Gabri, who put his large hand on Olivier's slender knee.

"I canceled choir practice," said Gabri. "Probably shouldn't have. Best to keep everything normal." He looked at Olivier. "I might've blown it."

"It?" asked Nichol.

After a surprised and strained pause, Gabri laughed.

"Atta girl," said Ruth.

And then the quiet descended again. The weight of waiting.

"Let me tell you a story," said Myrna, pulling her chair closer to the woodstove.

"We're not four-year-olds," said Ruth, but she put Rosa on her lap and turned to Myrna.

Olivier and Gabri, Clara, Gilles and Agent Nichol, all moved their chairs closer, forming a circle in front of the warm fire. Jérôme Brunel wandered over, but Thérèse stayed by the window, looking out. Henri lay beside Ruth and gazed up at Rosa.

"Is it a ghost story?" asked Gabri.

"Of sorts," said Myrna. She picked up a thick envelope from the coffee table. Written in a careful hand were the words: *For Myrna.*

An identical envelope lay on the table. It said, *For Inspector Isabelle Lacoste. Please Deliver by Hand.*

Myrna had found them dropped through her mailbox early that morning. Over coffee, she'd read the one addressed to her. But the envelope for Isabelle Lacoste remained sealed, though she suspected it said almost exactly the same thing.

"Once upon a time, a poor farmer and his wife prayed for children," said Myrna. "Their land was barren, and so, apparently was she. So desperate was the farmer's wife for children that she traveled all the way to Montréal, to the Oratory, to visit Brother André. She crawled up the long, stone stairs, on her knees. Reciting the Hail Mary as she went—"

"Barbaric," muttered Ruth.

Myrna paused to look over at the old poet. "Now, pay attention. This is important later."

Ruth, or Rosa, muttered, "Fuck, fuck, fuck." But they listened.

"And a miracle occurred," Myrna resumed. "Eight months later, on the day after Brother André died, five babies were born in a tiny farmhouse, in the middle of Québec, delivered by a midwife and the farmer himself. At first it was a terrible shock, but then the farmer picked up his daughters and held them and he discovered a love like none he'd ever experienced. As did his wife. It was the happiest day of their lives. And it was the last happy day."

"You're talking about the Ouellet Quints," said Clara.

"You think?" said Gabri.

"The doctor had been called," said Myrna, her voice melodic and calm. "But he didn't bother to go out in the blizzard to some dirt-poor farm where he'd be paid in turnips, if at all. So he went back to sleep and left it up to the midwife. But next morning, when he heard that it was quintuplets and all were alive and healthy, he got himself over there. Photos were taken with him and the girls."

Myrna paused and looked around the gathering, holding their eyes. Her voice was low, as though inviting them into a conspiracy.

"More than quintuplets were born that day. A myth was also born. And with it, something else came to life. Something with a long, dark tail." Her voice was hushed and they all leaned forward. "A murder was born."

Armand Gamache sped through the Ville-Marie Tunnel. He'd considered not taking it. Going around it. But this was the fastest way to the Champlain Bridge, and out of Montréal to Three Pines.

As he drove through the long, dark tunnel, he noticed the cracks. The missing tiles and exposed rebar. How could he have driven this route so often and never noticed?

His foot lifted from the accelerator and his car slowed, until other motorists were honking at him. Gesturing to him as they passed. But he barely noticed. His mind was going back over the interview with Monsieur Villeneuve.

He took the next exit and found a phone in a coffee shop.

"*Bonjour,*" came the soft, weary voice.

"Monsieur Villeneuve, it's Armand Gamache."

There was a pause on the other end.

"Of the Sûreté. I just left your place."

"Yes, of course. I'd forgotten your name."

"Did the police return your wife's car to you?"

"No. But they gave me back what was in it."

"Any papers? A briefcase?"

"She had a briefcase, but they didn't return it."

Gamache rubbed his face, and was surprised by the stubble. No wonder Villeneuve hadn't been all that anxious to invite him in. He must look like a vagrant, between the gray stubble and the bruise.

He focused his thoughts. Audrey Villeneuve had planned to go to the Christmas party. Had been excited, happy, perhaps even relieved. Finally she could pass on what she'd found to someone who could do something about it.

She must have felt a huge weight lift.

But she'd also realize that the Premier of Québec wouldn't just take her word for it, no matter how attractive she was in her new dress.

She'd have to give him proof. Proof she'd have carried with her to the party.

"*Allô?*" said Villeneuve. "You still there?"

"Just a moment, please," said Gamache. He was almost there. Almost at the answer.

Audrey might have carried a clutch with her to the party, but not a briefcase, or a file folder, or loose papers. So how did she plan to pass the proof to the Premier?

Audrey Villeneuve was killed because of what she'd found out, and what she'd failed to find. That one last step that would have taken her to the man behind it all. The very man she'd be approaching. Premier Georges Renard.

"May I come back?" Gamache asked. "I need to see what she had in the car."

"It's not much," said Villeneuve.

"I need to see anyway." He hung up, turned his car around, went back through the Ville-Marie Tunnel, holding his breath like a child passing a graveyard, and was back at the Villeneuve home a few minutes later.

Jérôme Brunel sat on the arm of Myrna's chair. Everyone leaned forward, to catch the story. Of miracles, and myth, and murder.

Everyone except Thérèse Brunel. She stood at the window, listening to the words, but looking out. Scanning the roads into the village.

The sun was bright and the skies clear. A beautiful winter day. And behind her, a dark story was being told.

"The girls were taken from their mother and father when they were still infants," said Myrna. "It was at a time when the government didn't need a reason, but they provided one anyway, by having the good doctor intimate that, though good people, the Ouellets were a little slow. Perhaps even congenitally so. Fit to raise cows and pigs, but not five little angels. They were a gift from God, Frère André's last earthly miracle, and as such they belonged to all of Québec, and not some subsistence farmer. Dr. Bernard also hinted that the Ouellets were well paid for the girls. And people believed it."

Clara looked at Gabri, who looked at Olivier, who looked at Ruth. They'd all believed that the Quints had been sold by their greedy parents. It was an essential part of the fairy tale. Not just that the Quints were born, but that they were saved.

"The Quints were sensations," said Myrna. "All over the world people crushed by the Depression clamored for news of the miracle babies. They seemed proof of good in a very bad time."

Myrna held the envelope containing the pages Armand Gamache had painstakingly written the night before. Twice. Once for his colleague. Once for Myrna. He knew Myrna had loved Constance, and deserved to know what had happened to her. He had no Christmas gift to give her, but he gave her this instead.

"To Bernard and the government it was clear that a fortune could be made from the girls. From films, to merchandise, to tours. Books, magazine articles. All chronicling their gilded life."

Myrna suspected Armand would not be thrilled to know she was telling everyone what he'd written. In fact, he'd printed *Confidential* across the first page. And now she was blabbing it freely. But when she'd seen the anxiety in their faces, felt the gravity of the situation pressing down on them, she knew she had to take their minds off their fears.

And what better way than a tale of greed, of love, both warped and real. Of secrets and rage, of hurt beyond repair. And finally, of murder. Murders.

She thought the Chief Inspector might forgive her. She hoped she'd get a chance to ask for it.

"And it was a gilded life for the five girls," she continued, looking around the circle at the wide, attentive eyes. "The government built them a perfect little cottage, like something out of a storybook. With a garden, a white picket fence. To keep the gawkers out. And the girls in. They had beautiful clothes, private tutoring, music lessons. They had toys and cream cakes. They had everything. Except privacy and freedom. And that's the problem with a gilded life. Nothing inside can thrive. Eventually what was once beautiful rots."

"Rots?" Gabri asked. "Did they turn on each other?"

Myrna looked at him. "One sibling turned on the others, yes."

"Who?" asked Clara quietly. "What happened?"

Gamache pulled into the driveway and got out of the car, almost slipping on the icy pavement underfoot. The door was opened before he could ring, and he stepped inside.

"The girls are at a neighbor's," said Villeneuve. He'd obviously realized the importance of this visit. He led the way back to the kitchen, and there on the table were two purses, one for everyday use and the other a clutch.

Without a word, Gamache opened the clutch. It was empty. He felt around the lining, then tipped it toward the light. The lining had been recently sewn back in place. By Audrey or the cops who'd searched it?

"Do you mind if I take out the lining?" he asked.

"Do whatever you have to."

Gamache ripped and felt around inside but came up empty. If there'd been anything there, it was gone. He turned to the other purse and quickly searched it but found nothing.

"Is that all there was in your wife's car?"

Villeneuve nodded.

"Did they give you back her clothes?"

"The ones she was wearing? They offered to, but I told them to throw them away. I didn't want to see."

While disappointed, Gamache wasn't surprised. He'd have felt the same way. And he also suspected whatever Audrey had hidden wasn't in her office clothes. Or, if it was, it had been found.

"The dress?" he asked.

"I didn't want it either, but it showed up with the other things."

Gamache looked around. "Where is it?"

"The garbage. I probably should've given it to some charity sale, but I just couldn't deal with it."

"Do you still have the garbage?"

Villeneuve led him to the bin beside the house, and Gamache rummaged through until he found an emerald green dress. With a Chanel tag inside.

"This can't be it," he showed Villeneuve. "It says Chanel. I thought you said Audrey made her dress."

Villeneuve smiled.

"She did. Audrey didn't want anyone to know she made some of her own clothes or dresses for the kids, so she'd sew designer labels in."

Villeneuve took the dress and looked at the label, shaking his head, his hands slowly tightening over the material, until he was clutching it and tears were streaming down his face.

After a couple of minutes, Gamache put his hand on Villeneuve's, and loosened his grip. Then he took the dress inside.

He felt along the hem. Nothing. He felt the sleeves. Nothing. He felt the neckline. Nothing. Until. Until he came to the short line at the bottom of the semi-plunging neckline. Where it squared off.

He took the scissors Villeneuve offered and carefully unpicked the seam. This was not machine-stitched like the rest of the dress, but done by hand with great care.

He folded back the material and found a memory stick.

THIRTY-EIGHT

—

Jean-Guy Beauvoir turned off the highway onto the secondary road. In the backseat Chief Superintendent Francoeur and Inspector Tessier were conferring. Beauvoir hadn't asked why they wanted to go to Three Pines, or why the unmarked Sûreté van was following them.

He didn't care.

He was just a chauffeur. He'd do as he was told. No more debate. He'd learned that when he cared, he got hurt, and he couldn't take any more pain. Even the pills couldn't dull it anymore.

So Jean-Guy Beauvoir did the only thing left. He gave up.

But Constance was the last Quint," said Ruth. "How could she have been killed by one of her sisters?"

"What do we really know about their deaths?" Myrna asked Ruth. "You yourself suspected the first one to die—"

"Virginie," said Ruth.

"—hadn't fallen down those stairs by accident. You suspected suicide."

"But it was just a guess," said the old poet. "I was young and thought despair was romantic." She paused, stroking Rosa's head. "I might've confused Virginie with myself."

"*Who hurt you once / so far beyond repair,*" Clara quoted.

Ruth opened her mouth and for a moment the friends thought she might actually answer that question. But then her thin lips clamped shut.

"Suppose you were wrong about Virginie?" Myrna asked.

"How can it matter now?" Ruth asked.

Gabri jumped in. "It would matter if Virginie didn't really fall down the stairs. Was that their secret?" he asked Myrna. "She wasn't dead?"

Thérèse Brunel turned back to the window. She'd allowed herself to glance into the room, toward the tight circle and the ghost story. But a sound drew her eyes back outside. A car was approaching.

Everyone heard it. Olivier was the first to move, walking swiftly across the wooden floor. He stood at Thérèse's shoulder and looked out.

"It's only Billy Williams," he reported. "Come for his lunch."

They relaxed, but not completely. The tension, pushed aside by the story, was back.

Gabri shoved another couple of logs into the woodstove. They all felt slightly chilled, though the room was warm.

"Constance was trying to tell me something," said Myrna, picking up the thread. "And she did. She told us everything, but we just didn't know how to put it together."

"What did she tell us?" Ruth demanded.

"Well, she told you and me that she loved to play hockey," said Myrna. "That it was Brother André's favorite sport. They had a team and would get up a game with the neighborhood kids."

"So?" asked Ruth, and Rosa, in her arms, quacked quietly as though mimicking her mother. "So, so, so," the duck muttered.

Myrna turned to Olivier, Gabri, and Clara. "She gave you mitts and a scarf that she'd knitted, with symbols of your lives. Paintbrushes for Clara—"

"I don't want to know what your symbol was," Nichol said to Gabri and Olivier.

"She was practically leaking clues," said Myrna. "It must've been so frustrating for her."

"For her?" said Clara. "It's really not that obvious, you know."

"Not to you," said Myrna. "Not to me. Not to anyone here. But to someone unused to talking about herself and her life, it must've seemed like she was screaming her secrets at us. You know what it's like. When we know something, and hint, those hints seem so obvious. She must've thought we were a bunch of idiots not to pick up on what she was saying."

"But what was she saying?" Olivier asked. "That Virginie was still alive?"

"She left her final clue under my tree, thinking that she wouldn't be back," said Myrna. "Her card said it was the key to her home. It would unlock all the secrets."

"Her albatross," said Ruth.

"She gave you an albatross?" asked Nichol. Nothing about this village or these people surprised her anymore.

Myrna laughed. "In a way. She gave me a tuque. We'd thought maybe she'd knitted it, but it was too old. And there was a tag sewn in it. MA, it said."

"Ma," said Gabri. "It belonged to her mother."

"What did you call your mother?"

"Ma," said Gabri. "Ma. Mama."

There was silence, while Myrna nodded. "Mama. Not Ma. They were initials, like all the other hats. Madame Ouellet didn't make that tuque for herself."

"Well then, whose was it?" Ruth demanded.

"It belonged to Constance's killer."

Villeneuve rang the doorbell and his neighbor answered.

"Gaétan," she said, "have you come to get the girls? They're playing in the basement."

"*Non, merci*, Celeste. I'm actually wondering if we could use your computer. The police took mine."

Celeste glanced from Villeneuve to the large unshaven man with the bruise and cut on his cheek. She looked far from certain.

"Please," said Villeneuve. "It's important."

Celeste relented, but watched Gamache closely as they hurried to the back of the house, and the laptop set up on the small desk in the breakfast room. Gamache wasted no time. He shoved the memory stick into the slot. It flashed open.

He clicked on the first file. Then the next. He made note of various words.

Permeable. Substandard. Collapse.

But one word made him stop. And stare.

Pier.

He clicked rapidly back. And back. And then he stopped and stood up so rapidly Celeste and Gaétan both jumped back.

"May I use your phone, please?"

Not waiting for an answer, he grabbed the receiver and began dialing.

"Isabelle, it's not the tunnel. It's the bridge. The Champlain Bridge. I think the explosives must be attached to the piers."

"I've been trying to reach you, sir. They won't close the tunnel. They don't believe me. Or you. If they won't close the tunnel, they sure as hell won't close the bridge."

"I'm emailing you the report," he said, retaking his seat and pounding on the keys. "You'll have the proof. Close that bridge, Isabelle. I don't care if you have to lie across the lanes yourself. And get the bomb disposal unit out."

"Yessir. *Patron*, there's one other thing."

By the tone of her voice, he knew. "Jean-Guy?"

"I can't find him. He's not in his office, he's not at home. I've tried his cell phone. It's shut off."

"Thank you for trying," he said. "Just get that bridge closed."

Gamache thanked Celeste and Gaétan Villeneuve and made for the door.

"It's the bridge?" Villeneuve asked him.

"Your wife found out about it," said Gamache, outside now and walking rapidly to his car. "She tried to stop it."

"And they killed her," said Villeneuve, following Gamache.

Gamache stopped and faced the man. "*Oui*. She went to the bridge to get the final proof, to see for herself. She planned to take that proof, and this"—he held up the memory stick—"to the Christmas party, and pass it on to someone she thought she could trust."

"They killed her," Villeneuve repeated, trying to grasp the meaning behind the words.

"She didn't fall from the bridge," said Gamache. "She was killed underneath it when she went to look at the piers." He got in his car. "Get your girls. Go to a hotel and take your neighbor and her family with you. Don't use your credit card. Pay cash. Leave your cell phones at home. Stay there until this is over."

"Why?"

"Because I emailed the files from your neighbor's home and used her phone. They'll know I know. And they'll know you know too. They'll be here soon. Go. Leave."

Villeneuve blanched and backed away from the car, then he ran stumbling over the ice and snow, calling for his girls.

Sir," said Tessier, looking down at his messages. "I need to show you this."

He handed his device over to Chief Superintendent Francoeur.

Gamache had returned to the Villeneuve house. And something had been emailed to Inspector Lacoste, from the neighbor's computer.

When he saw what it was, Francoeur's face hardened.

"Pick up Villeneuve and the neighbor," he said quietly to Tessier. "And pick up Gamache and Lacoste. Clean this up."

"Yessir." Tessier knew what "clean this up" meant. He'd cleaned up Audrey Villeneuve.

While Tessier made the arrangements, Francoeur watched as the flat farmland turned into hills, and forest, and mountains.

Gamache was getting closer, Francoeur knew. But so were they.

Chief Inspector Gamache craned his neck, to see what had stopped all the traffic. They were just inching along the narrow residential street. At a main intersection he spotted a city cop and a barricade. He pulled over.

"Move along," the cop commanded, not even looking at the driver.

"What's the holdup?" Gamache asked.

The cop looked at Gamache as though he was nuts.

"Don't you know? The Santa Claus parade. Get going, you're holding up traffic."

Thérèse Brunel stayed by the window, standing to the side. Staring out.

It wouldn't be long now, she knew.

But still she listened to Myrna's story. The tale with the long tail. That went back decades. Almost beyond living memory.

To a saint and a miracle, and a Christmas tuque.

"MA," said Myrna. "That was the key. Every hat their mother made had a tag with their initials. MC for Marie-Constance, et cetera."

"So what did MA stand for?" Clara asked. She went back over the girls' names. Virginie, Hélène, Josephine, Marguerite, Constance. No A.

Then Clara's eyes widened and shone. She looked at Myrna.

"Why did everyone think there were only five?" she asked Myrna. "Of course they'd have more."

"More what?" asked Gabri. But Olivier got it.

"More children," said Olivier. "When the girls were taken from them, the Ouellets made more."

Myrna was nodding slowly, watching them as the truth dawned. And, as with Constance and her hints, it now seemed so obvious. But it hadn't been obvious to Myrna, until she'd read it in Armand's letter.

When Marie-Harriette and Isidore had their beloved daughters taken away, what choice did they have but to make more?

In his letter, Chief Inspector Gamache explained that he'd had the tuque tested for DNA. They'd found his. They'd found Myrna's. Both of them

357

had recently handled the hat. They'd also found Constance's DNA, and one other. A close match to Constance.

Gamache admitted he'd assumed it was her father's or mother's, but the fact was, the technician had originally said a sibling.

"Another sister," said Clara. "Marie-A."

"But why didn't anyone know about this younger sister?" asked Gabri.

"Christ," snapped Ruth, looking at Gabri with disdain. "I'd have thought someone who was practically a work of fiction himself would know more about myths."

"Well, I know a gorgon when I see one." Gabri glared at Ruth, who looked like she was trying to turn him to stone.

"Look," Ruth finally said, "the Quints were supposed to be a miracle, right? A huge harvest from barren ground. Frère André's final gift. Well, how would it look if Mama starting popping out children all over the place? Kinda takes away from the miracle."

"Dr. Bernard and the government figured she'd laid the golden eggs, now she needed to stop," said Myrna.

"If I'd said that they'd castrate me," Gabri muttered to Olivier.

"But would people really care?" asked Olivier. "I mean, the Quints were pretty amazing no matter how many younger brothers and sisters they had."

"But they were more amazing if seen as an act of a benevolent God," said Myrna. "That's what the government and Bernard were peddling. Not a circus act, but an act of God. Through the Depression and war, people flocked to them, not to see five identical girls, but to see hope. Proof that God exists. A generous and kind God, who'd given this gift to a barren woman. But suppose Madame Ouellet wasn't barren at all? Suppose she had another child?"

"Suppose Christ hadn't risen?" said Gabri. "Suppose the water wasn't wine?"

"It was critical to their story that Madame Ouellet be barren. That's what made the miracle," said Myrna. "Without that the Quints became an oddity, nothing more."

"No miracle, no money," said Clara.

"So the new baby threatened to bring down everything they'd created," said Ruth.

"And cost them millions of dollars," said Myrna. "The child had to be hidden. Armand thinks that's what we were seeing, when Marie-Harriette closed the door on her daughters in the newsreel."

They remembered the image, frozen in their minds. Young Virginie howling. Trying to get back into the house. But the door had been closed. Shut in her face by her own mother. Not to keep the girls out, but to keep the younger child in. To keep MA away from the newsreels.

"Constance only told us one personal thing," said Gabri. "That she and her sisters liked to play hockey. But there're six players on a team, not five."

"Exactly," said Myrna. "When Constance told me about the hockey team, it seemed important to her, but I thought it was just some old memory. That she was sort of testing out her newfound freedom to reveal things, and had decided to start with something trivial. It never occurred to me that was it. The key. Six siblings, not five."

"I didn't pick up on it either," said Ruth. "And I coach a team."

"You bully a team," said Gabri. "It's not the same thing."

"But I can count," said Ruth. "Six players. Not five." She thought for a moment, absently stroking Rosa's head and neck. "Imagine being that child. Excluded, hidden. Watching your sisters grab the spotlight, while you're kept in the dark. Something shameful."

They paused and tried to imagine what that would be like. Not having one sister who was a favored child, but five of them. And not simply favored by the parents, but by the world. Given beautiful dresses, toys, candy, a fairy-tale house. And all the attention.

While MA was shoved aside. Shoved inside. Denied.

"So what happened?" asked Ruth. "Are you saying Constance's sister killed her?"

Myrna held up the envelope with Gamache's careful writing. "Chief Inspector Gamache believes it goes back to the first death. Virginie." Myrna turned to Ruth. "Constance saw what happened. So did Hélène. They told the other sisters, but no one else. It was their secret, the one that bound them together."

"The one they took to the grave," said Ruth. "And tried to bury. Virginie was murdered."

"One of them had done it," said Gabri.

"Constance came here to tell you that," said Clara.

"After Marguerite died, she felt she was free to finally talk," said Myrna.

"Matthew 10:36." Ruth's voice had dropped to a whisper. *"And a man's foes shall be they of his own household."*

Jean-Guy Beauvoir drove down the familiar road. It was covered in snow now, but when he'd first seen it, years before, it had been dirt. And the trees overhead hadn't been bare, but in full autumn color, with the sun shining through. Ambers and reds, warm yellows. Like a stained-glass window.

He hadn't remarked on the beauty of the place. Been too reserved and cynical to stare in open awe at the pretty, peaceful village below.

But he'd felt it. That awe. And that peace.

Today, though, he felt nothing.

"How far now?" Francoeur asked.

"Almost there," said Beauvoir. "A few more minutes."

"Pull over," said the Chief Superintendent, and Beauvoir did.

"If Chief Inspector Gamache was going to set up a post in the village," Francoeur asked, "where would it be?"

"Gamache?" asked Beauvoir. He hadn't realized this was about Gamache. "Is he here?"

"Just answer the question, Inspector," said Tessier from the backseat.

The van carrying the two agents and equipment idled behind them.

This was the moment of truth, Francoeur knew. Would Beauvoir balk at giving away information about Gamache? Up until now Francoeur hadn't asked Beauvoir to actively betray his former boss, but to simply do nothing to help him.

But now they needed more from Beauvoir.

"The old railway station," came the reply, without protest or hesitation.

"Take us there," said Francoeur.

Myrna still held the envelope containing the handwritten letter from Armand Gamache. In it he detailed all he knew, and all he suspected, about the murder of Constance Ouellet, and the murder of her sister Virginie over fifty years earlier.

Constance and Hélène had witnessed it. Virginie neither tripped, nor did she throw herself down those stairs. She was pushed. And behind that push was years and years of pain. Of being ignored, hidden, marginalized, denied. Years and years of the Quints getting all the attention. From the world, yes. But worse, from Mama and Papa.

When the girls came home for their rare visits, they were treated like princesses.

It warped a child. It wore a child down, until there was nothing recognizable left. And then it twisted them. The girls might have been spoiled, but their young sibling was ruined.

That little heart filled with hate. And grew into a big heart, filled with big hate.

And when Virginie teetered at the top of those long wooden stairs, the hand shot out. It could have saved her. But it didn't. It tipped her over the edge.

Constance and Hélène had seen what happened and chose to say nothing. Perhaps out of guilt, perhaps out of a near maniacal need for privacy, secrecy. Their lives, and their deaths, were nobody's business but theirs. Even their murders were private.

All this Gamache explained in his letter to Myrna, and now Myrna explained to those gathered in her home. Hiding in her home.

"The Chief Inspector knew he was looking for two things," said Myrna. "Someone whose initials were MA and who'd now be in their mid-seventies."

"Wouldn't there be birth records?" Jérôme asked.

"Gamache looked," said Myrna. "There was nothing in the official record or in parish records under Ouellet."

"The powers that be might not be able to create a person," said Jérôme. "But they could erase one."

He listened to the story, but kept his eyes on his wife. Thérèse was silhouetted against the window. Waiting.

"In considering the case, Armand realized he'd met four people who fit the description," Myrna continued. "The first was Antoine, the parish priest. He'd said he'd started as priest long after the girls had left, and that was true, but he'd failed to admit he'd actually grown up in the area. The Quints' uncle said he'd played with Antoine as a child. Père Antoine may not have lied, but he hadn't told the whole truth either. Why?"

"And the priest was in a position to alter the records," said Clara.

"Exactly Gamache's thinking," said Myrna. "But then there was the uncle himself. André Pineault. A few years younger than the girls, he described playing hockey with them, and he moved in with their father and looked after him until Isidore died. All the act of a son. And Monsieur Ouellet left the family farm to him."

"But MA would be a woman," said Clara. "Marie someone."

"Marie-Annette," said Myrna. "Annette is the name of Constance's neighbor. The only person the sisters socialized with. The only person allowed onto their porch. It sounds to us a small thing, almost laughable, but to the Quints, so traumatized by public scrutiny, letting anyone close to their home was significant. Could Annette be either Virginie, or the lost sibling?"

"But if Constance and Hélène saw her kill Virginie, would they have anything to do with her?" Gabri asked.

"Maybe they forgave her," said Ruth. "Maybe they understood that while they were damaged, their sister was too."

"And maybe they wanted to keep her close," said Clara. "The devil you know."

Myrna nodded. "Annette and her husband Albert were already in the neighborhood when the sisters moved in next door. If Annette was the sister, it suggests either forgiveness"—Myrna looked at Ruth—"or a desire to keep a close eye on her."

"Or him."

They looked at Thérèse. She was looking out the window, but had obviously been listening.

"Him?" asked Olivier.

"Albert. The neighbor," said Thérèse. Her breath fogged the windowpane. "Maybe she wasn't their sister, but he was their brother."

"You're right," said Myrna, carefully placing Gamache's letter on the table. "The Sûreté technician was sure the third DNA he'd found belonged to a man. That tuque with the angels was knitted by Marie-Harriette for her son."

"Albert," said Ruth.

When Myrna didn't respond they looked at her.

"If Isidore and Marie-Harriette had a son," she said, "what would they name him?"

There was silence then. Even Rosa had stopped muttering.

"Old sins have long shadows." They looked at Agent Nichol. "Where did this all begin? Where did the miracle begin?"

"Frère André," said Clara.

"André," said Ruth into the quiet room. "They'd have named him André."

Myrna nodded. "Gamache believes so. He thinks that was what Constance was trying to tell me, with the tuque. Marie-Harriette knitted it for her son, named after their guardian angel. A DNA test will confirm it, but he thinks André Pineault is their brother."

"But MA," asked Gabri. "What does the M stand for?"

"Marc. All the girls in Marie-Harriette's family were named Marie something and all the boys were named Marc something. Gamache found that out in the churchyard. He'd have been Marc-André, but called André."

"Brother André," said Gabri. "Literally."

"That's what Constance was trying to tell us," said Myrna. "What she did tell us. Me. She actually said that hockey was brother André's favorite sport. I was the one who capitalized the B, not her. Not Brother André, but brother André. The sixth sibling. Named after the saint who'd produced a miracle."

"He killed Constance so she wouldn't tell you that he'd killed Virginie," said Clara. "That was what the sisters had kept secret all those years, what kept them prisoners long after the public stopped prying."

"But how did he know she'd tell?" Olivier asked.

"He didn't," said Myrna. "But Gamache thinks they kept in touch. André Pineault claimed not to know where the girls lived, but he later said he'd written to tell them their father was dead. He knew their address. That suggested they kept in some contact. It was strange that Pineault would lie about that.

"Gamache thinks Constance must have told him what her plans were for Christmas. To visit her friend and former therapist. And Pineault got frightened. He must have suspected that with Marguerite dead, Constance might want to tell someone the truth, before her time came. She wanted the truth about Virginie's death to be known. She'd kept his secret all those years but now, for her own and Virginie's sake, she needed to be free of it."

"So he killed her," said Ruth.

Jérôme saw Thérèse's back stiffen, then he heard a sound. He got up and walked swiftly across to the window to join her.

He looked out. A large black SUV followed by a van were driving very slowly down the hill.

"They're here," said Thérèse Brunel.

THIRTY-NINE

———

Armand Gamache drove onto the Champlain Bridge. There was no sign, yet, of any effort to close it but he knew if anyone could do it, it would be Isabelle Lacoste.

The traffic was heavy and the road still snowy. He passed a car and glanced in. A man and a woman sat in the front and behind them an infant was strapped into a car seat. Two lanes over he could see a young woman alone in her car, tapping her steering wheel and nodding to music.

Red brake lights appeared. The traffic was slowing. They were now creeping along. Bumper-to-bumper.

And ahead, the huge steel span rose.

Gamache knew almost nothing about engineering. About load tests and concrete. But he did know that 160,000 cars crossed this bridge every day. It was the busiest span in Canada and it was about to be blown into the St. Lawrence River. Not by some enraged foreign terrorist, but by two of the most trusted people in Québec.

The Premier and the head of the police force.

It had taken Gamache a while, but finally he thought he knew why.

What made this different from the other bridges, the tunnels, the neglected overpasses? Why target this?

There had to be a reason, a purpose. Money, maybe. If a bridge came down, it would have to be rebuilt. And that would put hundreds of millions more dollars in pockets across Québec. But Gamache knew it was more than money. He knew Francoeur, and what drove the man. It was one thing. Had always been one thing.

Power.

How could bringing down the Champlain Bridge give him more than he already had?

One lane over, a young boy looked out his window and stared directly at the Chief Inspector. And smiled.

Gamache smiled back. His own car slowed to a stop, joining the column of stalled cars in the middle of the bridge. Gamache's right hand trembled a little, and he gripped the steering wheel tighter.

Pierre Arnot had started it, decades ago, on the remote reserve.

While up there he'd met another young man on the rise. Georges Renard.

Arnot was with the Sûreté detachment, Renard was an engineer with Aqueduct, planning the dam.

Both were clever, dynamic, ambitious and they triggered something in the other. So that over time, clever became cunning. Dynamic became obsessed. Ambitious became ruthless.

It was as though, in that fateful meeting, something had changed in each man's DNA. Up until then, both had been driven, but ultimately decent. There was a limit to how far they were willing to go. But when Arnot met Renard, and Renard met Arnot, that limit, that line, had vanished.

Gamache had known Pierre Arnot, had even admired parts of the man. And now, as he inched along the bridge toward the highest point of the span, Gamache wondered what might have become of Arnot, had he not met Renard.

And what might have become of Renard, had he not met Arnot?

He'd seen it in others, the consequences of failing to choose companions wisely. One slightly immoral person was a problem. Two together was a catastrophe. All it took was a fateful meeting. A person who told you your meanest desires, your basest thoughts, weren't so bad. In fact, he shared them.

Then the unthinkable was thought. And planned for. And put into action.

Georges Renard had put up the great La Grande hydroelectric dam. He could bring it down. With Pierre Arnot's help.

Arnot's part was simple and painfully easy. Recruiters, for terrorist cells and police forces and armies, relied on this simple truth: if you got people young enough, they could be made to do just about anything.

And that was what Arnot did. He'd left the Cree reserve years earlier and had risen to Chief Superintendent of the Sûreté du Québec. But he still had influence in the north. He was respected. His voice heard and often heeded.

Arnot put key officers in place on the reserve. Their task was to find, and if necessary create, the angriest, most disenfranchised native kids. To nurture that hatred. Reinforce it. Reward it.

Kids who didn't buy into it, or threatened to expose them, had "accidents." Committed "suicide." Disappeared into the bush forever.

Two abused and desperate children, nurtured into violent, glue-sniffing young men, were chosen. They were the angriest. The emptiest.

They were given two trucks loaded with explosives and told where to hit the dam. They would die, but they would die heroes, they were told. Celebrities. Songs would be written. Their brave stories told and retold. They would become legend. Myth.

Renard had provided the information on where to hit the dam. Where it was vulnerable. Information only someone who'd actually worked on the dam would know.

That had been the first plan, but Gamache had stopped it. Barely. And lost many young officers doing it. Had almost lost Jean-Guy.

Perhaps he had lost Jean-Guy, Gamache thought.

They were almost at the very top of the bridge now. The massive steel girders rose on either side of him. The boy in the next car had fallen asleep, his blond hair pressed against the window. His head lolling. In the front seat, Gamache could see Dad driving and Mom holding a large wrapped gift on her lap.

Yes, he'd stopped the dam from being brought down, but he'd failed to get at the rot. The dark core was still there and spreading. Recovering from the setback, it had grown darker and stronger.

Arnot had gone to prison and his second in command had taken over. In Sylvain Francoeur, Georges Renard had found his true muse. A man so like him they were two halves of a whole. And when put together, the results were catastrophic.

The target had shifted but not the goal.

What made the Champlain Bridge such a perfect target was finally very simple.

It was a federal bridge.

And when it came down, with a shattering loss of life, the government of Canada would be blamed for years of mismanagement, neglect, substandard materials, corruption.

All documented by the provincial Ministry of Transportation.

Audrey Villeneuve's department.

Footage of the dreadful event would run day and night on screens around the world. Photos of the parents, the children, the families who perished would stare out from newspapers and magazines.

Gamache's eyes swept the vehicles around him, and rested, again, on the boy in the car beside him. He was awake now. Staring out. Eyes glazed with boredom. Then he noticed his breath on the cold window. The boy brought his finger up, and wrote.

ynnaD, Gamache read.

His name was Danny.

This boy had the same name as his own son. Daniel.

If death came right now, would it be swift? Would Danny know?

Yes, their photographs would be on endless rotation on the news. Their names etched on monuments. Martyrs in the cause.

And the people responsible for the bridge, the Canadian government, would be villainized, demonized.

Je me souviens, Gamache read on the slushy license plate of the car ahead. The motto of Québec. I remember. They would never, ever forget the day the Champlain Bridge fell.

This was never about money, except as a means to corrupt. To buy silence and complicity.

This was about power. Political power. Georges Renard was not satisfied with being the Premier of a province. He wanted to be the father of a new country. He'd rather rule in hell than serve in heaven.

And to do that all he needed to do was to manufacture rage, then direct it at the federal government. He'd convince the population that the reason the bridge had come down was that Canada had willfully used substandard material. That the federal government did not care for the citizens of Québec.

And his words would carry great weight, not because he was himself a Québec separatist, but because he wasn't. Georges Renard was a lifelong Federalist. He'd built a political career as a supporter of Québec staying in Canada. How much stronger the argument for separation would be when coming from a man who'd never espoused it, until this hideous event.

By the New Year Québec would have declared its independence. The day the Champlain Bridge fell would be their Bastille Day. And the victims would pass into legend.

Where're they going?" Jérôme whispered.

As he, Thérèse and Agent Nichol watched from Myrna's window, the unmarked SUV drove slowly around the village green and over the stone bridge.

"To the old train station," said Nichol. "It's where Chief Inspector Gamache set up his Incident Room in the past."

"But how would they know that?" Jérôme asked.

"Could they have got the Chief Inspector?" Nichol asked.

"He'd never lead them here," said Thérèse.

"Someone needs to go down," said Clara.

They looked around the room at each other.

"I'll go," said Nichol.

"No, it needs to be one of us," said Clara. "A villager. When they find nothing at the old train station they'll come back to ask questions. Someone needs to answer them, or they'll take the place apart."

"I think we should vote," said Gabri.

They all, slowly, turned to look at Ruth.

"Oh, no you don't. I'm not going to be voted off the island," she snapped, then turned to Rosa, stroking her head. "They're all shits, aren't they? Yes they are, yes they are."

"I know who gets my vote," said Gabri.

"I'll go."

Olivier had spoken, and now he walked decisively toward the stairs down from Myrna's loft.

"Wait." Gabri ran after him. "Let Ruth."

"You need to go."

Superintendent Thérèse Brunel had spoken. Clearly, decisively. She'd taken charge, and everyone in the loft now turned to her. She'd spoken to Olivier.

"Go to the bistro and if they come in, act as though you don't know who they are. They're just tourists, nothing more. If they identify themselves as Sûreté, ask if they're looking for the Chief Inspector—"

She was cut off by their protests, but Thérèse held up her hand.

"They already know he was here, for the Ouellet case. No use denying it. In fact, you need to appear as helpful as possible. Three Pines has to look like it has nothing to hide. Got it?"

"Let me come too," said Gabri, his eyes wide.

"Yes, we vote he goes," said Ruth, putting up her hand.

"You're my best friend," said Olivier, looking at his partner. "My greatest love, but you couldn't lie to save your life. Fortunately, I can, and have." He looked at his friends. "You all know that."

369

There was a feeble attempt at denial, but it was true.

"Of course I was just practicing, for today," said Olivier.

"The dickhead's lying now," said Ruth, almost wistfully, and walked over to join him. "You'll need customers. Besides, I could use a Scotch."

Thérèse Brunel turned to Myrna and said, apologetically, "You need to go down too."

Myrna nodded. "I'll open the store."

Clara went to join them, but Superintendent Brunel stopped her.

"I'm sorry, Clara, but I've seen your paintings. I don't think you'd be a very good liar either. We can't risk it."

Clara stared at the older woman, then walked over to her friends at the top of the stairs.

"Myrna needs a customer too in her bookstore," said Clara. "I'm going."

"Call it a library, dear," said Ruth, "or they'll know you're just pretending."

Ruth looked at Jérôme and made a circular motion with her finger at her temple, and rolled her eyes.

"Release the kraken," said Gabri as he watched them leave.

"I think you mean crackers," said Jérôme, then he turned to Thérèse. "We're doomed."

Break it down."

Chief Superintendent Francoeur nodded at the door to the old train station.

Beauvoir strolled up, turned the handle and swung the door open. "No one locks their doors around here."

"They should pay more attention to the news," said Francoeur. The two large Sûreté officers followed Tessier into the building.

Jean-Guy Beauvoir stepped aside. Disengaged. He watched as though it was a film and nothing to do with him.

"Just a fire truck and some equipment," said Tessier, coming out a minute or two later. "No sign of anything else."

Francoeur examined Beauvoir closely. Was he screwing with them? "Where else could they be?"

"The bistro, I suppose."

They drove back over the stone bridge and parked outside the bistro.

"You know these people," Francoeur said to Beauvoir. "Come with me."

The place was all but empty. Billy Williams sat by the window, sipping a beer and eating pie. Ruth and Rosa were in a corner, reading.

Fireplaces at both ends of the bistro were lit, and maple and birch logs were burning and snapping.

Jean-Guy Beauvoir took in the familiar room, and felt nothing.

He met Olivier's eyes, and saw them widen in surprise.

And Olivier was indeed surprised. Shocked to see Beauvoir, in such company and in such condition. He looked hollowed out, as though a breeze or nasty word would knock him over.

Olivier put a smile on his face but his heart was pounding furiously.

"Inspector Beauvoir," he said, coming around the long polished bar. "The Chief Inspector didn't mention you were coming down."

Olivier spoke heartily and warned himself to dial it back.

"Chief Inspector Gamache?" The other man spoke and, despite himself, Olivier felt the attraction of the man, the immense charisma that came with confidence and authority. "Have you seen him?"

Here was a man used to commanding. He was in his early sixties, with gray hair and an athletic build. His eyes were searching, sharp, and he moved with casual grace, like a carnivore.

Beside this vibrant man, Beauvoir seemed to diminish even further. He became carrion. A carcass, that hadn't yet been devoured but soon would be.

"Sure," said Olivier. "The Chief Inspector's been here for..." he thought, "...almost a week, I guess. Myrna called him when her friend Constance went missing."

Olivier lowered his voice and looked around, leaning closer to Beauvoir. "Don't know if you heard, but Constance was one of the Ouellet Quints. The last one. She was murdered."

Olivier looked as though nothing could have pleased him more.

"Gamache has been asking questions. Showed us a film, an old newsreel of the Quints. Did you—"

"Where is he now?" the other man interrupted Olivier's babbling.

"The Chief Inspector? I don't know. Isn't his car here?"

Olivier looked out the window. "He was at the B and B for breakfast. My partner Gabri made—"

"Was he alone?"

"Well, yes." Olivier looked from the older man who'd spoken to Beauvoir. "He'd normally have you with him, but he said you were on another assignment."

"There was no one else with him?" Once again, the other man had spoken.

371

Olivier shook his head. He was a great liar, but he knew he was staring into the eyes of an even better one.

"Did the Chief Inspector set up an Incident Room?" the man asked.

Olivier shook his head and didn't dare speak.

"Where did he work?"

"Either in here or over at the B and B," said Olivier.

The man looked around the bistro, skimming past the old woman with the duck, and landing on Billy Williams. He walked toward him.

Olivier watched with growing anxiety. Billy Williams was likely to tell him everything.

"Bonjour," said Francoeur.

Billy Williams raised his beer glass. In front of him he had a huge wedge of lemon meringue pie.

"Do you know Chief Inspector Gamache?"

Billy nodded and picked up his fork.

"Can you tell me where he is?"

"Norfolk and chance."

"Pardon?"

"Norfolk and chance," said Billy, clearly.

"I'm trying to find Chief Inspector Gamache." Francoeur switched from French to English and spoke very, very slowly to this rustic. "I'm a friend of his."

Billy paused, and spoke equally slowly. "Whale oil beef hooked."

Francoeur stared at Billy, then turned away.

"Does he speak French or English?" Francoeur asked.

Olivier watched as Billy took a huge mouthful of pie, and quietly blessed him. "We're not sure."

"Do you know the B and B?" Francoeur asked Beauvoir, who nodded. "Take me there."

"Can I get you a coffee before you go? Have you had lunch?"

But Olivier was talking to their backs. He walked around the bar, not letting his guard down. Not daring to show how shattered he was.

Olivier Brulé knew he'd looked into the eyes of a man who could kill him, if need be. And maybe, Olivier knew, without need. But just because.

"Whale oil beef hooked," he whispered.

A<small>N</small> accident just off the bridge had backed up the traffic. A little fender-bender had caused a massive tie-up.

372

But Gamache cleared it, and watched as Danny, his sister and parents peeled off the highway, toward Brossard. Safe.

But other Dannys were just approaching the bridge. Other parents and grandparents and happy holiday children. He hoped Isabelle Lacoste would arrive soon.

Chief Inspector Gamache pressed down on the gas. He was an hour away from Three Pines, even on dry pavement. He went as fast as he dared. And then some.

Francoeur and Tessier searched the B and B. There was evidence of only one guest, and that was Chief Inspector Gamache. They found toiletries in his bathroom. The walls of the shower and the soap were still damp and clothes were hung in the closet and folded in the drawer. The room smelled slightly of sandalwood.

Francoeur looked out the window to the village green and the road that circled it. A few cars were parked, but not Chief Inspector Gamache's Volvo. But they knew that already. He'd been tracked to the penitentiary, then the Villeneuve home in Montréal. And then came word he'd emailed a large file to Inspector Lacoste, from the home next to Villeneuve.

Agents were on their way, to Lacoste's home, and to Villeneuve and his neighbor. And the search was on to find Gamache. They had his cell phone and the tracking device in his car, and they'd have him any moment now.

Francoeur turned to Beauvoir, who was standing in the middle of the room like a mannequin.

"Was the owner of the bistro lying?" Francoeur asked.

The direct question roused Beauvoir. "He might've been. He lies about a lot of things."

They heard swearing and turned to see Tessier punching his finger at his device.

"It's a fucking dead zone," he said, grabbing for the landline.

While Tessier called Sûreté headquarters, Francoeur turned to Beauvoir.

"Gamache was here, but where're the others?"

Beauvoir looked blank. "What others?"

"We're also looking for Superintendent Brunel and her husband. I think that man in the bistro was lying." Francoeur's voice was pleasant, reasonable. "Gamache might have left, but I think they're still here. We need to convince him to tell us the truth."

"The squads are closing in," Tessier whispered to Francoeur as they walked down the stairs toward the front door. "They have Gamache's signal. They'll get him in the next few minutes."

"They know what to do?"

Tessier nodded.

"That last message Gamache sent, in reply to the Granby Zoo," Francoeur asked, once they were on the porch. "What was it again?"

"*See Emilie.*"

"Right." Francoeur looked at Beauvoir and demanded, "Who's Emilie?"

"I don't know."

"Then what did Gamache mean when he told the Brunels to see Emilie?" snapped Francoeur. "Is there an Emilie in this village?"

Beauvoir's brows drew together. "There was one, but she's been dead for a few years."

"Where did she live?"

Beauvoir pointed to the right. There, just across the Old Stage Road, was Emilie Longpré's home, with its wide front verandah, wood cladding, mullioned windows, and brick chimney.

And the shoveled front path.

Last time Beauvoir had been in Three Pines, Emilie Longpré's home had been empty. Now it was not.

Christ," said Jérôme, standing to the side of Myrna's upstairs window and peering out. "He's leading them right to Emilie's place."

"Who is?" Gabri asked. He was seated by the woodstove with Agent Nichol, while the Brunels looked out the window and reported back.

"Inspector Beauvoir," said Thérèse. "He's with Francoeur."

"Impossible." Gabri got to his feet and went over to see for himself.

Glancing quickly out the frosted window, Gabri saw large men entering Emilie's home. Jean-Guy Beauvoir did not. Instead he stood on the snowy steps and looked around the village. Gabri swung away from the window a moment before Beauvoir's eyes reached him.

"I don't believe it," he whispered.

"Inspector Beauvoir's an addict," said Thérèse from the other side of the window. "Has been for a while."

"Since the factory," said Gabri quietly. "I know. But I'd thought . . ."

"Yes, we all thought," said Thérèse. "Hoped. Addiction's a terrible thing. It'll steal your health, your friends, family, careers. Judgment. It'll steal your soul. And when there's nothing left, it takes your life."

Gabri dared a quick glance out the window. Beauvoir was still on the porch, staring straight ahead. He looked like he had nothing left to steal.

"He'd never turn on Gamache."

"Jean-Guy Beauvoir wouldn't, you're right," said Jérôme. "But drugs have no friends, no loyalty. They'll do anything."

"Inspector Beauvoir may very well be the most dangerous person out there," said Superintendent Brunel.

They were here," said Francoeur, coming out of Emilie's home. "But they've gone. We need to get the truth out of the owner of the bistro."

"I know where they are."

Beauvoir stepped off Emilie Longpré's porch and pointed.

FORTY

———

It took a split second to break through the Yale lock, then they were in the schoolhouse.

Tessier stepped through first, followed by the two large agents. Sylvain Francoeur strolled in last and looked around. Monitors, cables, wires, and boxes were against one wall. Five empty chairs circled the still warm wood-stove.

Francoeur took off his gloves and let his hand hover over the cast-iron woodstove.

Yes. They'd been here, and not long ago. They'd gotten out in a hurry, leaving behind all that incriminating equipment. Gamache, the Brunels, and Agent Nichol were shut down and on the run. Incapable of more dam-age. It was just a matter of time before they were found.

"How'd you know?" Francoeur asked Beauvoir.

"The schoolhouse was closed," Beauvoir explained. "But the path to it's been cleared. Like the Longpré place."

"Gamache makes a habit of abandoning places," the Chief Superinten-dent said. "And people."

He turned his back on Beauvoir and joined the others at the computers.

Jean-Guy watched for a moment, then left.

His boots crunched on the snow, munch, munch, munch, as he walked across the village green, which was very, very, suspiciously, quiet. Nor-mally kids would be playing hockey, parents either watching or out cross-country skiing. Families would be tobogganing down the hill, shedding passengers as they flew over bumps.

But today, despite the sunshine, Three Pines was quiet. Not abandoned, he felt. Not a ghost town. Three Pines seemed to be waiting. And watching.

Jean-Guy walked over to the bench and sat down.

He didn't know what Francoeur and Tessier were about. He didn't know why they were here. He didn't know how Gamache figured in. And he didn't ask.

He pulled a pill bottle out of his pocket, shook two out and swallowed them. He looked at the OxyContin bottle. He had two more in his apartment, and a nearly full bottle of anti-anxiety pills.

Enough to do the job.

"Hello, numb nuts," said Ruth, as she sat on the bench beside Jean-Guy. "Who're your new friends?"

Ruth waved her cane toward the old schoolhouse.

Beauvoir watched as one of Francoeur's agents carried something from the van into the schoolhouse.

Beauvoir said nothing. He simply stared ahead of him.

"What's so interesting over there?" Ruth asked him.

Olivier had tried to stop her from going outside, but when Ruth saw Beauvoir sit on the bench alone, she put on her coat, picked up her duck, and left, saying, "Don't you think he'd find it strange if the village was completely deserted? I won't tell him anything. What do you think I am? Crazy?"

"As a matter of—"

But it was too late. The old poet had left the building. Olivier watched with trepidation. Myrna and Clara watched from the window of the bookstore. In the loft, Gabri, Nichol, and the Brunels watched as Ruth crossed the road and joined Beauvoir on the cold bench.

"Is this going to be a problem?" Thérèse asked Gabri.

"Oh, no. It'll be fine," said Gabri, and grimaced.

"I have a clear shot," said Nichol, her voice hopeful.

"I think Nichol and the crazy poet might be related," Jérôme said to Thérèse.

Down below, Ruth, Rosa and Jean-Guy sat side by side, watching the activity at the schoolhouse.

"*Who hurt you once,*" Ruth whispered to the young man, "*so far beyond repair?*"

Jean-Guy roused, as though finally noticing he wasn't alone. He looked at her.

"Am I, Ruth?" he asked, using her first name for the first time. "Beyond repair?"

"What do you think?" She stroked Rosa, but looked at him.

"I think maybe I am," he said softly.

Beauvoir stared at the old schoolhouse. Instead of taking the computers out, new equipment was being brought in from the van. Boxes and wires and cables. It looked familiar, but Beauvoir couldn't be bothered to dig through his memory for the information.

Ruth sat quietly beside him, then she lifted Rosa from her lap, feeling it warm where the duck had been. She carefully placed Rosa on Jean-Guy's lap.

He seemed not to notice, but after a few moments he brought his hand up and stroked Rosa. Softly, softly.

"I could wring her neck, you know," he said.

"I know," said Ruth. "Please don't."

She watched Rosa, holding her dark duck eyes. And Rosa looked at Ruth, as Jean-Guy's hand caressed the feathers of Rosa's back, coming closer and closer to the long neck.

Ruth held fast to Rosa's eyes.

Finally Jean-Guy's hand stopped, and rested.

"Rosa came back," he said.

Ruth nodded.

"I'm glad," he said.

"She took the long way home," said Ruth. "Some do, you know. They seem lost. Sometimes they might even head off in the wrong direction. Lots of people give up, say they're gone forever, but I don't believe that. Some make it home, eventually."

Jean-Guy lifted Rosa from his lap and attempted to return her to Ruth. But the old woman held up her hand.

"No. You keep her now."

Jean-Guy stared at Ruth, uncomprehending. He tried again to give Rosa back, and again Ruth gently, firmly declined.

"She'll have a good home with you," she said, now not looking at Rosa at all.

"But I don't know how to look after a duck," he said. "What would I do with her?"

"Isn't the question more what'll she do with you?" asked Ruth. She got up and fished in her pocket. "These are the keys to my car." She gave them to Beauvoir and nodded toward an old beat-up Civic. "I think Rosa would be better off away from here, don't you?"

Beauvoir stared at the keys in his hand, then at the thin, wrinkled, wretched old face. And the rheumy eyes that, in the bright sunshine, seemed to be leaking light.

"Leave here," she said. "Take Rosa. Please."

She bent down slowly, as though each inch was agony, and kissed Rosa on the top of her head. Then she looked into Rosa's bright eyes and whispered, "I love you."

Ruth Zardo turned her back on them and limped away. Her head erect, she walked slowly forward. Toward the bistro and whatever was coming next.

It's a joke, right?" the fat cop on the other side of the counter said to Isabelle Lacoste. "Someone's gonna blow this up?"

He waved at his monitors and all but called her "little lady."

Lacoste didn't have time for diplomacy. She'd shown him her Sûreté ID and told him what was about to happen. Not surprisingly, he hadn't been eager to close the bridge.

Now she walked around the counter and stuck her Glock under his chin. "It's no joke," she said, and saw his eyes widen in terror.

"Wait," he begged.

"Explosives are attached to the piers and will be set off any moment now. The bomb squad will be here in a few minutes but I need you to close the bridge, now. If you don't, you'll go down with it."

When the Chief Inspector had told her the target and ordered her to close the bridge, she'd been faced with a problem. Who to trust?

Then it struck her. The security guards on the bridge. They couldn't know what was about to happen, or they'd have gotten out of there fast. Anyone still working on the bridge could be trusted. The question now was, could they be convinced?

"Call your squad cars back in."

She waited, her gun still trained on him, while he radioed the cars and ordered them back.

"Download this." She handed the guard a USB key and watched as he put it in his computer and opened the files.

"What are these?" he asked, scanning them. But Lacoste didn't answer, and slowly, slowly his face went slack.

She returned her gun to its holster. He was no longer looking at it, or her. His eyes, and attention, were completely focused on the screen. A couple of his colleagues arrived back at the guard post. They looked at Lacoste, then at him.

"What's up?"

But the look on his face stopped any banter.

"What is it?" one asked.

"Call the Super, get the bomb squads out, close the bridge—"

But Lacoste didn't hear any more. She was back in her car and heading over the bridge. To the far shore. To the village.

Gamache sped along the familiar, snow-covered secondary road. His car fishtailed on a patch of ice and he took his foot off the accelerator. No time for an accident. Everything that happened from here on in needed to be considered and deliberate.

He spotted a convenience store and pulled into it.

"May I use your phone, please?" He showed the clerk his Sûreté ID.

"You have to buy something."

"Give me your phone."

"Buy something."

"Fine." Gamache picked up the closest thing he could find. "There."

"Really?" the clerk looked at the pile of condoms.

"Just give me the phone, son," said Gamache, fighting his desire to throttle this amused young man. Instead he brought out his wallet and put a twenty on the counter.

"If you want to use the can you'll have to buy something else," the kid said as he rang up the sale and handed Gamache the phone.

Gamache dialed. It rang, and rang. And rang.

Please, oh please.

"Francoeur." The voice was clipped, tense.

"*Bonjour*, Chief Superintendent."

There was a pause.

"Is that you, Armand? I've been looking for you."

The connection kept cutting in and out, but Sylvain Francoeur's voice had become happy, friendly. Not in a sly way, but he seemed genuinely pleased by the call. As though they were best friends.

It was, Gamache knew, one of the Chief Superintendent's many gifts, the ability to make an imitation appear genuine. A counterfeit man. Anyone listening, and there could be any number, would be in no doubt about Francoeur's sincerity.

"Yes, I'm sorry I've been out of contact," said Gamache. "Tying up loose ends."

"Exactly what I'm doing. What can I do for you?"

In the old schoolhouse, Francoeur watched as the agents worked.

He pressed the phone to his ear and stood by the window, barely able to get the signal. "You'll have to speak up. I'm in a village with very poor reception."

Gamache felt as though he'd swallowed battery acid.

So Sylvain was already in Three Pines. Gamache had miscalculated, thinking it would take Francoeur longer to find the place. But then another dose of acid hit his insides. Francoeur must have found someone who knew the way.

Jean-Guy.

Gamache took a deep breath and steadied his voice. Tried to make it sound casual, polite, slightly bored.

"I'm heading out your way, sir. I was wondering if we could meet."

Francoeur raised his brows. He'd expected to have to hunt Gamache down. It never occurred to him that Gamache's hubris was so great it consumed all good sense.

But apparently it did.

"Fine with me," said Sylvain Francoeur cheerfully. "Shall we meet here? Inspector Tessier tells me there's an interesting satellite dish set up in the woods. I haven't seen it yet. He thinks it might have been put there by the Aztecs. Do you know it?"

There was a pause.

"I do."

"Good. Why don't we meet there."

Francoeur hung up. He knew Gamache would never make the rendezvous. Agents were closing in and would pick up the Chief Inspector any moment now.

He turned to his second in command.

"They know what to do?" he indicated the two agents. One was under the desk, the other was at the door into the schoolhouse, working with wires.

Tessier nodded. The agents had been with him when he'd dealt with Pierre Arnot and Audrey Villeneuve, and others. They did as they were told.

"Come with me."

At the door, Tessier turned to the agents.

"Don't forget about Beauvoir. We need him here."

"Yessir."

Beauvoir was no longer on the bench, but Tessier wasn't worried. He was probably passed out in the SUV.

Wat do you think it means?" Jérôme whispered as they watched Francoeur and Tessier walk up the hill out of the village. "Are they leaving?"

"On foot?" asked Nichol.

"Maybe not," conceded Dr. Brunel. "But at least Beauvoir's gone."

They looked at the blank spot in the snow where Myrna's car had been.

Downstairs, Myrna turned to Ruth. "You gave him my car?"

"Well, I couldn't very well give him mine. I don't have a car."

"Where'd you get the keys?"

"They were on the desk where you always keep them."

Myrna shook her head, but she couldn't be angry at Ruth. Beauvoir might have taken Myrna's car, but he'd taken something far more precious from Ruth.

They heard the door to the bookstore close and looked over at it, then out the window. Gabri was walking swiftly along the road, without a coat or hat or boots. He slipped, but righted himself.

"Shit," said Nichol, racing downstairs, "where's he going?"

The Brunels were behind her, and Thérèse stopped the young agent before she followed Gabri outside.

"He's going to the church," said Clara. She threw on her coat and was almost at the door when Nichol grabbed her arm.

"Oh, no you don't," said Nichol.

Clara shook her arm free in a move so sudden and violent it took Nichol by surprise. "Gabri's my friend and I'm not going to leave him on his own."

"He's running away," said Nichol. "Look at him, he's scared shitless."

"I doubt that," said Ruth. "Gabri will never be shitless. He has an endless supply of it."

"Was that Gabri?" Olivier hurried through the connecting door from the bistro.

"He's going to the church," said Clara. "I'm going too."

"So'm I," said Olivier.

"No," said Thérèse. "You have to look after the bistro."

"You look after it." He tossed the tea towel at her and followed Clara out the door.

Once up the hill and in the woods, Francoeur's and Tessier's devices began to buzz. It was as though they'd crossed a membrane from one world to another.

Francoeur paused on the path and scanned his messages.

His orders had been followed, swiftly, effectively. The mess Gamache had created was being contained, cleaned up.

"*Merde,*" said Tessier. "We thought we had Gamache."

"You've lost him?"

"He threw his cell phone and the tracking device away."

"And it took your agents this long to figure that out?"

"No, they realized it half an hour ago, but that fucking village stopped the messages from getting through. Besides—"

"*Oui?*"

"They thought they were following him, but he put the tracking devices on a float in the Christmas parade."

"Are you telling me the elite of the Sûreté followed Santa Claus through downtown Montréal?"

"Not Santa. It was Snow White."

"Christ," Francoeur huffed. "Still, it doesn't matter. Gamache's coming to us."

Before putting his phone back in his pocket, Francoeur noticed a short text, sent to all points almost half an hour earlier, announcing Chief Inspector Gamache's resignation. So like Gamache, Francoeur thought. Thinking the whole world would care.

Thérèse Brunel saw one of the Sûreté officers emerge from the old schoolhouse. As she watched, he surveyed the village, then went into Emilie's home, then over to the B and B. A minute or so later he emerged and opened the passenger doors of the SUV.

Superintendent Brunel heard the car door slam and watched as the agent looked around in frustration.

He's lost something, Thérèse Brunel thought, and she could guess at what. Or whom. They were looking for Beauvoir. Then he looked in her direction, his sharp eyes just glancing past hers before she jerked back against the wall.

"What is it?" Jérôme asked.

"He's headed over here," said Thérèse, and brought out her gun.

The agent started toward the line of businesses. The bistro and bookstore and bakery. It was possible Beauvoir had gone in one of them, to rest. Or pass out.

This would be easy, the agent knew.

He could feel his gun on his belt, but he knew what would be most effective was in his pocket. The baggie of pills Tessier had given him, each a little bullet to the brain.

The other agent was making the final arrangements in the schoolhouse, and all they needed now was Beauvoir.

But the officer hesitated. A few minutes earlier he'd noticed a large black woman and an old woman with a cane heading to the church.

The same old woman who'd been talking to Beauvoir on the bench.

If Beauvoir was missing, she might know where he was.

He changed course and made for the church.

Armand Gamache parked beside the path into the woods. The one he and Gilles had forged just a few days earlier. It was freshly trodden, he could see.

He walked down the path, deeper and deeper into the forest. Toward the blind.

He saw Sylvain Francoeur first, standing at the base of the white pine. Then he looked up. Standing on the old wooden blind, beside the satellite dish, was Martin Tessier. Inspector Tessier, of the Serious Crimes division, was about to commit a very serious crime. He had an automatic trained on Chief Inspector Gamache.

Gamache stopped on the track, and wondered, fleetingly, if this was how the deer felt. He looked straight at Tessier and turned slightly toward him. Showing the marksman his chest. Daring him to pull the trigger.

If there was ever a time for that damned thing to collapse, thought Gamache, now was it.

But the blind held, and Tessier held him in his sights.

Gamache shifted his eyes to Francoeur and put his arms out at his sides.

The Chief Superintendent gestured and Tessier climbed rapidly and easily down the rickety ladder.

The agent entered the church and looked around. It appeared empty. Then he noticed the old woman, still in her gray cloth coat and tuque. She sat in a back pew. The large black woman sat in a front pew.

He stared into the corners but couldn't see anyone.

"You there," he said. "Who else is here?"

"If you're talking to Ruth, you're wasting your time," said the woman at the front. She stood up and smiled at him. "She doesn't speak French."

She herself spoke to him in very good, though slightly accented, French. "Can I help you?"

The agent walked down the aisle. "I'm looking for Inspector Beauvoir. You know him?"

"I do," she said. "He's been here before, with Chief Inspector Gamache."

"Where is he now?"

"Beauvoir? I thought he was with you," said Myrna.

"Why would I—"

But he didn't get to finish his sentence. The muzzle of a Glock was thrust into the base of his skull and an expert hand reached in and took his gun from its holster.

He turned around. The elderly woman in the cloth coat and knitted tuque was holding a service revolver on him.

And she wasn't old at all.

"Sûreté," said Agent Nichol. "You're under arrest."

Jean-Guy Beauvoir was on the highway heading toward Montréal. Rosa sat beside him, and hadn't made a sound. Nor had she stopped staring at him.

But Beauvoir kept his eyes forward. Moving further and further away from the village. He didn't know what Francoeur and Tessier and the others had planned, and he didn't want to know.

When he'd emerged from Three Pines his device had blipped, a few times. All messages from Lacoste. Wondering where he was.

Beauvoir knew what that meant. It meant Gamache was looking for him, probably to finish what he'd started the day before. But then he'd read her last message, sent across the system.

Gamache had resigned. He was out of the Sûreté.

It was over.

He glanced at the duck. Why in the world had he agreed to take her? Though he knew the answer to that. It wasn't that he'd agreed to take her, but that he hadn't the energy or willpower to fight.

Beauvoir wondered, though, why Ruth had given her to him. He knew how much she loved Rosa, and how much Rosa loved her.

I love you, Ruth had whispered to the duck.

I love you. But this time the voice didn't belong to the demented old poet, but to Gamache. In the factory. Bullets slamming into the concrete floor, into the walls. Bam, bam, bam. The clouds of choking, blinding dust. The deafening sounds. The shouts, the shots, the screams.

And Gamache dragging him to safety, and staunching his wound. Even as the bullets hit around them.

The Chief had stared into his eyes and bent over and kissed him on his forehead and whispered, "I love you."

As Gamache had the day before, when he thought Beauvoir was about to shoot him. Instead of struggling, of fighting back, as he could have, he'd said, *I love you*.

Jean-Guy Beauvoir knew then that he and Rosa hadn't been abandoned, they'd been saved.

FORTY-ONE

—

"Now what?" Gabri asked.

He, Olivier, and Clara had come out from behind the altar, where they'd watched. Clara and Olivier each held one of the simple candlestick holders, and Gabri gripped the crucifix, ready to brain the gunman if he got away from Nichol and Myrna.

But there was no need. The gunman was now gagged and handcuffed to a long wooden pew.

"There's one more," said Myrna. "In the schoolhouse."

"And the other two who went into the woods," said Clara. She looked at the gun in Myrna's hand, and the one in Nichol's. They were terrifying and repulsive, and Clara wanted one.

"So what do we do?" Gabri turned to Nichol, who managed to look both in charge and out of control at the same time.

Martin Tessier stripped the coat from Gamache and took his weapon, leaving him in his shirtsleeves.

Tessier placed Gamache's gun in Francoeur's outstretched hand.

"Where's Beauvoir?" Gamache demanded.

"He's in the village with the others," said Tessier. "Working."

"Let him be," said Gamache. "I'm the one you want."

Francoeur smiled. "'I'm the one you want,' as though this begins and ends with the great Armand Gamache. You really haven't grasped what's happening, have you? You even had your resignation broadcast, as though it was important. As though we might care."

"And you don't?" asked Gamache. "Are you sure?"

"Pretty sure," said Tessier, pointing his weapon at Gamache's chest.

389

Gamache ignored him and continued to watch Francoeur.

There was more buzzing and Francoeur checked his texts.

"We've picked up Isabelle Lacoste and her family. And Villeneuve and the neighbor. You're like the plague, Armand. Everyone you've come in contact with is either dead or soon will be. Including Beauvoir. He'll be found among the remains of the schoolhouse, trying to dismantle the bomb you connected to all those computers."

Gamache looked from Francoeur to Tessier and back to Francoeur.

"You're trying to decide whether to believe me," said Francoeur.

"For chrissake," said Tessier. "Let's get this over with."

Francoeur turned to his second in command. "You're right. Get that satellite dish down. I'll finish up here. Walk with me, Armand. I'll let you go ahead, for once."

Francoeur pointed down the path, and Gamache started to walk, slipping slightly in the snow. It was the trail that he and Nichol had made when they'd lugged the cable through the woods, back to Three Pines. It was, in effect, a shortcut to the old schoolhouse.

"Are they still alive?" Gamache asked.

"I honestly don't know," said Francoeur.

"Beauvoir? Is he still alive?"

"Well, I haven't heard an explosion yet, so yes. For now."

Gamache took another few steps.

"And the bridge? Shouldn't you have heard about the bridge by now?" Gamache asked, breathing heavily and grabbing a branch to catch his balance. "Something's wrong, Sylvain. You can feel it."

"Stop," said Francoeur, and Gamache did. He turned around and saw Francoeur bring out his cell phone. He touched it with his finger, then beamed.

"It's done."

"What's done?"

"The bridge is down."

At St. Thomas's Church the celebrations were short-lived.

"Look," said Myrna. She and Clara were peering through the stained-glass window.

The other gunman had come out the door of the old schoolhouse. His back was to them and he seemed to be working on the handle.

Locking it? Clara wondered.

Then he stood on the stoop and looked around, as his colleague had done a few minutes ago.

"He's looking for him." Olivier pointed to their handcuffed and gagged prisoner, guarded by Nichol.

As they watched, the gunman walked over to the van. He slung a large canvas bag into the back and slammed the door closed. Then he surveyed the village again. Perplexed.

At that moment, Thérèse Brunel left the bookstore. She wore a heavy coat, and a large tuque pulled down over her hair and forehead. Her arms were full of books and she walked slowly toward the Sûreté agent, as though infirm.

"What's she doing?" Clara asked.

"*Twas in the moon of wintertime,*" Gabri sang loudly. They turned to look at him. "*When all the birds had fled.*"

The gunman turned toward the singing coming from the church.

This village was giving him the creeps. It seemed so pretty, and yet was deserted. There was a menace about the place. The sooner he found Beauvoir and his partner and got out, the better.

He started toward the church. Clearly there were people in there. People who, with some persuasion, might tell him where Beauvoir was. Where his colleague was. Where everyone was.

An old woman with books was walking toward him, but he ignored her and made for the small clapboard chapel on the hill.

The gunman followed the sound of the singing, up the steps.

He didn't notice that the woman with the books had also changed direction, and was following him.

He opened the door and looked in. At the front of the church a bunch of people stood in a semi-circle singing.

An old woman in a cloth coat sat in a pew a few rows back. The singing stopped and the large man who seemed to lead the choir waved to him.

"Close the door," he called. "You're letting the cold in."

But the gunman didn't move. He stood on the threshold, taking in the scene. There was something wrong. They were looking at him strangely, except the hunched old woman, still wearing her tuque. She hadn't turned around.

He reached for his gun.

"Sûreté."

He heard the word. Heard the metallic click. Felt the muzzle against the base of his skull. He heard the books drop and saw them scattered at his feet.

"Lift your hands where I can see them."

He did as he was told.

He turned to see the old woman who'd followed him. The books she'd been carrying had been replaced by a service revolver. It was Superintendent Thérèse Brunel.

She was pointing her gun at him, and she meant business.

The bridge is down?" Gamache gaped at Francoeur.

"Right on time," said the Chief Superintendent.

A voice drifted to them from the village below, singing an old Québécois carol. It sounded like a lament.

"I don't believe it," said Gamache. "You're lying."

"You want proof?"

"Call Renard. Call the Premier. Confirm it with him," said Gamache.

"With pleasure. I'm sure he'd like a word with you too."

Francoeur hit a button on his cell. Gamache could hear the ringing. Ringing.

But no one answered.

"He's probably busy," said Gamache.

Francoeur gave him a sharp look and tried another number. Lambert in Cyber Crimes.

Ringing, ringing.

"Nothing?" asked Gamache.

Francoeur lowered the phone. "What've you done, Armand?"

"'Have Lacoste in custody. Family being held,'" Gamache recited. "A couple of minutes later you received another message, "'Villeneuve offered some resistance, but no longer.'"

Francoeur's face tightened.

"You didn't really think I'd let my department be destroyed, did you?" Gamache's eyes were penetrating, his voice hard, anger flaring. "All those agents who quit. All those agents who requested transfers. All over the Sûreté."

He spoke slowly, so that every word would hit its mark.

"Into the Traffic division. Serious Crimes. Public Safety. Emergency Response. Cyber Crime."

He paused, making sure Francoeur was with him, before he delivered the *coup-de-grâce*.

"The safety of public officials. The team that guards the Premier. You yourself dismantled my department and spread my agents into every division. My agents, Sylvain. Mine. Never yours. I didn't fight it because it served my purposes. While your plan progressed, so did mine."

Francoeur went as white as the snow.

"My people have taken over those departments and arrested any agents loyal to you. The Premier's in our custody, along with his staff. Had we been on water, this would've been called a mutiny.

"The announcement that I'd resigned was the signal for my officers to move in. I had to wait until I knew what you had planned, and had proof. There was no response to your phone calls because there was no one there to answer. And those texts you received? About the bridge? About the people picked up? Inspector Lacoste sent them. The bridge has been secured."

"Impossible."

Francoeur looked again at the device, just a quick glance down, but it was enough.

Gamache made his move.

Jean-Guy Beauvoir parked behind Gamache's Volvo. He cracked the window a little, to give Rosa air, then he got out.

He stood on the road, uncertain where to go. He'd thought to head right into Three Pines. He knew now what that equipment was he'd seen in the van. He'd probably known all along. It was explosives. And detonators. And trip wires.

They were attaching the wires to the door of the schoolhouse. When opened, it would detonate.

His plan had been to go into the village, to stop the agents, but the sight of the familiar car left him unsure.

He looked at the ground, at the fresh path into the woods, and he followed it.

Gamache plowed into Francoeur, grabbing for the gun, but it flew from Francoeur's hand and was buried in the snow.

Both men fell hard. Gamache brought his forearm to Francoeur's throat, leaning against it, trying to pin Francoeur. Francoeur lashed out, bucking and punching. His hand, grasping for the gun, closed around something hard and he swung with all his might, catching Gamache on the side of the head.

The Chief fell sideways, stunned by the rock. Francoeur scrambled to his knees and clawed at his parka, trying to get it open. Trying to get at the Glock on his belt.

Tessier?"

Beauvoir's voice surprised Martin Tessier as he climbed down the ladder. The satellite dish was on the ground where he'd tossed it from the platform, and Jean-Guy Beauvoir was standing beside it.

"Beauvoir," said Tessier, recovering himself and stepping off the last rung. His back to Beauvoir, he reached for his gun. "We've been looking for you."

But he got no further. Beauvoir's gun pressed into his neck.

"Where's Gamache?" he whispered into Tessier's ear.

Gamache saw Francoeur pull the gun out of the holster. He lunged before Francoeur could take aim, knocking him to the ground. But the gun remained in Francoeur's grip.

Now both men fought for the weapon, punching and twisting and thrashing.

Francoeur had hold of it, and Gamache had hold of Francoeur, grasping with both hands, but the snow was wet and he could feel his grip slipping.

Beauvoir gave a savage shove and ground Tessier's face into the bark of the tree.

"Where's Gamache?" Beauvoir repeated. "Does he know you plan to blow up the schoolhouse?"

Tessier nodded, feeling the flesh scrape off his cheeks and onto the bark. "He thinks you're in the schoolhouse."

"Why does he think that?"

"Because we thought that."

"You were going to kill me?"

"You and most of the people in the village, when that bomb explodes."

"What did you tell Gamache?"

"That the schoolhouse was wired to explode, and that you were in it," said Tessier.

Beauvoir turned him around and stared into Tessier's eyes, trying to get at the truth.

"Does he know the bomb's attached to the door?" Beauvoir demanded.

Tessier shook his head. "But it doesn't matter. He won't get that far. Francoeur's taking care of him in the woods."

Gamache could feel his grip slipping. He let go, and brought both hands down on Francoeur's nose. He felt it snap and blood gushed from it. Francoeur howled and heaved his body, sending Gamache sideways into the snow.

He twisted around just as Francoeur got to his knees.

Gamache saw something dark poking through the snow. It could be a rock, or a stick. Or the butt of a gun. He rolled toward it. And rolled once more, looking up just in time to see Francoeur raise his weapon and take aim.

And Armand Gamache fired. And fired. And shot again.

Until Chief Superintendent Sylvain Francoeur, his face blank, slumped sideways.

Dead.

Gamache got to his feet, wasting no more time on Francoeur, and ran.

Beauvoir heard the rapid-fire shots. A Glock.

"That's Gamache," said Tessier. "Dead."

Beauvoir turned his head toward the sound, and Tessier lurched, grabbing for the gun.

Beauvoir pulled the trigger. And saw Tessier fall.

Then he ran. And ran. Into the forest. Toward what was now silence.

Armand Gamache ran as though chased by the Furies. He ran as though the woods were on fire. He ran as though the devil was on his back.

He ran through the woods, between the trees, stumbling over fallen trunks. But he got up and ran. Toward the old schoolhouse. Toward the explosives. Toward Jean-Guy.

Jean-Guy Beauvoir saw a body facedown in the snow and ran to it, falling onto his knees.

Oh, no, no, no.

He turned it over.

Francoeur. Dead.

Beauvoir got to his feet and looked around, frantic. Then he forced himself to calm down. To listen. As the quiet of the forest descended, he heard it. Up ahead. Someone running. Away from him. Toward Three Pines.

Toward the schoolhouse.

Jean-Guy Beauvoir took off. Running. Screaming. Screaming. Running.

"Stop! Stop!" he screamed.

But the man ahead didn't hear. Didn't stop.

Beauvoir ran as fast as he could, but there was too great a distance between them. Gamache would reach the schoolhouse. Believing Beauvoir was inside. Believing Beauvoir was in danger.

Gamache would take the stairs two at a time, rip the door open, and . . .

"Stop! Stop!" Beauvoir screamed. And then he shrieked. Not words, just a sound. All his fear, all his rage, everything he had left he put into that howl.

But still the Chief ran, as though pursued by demons.

Beauvoir stumbled to a stop. Sobbing.

"No. Stop."

He couldn't catch him. Couldn't stop him. Except . . .

Isabelle Lacoste knelt beside Tessier but sprang to her feet at that godawful sound. She'd never heard anything like it. It was like something breaking, being torn apart. She ran toward it, following the unholy scream deeper into the forest.

Armand Gamache heard the shot. Saw the bark fly off the tree ahead of him. But still he ran, and he ran. Unswerving. As fast and as true as he could.

Straight for the schoolhouse.

He could see it now, red through the white and gray of the forest.

Another shot hit the snow beside him, but still he ran. Tessier must have found Francoeur, and was now trying to stop him. But Gamache would not be stopped.

Jean-Guy's hand quivered and the gun wavered, sending his shots off the mark. He'd been aiming at the Chief's legs. Hoping, praying, to graze him. Enough to bring him down. But it wasn't working.

"Stop, oh, please stop."

Beauvoir's vision was blurred. He dragged his sleeve across his face, then tilted his head back, for a moment, and looked through the bare limbs. To the blue sky above.

"Oh, please."

Gamache was almost out of the woods. Almost at the schoolhouse.

Beauvoir closed his eyes briefly.

"Please," he begged.

He brought his gun up again. His hands steady now. The gun unwavering. The aim sure. No longer for Gamache's legs.

Stop," screamed Lacoste, her gun trained on Beauvoir's back.

She could see, ahead through the woods, the Chief Inspector racing toward Three Pines. And Jean-Guy Beauvoir about to gun him down.

"Drop it," she commanded.

"No, Isabelle," Beauvoir called. "I have to."

Lacoste braced herself and took aim. From there it would be impossible to miss. But still, she hesitated.

There was something in his voice. Not pleading, not begging, not madness.

Beauvoir's voice was strong and certain. His old voice.

She had no doubt what he intended to do. Jean-Guy Beauvoir was going to shoot Chief Inspector Gamache.

"Please, Isabelle," Beauvoir called, his back still to her, his weapon raised.

Isabelle Lacoste steadied herself. Steadied her gun with both hands. Her finger pressed against the trigger.

Jean-Guy Beauvoir had Armand Gamache in his sights.

The Chief was at the tree line, just steps from the schoolhouse.

Beauvoir took a deep breath in. A deep breath out.

And pulled the trigger.

Armand Gamache could almost touch the schoolhouse now. The shooting had stopped.

He'd make it, he knew. He'd get Jean-Guy out.

He had just cleared the trees when the bullet hit. The force lifted him

397

off his feet and spun him around. In the instant before he hit the ground, in the split second before the world disappeared, he met the eyes of the man who'd shot him.

Jean-Guy Beauvoir.

And then Armand Gamache fell, spread-eagled, as though making an angel in the bright snow.

FORTY-TWO

St. Thomas's Church in Three Pines was quiet, just a slight rustle of paper as the guests read the order of service. Four monks walked in, heads bowed, and formed a semi-circle in front of the altar.

There was a pause, and then they began to sing. Their voices blending, joining. Swirling. Then becoming one. It was like listening to one of Clara's paintings. With colors and swirls and the play of light and dark. All moving around a calm center.

A plainchant, in a plain church.

The only decoration in St. Thomas's was a single stained-glass window, of perpetually young soldiers. The window was positioned to catch the morning light, the youngest light.

Jean-Guy Beauvoir bowed his head, weighed down by the solemnity of the moment. Then, behind him, he heard a door open and everyone rose to their feet.

The chant came to an end and there was a moment of quiet before another voice was heard. Beauvoir didn't need to look to know who it was.

Gabri stood at the front of the church, looking down the aisle, past the wooden pews, and sang in his clear tenor,

> *Ring the bells that still can ring,*
> *Forget your perfect offering,*

Around Beauvoir, the congregation joined in. He heard Clara's voice. Olivier's and Myrna's. He even made out Ruth's thin, reedy, unwavering voice. A doughboy voice. Unsure but unyielding.

But Jean-Guy had no voice. His lips moved, but no sound came out. He looked down the aisle, and waited.

There is a crack in everything
That's how the light gets in.

He saw Madame Gamache first, walking slowly. And beside her, Annie. Radiant in her wedding dress. Walking down the aisle on her mother's arm.

And Jean-Guy Beauvoir began to cry. With joy, with relief. With sorrow for all that had happened. For all the pain he'd caused. He stood in the morning light of the boys who never came home, and he wept.

He felt a nudge on his arm and saw a linen handkerchief being offered. Beauvoir took it, and looked into the deep brown eyes of his best man.

"You need it." Jean-Guy gave it back.

"I have another." Armand Gamache brought one from his breast pocket and wiped his eyes.

The two men stood shoulder-to-shoulder at the front of the packed chapel, weeping and watching as Annie and her mother walked down the aisle. Annie Gamache was about to marry her first, and last, love.

*N*ow *there will be no more loneliness,*" said the minister, as he gave his final blessing on the couple.

Go now to your dwelling place to enter into
the days of your togetherness.
And may your days be good and long upon the earth.

The party on the sunny village green started in mid-morning on the early July day, and lasted well into the night. A bonfire was lit, fireworks set off, a barbeque was held and all the guests brought salads and desserts, pâtés and cheeses. Fresh bread. Beer and wine and pink lemonade.

As the first song started, Armand, in morning coat, gave his cane to Clara and limped slowly to the very center of the circle of guests, the center of the green, the center of the village, and put out his hand.

It was steady, not a quiver, as Annie placed her hand in his. He bent over and kissed it. Then he held her to him, and they danced. Slowly. In the shadow of the three huge trees.

"You're sure you know what you're taking on?" he asked.

"Did Mom?" his daughter replied with a laugh.

"Well, she was lucky. I happen to be perfect," said Gamache.

"Shame. I hear that things are strongest where they're broken," she said, as her father moved her slowly around the village green, and she rested her head on his strong shoulder. The place he reserved for people he loved.

They danced past Gabri and Olivier, past Myrna and Clara, past the shopkeepers and villagers. Past Isabelle Lacoste and her family, past the Brunels, standing beside Agent Nichol. Yvette Nichol.

They smiled and waved as Armand and his daughter danced by. Across the green Jean-Guy and Reine-Marie danced past Daniel and Roslyn and the Gamache grandchildren, who were stroking Henri.

"You know how happy we are, Jean-Guy," Reine-Marie said.

"Are you really?"

He still needed reassurance.

"None of us is perfect," she whispered.

"I tried to kill your husband," said Jean-Guy.

"No. You tried to save him, to stop him. And you did. I will be forever in your debt."

They danced in silence, as both thought of that moment. When Jean-Guy had been faced with a choice.

To continue shooting at, and missing, Gamache's legs. Or to raise his sights, and aim for his back. A shot that might kill the very man he was trying to save. But to not shoot would mean the Chief would certainly die. Be blown up as soon as he reached the door to the schoolhouse. Believing he was saving Jean-Guy.

It had been a terrible, terrible choice.

As had Isabelle Lacoste's.

She'd gone with her instincts, and lowered her gun. And watched in horror as Beauvoir had fired, and the Chief had fallen.

The only thing that had saved Gamache was the presence of Jérôme Brunel, the former emergency room physician. He'd raced from the church while others called 911.

Reine-Marie wondered, as her new son-in-law led her around the sunny village green, what she'd have done. Could she have taken that shot, knowing she'd almost certainly kill the man she loved?

And yet, not to would condemn him.

Could she have lived with herself either way?

When she'd heard the story, she knew then that if he got to rehab, and Annie still wanted him, she would consider herself blessed to have such a man in her family. And now, in her arms.

Annie was safe with him. Reine-Marie knew that, as few mothers ever could.

"Shall we?" Jean-Guy asked, and indicated the other couple, dancing closer.

"*Oui,*" said Reine-Marie, and released Beauvoir.

A moment later, Armand Gamache felt a tap on his shoulder.

"May I?" asked Jean-Guy, and Gamache stepped aside, bowing slightly.

Beauvoir looked at Annie with such tenderness, Gamache felt his own heart skip a beat, surprised by joy.

Then Jean-Guy turned and took Gamache in his arms, while Reine-Marie danced with Annie.

There was a whoop of laughter and applause from the guests. Gabri and Olivier were the first to join them, followed by the entire village. Even Ruth, with Rosa in her arms, danced with Billy Williams, whispering sweet swear words in each other's ears.

"Is there something you need to tell me, young man?" Gamache asked, as he felt Jean-Guy's strong hand on his back.

Beauvoir laughed, then paused before speaking. "I want to say I'm sorry."

"For shooting me?" asked Gamache. "I forgive you. Just don't do it again."

"Well, that too. But I meant I'm sorry you've retired from the Sûreté."

"When senior officers start shooting each other, it's time to leave," said Gamache. "I'm sure it's somewhere in the regulations."

Beauvoir laughed. He could feel the older man leaning on him, tiring a bit and still uncertain on his feet without his cane. Allowing Jean-Guy to take his weight. Trusting that Jean-Guy would not let him fall.

"Did it feel strange," Beauvoir asked, "seeing Madame Gamache walk Annie down the aisle?"

"You must call her Reine-Marie," said Gamache. "Please. We've asked you before."

"I'll try." It was difficult to break the habit of years, just as he found it almost impossible to call the Chief Inspector Armand. But one day, perhaps, when the children were born he might call him "Papa."

"I walked Annie down the aisle in her first wedding," said Armand. "It seemed only fair for her mother to do it this time. I'll do it at her next wedding."

"Wretched man," whispered Beauvoir.

He held the Chief and thought about the moment he'd pulled the trigger and seen Gamache propelled from the forest by the force of it. He'd dropped his gun and run and run and run. Toward the prone man, and the red stain spreading on the snow, like wings.

"My heart broke, you know," Beauvoir whispered, and resisted the urge to lower his head onto Gamache's shoulder. "When I shot you."

"I know," said Armand softly. "And my heart broke when I left you in that factory." There was silence for a few steps before Gamache spoke again. "There really is a crack in everything."

"Yes."

By midnight Armand and Reine-Marie were sitting on the wide verandah of Emilie's home. They could see Annie and Jean-Guy, silhouetted against the bonfire on the village green, swaying in each other's arms to the soft music.

Clara and Myrna had joined Armand and Reine-Marie on the porch. Daniel, Roslyn and the grandchildren were asleep upstairs, and Henri was curled up by Reine-Marie's feet.

No one spoke.

It had taken several months for Gamache to recover enough to leave the hospital. While he was there, Jean-Guy had been in rehab.

There was, of course, an inquiry into the plot to bring down the bridge and a Royal Commission had been struck to investigate the corruption.

Arnot, Francoeur, and Tessier were dead. Georges Renard was in the SHU awaiting trial, along with all the others who'd plotted and colluded. At least the ones they'd caught so far.

Isabelle Lacoste was the acting Chief Inspector of homicide, and would soon be confirmed. Jean-Guy was on part-time duty, and continued, as he would the rest of his life, to recover from his addictions.

Thérèse Brunel was the acting Chief Superintendent. They'd offered Gamache the job but he'd refused. He might recover physically, but he wasn't sure if he'd ever recover in other ways. And he knew Reine-Marie would not.

It was someone else's turn now.

When it came to deciding what to do next, it had been an easy decision. They'd bought Emilie Longpré's house on the village green in Three Pines.

Armand and Reine-Marie Gamache had come home.

He held her hand now, stroking it with his thumb, while a single fiddler played a soft familiar tune, and Armand Gamache knew he was fine where he was.

Reine-Marie held her husband's hand and watched her daughter and son-in-law on the village green and she thought about her conversation with Jean-Guy, as they'd danced. He'd told her how much he'd miss Armand. How much the Sûreté would miss him.

"But everyone understands his decision to retire," Jean-Guy had hurriedly reassured her. "He's earned his rest."

She'd laughed, and Jean-Guy had pulled back to study her.

"What was that?" he asked.

"Armand was made to do what he was doing. He might retire, but he can't quit."

"Really?" asked Jean-Guy, not exactly convinced. "'Cause the Chief seems pretty sure."

"He doesn't know it yet."

"And you? Would you be all right if he wants to rejoin the Sûreté one day? If you said no, he'd listen to you."

The look on her face told Jean-Guy that he wasn't the only one to face a terrible choice.

And now Reine-Marie held her husband's hand and looked at him as he watched Jean-Guy and Annie dance.

"What're you thinking of, *mon beau*?" she asked.

"*Now there is no more loneliness*," Gamache said, and met her eyes.

> *Go now to your dwelling place to enter into*
> *the days of your togetherness.*

When he'd handed Beauvoir back to Annie, in the middle of the first dance, Armand had seen something in Jean-Guy's eyes. Beyond the happiness, beyond the sharp intelligence, beyond even the suffering, Armand Gamache had seen something luminous. A glint. A gleam.

> *And may your days be good and long upon the earth.*

AUTHOR'S NOTE

As a Canadian, I was raised on lore of the famous Dionne quintuplets, born in Callander, Ontario, in 1934. They were a phenomenon and a sensation. Many of you might have recognized them in my Ouellet Quints, and the truth is, the fictional Ouellets were certainly inspired by the Dionne girls. But in researching *How the Light Gets In*, I was careful not to delve into the real lives of the Dionne quintuplets. I felt it would be both an intrusion on them, and far too limiting for me. I honestly didn't want to know what life was really like for the Dionnes. That freed me up to create whatever life I wanted and needed for *my* Quints.

There are clearly similarities—how could there not be? But the Ouellets are fictional, and their struggles not real. The Dionnes are real. The fact that both families are quints is where the similarity ends. I felt I owed you, and certainly the surviving Dionne Quints, this acknowledgment. They were a wonderful inspiration.

055526959